ROSE

Also by Martin Cruz Smith

The Indians Won
Gypsy in Amber
Canto for a Gypsy
Nightwing
Gorky Park
Stallion Gate
Polar Star
Red Square

MARTIN CRUZ SMITH

ROSE

MACMILLAN

First published in Great Britain 1996 by Macmillan

an imprint of Macmillan General Books
25 Eccleston Place, London SW1W 9NF
and Basingstoke

Associated companies throughout the world

ISBN 0 333 63292 3

Copyright © Martin Cruz Smith 1996

The right of Martin Cruz Smith to be identified as the
author of this work has been asserted by him in accordance
with the Copyright, Designs and Patents Act 1988.

1 3 5 7 9 8 6 4 2

A CIP catalogue record for this book is available from
the British Library

Typeset by CentraCet Limited, Cambridge
Printed by Mackays of Chatham PLC, Chatham, Kent

For Em

Acknowledgements

I would like to thank Christopher Maclehose and Anne O'Brien for setting me on the road to Wigan, Nikki Sheriff for the map room, Kristin Jakob for the right garden, Jean Sellars for the proper attire, George Thompson for the poetry and Ian Winstanley for the world underneath the surface.

Most of all, I owe Joe Fox, who for five books over fifteen years lit the way.

Chapter One

THE MOST BEAUTIFUL women in the world were African.

Somali women wrapped in robes suffused with purple, vermilion, pink. Around their necks beads of amber that, rubbed together, emitted electricity and the scent of lemons and honey.

Women of the Horn who peered through veils of gold, strands in the shape of tinkling teardrops. They stood veiled in black from head to toe, their longing compressed into kohl-edged eyes. In the Mountains of the Moon, Dinka women, dark and smooth as the darkest smoothest wood, tall and statuesque within beaded corsets that would be cut open only on their wedding nights.

And the women of the Gold Coast in golden chains, bells, bracelets, dancing in skirts of golden thread in rooms scented by cinnamon, cardamom, musk.

Jonathan Blair awoke tangled in damp sheets and shivering to the rain, gas fumes and soot that pressed against his lodging's single window. He wished he could slip back into his dream, but it was gone like smoke. The Africa in his bloodstream, though, that was for ever.

He suspected he had typhoid. His bedclothes were dank from sweat. The week before, he had been yellow from his eyeballs to his toes. He pissed brown water, a sign he had malaria. Which last night had demanded quinine and gin – at least he had demanded it.

Outside, morning bells rang in another foul day, resounding like blood vessels exploding in his brain. He was freezing and on the room's miniature grate a pitiful mouthful of coals was fading under ash. He swung his feet to the floor, took one step and collapsed.

He came to an hour later. He could tell by another outburst of bells, so there was some point to God after all – as a celestial regulator with a gong.

From the floor Blair had a low but excellent view of his sitting room: threadbare carpet of tea stains, bed with wrestled sheets, single chair and table with oil lamp, wallpaper patched with newspaper, window of weepy grey light that showed dead ashes on the grate. He was tempted to try to crawl to the chair and die in a sitting position, but he remembered that he had an appointment to keep. Shaking like an old dog, he struck out on all fours towards the fireplace. Chills squeezed his ribs and twisted his bones. The floor pitched like the deck of a ship, and he passed out again.

And came to with a match in one hand and a newspaper and kindling in the other. He seemed to do as well unconscious as conscious; he was pleased with that. The paper was folded to the Court Circular for 23 March 1872. 'HRH The Princess Royal will attend a Patrons' meeting at the Royal Geographical Society with Sir Rodney Murchison, President of the RGS, and the Right Reverend Bishop Hannay. In attendance will be ...' That was yesterday, which meant he had missed the festivities, had he been, well, invited, and possessed the cab fare. He struck the match and used all his strength to hold the sulphurous flame under the paper and sticks, and to push them under the grate. He rolled on his side to the scuttle. Please God, he thought, let there be coal. There was. He laid a handful on the fire. A kettle hung over the grate. Please God, he thought, let there be water. He tapped the kettle and heard its contents slosh from side to side. He fed the fire more paper and more coal, and when the coal had caught he lay as close as he could to the fire's warming breath.

He didn't like English tea. He would have preferred sweet Moroccan minted tea served in a glass. Or thick Turkish coffee. Or a tin cup of American boiled coffee. In London, however, he thought this was probably about as pleasant as life could get.

Once he'd had his tea, Blair chanced getting dressed. Fashioning his scarf into a sort of tie gave him problems, since he couldn't raise his arms without triggering the shakes. Because he hadn't dared put a razor near his throat for days he had the beginnings of a beard. He did still have decent clothes and a pocket watch to tell him that if he was going to walk from Holborn Road to Savile Row – he certainly didn't have money to ride – he had to leave at once. Ordinarily the route was an hour's stroll. Today it lay before him like a passage through mountains, deserts, swamps. He leaned against the window and stared down at the hunched backs of cabs and vying streams of umbrellas on the pavements. The glass reflected a face that was raw and high-coloured by a life spent out of doors. Not a friendly or comfortable face even to its owner.

Going down the stairs he swayed like a sailor. As long as he didn't break a leg he'd be fine, he told himself. Anyway, this was an appointment he couldn't afford to miss, not if he wanted to get out of England. He'd crawl on his elbows to do that.

London assaulted him with the steaming smell of horse drop-pings, the shouts of a rag-and-bone man contending with a line of hackney cabs, the argument punctuated with explosive discharges of phlegm. The boulevards of Paris were washed once a day. In San Francisco dirt at least rolled down to the bay. In London filth accreted undisturbed but for the daily piss from the heavens, creating a stench that made the nose weep.

Well, that was what England itself was like, a snuffling nose set by the blue eye of the North Sea, Blair thought. This other Eden, this sceptred isle, this chamberpot beneath the sky. And every subject proud of his umbrella.

At this end of Holborn Road the local tribes were Jews, Irish and Romanians, all dressed in bowlers and drab rags. Every street had its pawnshop, mission hall, tripe house, oyster stall, brace of beerhouses. If the surrounding stench was a miasma, the inhabitants on the street took no more notice than fish took of salt water. Horse-drawn buses with open upper decks lurched through layers of drizzle and fog. Men in sandwich boards carried the offers of chiropractors, dentists, psychics. Women in sodden boas offered glimpses of rouge and venereal disease. Corner vendors sold French rolls, penny rolls, hot potatoes and newspaper headlines announcing 'HEARTSICK STRANGLER KILLS BABE, MUM!' How the editors sorted out which of the daily multitude of urban atrocities to sell, Blair couldn't imagine.

Halfway, by Charing Cross, billboards advertised the staples of middle-class life: liver pills and elderberry, Nestlé's milk and Cockburn's sherry. Here the population was transformed to a masculine society in black suits and top hats: clerks with one hand clutching their collars, tradesmen with cotton gloves and ribboned boxes, barristers in waistcoats festooned with silver fobs, all jostling with umbrellas. Blair had no umbrella himself, only a broad-brimmed hat that diverted rain on to the shoulders of his mackintosh. On his feet he had a pair of leaky wellingtons, the soles lined with pages torn from a mission hymnal: 'A Closer Walk with Thee' in the left boot. He stopped every five minutes to rest against a lamp-post.

By the time he reached St James's, the chills had returned as spasms that made his teeth chatter. Although he was late, he turned into a public house with a blackboard that declared 'Cheapest Gin'. He laid his last coin on the bar and found himself given ample room by the regulars, a lunchtime gallery of shop assistants and apprentices with the drawn faces of mourners in training.

The bartender delivered a glass of gin and said, 'There's pickled eggs or oysters comes with that, if you want.'

'No, thanks. I'm off solids.'

Every eye seemed to watch him down the glass. It wasn't simply that their faces were white. Compared with other complexions, British skin had the sallow shine that reflected a sun long lost in a pall of smoke. A boy with brighter eyes edged along the counter. He wore a green band on his hat, a purple tie squashed as flat as a cabbage leaf, and yellow gloves with rings on the outside.

'*Illustrated London News*,' he said and extended a hand.

A reporter. Blair didn't wait for his change. He pushed himself away from the bar and plunged through the door.

The boy had the grin of someone who had found a pearl in his oyster. 'That was Blair,' he announced. 'Blair of the Gold Coast. Nigger Blair.'

His destination was in the sort of Savile Row townhouse that merchant banks and clubs were fond of: an entrance between banded columns, three floors of windows overhung with marble crenellation that expressed confidence, propriety, discretion. A brass plaque on a column read 'The Royal Geographical Society'.

'Mr Blair.' Jessup, the steward, was always solicitous for reasons Blair never understood. He helped Blair off with his hat and coat, led him to the rear of the cloakroom and fetched him tea and milk. 'How are you feeling, sir?' he asked.

'A little chilled, just the smallest bit.' Blair was trembling so hard from the short dash from the pub that he could barely keep the tea in the cup.

'Gunpowder tea will set you straight, sir. It's good to see you again, sir.'

'A pleasure to see you, Jessup. The Bishop is still here?'

'His Grace is still here. One of the men just took him some cheese and port. You catch your breath. I read the reports of your work with great interest, sir. I hope there will be more accounts to come.'

'I hope so, too.'

'Do you think you can stand, sir?'

'I believe I can.' The shakes were subsiding. He got semi-briskly to his feet and Jessup brushed his jacket.

'Gin will rot your insides, sir.'

'Thank you, Jessup.' He started to move while he was still faintly refreshed.

'You'll find the Bishop in the map room, sir. Please be careful. He's in a mood.'

The map room was testimony of the Society's contribution to exploration and knowledge. It had started as the African Association. A great map delineated expeditions the Society had sponsored: Mungo Park up the Niger, Burton and Speke to Lake Victoria, Speke and Grant to the White Nile, Livingstone to the Congo, Baker to Uganda in search of Speke. The walls were two levels of book and map shelves, the upper gallery supported by cast-iron columns and a spiral stairway. Watery light showed through the glass roof. In the middle of the room a mounted globe showed the British possessions as an earth-girdling corporation in Imperial pink.

By the globe stood Bishop Hannay, a tall man of middle age

in a black woollen suit and the inverted V of an ecclesiastical collar. Because most English dressed in black they seemed a nation in perpetual grief, but the sombre cloth and white collar only emphasized the Bishop's inappropriate vigour and the bluntness of his gaze. He had ruddy skin with red lips, and dark hair gone grey and wild at the temples and brows as if singed.

He said, 'Sit down, Blair. You look like Hell.'

Two high-backed chairs were at a map table set with cheese and port. Blair accepted the invitation to collapse.

'It's good to see you again, too, Your Grace. Sorry about being late.'

'You stink of gin. Have some port.'

Hannay poured him a glass, taking none for himself.

'You're in bad odour altogether, Blair. Embezzlement of charitable funds, wilful disobedience of orders, abetting slavery, for God's sake! You embarrassed the Society and the Foreign Office. And you were my recommendation.'

'I only took funds that were owed me. If I could meet with the Board of Governors—'

'If you did, they'd slap your face and turn you out of the door.'

'Well, I'd hate to provoke them to violence.' Blair refilled the glass and looked up. 'You'll listen to me?'

'I'm not as easily shocked as the others. I expect moral turpitude.' The Bishop sat back. 'But, no, I won't listen because it would be a waste of time. They resent you for reasons that have nothing to do with the accusations.'

'Such as?'

'You're American. I know you were born here, but you're American now. You have no idea how abrasive your style and voice can be. And you're poor.'

Blair said, 'That's why I took the money. There I was in Kumasi on survey. I'm not like Speke, I don't need an army, just

7

five men, assay equipment, medicine, food, gifts for the chiefs. I had to pay the men in advance, and I'd already spent all my own funds. Those people depend on me. Twenty pounds. It's little enough money anyway and half the men die. Where was all the money promised by the Foreign Office and the Society? Spent by the colonial administration in Accra. The only thing I could get my hands on was the Bible Fund. I used it. It was food or books.'

'Bibles, Blair. The food of souls. Even if it was for Methodists.' The Bishop whispered so low that Blair couldn't tell whether he was inviting a laugh.

'You know what the office in Accra spent my money on? They splurged on ceremonies and honours for a murderous cretin – your nephew.'

'It was an official visit. Of course they put on a show. If you weren't so poor it wouldn't have been a problem. That's why Africa is a field for gentlemen. Whereas you are—'

'A mining engineer.'

'Let's say more than just a mining engineer. A geologist, a cartographer, but definitely not a gentleman. Gentlemen have sufficient private means so that unexpected situations don't become painful embarrassments. Don't worry, I made good on the Bible Fund for you.'

'With the money I spent in Kumasi, the Society still owes me a hundred pounds.'

'After the way you disgraced them? I don't think so.'

The Bishop stood. He was as tall as a Dinka. Blair knew for sure because Hannay was the only member of the Board of Governors ever to go to Africa, the real Africa south of the Sahara. Blair had taken him into the Sudan, where they encountered first the flies, then the cattle, and finally the camp of nomadic Dinkas. The women ran from the visitors' white

8

faces. Africans usually did: the story was that whites ate blacks. The Dinka men stood in a bold line, naked except for a ghostly dusting of ash and armbands of ivory. Out of curiosity the Bishop stripped off his suit and matched himself limb for limb with the largest warrior. From the shoulders down in every physical particular the two giants were identical.

Hannay rose. He gave the globe a light spin. 'This slavery business. Explain that.'

Blair said, 'Your nephew, Rowland, came inland slaughtering animals.'

'He was gathering scientific specimens.'

'Specimens with holes. When someone shoots fifty hippos and twenty elephants in half a day, he's a butcher, not a scientist.'

'He's an amateur scientist. What has that to do with slavery?'

'Your nephew revealed he had a commission from the Foreign Office to investigate native affairs, and he declared that he was shocked to find slavery in a British colony.'

'British *protectorate*.' Hannay put up his hand.

'He had troops and a letter from you retaining me as his guide. He announced he would free the Ashanti's slaves and put the king in irons. It was a statement designed to provoke an Ashanti reaction and bring in British troops.'

'What's wrong with that? The Ashanti grew fat off slavery.'

'So did England. England and the Dutch and the Portuguese set up the slave trade with the Ashanti.'

'But now England has shut the slave trade down. The only way to do it completely is to crush the Ashanti and make British rule secure throughout the Gold Coast. But you, Jonathan Blair, my employee, took the side of black slavers. Just when did you find it in your competence to frustrate the policies of the Foreign Office or to question the moral vision of Lord Rowland?'

Blair knew Hannay used Rowland's title to emphasize his

own far inferior status. He swallowed the impulse to make an angry, democratic exit.

'All I did was advise the king to retreat and live to fight another day. We can slaughter him and his family a few years from now.'

'The Ashanti fights well. It won't be a slaughter.'

'The Ashanti goes into battle with a musket and boxes of verse from the Koran stitched to his shirt. The British infantryman goes into battle with a Martini-Henry rifle. It will be a glorious slaughter.'

'Meanwhile the evil of slavery goes on.'

'England doesn't want their slaves, it wants their gold.'

'Of course it does. That's what you were supposed to find and didn't.'

'I'll go back for you.' He had meant to introduce the offer slowly, not to blurt it out as desperately as this.

The Bishop smiled. 'Send you back to the Gold Coast? So you could abet your slaver friends again?'

'No, to finish the survey I've already started. Who knows the land as well as I do?'

'It's out of the question.'

Blair was familiar enough with Hannay to understand that the Bishop answered personal appeal with contempt. Well, there were many routes to Africa. He tried a different one. 'I understand there'll be an expedition to the Horn next year. There's gold there. You'll need someone like me.'

'Someone *like* you, not necessarily you. The Society would prefer anyone to you.'

'You're the major sponsor, they'll do what you say.'

'At the moment that does not work to your benefit.' Hannay managed to look amused without a smile. 'I see through you, Blair. You hate London, you detest England, every hour here is odious to you. You want to get back to your jungle and your coffee-coloured women. You are transparent.'

Blair felt a warm flush on his cheeks that had nothing to do with either malaria or port. Hannay had diagnosed him in a brutally accurate way. And perhaps dismissed him, too. The Bishop crossed to the bookshelves. Burton's *First Footsteps in East Africa* was there. Also Livingstone's *Missionary Travels*. Both had been bestsellers on a scale usually reserved for Dickens's maudlin myths of London. Hannay ran his fingers lightly across Society reports: 'Trade Routes of the Arab Dhow', 'Superstitions and Rituals of the Hottentot', 'Mineral Resources of the Horn of Africa', 'Certain Practices among the Peoples of the Horn'. The latter two had been Blair's own minor contributions. As if he were alone, Hannay moved in a leisurely fashion to the shelf devoted to South Africa, to Zulus and Boers.

No protest or exit line came to Blair's mind. Perhaps he had been expelled and the expulsion had been so swift that he had missed the kick. In the silence he calculated how much he owed for his miserable lodging. Besides the clothes on his back he owned nothing that didn't fit into a pack. His only valuable possession was his surveying equipment: chronometer, brass sextant, telescope.

'What are your prospects?' Bishop Hannay asked, as if Blair had been wondering aloud.

'There are other mining companies in London. The East India Company or an Egyptian interest. I'll find something.'

'Any employer will ask for a recommendation, and you'll be publicly infamous before the week is out.'

'Or go to New York or California. There's still plenty of gold there.'

'Not without a steamship ticket. Your hat is soaked. You didn't have enough for a cab here.'

'For a bishop you are a mean son of a bitch.'

'I'm Church of England,' Hannay said. 'That gives me a great deal of latitude. That's why I tolerate you.'

'I've engineered Hannay mines in America, Mexico, Brazil. You're the one who sent me to Africa.'

'Asked, not sent, and you were off like a shot.'

'I'm not asking for money, not even what the Society owes me. Just a ticket to New York, nothing more.'

'That's all?'

'The world is full of mines.'

'And like the white rabbit, you'll pop down a hole and never be seen again.' To emphasize his point, Hannay dropped his own frame into the chair opposite Blair.

'Right.'

'Well, I would miss you, Blair. You may be many things, but a rabbit is hardly one of them. I do feel responsibility for you. You've done some good work in difficult places, that's absolutely true. Your company, when you control your language, isn't disagreeable. It's pathetic to see you reduced to this condition. Tomorrow you'll be boiling your boots and dining on them. Or dining on the citizens of London. No, you're not a rabbit.'

'Then get me out of this place.'

The Bishop put his hands together in a way that on anyone else would have looked like prayer; on him it was simply concentration. 'You'd ship to New York out of Liverpool?'

Blair nodded, for the first time with a little hope.

'Then there might be something for you on the way,' Hannay continued.

'What's "on the way"?'

'Wigan.'

Blair laughed, surprised that he had the strength. He said, 'Thanks, I'd rather starve.'

12

'Wigan is mining country. The world is full of mines, you said so yourself.'

'I meant gold mines, not coal.'

'But you started in coal mines.'

'So I know the difference.'

'A hundred pounds,' Hannay said. 'And expenses.'

'You owe me the hundred. Expenses in Wigan? You mean all the meat pie I can eat?'

'And a place on next year's expedition. They'll be mustering in Zanzibar and attempting to cross the continent from the east coast of Africa to the west, aiming for the mouth of the Congo. I can't guarantee the position – I'm only a sponsor – but I will speak for your character.'

Blair refilled his glass and tried to keep the decanter steady. This was all he could have hoped for, weighed against Wigan.

'Just to look at a coal mine? There are a hundred better men for that already in Wigan.'

'No. What I want you to do is for the Church.'

'Lectures? Lantern slides of Africa? Missionaries I have admired, that kind of thing?'

'That would strain credulity too much. No, something better suited to your nature, your curiosity, your peculiar background. Something private. I have a young curate in Wigan. A "low church" kind of curate, the evangelical kind. Practically Methodist, almost Wesleyan. A zealot for preaching to fallen women and convicted men. The problem is not that he's a fool but that I can't find him. Like the white rabbit, he has gone down a hole and disappeared.'

'You mean he went down a mine?' Blair asked.

'No, no, just that he's vanished. It's been two months since he was seen in Wigan. The police have asked questions, but our constables are local lads trained mainly for subduing drunks and finding poachers.'

'Bring in a detective from the outside.'

'Miners despise detectives as strikebreakers, which they usually are. You, on the other hand, blend in. You did it in Africa as well as a white man could.'

'You could get someone from London.'

'Someone from London would be lost. They wouldn't understand five words a Lancashireman said. Your mother was from Wigan, wasn't she? I seem to remember the two of us sitting at a campfire in the middle of the Sudan and your confiding that information.'

'We'd talked about everything else.'

'It was completely natural. My home is Wigan. It's a mutual bond between us. You lived in Wigan before your mother took you to America.'

'What's your point?'

'That when someone in Wigan speaks to you, you will comprehend what he's saying.'

Gin and port was not a bad combination. The chills faded. The mind focused.

'There's more to it,' Blair said. 'You're not going to all this trouble simply for a wayward curate. Especially a fool.'

Bishop Hannay sat forward, pleased. 'Of course there's more. The curate is engaged to my daughter. If he was outside a pub and skulled by an Irishman, I want to know. If he was saving a prostitute and seduced in turn, I want to know. Quietly, through an agent of mine, so my daughter and I and the rest of the nation won't be reading about it in the newspapers.'

'Anything could have happened. He could have fallen down a shaft, into a canal, under a coal wagon. Maybe he dipped into *his* Bible Fund and ran off with gypsies.'

'Anything. But I want to know.' From under his chair the Bishop drew a cardboard envelope tied with a red ribbon. He untied it and showed Blair the contents. 'John.'

'His name is John?'

'His Christian name. Also, fifty pounds in advance for any costs that you incur.'

'What if he walks into church tomorrow?'

'You keep it all. Get a decent meal in you and some more medicine. I've had you booked into a hotel in Wigan. The bills will go to me.'

'You mean, the bills will go to Hannay Coal?'

'Same thing.'

A hundred pounds was still owed to him, Blair thought, but fifty pounds was generous. The Bishop was a host who offered a spoon of honey for a spoon of bile. Blair was sweating so hard he was sticking to the back of the chair.

'You think I'll do this?'

'I think you're desperate, and I know you want to return to Africa. This is an easy task. A personal favour. It's also a form of minor redemption.'

'How is that?'

'You think I'm the hard man, Blair? Anyone but you would have inquired about my daughter, what condition she was in when she realized that her fiancé had gone to ground. Was she distressed? Hysterical? Under a doctor's care? You ask not a single word.'

The Bishop waited. Blair watched rain tap on the window, collect in beads, coalesce, and then sluice to the bottom of the pane.

'Very well, how is your daughter?'

Hannay smiled, getting the performance he was paying for. 'She's bearing up, thank you. She'll be relieved to know you've consented to help.'

'What's her name?'

'It's all in there.' The Bishop closed the envelope, tied it and placed it on Blair's lap. 'Leveret will be in contact with you at the hotel. He's my estate manager. Good luck.'

This time there was no doubt Blair was being dismissed. He stood, steadying himself with the chair, holding on to the envelope and its precious money. 'Thank you.'

'You overwhelm me,' Hannay said.

On his way out, Blair had negotiated the globe and was at the door when the Bishop called after him.

'Blair, since you will be working for me and near my home I want to remind you that some parts of the public do think of you as a sort of explorer. You have a reputation for getting close to the natives, first in East Africa, then in the Gold Coast. Picking up the language is one thing; dressing like them and acting like them is something else. People like to call you "Nigger Blair". Discourage that.'

Chapter Two

BLAIR RODE IN a railway car as hushed and polished as a hearse, with oil lamps that were as low as candles. He thought all he was missing were lilies on his chest. It didn't help that mourners seemed to have climbed in with him, because the rest of his compartment was occupied by two men and a woman returning from a Temperance rally. They wore militant black with red sashes that said 'Tea – The Drink That Cheers and Does Not Inebriate'. Since he still hadn't shaved, he hoped that he made a travelling companion too unsavoury to speak to, but they eyed him like vultures presented with a dying lion.

Though Blair had invested in quinine and brandy, fever came in tides that lifted him from crest to crest of sweat and left him exhausted between waves. Not that he could complain. Malaria was the minimum, the price of admission in Africa. There were far more extravagant tropical souvenirs for the unlucky – sleeping sickness, marsh fever, yellow jack, unnamed exotic diseases that caused haemorrhaging, paralysis or swelled the tongue like a pig's bladder until the air passage was choked. In comparison, malaria was minor discomfort, a sneeze, a bagatelle.

He rested his forehead against the cold window. Outside passed the bucolic scene of a farmer ploughing behind a shire horse, man and beast plunging into a sea of mud. The English monsoon. Mud rose in brown waves, carrying the farmer away. When he closed his eyes, a conductor shook him and asked if he was ill. My eyes are as yellow as your brass buttons; does that look well to you? Blair thought.

'I'm fine.'

'If you're sick, I'll have to put you off,' the conductor warned.

There was a moment of embarrassment among the tee-totallers after the conductor left. Then the one across from Blair licked his lips and confided, 'I was once as you are, brother. My name is Smallbone.'

Smallbone's nose was a rosy knob. His black suit shone, the sign of wool revived with polish. Blue lines tattooed his forehead. The blue was permanent, Blair knew: dust in the scars every miner collected from coal roofs.

'But my husband was saved,' said the woman at his side. She pressed her mouth into a line. 'Weak and worthless though we may be.'

There was no access to another compartment unless he crawled along the outside of the train. He considered it.

'Would you mind if we prayed for you?' Mrs Smallbone asked.

'Not if you do it quietly,' Blair said.

Smallbone whispered to his wife, 'Maybe he's a Papist.'

'Or a thug,' said the other man. He had a full beard with a black, curly nap that crept nearly to his eyes. An almost Persian beard, Blair thought, one of which Zoroaster would have been proud.

'I would have said a cashiered officer until you opened your mouth, which pronounces you American. I can see that you are usually clean-shaven, which is the habit of artistic types, Italians or French.'

The miner's wife told Blair, 'Mr Earnshaw is a Member of Parliament.'

'That must account for his manners.'

'You make enemies quickly,' Earnshaw said.

'It's a talent. Good night.' Blair closed his eyes.

Gold was what drew the British. The Ashanti had so much that they seemed the Incas of Africa. Their rivers were flecked with gold, their hills veined with it. What better investment than a man with a tripod and sextant, auger and pan, and bottles of quicksilver? Let heroes discover the source of the Nile and the Mountains of the Moon, slaughter lions and apes, baptize lakes and peoples. All Blair searched for was pyrites and quartz, the telltale glitter of aurora.

In a feverish dream he was back on the golden sea-sands of Axim. This time Rowland was with him. He knew the Bishop's nephew was insane, but he hoped the ocean would soothe his blue eyes. The sea breeze tugged at Rowland's golden beard. Surf rolled in with the steady pace of wheels. 'Excellent,' Rowland murmured. 'Excellent.' At Axim, women panned the sands with wooden plates painted black to let the sun find the gold. Naked, they waded into the water to rinse the sand away, and rose and fell in the waves, holding the pans high. 'Wonderful ducks,' Rowland said and raised his rifle. A pan flew and the woman who had been holding it sank into a reddening wave. While he reloaded, the other women waded for shore. Rowland shot again, methodically, casually. As a woman fell, gold dust dashed across the sand. He rolled her with his foot so that she was dusted with sparkling flecks. Blair gathered the remaining women to lead them to safety, and Rowland reloaded and turned the rifle on him. He felt the barrel press against the back of his neck.

19

Sheer terror brought Blair half awake. It was sweat on his neck, not a rifle. It was only a dream. Rowland had never done anything like that – at least not at Axim.

We live equally in two worlds, an African had told Blair. Awake, we plod on with our eyes downcast from the sun, ignoring or not seeing what lies around us. Asleep, eyes open behind their lids, we pass through a vibrant world in which men become lions, women become snakes, in which the vague fears of the daytime become, through heightened senses, revealed and visible.

Awake, we are trapped in the present like a lizard in an hour-glass that crawls for ever over the falling sand. Asleep, we fly from the past into the future. Time is no longer a narrow, drudging path but an entire forest seen at once. Blair's problem, the African said, was that he lived only in the waking world. That was why he needed maps, because he saw so little.

Blair claimed he rarely dreamed, and this sent the African into paroxysms of laughter. Only a man without memory couldn't dream. What about Blair's parents? Even if they were far away, he could visit them in dreams. Blair said he had no memory of his parents. His father was anonymous, his mother was buried at sea. He was about four then. How could he have any memories?

The African offered to cure him so he would have memories and dreams.

Blair said, No!

He opened his eyes. On his lap was a Temperance pamphlet. 'Drink drowns all feelings of Sorrow and Shame! Drink turns the Labourer into the Sluggard, the Loving Father into the Prodigal! Does this sound Familiar to You?'

It certainly did. He would never get back to the Gold Coast.

With open eyes, with the clarity of fever, he saw that Hannay's promise was like a bauble dangled above a child's hand. Missionaries were the rage, and none of them would accept a man with Blair's reputation as a member of his team, no matter what the Bishop said, and Hannay knew it. So all that was really being offered was the hundred and fifty pounds, one hundred of which was already owed him. Which left whatever he could steal from expenses.

Wigan? A single minute spent there was money wasted. Blair thought he might even forget the hundred pounds that was owed. He could stay on the train to Liverpool and catch the first steamer to West Africa. The problem was that as soon as he set foot in the Gold Coast, the consulate would have him put back on board the ship. If he went into the bush to find his daughter, soldiers would follow. They had before. In which case she was better off without him.

He saw her dancing on a mat, winding and unwinding herself within her mother's golden cloth back in his house in Kumasi. The girl glowed from the threads. An entire language was spoken by the hands during a dance and her hands said: No, go away. Stop, stay there. Come here. Closer, closer. Dance with me.

He had no talent as a dancer, whereas the Ashanti seemed to have extra joints in their bodies just for dancing. She would cover her mouth because he was so clumsy. He watched her dance and wondered, Where am I in her? She had distilled everything that was decent in him and he wondered what she had done with all the rest. Perhaps there was some other child, black on the inside. It wasn't the gold that made her shine, the glow came from herself. If she was at all a mirror of him, why was the mirror brighter?

*

'The prostitute, at least, plays a traditional role in society. She is a fallen woman, perhaps weak, perhaps depraved, usually ignorant and poor, pawning her greatest prize for a few coins. A pathetic creature but understandable. The pit girls of Wigan, however, are a far greater threat for two reasons.' Earnshaw paused.

His eyes closed, trying to sleep, Blair listened to the sleepers passing underneath to the endless formula, *wiganwiganwiganwigan*, over a trestle bridge, *africafricafrica*, then again, *wiganwiganwigan*.

'For two reasons,' Earnshaw went on. 'First, because she has traduced her very sexuality. She has denied it and perverted it. A prostitute is, at least, a woman. But what is a pit girl? I have seen pictures of them for sale throughout England. Freaks wearing mannish pants, looking at the camera with mannish stares. The reaction of any decent woman is repulsion and disgust. Indeed, the instinctive reaction even of fallen women is the same.

'The second reason is that pit girls do the work that should be done by men. There is no other instance in industrial England of women shouldering labour meant for the stronger, more responsible sex. By doing so, the pit girl steals food not only from men but from the families of those men. Wives and children are the victims, a suffering to which mine owners turn a blind eye because they can pay less to a pit girl than they would to a man.'

'The union is with you,' the miner said. 'The lasses are a danger to labour and a threat to the institution of family life.'

Earnshaw said, 'Parliament has twice before tried to chase them from the pits and failed, which has only made the women more brazen. This time we cannot fail. Christ has made this my crusade.'

Blair looked through slitted lids. Earnshaw's brows looked

electrified, as if Jehovah had anointed him with a lightning bolt. Besides his wiry beard, subsidiary tufts exploded from his nostrils and ears. Blair thought of suggesting butter to train the beard, the way Somali women groomed their hair, but Earnshaw didn't look receptive to new ideas.

As afternoon faded, the conductor came through the car to turn up the lamps. Earnshaw and the Smallbones perused their Bibles. Blair's pulse was too rapid for him to sleep, so he opened his knapsack and extracted the envelope Bishop Hannay had given him. He had removed the money before without bothering with the rest of the contents, which consisted of two onionskin pages and a photograph of a rugby team. The pages were written in the meticulous hand of a bookkeeper. Blair glanced at the signature at the end. O. L. Leveret, Hannay's man. He returned to the beginning.

I write these words as a friend and confidant of Revd John Edward Maypole, whose disappearance and continued absence has deprived the Wigan Parish Church and the town of Wigan of a vigorous and earnest spirit.

As Curate of our Parish Church, Mr Maypole assisted Revd Chubb in every regular parish duty, such as services, instruction in the Catechism, Bible School, calls on the sick and poor. On his own, Mr Maypole gathered the funds and founded the Wigan Home for Single Women Who Have Fallen for the First Time. It was during his work for the Home that he met a soulmate in Bishop Hannay's daughter, Charlotte. They were engaged to be married this July. She has been inconsolable. Otherwise it is the working class that has most keenly suffered the absence of Mr Maypole. He was a constant visitor to the poorest households, and although much of his social work was among women, he was a man's man who could take the rugby field with the brawniest miner, play fair and hold his own.

I apologize if what follows sounds like the contents of a police blotter. It is merely an attempt to reconstruct John Maypole's activities on 18 January, the last day he was seen. He performed the Morning Service for Revd Chubb, who was ill, and from then until noon visited convalescents. Dinner for Mr Maypole was bread and tea taken at the home of Mary Jaxon, widow. In the afternoon, he gave Bible class at the parish school, delivered food to the town workhouse and visited the Home for Women, where he oversaw instruction in nursing and domestic service. By this hour the work day was done. Mr Maypole spoke to returning miners, inviting them to a social at the parish rectory the following Saturday. The last person he is known to have invited was Rose Molyneux, a pit girl at the Hannay Pit. He was not seen afterwards, Since he often took tea alone with a book and had no obligations for the evening, Mr Maypole may well have concluded what was for him a normal day. Likewise, the following day, because his duties and interests were so wide and various, his absence was not commented on until evening, when Revd Chubb asked me to visit John's rooms. I reported that his housekeeper told me that his bed had not been slept in. Inquiries through the police have, since then, proved fruitless.

It is the desire and expectation of the Parish Church, of the Hannay family and of John's friends that any questions into his whereabouts be conducted in a manner that ensures that no scandal or public sensation attaches to the modest, Christian life he led.

O. L. Leveret, Estate Manager, Hannay Hall.

The photograph was stiffened with pasteboard. Twenty rugby players in makeshift uniforms of sweaters and shorts posed in two rows, one sitting and one standing, before a painted backdrop of a garden. Instead of shoes, they wore clogs with leather uppers and wooden soles. The men were slope-shouldered, powerful, some with legs as bowed as a bulldog's. The middle man in front marked the occasion by holding a rugby ball on which was written in white ink, 'Wigan 14–Warrington 0'. The group was balanced by the placement of the only two tall men at opposite ends of the back row. One was dark, with thick hair and a fierce glare directed at the lens. The other was fair, with eyes as placid as a veal calf's. By this figure was the notation in Leveret's hand, 'Revd John Maypole'. Etched on the reverse was 'Hotham's Photographic Studio, Millgate, Wigan. Portraits, Novelties, Stereoscopics'.

Even taking into consideration the dramatized language of letters, Leveret's words were a eulogy. A confused eulogy since he didn't know what tense to use in writing about the missing curate, past or present, dead or alive. It also struck Blair that for such a public figure as Maypole there was little indication of much hue and cry when he disappeared.

He studied the photograph again. About the other men there was a worn quality. In the youngest this was a gauntness around their eyes, in the oldest a trademark smudging on the foreheads and hands that wasn't ordinary dirt. By comparison, John Edward Maypole's hair was brushed back from a smooth brow. A chinless quality marred his profile, but it made him look more sincere.

Blair put the letter and picture away. He liked the name. Maypole. A good English name with both rustic and erotic connections, a hint of maids honouring pagan gods as they braided garlands around an ancient symbol of fertility. He doubted such a picture had ever come to the curate's mind, no more than thought could penetrate solid marble, he decided. The same could probably be said for the 'inconsolable soulmate', Miss Charlotte Hannay. Blair imagined different possible Miss Hannays. A virtuous Miss Hannay with a corset and a bun, dressed in mourning just in case? A pretty and brainless Miss Hannay who would ride a pony cart to visit the poor? A practical Miss Hannay ready with bandages and remedies, a local Florence Nightingale?

The dark sky turned darker, not with clouds but with a more pungent ingredient. From the window, Blair saw what could have been the towering effluent plume of a volcano, except that there was no erupting volcanic cone, no mountain of any size, in fact, between the Pennines to the east and the sea to the west, nothing but swale and hill above the long tilt of underground carboniferous deposits. The smoke rose not from a single point but as a dark veil across the northern horizon, as if all the land thereafter was on fire. Only closer could a traveller tell that the horizon was an unbroken line of chimneys.

Chimneys congregated around cotton mills, glass works, iron foundries, chemical works, dye works, brick works. But the most monumental chimneys were at the coal pits, as if the earth itself had been turned into one great factory. When Blake wrote of 'dark Satanic mills', he meant chimneys.

The hour was almost dusk, but this darkness was premature. Even Earnshaw stared through the window with some awe. When enough chimneys had passed one by one, the sky turned the ashen grey of an eclipse. On either side private tracks connected pits to the canal ahead. Between the pall and the lines of steel lay Wigan, at first sight looking more like smouldering ruins than a town.

Coal was worked into the town itself, creating coal tips that were black hills of slag. On some, coal gas escaped as little flames that darted from peak to peak like blue imps. The train slowed beside a pit as a cageload of miners reached the surface. Coated in coal dust, the men were almost invisible except for the safety lamps in their hands. The train slid past a tower topped by a headgear that, even in the subdued light, Blair saw was painted red. On the other side, figures crossed in single file across the slag, taking a shortcut home. Blair caught them in profile. They wore pants and coal dust too, but they were women.

The track bridged the canal, over barges heaped with coal, then travelled by a gas works and a rank of cotton mills, their high windows bright and the chimneys that drove their spinning machines spewing as much smoke as castles sacked and set ablaze. The locomotive slowed with its own blasts of steam. Tracks split off to goods sheds and yards. In the middle, like an island, was a platform with iron columns and hanging lamps. The train approached at a creep, gave a last convulsive shake and stopped.

The Smallbones were up at once and in the corridor, ready to engage the forces of darkness. Earnshaw pulled a bag off the rack overhead. 'Getting off?' he asked Blair.

'No, I think I'll ride to the end of the line.'

'Really? I would have thought that Wigan was your sort of place.'

'You'd be wrong.'

'I hope so.'

Earnshaw joined the Smallbones outside on the platform, where they were greeted by a priest in a cassock, making a happy circle of wraiths. At something Earnshaw said, the priest lifted an owlish gaze towards the train. Blair sat back and the group's attention was diverted by the arrival of a tall man in a bowler.

Blair was two hundred pounds ahead – well, one hundred

pounds ahead. Passage from Liverpool to the Gold Coast was ten pounds, and he knew he'd have to use a different name and disembark north of Accra, but doctors always ordered ocean voyages, didn't they, so he'd recuperate on the way. With luck, he could be gone tomorrow.

He replaced his hat over his eyes and was attempting to get comfortable when a hand prodded his shoulder. He tipped the hat back and looked up. The conductor and the tall man from the platform stood over him.

'Mr Blair?'

'Yes. Leveret?' Blair guessed.

Silence seemed to be Leveret's form of assent. A young man and a creature of contradiction, Blair thought. Leveret's bowler was brushed but his jacket was crushed. His striped silk waistcoat looked uneasy. His earnest, deep-set eyes pondered Blair's lack of movement.

'It's Wigan.'

'So it is,' Blair agreed.

'You don't look well.'

'You're an astute observer, Leveret. Not quite well enough to rise.'

'You were thinking of staying on, from what I hear.'

'The idea occurred to me.'

'Bishop Hannay advanced you funds to perform a task. If you don't, I'll have to ask for those funds.'

'I'll rest in Liverpool and return,' Blair said. The hell I will, he thought, I'll be on deck and at sea.

The conductor said, 'Then you'll have to buy another ticket in the station.'

'I'll buy it from you.'

'That may be the way you do things in America,' Leveret said. 'Here you buy tickets in the station.'

When Blair pushed himself to his feet, he found his legs frail and his balance untrustworthy. He fell in one long step to the platform, stood and gathered his dignity. The last disembarking travellers – shop girls with hat boxes – leaned away as he reeled by at a leper's pace into the station. A stove sat between two empty benches. No one was at the ticket window, so he leaned against the window sill and hit its bell. At the same time it rang, he felt a shudder; he turned and saw the train pulling away from the platform.

Leveret came in the station door with Blair's pack under his arm. 'I understand it's been a long time since you were in Wigan,' he said.

Leveret had the long face and shamble of an underfed horse and he was tall enough to have to duck under shop signs. He led Blair up the station steps to a street of shops of greasy red brick. Despite the gloom of gas lamps, the pavement was crowded with shoppers and outdoor displays of waterproof coats, wellington boots, silk scarves, satin ribbons, Pilkington glass, paraffin oil. Stalls offered sides of Australian beef, glutinous tripe, herring and cod arrayed in tiers, iced baskets of oysters. The smells of tea and coffee insinuated like exotic perfumes. Everything lay under a faintly glittering veil of soot. The thought occurred to Blair that if Hell had a flourishing main street it would look like this.

They slowed by a shopfront with the newspaper placard: 'LONDON SLASHER'. 'The local newspaper,' Leveret said, as if they were passing a brothel.

The Minorca Hotel was in the same building. Leveret ushered Blair up to a second-floor suite furnished in velvet and dark panelling.

'Even a rubber tree,' Blair said. 'I do feel at home.'

'I reserved the suite in case people would be visiting you in the course of your inquiry. This way you have an office.'

'An office? Leveret, I have the feeling that you know more about what I'm supposed to do than I do.'

'I care more about this investigation than you do. I'm a friend of the family.'

'That's nice, but I'd appreciate it if you stopped calling this an "investigation". I'm not the police. I'll ask a few questions that you have probably already asked, and then I'll be on my way.'

'But you'll try? You took the money for it.'

Blair felt his legs start to buckle. 'I'll do something.'

'I thought you'd want to get started right away. I'll take you around now to the Reverend Chubb. You saw him at the station.'

'And more fun than a barrel of monkeys, from what I saw.' Blair aimed himself into a chair and sat. 'Leveret, you found me on the train and you have dragged me here. Now you can go.'

'The Reverend Chubb—'

'Does Chubb knows where Maypole is?'

'No.'

'Then what's the point in talking to him?'

'It's a matter of courtesy.'

'I haven't got time.'

'You ought to know that we've warned the ship's captains in Liverpool that if you show up there with any funds, they've been stolen.'

'Well, so much for courtesy.' Blair gave Leveret a broad wink. 'The English are so grand to work with, such a smug little nation.' Talking was exhausting. He let his head loll back and shut his eyes. He heard scribbling.

'I'm putting down addresses,' Leveret said. 'I wasn't trying

30

to offend you about the captains, but I do want to keep you here.'

'And a great pleasure it is.' Blair sensed welcome oblivion on the rise. He heard Leveret open the door. 'Wait.' Blair stirred from his torpor for a moment. 'How old is he?'

Leveret took a moment.

'Twenty-three.'

'Tall?'

'Six feet. You have the photograph.'

'An excellent photograph. Weight, about?'

'Fourteen stone.'

Almost two hundred pounds, to an American. 'Fair hair,' Blair remembered. 'Eyes?'

'Blue.'

'Just in case I bump into him on the stairs. Thanks.'

His eyelids dropped like leaden gates. He was asleep before Leveret was out of the door.

When he awoke, it took Blair a moment to comprehend where he was. The fever had ebbed, but in the dark the unfamiliar furniture seemed suspiciously animated, especially chairs and tables so draped in tassels and cloths that they were virtually dressed. Standing, he felt lightheaded. He thought he heard horses but when he made his way to the window and looked down on the street he saw only people, which puzzled him until he realized that half of them wore clogs. Clogs were leather shoes with wooden soles protected by iron rails that could last a working man ten years. The perfect sound for Wigan: people shod like horses.

It was eight o'clock by his watch. The thing to do, it seemed to him, was to talk to the smallest number of locals in the shortest amount of time and get out of town. In Africa he had marched with eyes sealed shut with infection, with feet covered in sores; he could overcome a little chill to get out of Wigan.

He read Leveret's note on the table. The Reverend Chubb's address was the parish rectory, John Maypole's seemed near by, the widow Mary Jaxon's was in Shaw's Court, Rose Molyneux's was in Candle Court. There was no address for Miss Charlotte Hannay.

The widow Jaxon sounded like the best choice, more likely to be home, readier to gossip. As he picked up the paper he caught sight through the open bedroom door of a man in a mirror. Someone in a slouch hat, bad beard and eyes staring back like two dim candles.

Blair was not quite as ready for an excursion as he'd imagined. He had no sooner climbed into a cab before he passed out. Between black spells he was vaguely aware of shopping streets giving way to foundries, the sharp fumes of dye works, a bridge and then row upon row of brick houses. He revived as the carriage pulled up.

The driver said, 'This is Candle Court.'

Blair said, 'I wanted Shaw's Court.'

'You told me Candle Court.'

If Blair had made a mistake, he didn't have the strength to correct it. He got out and told the driver to wait.

'Not here. I'll be on the other side of the bridge.' The driver turned his cab around briskly in retreat.

The street was a paved trench between terraced houses built for miners by mine owners, two storeys back to back, under a single roofline of Welsh slate so that it was impossible to tell one house from another except by their doors. It was a maze of shadow and brick. The gas jets of street lights were far apart, and most illumination came from the paraffin lamps of beerhouses and pubs, or open windows where sausages, oysters or hams were for sale. Everyone else seemed to be at the evening meal; he heard a sea sound of voices within.

According to Leveret the Molyneux girl lived at number 21. When he knocked on the door it swung open.

'Rose Molyneux? Miss Molyneux?'

As he stepped into a parlour the door closed behind him. Enough of the street's faint light entered for him to see chairs, table and a cabinet filling the tight space. He had anticipated worse. Miners' houses usually had families of ten or more, plus lodgers stepping over and on top of each other. This was as quiet as a sanctuary. Relatively prosperous, too. The cabinet displayed ornamental pots: a ceramic Duke of Wellington, with his hook nose, was the only one Blair could identify.

The next room was lit by a rear window. Heat and the aroma of milk and sugar emanated from a kitchen range. A large pan of hot water sat on top. Blair opened the oven and raised the lid of the pot inside. Rice pudding. Two plates for it lay on a table. Wash tubs crowded in the corner and, curiously, a full-length mirror. A hook rug softened the boards of the floor. On the wall opposite the range a flight of stairs rose to a quiet bedroom floor.

Feet shuffled outside. Blair looked through the window at a miniature yard with a wash boiler, slop stone for washing and a pig rubbing against the slats of its pen. The pig raised its eyes yearningly. Someone was expected home.

Blair knew that to wait outside would be self-defeating because any loitering stranger was, until proven otherwise, a debt collector to be avoided. He went into the parlour to sit, but neighbours were passing by the front window and he couldn't lower the curtain without drawing attention: a lowered curtain was a public notice of death among miners. Odd he remembered that, he thought.

He retreated to the kitchen and sank into a chair set in the shadow of the stairs. The fever was between swings, leaving him limp. He told himself that when he heard the front door open he could return to the parlour. As he tipped back into shadow the wall pushed his hat forward over his face. He closed his eyes – just for a second, he told himself. The sweetness of the pudding scented the dark.

He opened his eyes as she stepped into the bath. She had lit a lamp but turned the wick low. She was black with silvery glints of mica, and her hair was twisted up and pinned. She washed with a sponge and cloth, watching in a full-length mirror not in admiration but because fine coal dust had insinuated itself so completely into the pores of her skin. As she washed she progressed from ebony to blue, and from blue to olive, like a watercolour fading.

She stepped into a second tub and directed a pitcher's stream of water over her face and shoulders. Turning within the confines of the tub her movements were a private, narrow dance. Steam hung as an aureole around her face, water ran in braids down her back and between her breasts. Minute by minute she transformed from black to grey to shell-like pink, though her eyes revealed a cool disregard for the flesh, as if another woman were bathing.

When she was done she stepped out of the tub on to the rug. For the first time Blair noticed a towel and clothes laid over a chair. She dried herself, raised her arms and let a chemise slip over her and stepped into a skirt of linen that was thin but of good quality, what a maid might steal from a house. Finally she released her hair, which was dark copper, thick and vigorous.

As Blair let his chair settle forward she stared into the dark like a fox startled in its den. If she cried for help, he knew that the house would quickly fill with miners happy to mete out punishment to any stranger who violated the privacy of their hovels.

'Rose Molyneux?'

'Aye.'

'Bishop Hannay asked me to look into the matter of John Maypole. Your door was open. I came in and fell asleep. I apologize.'

'When did you wake up? If you was a gentleman you'd have spoke up right away.'

'I'm not a gentleman.'

'That's clear.'

She looked towards the front door but made no move to it, and though the shift clung damply to her, she left her dress on the chair. Her eyes were dark and direct. 'I know nowt about the priest,' she said.

'On January 18th, Maypole was seen talking to you, and then he wasn't seen again. Where was that?'

'Scholes Bridge. I told the constables. He asked me to a social, a dance with songs and lemonade.'

'You were friends?'

'No. He asked all the girls. He was always at us for one thing or another.'

'What kind of things?'

'Church things. He was always trying to save us.'

'From what?'

'Our weaknesses.' She watched his eyes. 'I fell into a coal car, that's why I had t'wash.'

'Did you go to the social?'

'There was no social.'

'Because Maypole was missing?'

She gave a laugh. 'Because there was an explosion down the

pit. Seventy-six men died that day. Nobody here gave a damn about a priest.'

Blair felt as if the bottom had dropped out of his chair. Seventy-six men had died the same day Maypole vanished from sight and Leveret hadn't mentioned it?

From next door came a cannonade of clogs down a stairway. Bricks between houses were a membrane so thin that the stampede sounded as if it had descended the steps above Blair's head. A bead of water like a ball of light ran down the girl's cheek, coursed down her neck and disappeared. Otherwise she was still.

'No more questions?' she asked.

'No.' He was still trying to assimilate the news of the explosion.

'You're really not a gentleman, are you?'

'Not a bit.'

'Then how do you know the Bishop?'

'You don't have to be a gentleman to know the Bishop.' He got to his feet to go.

Rose said, 'What's your name? You know mine, I don't know yours.'

'Blair.'

'You're a bastard, Mr Blair.'

'That's been said. I'll see myself out.'

He was so dizzy the floor seemed to be on a slant. He guided himself with seatbacks through the parlour to the front. Rose Molyneux followed as far as the kitchen door, more to make sure he went than to say goodbye. She was framed by the sash and the kitchen light, white muslin and red hair. From the house on the other side came a volley of cabinets slamming and domestic denunciations joined by the wails of a baby.

'It's a small world, Wigan?' Blair asked.

Rose said, 'It's a black hole.'

Chapter Three

IN THE MORNING Blair found himself feeling strangely better. Malaria did that, came and went like a house guest. He celebrated with a bath and shave and was eating a breakfast of cold toast and dry steak when Leveret arrived.

'There's some terrible coffee on the table,' Blair offered.

'I've eaten.'

Blair went back to his meal. He'd had nothing but soup or gin for a week and he intended to finish the remains on his plate.

Leveret removed his hat respectfully. 'Bishop Hannay is up from London. He has asked you to dinner tonight. I'll gather you here at seven.'

'Sorry. I don't have anything to wear.'

'The Bishop said you would say that and I should tell you not to worry. Since you are American, people will assume you don't know how to dress for dinner.'

'Very well, you can go back to His Grace and tell him that his insult has been delivered. See you at seven.' Blair returned to his steak, which had the texture of incinerated rope. He became aware that his visitor hadn't moved. 'You're just going to stand there? You look like a doorstop.'

Leveret edged towards a chair. 'I thought I'd accompany you this morning.'

'Accompany me?'

'I was John Maypole's best friend. No one can tell you as much about him as I can.'

'You assisted the police?'

'There hasn't been a real investigation. We thought he was away and then . . . well, he still may be away. The Bishop doesn't want the police involved.'

'You're the Hannay estate manager, haven't you got things to do, cows to tend, tenants to evict?'

'I don't evi—'

'What's your first name, Leveret?'

'Oliver.'

'Oliver. Ollie. I know Russians in California. They'd call you Olyosha.'

'Leveret will do.'

'How old are you?'

Leveret paused, like a man stepping into high grass. 'Twenty-five.'

'The Hannay estate must be quite a responsibility. Do you evict aged tenants personally or do you have a bailiff for that?'

'I try not to evict anyone.'

'But you do it. You get my point? No one is going to talk confidentially to me if I have you at my side.'

Leveret looked pained. Besides making his point, Blair had meant to offend him; if brushing him aside with a paw left him scratched that was fine, but Leveret seemed to take the exchange as his own fault, which irritated Blair more. The man had an inward expression, as if the failing of the world was due to himself.

'I was in Africa, too. In the Cape Colony,' Leveret said.

'So?'

'When I heard you might be coming here, I was thrilled.'

*

38

Blair visited the newspaper office next to the hotel and Leveret followed.

Eight pages of the *Wigan Observer* were posted on the wall, announcing auctions of farm stocks and saw mills, vivid church pantomimes, complete railway timetables. Advertisements, too, of course. 'Glenfield's Starch Is the Only Kind Used in Her Majesty's Laundry.' The *Illustrated London News* was also offered; its front page was devoted to the Lambeth Slasher.

'You notice there are no washday encomiums from the Slasher,' Blair pointed out. 'Now there would be an endorsement.'

Punch, the *Coal Question* and the *Miners' Advocate* were offered to men, *Self-Help*, *Hints on Household Taste*, the *English-woman's Review* to ladies. There were local histories like *Lancashire Catholics: Obstinate Souls* and for the popular reader a selection of sensational novels about Wild West cowboys and Horse Marines. Glass cases displayed stationery, fountain pens, stamp boxes, steel nibs, Indian ink. A wooden rail divided the shop from an editor in an eye shade scribbling at a desk. On the walls around him were framed photographs of derailed locomotives, gutted houses and mass funerals.

Blair called Leveret's attention to the railway timetable in the newspaper. 'Have you noticed this? Timetables are the most reassuring information of modern life. Yet according to the *Observer*, same page, we read that five local people were run over in separate railroad accidents on Saturday night. Are these regularly scheduled executions?'

'On Saturday night workers drink and to find their way home they follow the tracks.'

'Look at this, steamship notices that include free transport to Australia for female domestics. In what other nation would a ticket to a desert on the far side of the world be a lure?'

'You're not an admirer of England.' The idea pained Leveret so that he almost stuttered.

'Leveret, go away. Count the Bishop's sheep, set mantraps. whatever you usually do, but leave me alone.'

'Can I get you something?' the editor said. His speech was lengthened by the Lancashire 'o' and shortened by a 'g': 'soomthin'.'

Blair pushed through the gate of the bar to study the photographs more closely. It was always educational to see what gas and steam could do to metal and brick. In one picture a building façade was sheared away like the front of a doll's house, exposing a table and chairs set for tea. In another a locomotive had propelled itself like a rocket on to the roof of a brewery. Two pictures were labelled 'Unfortunate Victims of the Hannay Pit Explosion'. The first was of the coal-mine yard. Standing figures were blurred while the bodies laid on the ground were in deathly focus. The other was of a long line of hearses drawn by horses with black plumes.

The editor said, 'Miners believe in a proper send-off. The *Illustrated London News* covered that one. Still the biggest disaster of the year so far. Intense interest. You must have read about it.'

'No,' Blair said.

'Everyone read about it.'

'Do you have copies of that edition?'

The man pulled out a drawer of newspapers hung on rods. 'Most of the inquest nearly verbatim. Otherwise you have to wait for the official report of the Mines Inspector. You seem familiar.'

Blair flipped through the newspapers. He had no interest in the explosion at the Hannay Pit, but the editions that covered the accident, rescue attempts and inquiries into the disaster also covered the weeks after John Maypole disappeared.

In the 10 March issue, for example: 'There will be a meeting of the patrons of the Home for Women Who Have Fallen for

40

the First Time despite the absence of Revd Maypole. It is thought that Revd Maypole has been called away by urgent family affairs.'

In the 7 February issue: 'Revd Chubb led prayers for the souls of parishioners who tragically lost their lives in the Hannay Pit Explosion. They are now with Christ. He also asked the congregation to pray for the safety of the curate, Revd Maypole, who has not been heard from for two weeks.'

And on 23 February: 'All Saints' Parish Church 21–St Helen's 6. Marked by William Jaxon's two tries, the victory was dedicated to Revd John Maypole.'

The rest of the editorial columns were taken up with the disaster. An engraved illustration showed rescuers assembled around the base of a pit tower that was decorated at the top with a Lancashire rose.

'Could I buy these?'

'Oh, yes. We did special editions.'

'I'll pay for the gentleman,' Leveret said.

'And a notebook, red ink, black ink and your best local map,' Blair said.

'An Ordnance Survey map?'

'Perfect.'

The editor wrapped the purchases without taking his eyes off Blair. 'The Hannay Pit explosion was a major story. It's things like that put Wigan on the map.'

On the way out, Blair noticed among the books for sale one titled *Nigger Blair*, with a cover illustration of him shooting a gorilla. He had never worn a moustache and never seen a gorilla. They got his slouch hat right, though.

New country was best seen from a high point. Blair scrambled through a trapdoor to the open top of the Parish Church tower, startling doves off the finials. Leveret struggled to pull his long frame through, picking up feathers and dust on his bowler as he did. It was midday, but the sky was as oily as dusk. When Blair opened and spread his map, granules of dirt immediately, visibly appeared on the paper.

Blair loved maps. He loved latitude, longitude, altitude. He loved the sense that with a sextant and a decent watch he could shoot the sun and determine his position anywhere on earth, and with a protractor and paper chart his position so that another man using his map could trace his steps to the exact same place, not a second or an inch off. He loved topography, the twist and folds of the earth, the shelves that became mountains, the mountains that were islands. He loved the inconstancy of the planet – shores that washed away, volcanoes that erupted from flat plains, rivers that looped first this way, then that. A map was, admittedly, no more than a moment in that flux, but as a visualization of time it was a work of art.

'What are you doing?' Leveret asked.

From a chamois purse Blair unwrapped a telescope; it was a German refractor with a Ramsden eyepiece, and easily his single most precious possession. He turned in a slow 360 degrees, sighting off the sun and checking a compass. 'Getting my bearings. There's no north indicated on the map, but I think I've got it now.' He drew an arrow on the map, an act that brought him a small, reflexive satisfaction.

Leveret stood, grabbing his bowler to keep it from being snatched by the wind. 'I've never been up here before,' he said. 'Look at the clouds, like ships from the sea.'

'Poetic. Look down, Leveret. Ask yourself why this seems to be an especially senseless jumble of streets. Look at the map and you see the old village of Wigan that was the church, market place and medieval alleys, even if the green is overlaid now by cobblestones and the alleys are turned into foundry yards. The oldest shops have the narrowest fronts because everyone wanted to be on the only road.'

Leveret compared eyesight and map, as Blair knew he would. People could no more resist maps of where they lived than they could portraits of themselves.

'But you're looking at other places,' Leveret noticed.

'Triangulation is the mapmaker's method. If you know the position and height of any two places and you see a third, you can work out its position and height. That's what maps are, invisible triangles.'

Blair located Scholes Bridge, which he had crossed the night before. In the dark and with his fever, he hadn't appreciated how completely the bridge divided the town. West of the bridge was prosperous, substantial Wigan, an orbit of business offices, hotels and stores topped by the terracotta coronets of chimney-pots. East of the bridge was a newer, densely packed community of miners' terraced houses with brick walls and blue slate tiles. North from the church, avoiding the bridge completely, a boulevard of well-to-do townhouses with a blaze of gardens ran to a thickly wooded area. A note on the map read, 'To Hannay Hall'. South lay the battlefield smoke of coal pits.

What was obscured to the eye but apparent on the map was that Wigan was vivisected and stitched back together by railways: the London & Northwest, the Wigan and Southport, Liverpool and Bury and Lancashire Union lines extended with sweeping geometric curves in every direction, connecting to the private tracks that ran to the mines. Haze veiled the southern horizon, but on the map Blair counted a full fifty active coal pits, incredible for any town.

He turned his glasses to the miners' terraces across the bridge. Perhaps they had been erected on straight lines, but since they were built over older, worked-out mines where underground props rotted and tunnels gave way, the walls and roofs above had shifted in turn until the houses presented a rolling, sagging, slowly collapsing landscape that was as much a product of nature as man-made.

Leveret said, 'I heard the story about the Bible Fund. And the, the—'

'Debauchery?'

'Fast living. However, it seems to me from a careful reading of the facts that you've been a champion of the African.'

'Don't believe what you read. People have many reasons for what they do.'

'But it's important to let people know, otherwise you'll be misjudged. It sets an example.'

'Like Hannay? Now there is one hell of a bishop.'

'Bishop Hannay is ... different. Not every bishop will support costly expeditions to the far corners of the world.'

'It's a luxury he can afford.'

'It's a luxury you need,' Leveret pointed out gently. 'Anyway, no matter how private your reasons for doing good in Africa, don't let people paint you quite so black.'

'Leveret, let me worry about my reputation. Why didn't you mention the explosion at the Hannay Pit in the information about John Maypole?'

Leveret took a moment to adjust to the change in subject.

'Bishop Hannay felt that information didn't apply. Except that everyone was so occupied with the explosion that we didn't take proper notice at first that John was gone.'

'You read Dickens?' Blair asked.

'I love Dickens.'

'Miraculous coincidence doesn't bother you?'

'You don't like Dickens?'

'I don't like coincidence. I don't like it that Maypole disappeared on the same day as a mine explosion. Particularly when the Bishop chose me, a mining engineer, to find him.'

'It's simply that we didn't pay sufficient attention to John's disappearance because of the explosion. The Bishop selected you, I believe, because he wanted someone from the outside whom he could trust. Your mining background is appropriate for Wigan, after all.'

Blair was still unconvinced. 'Was Maypole ever down in the mine?'

'It's not allowed.'

'He could only preach to the miners when they were up?'

'That's right.'

'But he did preach to them?'

'Yes, as soon as they came to the surface. And to pit girls. John was a true evangelist. He was of selfless, absolutely stainless character.'

'He sounds like someone I would cross streets of deep mud to avoid.'

With red ink Blair initialled the addresses of John Maypole, the widow Mary Jaxon and Rose Molyneux.

His mind stayed on Rose. Why hadn't she called for help? Why hadn't she even dressed? Her clothes were on the chair. Instead she had stayed in her damp chemise. When she had looked towards the door, was she as afraid of being discovered as he was?

John Maypole's room was near Scholes Bridge in an alley of brick walls leaning together so acutely that their roof lines almost touched. Between them a slice of grey air dropped on to Leveret and Blair. Maypole was obviously the sort of evangelist who chose to mingle with his congregation day and night, a man who was willing not only to descend to the depths but to sleep there.

Leveret opened a room furnished with bed, table and chairs,

45

cast-iron range, chest of drawers, wash basin, chamberpot set on linoleum of a dark, indecipherable pattern. Blair lit an oil lamp hanging on the wall. Its wan illumination reached to the glory of the room, an oil painting of Christ in a carpenter's shop. Jesus appeared delicate and unaccustomed to hard work, and in Blair's opinion His expression was overly abstracted for a man handling a saw. Shavings curled around His feet. Through His window was a glimpse of olive trees, thorn bushes and the blue Sea of Galilee.

Leveret said, 'We left the room as it was, in case he returned.'

A pewter crucifix hung in the centre of another wall. On a shelf leaned a Bible, well-thumbed theological books and a single slim volume of Wordsworth. Blair opened the chest of drawers and felt through the black woollen cassocks and suits of a poor curate.

'John wasn't interested in material goods,' Leveret said. 'He owned only two suits.'

'And they're both here.' Blair returned to the shelf, flipped through the Bible and books and stood them upright. They stayed. They hadn't leaned long enough for the bindings to warp. 'Is anything missing?'

With a deep breath, Leveret said, 'A journal. John recorded his thoughts. It's the one item that's gone. It was the first thing I looked for.'

'Why?'

'In case it might tell where he was going or what he was thinking.'

'Have you ever read it?'

'No, it was private.'

Blair walked around the room and to the window, which was dirty enough to serve as a shade. 'Did he ever have visitors?'

'John chaired meetings here for the Explosion Fund and the

Society for the Improvement of the Working Classes, not to mention the Home for Women.'

'Practically a radical.' Blair sniffed. 'He didn't smoke?'

'No, and he didn't allow smoking here.'

'Leveret, you described yourself in your letter as not only Maypole's friend but his confidant. Which suggests that he confided in you. What?'

'Personal matters.'

'Do you think this is a good time to hold out, after he's been gone for two months?'

'If I thought that the sentiments John shared with me in the intimacy of friendship had anything to do with his disappearance, naturally I would divulge them to you.'

'How intimate were you? Damon and Pythias, Jesus and John, Punch and Judy?'

'You're trying to provoke me.'

'I'm trying to provoke the truth. The sort of saint you describe doesn't exist. I'm not writing his tombstone, I'm trying to find the son of a bitch.'

'I wish you wouldn't use that language.'

'Leveret, you're a specimen, you really are.'

Even in the dusk of the room, Blair saw the estate manager's face heat to red. He lifted the painting and felt the back of the canvas. He paced off the linoleum: ten by twenty feet, ending in walls of whitewashed brick. He touched the plaster ceiling: seven feet high in one corner, six in another. He went to the centre of the room and knelt.

'Now what are you doing?' Leveret asked.

'The way Bushmen teach their children to track is to give them turtles as pets. The father releases the turtle and the child has to find it by following scratches the turtle claws make on bare rock.'

'You're looking for scratches?'

47

'I was looking for blood, actually, but scratches would do.'

'What do you see?'

'Not a damn thing. I'm not a Bushman.'

Leveret pulled out his watch. 'I'll leave you now. I have to invite the Reverend Chubb for tonight.'

'Why will he be there?'

Leveret answered reluctantly. 'Reverend Chubb has expressed some concerns about your fitness.'

'My fitness?'

'Not your intelligence,' Leveret said quickly. 'Your moral fitness.'

'Thank you. This promises to be a delightful dinner party. Will there be other guests concerned about my moral fitness?'

Leveret backed towards the door. 'A few.'

'Well, I'll try to stay sober.'

'The Bishop has faith in you.'

'The Bishop?' Blair could hardly keep from laughing.

The night before, darkness had softened the terraced houses on the eastern side of Scholes Bridge; now daylight and soot outlined every brick and slate. The mystery cast by gas lamps was replaced by a meanness of block after block of back-to-back construction that showed in leaning walls and the reek of privies. The daytime sound was different because women and children were in the streets and the din of their clogs on stone rang through the singsong of vendors and tinkers. Miners wore clogs, mill workers wore clogs, everyone in Scholes wore clogs. What had Rose Molyneux called Wigan? A black hole? It was a loud hole.

John Maypole had met her at the bridge. It was a logical place to follow the martyr's steps.

It wasn't quite the Via Dolorosa. The corner beerhouse was a parlour with long tables, barrels of beer and cider, and the commercial hospitality of pickled eggs. Blair introduced himself to the owner as Maypole's cousin and suggested that the family would reward good information about the priest, last seen two months ago at the bridge.

The owner reminded Blair that in March dark came early. And, as the man put it, 'Your Maypole might be a curate, he could be the Pope with a bell on, but unless a man comes in with his mates for a drink he's pretty much invisible this end of Wigan.'

A butcher's shop looked out on the next block. The butcher was Catholic, but he recognized Maypole from rugby. He said the curate had been walking at a stiff pace with the Molyneux girl, lecturing her or being lectured by her.

'She's a Catholic girl, she stood right up to him. It caught my eye how Maypole was pulling off his choker – you know, his ecclesiastical collar.' He paused significantly. 'In a furtive manner.'

'Ah.' Blair brushed a fly away.

The fly returned to a swarm browsing on what looked like torn flannel: tripe. Pigs' feet and black pudding lay under a glass as scummy as a pond. The butcher leaned across to whisper, 'Priests are human. The flesh is weak. It never hurt a man to wet his willy.'

Blair looked around. He wouldn't have been too surprised to see a willy or two hanging from hooks. 'They looked friendly, then? I thought you said that one seemed to be lecturing the other.'

'That's Rose, complete with thorns, as the saying goes.'

The butcher was the last person who recalled anyone resembling Maypole. These things happened in Africa, Blair thought. Missionaries vanished all the time. Why not in darkest Wigan?

Blair spent the afternoon asking about his missing cousin John Maypole at the Angel, Harp, George, Crown and Sceptre, Black Swan, White Swan, Balcarres Arms, Fleece, Weavers' Arms, Wheelwrights' Arms, Windmill, and the Rope and Anchor. Along the way he bought not new but old clothes from a 'shoddy shop'. 'Shoddy' were clothes so old they were ready to be torn up and used as fertilizer; in fact, they were more valuable as fertilizer than as clothes. Perfect miner's clothes.

By six he was in a pub called the Young Prince. Outside, the establishment looked to be falling down. Corner bricks had dropped like rotted teeth; slate tiles had skated off the roof. Yet the interior boasted a mahogany bar, a glowing hearth and the Young Prince himself, mounted on a pedestal beside the door. The Prince was apparently a fighting dog of some renown, a bull terrier white when alive, now stuffed and turning grey with immortality.

Miners were just arriving. A few had been home, washed and returned in clean caps and white silk scarves. The majority, however, had stopped on their way from the pit to rinse their throats first. Where their caps tipped back was a peek of white skin and hairlines tattooed from coal scars; the older men smoked long clay pipes and wore scars on their foreheads as blue as the veins in Stilton cheese. Blair ordered a hot gin for his fever, which was returning in a spiteful manner, as if it had left him alone too long, and listened to arguments about racing doves, the decline of rugby, whether a ferret or a dog could kill more rats. This was edifying company, he thought. He had once spent a day listening to an Ethiopian describe different ways to skin and cook a snake, which was a discourse by Socrates compared with this.

This was not a job for him, he thought. He was serious with Leveret: Maypole was too opposite. How could he retrace the steps of a man who was practically a martyr? The curate was an Englishman who saw the world as a battle between Heaven and Hell, whereas he saw it as geology. Maypole thought of England as a shining lamp unto all nations, which to him was like claiming that the world was flat.

Blair became aware that he had been joined at his table by a familiar face, Mr Smallbone from the train, except that he had traded his suit for a miner's moleskin jacket and a leather pouch like the kind used by bookmakers at race courses hung from his shoulder. His prominent nose, set off by blank smudges on his cheeks, was in crimson bloom.

'I'm not drinking,' Smallbone said.

'I can see that.'

'I came in with the lads, I didn't spend a penny, I was only being sociable. It's a very friendly situation, the Young Prince.'

'That's what you tell Mrs Smallbone?'

'Mrs Smallbone is another story.' Smallbone sighed as if his wife was a volume to herself, then brightened. 'You're come to the right place, especially tonight. Oh, if you'd gone to the Harp.'

'I was at the Harp.'

'Irish. Is it me or is it dry in here?'

Blair caught the barman's attention and held up two fingers.

'The fights at the Harp. Every night it's one Irishman biting off the nose of another Irishman. They're good men. Oh, there's no one better for digging a hole than an Irishman. But for the day-in, day-out getting of coal there's nothing like a

Lancashireman.' Smallbone sighed as the gins arrived and took
his before it hit the table. 'Your Welshman, your Yorkshireman,
but above all, your Lancashireman.'

'Underground?'

'So to speak. Your health.'

They drank, Blair half his glass at a go, Smallbone with a
careful, parsimonious sip – a man for the long haul.

'You must have known the men who died in the fire.'

'Knew them all. Worked with them thirty years, fathers and
sons. Absent friends.' Smallbone doled himself another sip.
'Well, not all. There are always miners from outside Wigan. Day
workers. You never even know their last names. If they're Welsh
you call them "Taffy", if they're Irish they're "Paddy", and if
they're missing two fingers you call them "Two Pints". As long
as they can get coal, that's all that matters.'

A group of women entered. Respectable women were rele-
gated to an area called the snug; their bustles would upset
glasses if they even tried to make their way to the bar. These
four, however, pushed through. Boldness was not the only
difference: from the waist up they dressed in woollen head
shawls and flannel shirts, but their sack skirts were rolled up to
the waist like cummerbunds and sewn to stay permanently out
of the way of their corduroy trousers. Their hands were blue on
one side, pink on the other, their faces raw and damp from
washing.

The bartender didn't seem surprised. 'Beers?'

'Ales,' said a big girl with ginger hair. She told the other
girls, 'He'd forget his balls if they weren't in a bag.' Her eyes
roamed the pub until she noticed Blair. 'You're a photographer?'

'No.'

'I do photographs. My friend Rose and I pose in work
clothes or Sunday dresses. We're very popular.'

'Rose who?'

'My friend Rose. No artistic poses, if you know what I mean.'

'I know what you mean,' Blair said.

'Call me Flo.' Ale in hand, she approached his table. Her features were plain but she had painted her lips and cheeks with enough rouge to look like a tinted photo. 'You're American.'

'You have a good ear, Flo.'

The compliment brought pink to her face. Her hair seemed to spring electrically from her shawl. She put Blair in mind of Queen Boadicea, the mad queen of the Britons who almost drove Caesar's troops back into the sea.

She said, 'I like Americans. They don't stand on ceremony.'

'I don't stand on any ceremony at all,' Blair promised her.

'Not like someone from London.' There was a dramatic quality to Flo; London was clearly her equivalent of a nest of lice. 'Members of Parliament who wanted to put honest girls out of work.' Her gaze swooped down on Smallbone. 'And the little arse-kissers who help them.'

Smallbone listened unprovoked, a pat of butter that wouldn't melt in a furnace. She turned her attention back to Blair. 'Could you see me in a factory? Flouncing around in a skirt, seeing to a bobbin here and a spool there? Going pale and deaf and tied to a machine? Not me. And not you, because you never see any photographers in a factory. People only want to buy pictures of women at a mine.'

A voice behind them said, 'He's no photographer.'

Blair looked up at a young miner wearing a jacket with a velvet collar and a silk scarf with brown spots. He recognized Bill Jaxon from the picture of the rugby team.

Jaxon said, 'Last night he visited Rose.'

The rest of the pub was silent, a tableau. It struck Blair that Jaxon's entrance was expected. Relished. Even the Young Prince's glass eyes seemed to show a fresh gleam.

Jaxon said mildly, 'You didn't knock, did you? She said she was lucky to be dressed.'

'I apologized.'

Flo said, 'Bill, he's drunk. Besides, he's got no clogs. He'd be no sport at all.'

Jaxon said, 'Hush up, Flo.'

What clogs had to do with sport, Blair didn't know.

Jaxon delivered his attention back to Blair. 'You're from the Bishop, Rose says.'

'From Reverend Maypole's family, I heard,' Smallbone said.

'Both.'

'A distant relation?' Jaxon asked.

'Very distant.' When Blair twisted in his chair to look up at Jaxon he had a sensation of envelopment, like a mouse in a large hand. It wasn't comfortable. Bill Jaxon had fair features and straight dark hair, exceedingly combed, a pearly scarf tucked under a ploughshare of a jaw, the sort that could make an actor's career. Blair said, 'I was asking Rose about Reverend Maypole. Weren't you on the same rugby team?'

'We were.'

'Maybe you can help.'

At a signal Blair hadn't caught, Smallbone jumped from the chair and Jaxon sat. The man was the centre of attention, a sun in the benighted universe of this pub, Blair thought. He remembered how in the photograph Maypole had been looking at Jaxon instead of at the camera. Jaxon's eyes said he took questions as seriously as charades.

'Ask away.'

'Did you see Reverend Maypole that last day?'

'No.'

'Do you have any idea what happened to him?'

'No.'

'Did he seem unhappy?'

54

'No.'

That seemed to cover it, Blair thought. For form's sake, he added, 'What did you talk about with John Maypole?'

'Sports.'

'Did you ever talk about religious matters?'

'The Reverend said Jesus would have been a champion rugby player.'

'Really?' This was a revelation, a contribution of muscular theology: Christ in a scrum, breaking tackles, dashing upfield between centurions.

'The Reverend said Jesus was a working man. He was a carpenter and fit, so who can say He wasn't a great athlete as well? John said that Christian competition was a joy to God. He said he'd rather be on the field with our team than in church with all the dons at Oxford.'

'Makes sense to me.'

'All the disciples, the Reverend said, were working men, fishermen and the like. John said that impure thoughts undermined the athlete as much as any archbishop, and that it was the special duty of the strong to be patient with the weak.'

'I'm glad to hear that.' Blair didn't feel at his own physical peak. 'Exactly what positions did the disciples play?'

'What do you mean?'

'What positions on the team? Peter and Paul? Wingmen, you think? And John the Baptist? Lots of brawn, I would guess. Right wing?'

The pub became quiet. Jaxon liked sending up a visitor, he didn't like being sent up himself.

'You shouldn't make fun.'

'No, you're right.' Blair caught a glow in Jaxon's eyes. It was a bit like stirring coals. 'So my lost cousin John was a theologian and a saint?'

'That's one way of putting it.'

'Two ways, actually.' Blair decided to get out while he could navigate. He picked up his knapsack. 'You've been so helpful I can't say.'

'Are you going back to America now?' Flo asked.

'Maybe. Leaving Wigan, at any rate.'

'Too quiet?' Jaxon asked.

'I hope so.'

Blair wove to the door. Outside, an early twilight was turning to the dark of a cave. The street was a tunnel of gas lamps and beerhouse doors. Too late he remembered the fear expressed by his driver the night before. The man had plainly exaggerated, but there wasn't a cab in sight.

Mill girls in wool shawls and cotton dresses and carrying food cans rushed by, and the sound of their clogs was deafening. He felt the gin circulating sluggishly in his brain. When he had walked a couple of blocks, however, he realized what Bill Jaxon had said – or not said. When Blair had asked if he had seen Maypole that last day, Jaxon's answer shouldn't have been 'No'; it should have been, 'What day was that?'

Though it was a small point and Blair knew he should hurry to meet Leveret, he turned around and made his way back to the Young Prince. When he arrived, he wondered whether he had walked into the wrong pub because the room that had been full was empty. From his pedestal the Young Prince presided stiffly over abandoned chairs, fireplace and counter.

Blair knew that no crowd had passed him. Through the rear door of the pub he heard shouts. He opened it and edged carefully past a hole used as a pissoir to a junction of back alleys. Here, where there were no gas lamps, there was light from lanterns held on poles and clamour from at least two hundred people, including patrons and employees of the Young Prince, other miners, women in skirts, pit girls in trousers, families with babes, all of them festive as if at a fair.

56

It was a scene from Bosch's *Garden of Earthly Delights*. Or an ancient Olympic contest, Blair thought. Or a nightmare. He stayed in the dark unseen, though he could see Bill Jaxon standing naked in the middle of the crowd. He had a miner's overly defined body, the pinched waist and stark muscles that were the result of hard labour in extreme heat. His skin, pale as polished marble, contrasted with his dark hair, which now looked ruffled and wild. A second man had also stripped. He was shorter, older, with a barrel chest and bow legs. His head was shaved and his shoulders bore a backlit nimbus of curls. Behind him waved a green satin banner embroidered with an Irish harp.

Jaxon bent and laced on his clogs tight. Lancashire work clogs were leather uppers on ash soles, irons shaped like horseshoes on the soles for wear. Jaxon's were tipped with brass studs. He draped his scarf lightly around his neck and paraded like a thoroughbred in a paddock.

Jaxon's opponent advanced with the intent rolling gait of a bulldog. His shins were crosshatched with scars. His clogs were tipped with brass, too.

It wasn't human, Blair thought. More like cockfighting between rooster men wearing razors. In California they would have boxed with bare knuckles, which was effete by comparison. The mining-camp behaviour was familiar: backbreaking work relieved by blood sport. The wagering was also familiar; now Smallbone's money pouch made sense.

The bartender from the Young Prince said, 'The rules are: no high kicking, punching or biting. No wrestling to the ground. When a man goes down or breaks off or calls "Quit", the match is over.'

The other man was Irish. He told Jaxon, 'You'll look grand with a tin dick.'

'Fuck the rules,' Jaxon told the bartender. The smile released on his face was reckless, nearly gleeful.

The two opponents stepped back for a moment. A brass-tipped clog made a massive club, especially when swung with the full force of a miner's leg, and particularly against unprotected flesh. A miner could batter down a wooden door with his clogs.

In the lull Blair took in the feverish brightness of the bartenders' aprons, the whiteness of the two men in the swaying lights of the lanterns. It was a saturnalia, he thought, nothing English about it. It was clear from their faces that Jaxon was the favourite of Flo and the other pit girls and the object now of their anxiety.

The two men placed their hands on each other's shoulders and touched their foreheads together. Even while the bartender tied them loosely together at the neck with Jaxon's scarf they started pushing and angling for position. At close quarters a shorter, more experienced man had the advantage. The Irishman's threat was a veteran's trick, Blair thought. Let Jaxon try to protect his manhood and he'd be fighting on one leg. More likely he would go down with a shattered leg than a ruptured testicle.

The bartender held another scarf high. Waiting for it to drop, the two fighters leaned forward, heads touching. Flo and her friends put their hands together in prayer.

The bartender snapped the scarf down.

Ballet, Blair thought, as danced in Wigan. The first kicks were so swift that he couldn't follow them. Both men were bleeding from the knees down. With each hit a violent red blush spread on their skin. The Irishman tried to cave in Bill Jaxon's knee from the side. As Jaxon slipped the Irishman slashed his clog up, slicing Jaxon from knee to groin.

Jaxon leaned away and hammered his forehead down on the other man, whose shaved head split like a porcelain bowl of blood. Jaxon sidestepped a blind, retaliatory butt and swung his own leg from the outside, scooping the smaller man into the air. The scarf shot up into the air. As the Irishman hit the ground Jaxon swung his foot with his full weight. Clog and ribs met with a crack. A moan rose from the men below the banner of the harp.

The Irishman rolled and coughed black phlegm on to the dirt. As he hopped to his feet he struck back, stripping skin from Jaxon's flank. Jaxon's next blow caught the Irishman in the stomach and lifted him into the air again. The Irishman bounced from the ground to his knees and swayed. A bright effusion of blood flowed from his mouth. In that moment the fight was already over, except that it wasn't.

Jaxon announced, 'The man who bothered Rose, he's put me in a mood,' and his kick swung forward like the blur of a wing.

Chapter Four

THE CANNEL ROOM was the strangest formal dining room Blair had ever seen.

Bishop Hannay sat at the head of the table. Around it were his sister-in-law, Lady Rowland; the Reverend Chubb; a union man named Fellowes; Lady Rowland's daughter, Lydia; Earnshaw, the Member of Parliament from the train; Leveret; Blair; and at the foot of the table an empty chair.

The Cannel Room's ceiling, walls and wainscoting were panelled in polished black stone. Table and Queen Anne chairs were hand-turned work of the same material. Chandelier and candelabra seemed carved of ebony. Yet the walls showed no marble veins. The weight of the chairs was wrong. The temperature was wrong; marble always felt cooler than the air around it, but when Blair laid his hand on the table it was almost warm. Properly so, since cannel was jet, a form of clean, exceedingly fine coal. He had seen sculptures in black cannel. The Cannel Room was the only room made entirely of coal and it was famous. Its effect was heightened by contrasts: the luminous shimmer of silver and crystal on the black table, the deep purple of Lady Rowland's gown, the camellia white of Miss Rowland's dress.

The men – except for Blair of course – were all dressed for dinner in black, Hannay and Chubb in cassocks. The butler was

60

assisted by four footmen in black satin livery. The floor was carpeted in black felt to silence the sound of their feet. The effect was as if they were dining in an elegant hall far below the surface of the earth. Blair ran his hand over the table and looked at his palm. Clean: not a speck of carbon dust, not an atom, not a mote.

'Mr Blair, exactly what is it that you do?' Lady Rowland asked.

Blair felt Leveret watching anxiously. He also felt contending waves of gin on one side of his brain and fever on the other. He wished the room were a little less hallucinatory. The only reassuring note of reality was a pail of sand by each footman in case of fire.

'The Hannay interests own different kinds of mines in different parts of the world. North America, South America, England. I work as a mining engineer.'

'Yes, I know that.' Lady Rowland had the theatrical quality of a flower that was slightly past its prime, still beautiful but pouty. She asserted the ancient right of aristocratic *décolletage*, and had a manner of playing with the string of pearls that lay upon it. 'I meant, what were you doing in Africa? We read about explorers and missionaries. It seems to me so important that the first white man that Africans encounter be the right sort. They frame their impression from the first contact, don't they?'

'Well said,' agreed Hannay, a host who liked to see the conversational ball in play. Lady Rowland was young Lord Rowland's mother, the same Rowland whom Blair had described to Hannay as a 'murderous cretin'. Maybe this was family courtesy, he thought.

Blair refilled his wine glass, prompting a footman to come to life and bring out another bottle. Leveret lowered his eyes from the sight. The estate manager had tried to be a social palliative and was obviously dazzled by the sheer radiance of Lydia Rowland, but small talk was not in his nature, no matter how well he dressed for the occasion. It was like asking a walking stick to be an umbrella.

'Well, explorers are good at finding lakes, and missionaries are good at singing psalms, but neither of them are good at finding gold,' Blair said. 'That's what I was in West Africa for, to map where gold was most likely to be found. It's there; that's why they call it the Gold Coast. As for being the first white man, the Ashanti have already met Arab slavers, Portuguese slavers and English slavers, so I'm probably not going to lower their respect for the white race too much.'

Lydia Rowland was seventeen or so, Blair guessed. She was as fresh and milk-white as her dress. Her hair swept back in golden wings tied with velvet bows, and everything she said was with a breathless sense of discovery. 'I understand that you're the only man in England who can say what Ashanti women are like. Flirtatious?'

'Don't be grotesque, dear,' Lady Rowland said.

'It's a rash matter to send men who have no moral base,' the Reverend Chubb said. 'Missionaries don't just sing psalms, Mr Blair. They also conduct the saving of souls and the introduction of civilization. That never requires fraternization.'

Blair said, 'You can always stay ignorant of people you're supposed to save. Anyway, the missionary is there to introduce English business, not civilization.'

Earnshaw said, 'Surely the second white man into such places is the scientist. Your Grace, the Royal Society sponsors botanical expeditions around the world, does it not?'

'The rhododendrons at Kew Gardens were spectacular this year,' Lady Rowland said.

'Yes,' Blair said, 'but the botanist who brings rhododendrons from Tibet also smuggles out tea plants, and the botanist who brings orchids out of Brazil also smuggles out rubber trees, and that's why there are tea and rubber tree plantations in India. That's also why botanists are knighted, not because they find flowers.'

'That's a very jaundiced view of the world, isn't it?' Earnshaw looked over his beard. If on the train from London he had regarded Blair with suspicion, he now had the certain air of a man who had identified a snake by species and size.

'It may be a different point of view, but it's rather exciting,' Lydia Rowland said.

'It's not exciting to support slavery. Isn't that what you were doing in the Gold Coast?' Earnshaw asked.

'I think the stories we've heard about Mr Blair are just that – stories,' Leveret said.

'But there are so many stories,' Earnshaw said. 'How did you ever pick up that interesting sobriquet "Nigger Blair"? From your close association with Africans?'

Blair said, 'Funny you should ask. In the Gold Coast if you called a free African a "nigger", he could sue you. There "nigger" means slave, nothing else. He'd sue you for libel in a Gold Coast civil court and he'd win. The word was fixed on me by the newspapers in London, that's all. I can't sue here.'

'They have lawyers there?' Lydia Rowland asked.

'African lawyers, the first crop of civilization,' Blair said.

'So you're not offended when someone says, "Nigger Blair"?' Earnshaw asked.

'No, no more than I would be if another man called a springbok a spaniel because he doesn't know the difference. I can't be offended if someone is uninformed.' Blair was so pleased with himself for producing such a moderate response that he accepted another glass of wine. 'Whether he's a Member of Parliament or not.'

Teeth showed in Earnshaw's beard. It was a smile. He said,

'The interior of the Gold Coast is not civilized, it is the kingdom of the Ashanti. Just where did you stand in the Ashanti War?'

Blair said, 'There was no war.'

'Pardon?'

'There was no war,' Blair repeated.

'We read about it in *The Times*,' Earnshaw said.

'They marched out to have a war. They had dysentery instead. No war.'

'The disease?' Lydia Rowland asked, to be certain.

'An epidemic. Wiped out whole villages, and also hit the armies, British and Ashanti. They were both too sick to fight. And many people died.'

Earnshaw said, 'I read that you helped the Ashanti escape.'

'Members of the king's family were sick, some dying. Women and children. I led them out.'

'So you were practically a member of the Ashanti retinue. Why else would they trust you with their women?'

'Don't worry, Earnshaw, there'll be another Ashanti war and this time you'll get to kill the king and his family, too. Or maybe we can introduce syphilis.'

'He really is fully as awful as my son promised,' Lady Rowland told the Bishop.

'Then you're not disappointed,' Hannay said.

Turtle soup was followed by poached trout. Aspic made Blair queasy. He had more wine and wondered whether anyone was ever going to take the empty chair at the end of the table.

'I read something fascinating,' Lydia Rowland said. 'That the African explorer Samuel Baker bought his wife at a Turkish slave auction. She's Hungarian – I mean, she's white. Can you imagine?'

Bishop Hannay had more wine himself. 'Is this what all the young ladies of your set are imagining, Lydia?'

'I meant that it's terrible. She speaks four or five languages, goes to Africa with him and shoots lions.'

'Well, as you said, she's Hungarian.'

'And he's famous and successful. He was received at court by the Queen.'

'But his wife was not, dear, and that's the point,' Lady Rowland said.

'Whom we receive at court and whom we send to Africa can be two different sorts,' Hannay said. 'We could send a thoroughbred horse, for example, but it would be a total waste. Most of Central Africa is fly country. The insects carry some sort of malady that kills horses, even the best, within weeks. What you want is any four-legged animal that has been "salted" – bitten by the flies and survived. The same with men. The Royal Society selects its explorers from gallant officers. Then they get into the jungle and rot with fever or blow their brains out. But you could cut Blair's leg off and he would walk on the other. Cut off both and he would walk on the stumps. That's his gift: he absorbs punishment.'

Lady Rowland said, 'May I change the subject from Africa? Mr Earnshaw, what is it that brings you to Wigan?'

Earnshaw laid his knife and fork down. 'It's kind of you to ask. I am a member of a parliamentary committee looking into the employment of women called "pit girls" in the coal mines. They're women who work on the surface, sorting and moving coal as it comes up. We are, in fact, the third parliamentary committee that has tried to remove these women from the mines, but they are obstinate. That's why I've been talking to the Reverend Chubb and Mr Fellowes.'

Fellowes had spent the evening trying to choose between different knives and forks. He spoke for the first time; his voice was geared to union halls. 'It's an economic issue, Your

Ladyship. It should be men doing that work and getting decent wages, with the women staying at home. Or if they do want to work, work in the cotton mills like decent girls.'

'It's a moral issue,' the Reverend Chubb said. 'The sad truth is that Wigan is the most degraded city in England. The cause is not the men, who are the coarser sex. The reason is the women of Wigan, who are so unlike their softer gender anywhere, except perhaps for Africa or along the Amazon. Earnshaw tells me he has seen picture cards sold in London, sordid cards for low tastes, of French "models" and Wigan pit girls. Their notoriety only makes them more brazen.'

'Why Wigan?' Lady Rowland asked. 'Surely women work at pits in Wales and other parts of the country?'

'Not in trousers,' Chubb said.

Revulsion was shared by Lady Rowland and her daughter; for a moment they were mirrors of each other.

'Not dresses?' the girl asked.

'A mockery of a dress rolled up and pinned above the trousers,' Fellowes said.

Earnshaw said, 'They claim for reasons of safety, but the fact is that factory girls in full skirts work surrounded by intense heat and spinning gears. So we have to ask ourselves, why do pit girls *choose* to unsex themselves? It seems a deliberate provocation.'

'An insult to every decent woman,' Fellowes said.

'And damage to marriage itself,' Earnshaw said. 'The commission has gathered information from medical experts, including Dr Acton, the author of *The Functions and Disorders of the Reproductive Organs*. With your permission?' Earnshaw waited for a nod from Lady Rowland. 'Dr Acton, who is *the* authority, says that a young man unfortunately often forms his ideas of the feminine sensibility from the lowest and most vulgar women, hence has the mistaken impression that the sexual feelings of the female are as strong as his, an error that only leads to heartbreak when he forms a union with a decent woman.'

Lydia Rowland lowered her eyes, held her breath and blushed delicately; the effect was like a faint stain on fine porcelain. Blair marvelled at her; a person didn't need language if she could manage the colour of her cheeks so well.

'I want to be fair,' Earnshaw added, 'but there does seem to be a scientific correlation between dress and behaviour, because statistically pit girls have the highest rate of illegitimate births in the country.'

'We see them carousing naked in and out of the beerhouses every night,' Chubb said.

'Pit girls?' Blair asked.

'Yes,' Chubb said.

'Totally undressed?'

'Their arms bare,' Chubb said.

'Ah,' said Blair.

The main course was saddle of mutton, beetroot, mustard. The empty chair was still unclaimed.

'Actually, what I saw, besides bare arms, was a fight between miners. A kicking fight,' Blair said.

'It's called "purring",' Hannay said. 'Lord knows why. A traditional local sport. The miners love it. Barbaric, isn't it?'

'It vents the tension,' Fellowes said.

Hannay said, 'They vent their tension on their wives, too. Taking clogs off a drunken miner is like unloading a cocked gun.'

'How horrible,' Lydia Rowland said.

'There's a pit girl or two knows how to use her clogs, too,' Fellowes said.

'That's a domestic scene to contemplate, isn't it?' Hannay said.

Blair asked, 'What did John Maypole think of pit girls?'

There was quiet the length of the table.

'Maypole?' Earnshaw asked.

The Reverend Chubb explained that the curate of the parish church was missing. 'We continue to trust that John's fate will become known to us. In the meantime, the Bishop has imported Mr Blair to make unofficial inquiries.'

'Looking for John?' Lydia Rowland asked her mother.

'Like setting a black sheep after a white,' Earnshaw said.

'Does Charlotte know about this?' Lady Rowland asked her brother.

Chubb set his fork down. It rattled with the fury transmitted by his body. 'The truth is that John Maypole was naïve about the character of pit girls. The fact that more illegitimate children are born here than even in Ireland marks Wigan as a moral cesspool. They are women totally beyond the bounds of decency or social control. It is my duty, for example, to disburse church funds to unwed mothers who apply, making sure not to give money so lavishly as to encourage animal conduct. It would be a lesson to pit girls for me to withhold money from them, but since they refuse to request assistance the lesson is utterly lost.'

There was a silence after Chubb's explosion.

'Do you think they'll find a lake in Africa for Princess Beatrice?' Lydia Rowland asked Blair finally.

'For Princess Beatrice?'

'Yes. They've found lakes and falls to name for the rest of the royal family. The Queen and Albert, of course. Alexandra, the Prince of Wales, Alice, Alfred, Helena, Louise, Arthur, even poor Leopold, I think they all have something discovered and named after them. All but Beatrice, the baby. She must be feeling left out. Do you think there's anything left worth finding and naming for her? It just makes it more personal if you can find your own lake on the map.'

Lady Rowland gave her daughter's hand a touch of maternal concern. 'Dear, it doesn't matter what Mr Blair thinks.'

Meat was followed by fowl. Fellowes chased a round plover egg around his plate with a knife and spoon. In the shifting light of the candles Blair detected a Paisley pattern on the opposite wall like a watermark in black stone. Not Paisley, he realized, but ferns fossilized within the cannel. He moved the candelabra and other small, graceful, intricately delicate fronds came into focus. They were seen best in the corner of the eye. On a second wall what he had first taken to be irregular striation was in fact ghostly fossil fish. Moving diagonally across another wall were the imprints of a great amphibian.

He said, 'If it's all right, I'd like to visit the mine where you had the explosion.'

'If you want,' Hannay said. 'It seems a waste of time since Maypole was never below. The last thing we'd allow is preachers down the shaft, the men's work is difficult and dangerous enough. But when you want to, Leveret will arrange it.'

'Tomorrow?'

Hannay took a moment. 'Why not? You can tour the surface too, and see the notorious pit girls in action.'

Earnshaw rose to the bait. 'I'm surprised, My Lord, that you tolerate those women for a moment, considering the reputation they give Wigan. It seems to me that the question is not whether a handful of brazen women wear skirts or not, it's whether Wigan joins the modern world.'

Hannay asked, 'What do you know about the modern world?'

'As a Member of Parliament, I know the spirit of the age.'

'Such as?'

'The upwelling political reform, the social conscience of modern theatre and books, the call for elevated subjects in the arts.'

'Ruskin?'

'John Ruskin is a perfect example, yes,' Earnshaw agreed.

'Ruskin is the greatest art critic of our time, and also a friend of the working man.'

'Tell him, Leveret,' Hannay said.

Earnshaw was wary. 'What?'

'We invited Ruskin.' Leveret told the tale as deferentially as he could. 'We invited him to give a lecture on the arts to the workers. But when he arrived he looked out of the window at Wigan and he wouldn't leave the train. He refused. No entreaty made him budge. He stayed on the train until it left.'

Hannay said, 'It's public knowledge that Ruskin couldn't consummate his marriage, either. He does seem to be easily shocked.'

Lady Rowland's blush burned through her pallor. 'We will leave the table if you speak like that.'

Hannay ignored her. 'Earnshaw, I appreciate that unlike other visitors from London, you had the courage to leave the train. Before you lecture us about Wigan's place in the modern world, though, let me suggest that the question is not one of politics or art, but one of industrial power. The best measure of that is steam engines *per capita*. Between mines and mills and factories, there are more steam engines per person in Wigan than in London, Pittsburgh, Essen or anywhere else. It happens to fit nicely that the palm oil we import from Africa lubricates those engines. The world runs on coal, and Wigan leads it. As long as we have coal we will continue to do so.'

'What about religion?' Chubb asked.

'That's the next world,' Hannay said. 'Perhaps there'll be coal there, too.'

'Does this mean you insist on employing pit girls?' Earnshaw asked.

Hannay shrugged. 'Not at all, as long as someone sorts the coal.'

'How long will the coal in Wigan last?' Lydia Rowland asked. The thought had never occurred to her before.

'A thousand years,' Leveret assured her.

'Really? The price of coal shot up last year because of a supposed shortage. We heard in London that English coalfields were running out,' Earnshaw said.

Hannay said blandly, 'Well, the good news is that we aren't.'

Dessert was pineapple cream and a meringue that rose to a snowy peak in the middle of the table.

'The importance of family,' Lady Rowland said.

Fellowes said, 'Social reform.'

'Moral life,' said Chubb.

'Blair, what do you think has been the Queen's greatest gift to England?' Hannay asked.

Before he could answer, a new voice said, 'Chloroform.'

A new arrival had slipped in through a service door. She was not much more than twenty but wore a matron's soberly purple dress and long gloves and apparently had just arrived at the house because her hair of brooding Celtic red was dragged under a dark bonnet that shadowed a face of sharp features and small, severe eyes. Blair was put in mind of a fierce sparrow.

The men, all but Hannay, stood. He said, 'Charlotte, how flattering of you to join us.'

'Father.' She took the chair that had been empty opposite Hannay and waved off a footman bearing wine.

The men sat.

'Chloroform?' Blair asked.

'That the Queen had chloroform for labour and made it acceptable not to give birth in agony will go down in history as her greatest gift.' Charlotte Hannay redirected her gaze. 'Cousin Lydia, you look like a freshly picked peach.'

'Thank you,' Lydia said uncertainly.

Hannay introduced the table and said, 'Charlotte doesn't

often join us for dinner, although we always hope. Remove your hat and stay.'

Charlotte said, 'I just wanted to see your white African.'

'American,' Blair said.

'But your reputation is from Africa,' she said. 'Slaves and native women, isn't that what you're known for? What was it like to be in a position of such power? Did it make you feel like a god?'

'No.'

'Perhaps you have a charm that only works on black women.'

'Perhaps.'

'Mr Blair is actually very charming,' Lydia Rowland said.

Charlotte said, 'Really? I look forward to seeing that.'

'Many of us do,' Earnshaw said drily.

'And you've been hired by my father to inquire after John Maypole. What a bizarre proposition,' Charlotte said.

'Tell him to go away, Charlotte,' Lady Rowland said.

Hannay said, 'I'm sure Charlotte wants to know what happened to Maypole. After all, he was her fiancé.'

'Is, until I know otherwise,' Charlotte said.

'I know we will receive a letter from the Reverend Maypole that will explain everything. You have to carry on,' Lydia Rowland said.

'I do. I just don't carry on like you.'

Lydia Rowland blinked as if she'd been slapped, and for the first time Blair felt sympathy for the girl. She might be a fool, but in contrast to Charlotte Hannay a fool was positively attractive. He instantly saw Charlotte's future: she had a mouth on which no smile would ever perch, eyes that would never soften, a body that would never be unbound from mourning. She might have arrived late but she was a proper mistress for the Cannel Room.

From his end of the table, Hannay said, 'Charlotte, it seems to me that your devotion to Maypole grows in proportion to his absence.'

'Or in proportion to your inconvenience,' she suggested.

'Maybe Blair will put an end to both,' Hannay said.

Charlotte regarded Blair with, if possible, increased hostility. 'You'll do anything to get back to Africa?'

'Yes.'

She told her father, 'Congratulations, you certainly have found your man. And, Blair, are you being adequately recompensed?'

'I hope so.'

Charlotte said, 'You had better hope. My father is like Saturn, except that he doesn't eat all his children. He lets them fight it out, and then he eats the survivor.'

Lydia Rowland put her hand over her mouth.

Hannay stood. 'Well, it's been a very successful party.'

The men moved to a library fully as large as the Royal Society's. Two storeys of stacks and chart drawers with an iron balcony surrounded birds of paradise in bell jars, tables of fossils and meteorites, a rose-marble fireplace, ebony desk and deep leather furniture. Blair noticed the steady gas glow of wall lamps. Apparently only the Cannel Room was lit with candles.

'The women are happy in the study.' Hannay poured port left to right. 'The family has been building Hannay Hall for eight hundred years, so that now it's a perfect monster. You exit from a Gothic gallery and enter a Georgian ballroom. Step out of a Restoration library and run into the plumbing of a modern water closet. The scullery dates back to the Black Prince. Pity the wretches who work there.'

'My aunt works there,' Fellowes said.

'Excellent.' Hannay proposed a toast. 'Your aunt.'

'Very kind, Milord,' Fellowes said.

They drank. Blair asked, 'Do you mean there's another library?'

'Yes. This was a chapel,' Hannay said.

'Roman Catholic,' Chubb whispered.

Hannay pointed to a small oil portrait of a long-haired man wearing an ear-ring and a flamboyant Elizabethan collar. 'The Hannays were resolute Catholics, hiding and running priests from here to the Highlands. The tenth earl, whom you see there, was an abject coward who converted to save his neck and estate, for which his descendants eternally thank him. The chapel was allowed to go to rack and ruin. The lead was stripped, roof and windows fell in. Being in a back courtyard no one much noticed. I decided to make something of it.'

Earnshaw and Chubb were reduced to reverence by a framed manuscript of gilded Latin designed into Celtic knots. Leveret and Blair lingered over the fossils: a fiddlehead fern curled like the scroll of a cello, the cross-section of a fossilized tree as iridescent as a peacock's tail.

Hannay opened drawers with maps in Greek, Persian and Arabic drawn on tree bark, papyrus, vellum, and pilot charts written in Dutch and Portuguese. On them Africa evolved and grew from Egyptian delta, to Carthaginian empire, to indeterminate land mass guarded by boiling waters, to the saints' names of a newly navigated but still ominous continent, to a modern, well-plotted coastline and beckoning interior.

'Africa does seem to be your special interest,' Earnshaw said.

'Not entirely. This is the prize of the library.' Hannay opened a velvet slipcase and as painstakingly as if he were lifting air brought out a book with a badly worn leather cover faded to a powdery mauve. He raised the front just enough for Blair and Earnshaw to read, handwritten on the frontispiece, 'Roman de la Rose'. 'Every fine medieval lady had her copy of *The Romance of the Rose,*' Hannay said. 'This was written, fittingly enough, in 1323 for Céline, Dame de Hannay.'

'What is it about?' Fellowes asked.

'Chivalry, spirituality, carnality, mystery.'

'Sounds interesting.'

'Would you like to take it home with you, share it with the wife?' Hannay handed it to him.

'No, no!' Fellowes backed away, horrified.

'Very well.' Hannay took it back.

'She doesn't speak French,' Fellowes told Blair.

The library doors flew open. The book emitted a faint bouquet of roses as the room was invaded by Charlotte, still in her bonnet, driving her aunt and cousin before her like a demon.

Charlotte announced, 'I want to know what new arrangements you're making behind my back. Your Blair has probably the most loathsome reputation on the face of the earth, and you've hired him to foul the name of a better man under the pretence of an investigation. I would no more answer questions from Blair than I would willingly sit in stinking offal.'

'But you *will* answer them,' Hannay said.

'Father, when you rot in Hell. Since you're a bishop of the Church, that's not very likely, is it?'

She gave the company in the library a contemptuous rake of her small, hard-set eyes and marched away. If this were Joan of Arc, Blair thought, he'd light the first torch. Gladly.

Chapter Five

BLAIR ROSE AT the sound of clogs ringing on the cobblestones like gongs. In the light of the street lamp he could make out miners and women heading for the pits on the west side of town, and mill girls in dresses and shawls streaming in the opposite direction.

He had dressed in the secondhand clothes he had bought the day before and had his coffee by the time Leveret arrived. They climbed into the state manager's modest one-horse gig and took the road south towards the Hannay Pit. In dark fields on either side Blair could make out miners in the dark by the glow of their pipes and the mist of their breath. The fields smelled of manure, the air of ash. Ahead, from a high chimney, issued a silvery column of smoke that at its very peak was coloured by dawn.

'Last night was a rare appearance by Charlotte,' Leveret said. 'For weeks you can't find her, and then she bursts on to the scene. I'm sorry that she was rude.'

'The nastiest little monster I ever met. You know her well?'

'I grew up with her. Not actually *with* her, but on the estate. My father was manager before me. Then I was John's best friend when he came here and he and Charlotte became allied. It's just that she feels strongly about things.'

'Are there any brothers or sisters?'

'Deceased. Charlotte's oldest brother had a hunting accident. Tragic.'

'So in the house it's just the Bishop and her and a hundred and forty staff?'

'No. The Rowlands live at Hannay Hall with the Bishop, but Charlotte lives in a separate cottage. A nice house, actually. Very old. She lives her own life.'

'I bet she does.'

'She used to be different.'

'She *is* different,' Blair said.

Leveret laughed timidly and changed the subject. 'I'm surprised you want to take the time to go down the mine. You were in such a rush to look for John.'

'I still am.'

There was no gate or clear demarcation between farmland and the Hannay Pit. Miners on either side converged, and Blair found himself entering a yard lit by gas lamps and surrounded by sheds where sound and light seemed to have been stored and at that moment unleashed: the heavy breath and hoofbeats of horses pulling wagons across stones, the amber glow and rhythm of farriers shaping iron, the sparks and whine of picks being sharpened. Donkey engines chuffed out of railway sheds. Tram wagons, chained, not coupled, crashed together. Barely audible overhead, like a bow drawn across a cello, came a vibration from the cables running from the winding gears in the tower that stood above the shaft.

Metal tubs full of coal rolled off the cage on to a scale, connected to an 'endless chain' and moved mechanically on rails up to the shed to be sorted and graded. Blair hopped off the gig and kept pace with the parade of tubs. Each full tub weighed, according to the scale, at least two hundred pounds.

The shed had a cover, no sides, more to protect coal from water than workers from weather. All the workers in it were pit girls. Those at the top unlinked arriving tubs, rolled them to a tippler, locked a tub in and slowly released a brake lever so that as the tippler rocked, the tub disgorged a black stream of coal on to a conveyor belt where, by the light of a lamp, other women cleaned the coal of dirt and stones.

The pit girls wore flannel shirts, corduroy trousers and vestigial skirts greasy with coal. Their hair was hidden in shawls from the dust. Their hands were black and their faces blurred from clouds of pulverized carbon that erupted as coal from the belt flowed down a slanted screen, or fell through to finer screens.

Cleaned and graded coal poured down a chute to the shed's railway siding, where two girls manhandled the chute mouth over wagons. Blair recognized Flo from the Young Prince and Rose Molyneux.

Flo had a voice that sawed through the din. 'It's him.'

Blair shouted to Rose, 'I want to talk to you.'

Rose turned towards him and put one hand on her hip. Her eyes were two prisms of concentration, accentuated by the black dust that covered her face. It was the sort of unhurried gaze a man might receive from a cat at ease on a chair she claimed for her own. She took in Blair, engine drivers, haulers and miners, as if they were all of equal unimportance.

'You look debonair,' she said.

He glanced down at his shabby jacket and trousers. 'For the occasion.'

Somehow she managed to imbue her own dirty apparel with stylish impudence. 'Going down pit? You'll be black as a pipe cleaner when you come back.'

'We have to talk.'

'Was it such a fascinating conversation the first time?'

'It was interesting.'

She held his gaze. In that moment he saw that she knew she had the power to catch his eye when she wanted.

'Bill won't like that,' Flo said.

'Bill Jaxon?' Blair asked.

Rose laughed at Blair's reaction. 'Did that make your pecker drop?'

'Blair!' Leveret shouted from a shed across the yard.

Because the lamp shed was where the miners were issued their safety lamps it burned on the inside like a chandelier. On the lower shelves were lamp oil, rolls of wick cord and caulking in cans that read 'Good Enough for the Royal Navy!' Hanging on the back wall, six canary cages sounded a chorus. Yellow heads peeked through the grilles.

'Maybe you should wait here,' Blair told Leveret. In the light he could see that under a borrowed leather jacket the estate manager wore a silk waistcoat and white shirt, not to mention a nicely brushed bowler.

'No, I've always wondered about the mining experience. I've never been more than ten feet deep in an old mine before.'

'You could tie yourself into a sack of coal and jump up and down,' Blair suggested.

The safety lamps were eight inches tall, with brass caps and bases and, in between, a cylinder of brass gauze to cool the heat of the flame below the ignition point of explosive gas. The lamp man lit and locked lamps for Leveret and Blair. Within the safety gauze, the flames were murky embers. Scratched into each lamp base was a different number that the lamp man wrote into a ledger that he turned for Blair and Leveret. 'That's how we know who went down pit and who come up. Just in case. I should warn you, gentlemen, the Hannay Pit's a mile down, the deepest pit in Lancashire. If closets make you uncomfortable, best to think twice.'

They went back into the dark to join men waiting under the tower at the pit head. The miners wore dirty wool jackets and moleskin trousers; moleskin had no nap to rub the wrong way underground. Cloth caps and clogs, of course. Tommy tins of food hung on straps over their shoulders. The men lounged against one another with an ease particular to soldiers, athletes, miners. In spite of himself, Blair felt at home among them, just as Leveret showed signs of middle-class unease. Air whistled down the shaft – it was the ventilation intake for eight miles of workings underground – and the wind set the flames in the safety lamps trembling. Blair could just see the white warning fence around a ventilation upshaft fifty yards away; at the bottom was a furnace that drove foul air from the pit and drew in good – at least, that was the theory.

The wind subsided at the same time as the improbable sound of a freight train approached from beneath the ground. Blair watched the winding wheel slow, the vertical line of cable shake as the load lessened, a hook emerge, followed by a cage – an iron square with two wooden sides and ends open except for two loose chains. Immediately the chains were unhooked and tubs of glossy coal were rolled from the cage to the scale. Just as quickly, the miners pushed into the cage, taking the place of the tubs, putting their feet around the rails, and Blair and Leveret joined them.

Everyone crowded in; miners were paid by coal they produced, not the time they spent waiting for a ride. They didn't force Blair or Leveret to the open ends, and that was courtesy enough, Blair thought. In the glow of the lamps, fainter than candles, he saw coal dust on Leveret's collar and knew the same inescapable smudges were on him.

'Last chance. You'll look like a pipe cleaner when we come back,' Blair said. He liked Rose's expression. Another woman would have said 'chimney sweep'. Leveret was tall, so 'pipe cleaner' fitted him.

Leveret's bravado was lost in the deafening clatter of a bell. One ring: going down.

The cage started slowly, down through the round, brick-lined upper mouth of the shaft, past round garlands of Yorkshire iron, good as steel, into a cross-hatched well of stone and timber and then simply down. Down into an unlit abyss. Down at twenty, thirty, forty miles per hour. Down faster than any men anywhere else on earth could travel. So fast that breath flew from the lungs and pressed against the ears. So fast that nothing could be seen at the open end of the cage except a blur that could whip away an inattentive hand or leg. Down seemingly for ever.

Past the lamplight of an older landing. It could have been a firefly. Blair caught Leveret crossing himself and shook his head; the less movement the better. At its fastest, the cage dropped so smoothly that the men almost floated. In a shaft it was always the moment of greatest danger and greatest bliss. Blair thought that with their massed lamps they might resemble a meteor to a spectator, to a dazzled worm.

Brunel, the great railway engineer, claimed that the drivers of trains should be illiterate because only the unlettered man *paid attention*. Miners paid attention, Blair thought. The faces in the cage were more concentrated than the School of Plato for the way they listened to the unravelling of round steel cable, the slightest yawing of the cage, the growing pressure on the wooden soles of their clogs.

They were slowing. At two minutes by Blair's watch at an estimated average speed of thirty miles per hour, a mile down, the cage settled into a subterranean well of lights and stopped.

At once the miners poured out, followed by Blair and Leveret, the latter in a state of confusion.

For good reason. There was the converging traffic of underground roads, out of which emerged ponies in heavy harness and boys in caps and jackets, both beasts and tenders even more stunted by dim lamps hanging from the timbers. Behind each pony followed a row of loaded tubs on rails.

There was the smell emanating from a long row of low pony stalls. Underground stables were always placed by the downshaft and built on planks, but they never totally dried out; instead, the pungent aroma of horse manure and urine seemed both ancient and distilled.

There was the gale-force wind that whistled down the shaft, fresh air now tainted by the stable it passed through.

There was the heat, the opposite of a dank cave. A stifling heat ripe with sweat, muck, carbon dust. A reminder that the earth was a living organism with a burning core.

All these were sensory evidence that a visitor took notice of, sorted through, made order of. It took a minute for a visitor to comprehend that the pit eye was a hundred yards across. What the visitor had simply to ignore was the subtler, stronger report of his senses that a mile of earth stood over him, or that he was that far from escape. Blair checked his compass anyway.

Just as there was a manager's office on the surface there was an underlooker's office below, a square and simple room of brick. The underlooker was named Battie, a happy Vulcan in shirtsleeves, bowler and braces.

Battie was expecting them; he had cleared his desk, spread a map and weighted the corners with lamps. On the north end of the map were the cage and furnace shafts. The south was a gridiron of large and small tunnels that ran to an irregular border.

Battie registered with a noncommittal glance the different

fashions of his visitors' dress. 'Mr Leveret, Mr Blair, will you please turn your pockets inside out?'

Blair pulled out his watch, compass, handkerchief, penknife and loose change; Leveret produced a more substantial pile of watch, purse, wallet, locket, comb, visiting cards, briar pipe, tobacco, matches. Battie locked the pipe, tobacco and matches in his desk.

'No smoking, Mr Leveret. I wouldn't want you to even think about it.'

The map was dated the day of the explosion and bore circles with numbers ranging from one to three digits. Lamp numbers, Blair realized. There were seventy-six victims in the fire and that was the total he counted. It wasn't difficult because so many were clustered in a central tunnel, while others were evenly spaced along the coal face. One number, however, was right outside the underlooker's office.

'What happened here?' he asked.

'The cage was up. The shaft itself goes further down, you know. A boy had just come with his pony and tubs. When the smoke reached here, the pony backed over the edge. The boy tried to save it. That's how they went – pony, tubs and then the boy.' Battie paused. He lifted the lamps and let the map roll up, and put it in a leather satchel along with a ledger. He replaced his bowler with a red bandanna tied around his forehead. In a second, he had regained his poise, as if he were about to stroll through a park. 'Well, gentlemen, I have to make my rounds. If you still want to, we have a long way to go.'

'You can wait here or go up in the cage,' Blair offered Leveret again.

'I'm with you,' Leveret said.

'"Onward, Christian Soldiers"?' Blair asked.

'I won't hold you back,' Leveret promised.

Swinging his satchel, Battie led the way around the shaft and darted into the right-hand tunnel. 'Tunnels we call "roads",' he said over his shoulder. 'When they're as wide as this, it's a "main road".'

There was nothing high about it, however, and as soon as they entered, Leveret was in trouble. The only light was the safety lamps, three flames so obscured by wire gauze that they barely lit the rails on the floor or the timbers on the ceiling, and when Leveret tried to avoid one he stumbled into the other, and he didn't know when to step and when to duck.

Battie slowed but didn't stop. 'When you want to turn around, Mr Leveret, look for a sign saying, "Out". If you don't find one, just follow the air in your face. If the wind's at your back, you're going further in. Mr Blair, you've done this before.'

Blair hadn't even realized he'd slipped into the miner's stride: a half crouch with the head up, steps unconsciously measuring the sleepers of the track.

'When do we reach the coal?' Leveret asked.

'We're in it now. You're in the middle of the Hannay Seam, one of the richest coal seams in England,' Battie said. 'That's what's holding up the roof.'

Black walls. Black roof, too, Blair thought, because coal cushioned timbers better than stone. The irises of his eyes had dilated so that dark became shadow, and shadow took on form. Ahead of Battie a shaggy outline and lamp came from the opposite direction.

'Pony,' Battie said and stepped into a refuge hole that not even Blair had seen. Blair followed and they pulled in a startled Leveret the moment before a pony passed, a Shetland with sooty locks tended by a boy with a lamp and trailed by four full tubs. Leveret looked a little shorter.

'Lost your hat?' Blair asked.

'Actually, yes.' Mournfully Leveret watched the tubs roll by.

Blair asked Battie, 'You can tell when someone's been in mines before no matter how they're dressed?'

'With their first step. And whether they're drunk or not. If they are, I send them up. You're only as safe as the stupidest man in the mine.'

To join the conversation, Leveret asked, 'Why do the men wear clogs? I understand that most people in Wigan do, but I'd think that down in a mine they would be clumsy.'

Battie said, 'Rockfalls, sir. When the roof comes down on you it doesn't crush a clog's wooden sole the way it does a shoe. Then they're easier to squirm and get your foot out of, too.'

Leveret fell silent.

Walking underground was called travelling. They travelled twenty minutes, encountering only ponies and tub trains. The road became lower and narrower and began to slant down, and the sound of the trains was muffled by the constricted breath of the wind and the press of weight on wooden timbers. Battie halted regularly to hold his lamp where stones packed into dry walls or timbers propped up the roof.

He explained to Leveret, 'When we cut the coal, we let out firedamp. A funny word, isn't it, gentlemen?'

'It is a funny word,' Leveret agreed.

'As if it would put out fire.' Battie poked into a niche.

'And it does?'

'From the German *Dampf*. Meaning vapour. Explosive gas.'

'Oh,' said Leveret.

'Methane. It likes to hide in cracks and along the roof. The point of a safety lamp is that the gauze dissipates enough of the heat so that you won't set the gas off. Still, the best way to find it is with a flame.' Battie lifted the lamp by a rough column of rock and studied the light wavering behind the screen of the gauze. 'See how it's a little longer, a little bluer? That's methane that's burning.'

'Should we evacuate?' Leveret asked.

The flame lit Battie's grin as he pulled off his waistcoat and fanned the rock. He went back in the tunnel and returned a minute later with a folded frame of canvas and wood that he opened into a standing panel that redirected the flow of air at the rock.

'Mr Leveret, if we closed a pit every time we found a whiff of firedamp, England would freeze.' He took the ledger from his pack and noted the time, location and amount of gas. 'We watch the firedamp, we chase the firedamp, and we don't let it blow us to kingdom come.'

From here the road got worse, which didn't slow Battie in the least. 'This is a "sit",' he said at a place where the ceiling buckled, and made a note in his book. 'This is a "creep",' he said where the floor rose, lifting the track. 'There's pressure up and down. We have limestone above and gritstone below. We haven't lost the coal yet, though.'

The further they walked the more Blair understood that Battie didn't need the map. The man knew the Hannay Seam the way a riverman knew a river. Probably his father and grandfather had worked the same coal. A man like Battie knew where the black banks twisted left, right, up and down, or plunged from sight at a geologic fault. He knew the Hannay Seam's density, cohesion, water content, lustre, lighting point and ash. He could follow it in the dark.

Leveret was falling behind. Blair was about to ask Battie to relent when the underlooker stopped on his own and set his lamp by a coal pillar. He spread his map across the floor and pointed to two lamp numbers. 'This is where we found these two lads. They were the nearest casualties to the cage except for the boy and pony.'

A trail of numbers led to the west coal face, still twice as far as they had gone so far. The victims on the main road had fallen in groups, some huddled in refuge holes.

Leveret arrived, gasping and covered in coal dust as if he'd been dragged behind a pony.

'I'm ... fine,' he said and sank to his knees.

Blair and Battie returned to the map.

'Were they burned?' Blair asked.

'No. No one was burned until we get to the end of the main road, close to the face. The lads here were stretched out like they'd gone to sleep.'

'But facing the air? Running when they'd dropped?'

'Right.' Battie seemed darkly satisfied. 'Mr Leveret, your friend here knows something about coal.'

'They were crushed?' Leveret asked.

'No,' Battie said. 'When firedamp explodes it turns to afterdamp. Carbon monoxide. The strongest man in the world could be running through here at top speed, but two breaths of that and he'll drop to the floor. Unless you drag him out, he'll die. In fact, I've seen rescue attempts where one, two, three men will drop trying to pull one man out.'

The floor jumped, followed by a roar that rolled through from one end of the tunnel to the other. Pebbles rained in the dark.

Leveret was on his feet. 'Fire!'

'Just blasting, Mr Leveret. There's a difference. When there's an explosion you can feel it in Wigan. I'll let you know.' Battie rolled up the map and added, 'There won't be any more demonstrations like that, I hope, Mr Leveret. Around the men, I mean.'

Battie's lamp led the way again, pausing only as he mentioned that three miners had died here, four there, all trying to outrun afterdamp. It wasn't an unsafe mine, as mines went, Blair thought. It was dirty and close and uncomfortable, of course, but tunnels were kept clear, tracks well maintained, and Battie seemed to be a punctilious supervisor. It was just that all mines were an inversion of the natural order, and coal mines in particular were stupid and deadly.

The tunnel started to plunge. It would go deeper as the whole underground strata tilted south, Blair thought. The seam had likely first been worked as an easy outcropping north of Wigan. Roman troops had probably dried their sandals by fires of Hannay coal. With each step down, he was more aware of heat. The mine's breath parched the throat even as the skin turned to a slough of black sweat.

The tunnel opened into a crypt-sized chamber where a boy walked a pony on a ring of track, making a ghostly carousel. When the pony stopped, a man silvery with coal dust, naked except for improvised kneepads and clogs, emerged from a low tunnel and hooked full tubs to the animal's harness. Giving Battie the briefest of nods, he disappeared like an apparition back into the tunnel, pushing an empty tub ahead of him. Pony and boy vanished in the opposite direction.

'Hot.' Leveret found his voice.

'Tea, sir?' Battie offered a tin flask from his pack.

Leveret shook his head and dropped to the track in exhaustion. The first time in a mine was always the worst, no matter how fit you were, Blair thought. Even with malaria, he was simply doing what he had done all his life.

Leveret said, 'Sorry to be so clumsy.'

'No bother, sir,' Battie said. 'Miners get too comfortable. They know a single spark is dangerous, but they will come skating down the rails here on the irons of their clogs, sparks flying like fireworks. Or sneak away from work into a side tunnel and sleep like a fieldmouse.'

'Sounds quite cosy,' Leveret said.

Battie said, 'Sometimes. There was a pony here the day of

the fire. Dropped and blocked that tunnel. We found ten men on the other side.'

'Afterdamp?' Blair asked.

'Yes. You know, I read a London paper that said the greatest modern fear is being buried alive. There were advertisements for coffins with speaking tubes and semaphores. Why would they worry about being buried alive in London?' Battie turned to Leveret. 'Better?'

'I'm ready to move.'

'Good.'

They ducked into the tunnel that the miner had vanished into. There were rails and just enough room for a crouching man to manoeuvre a tub through a gallery of wooden props. Through the tunnel came a concussive sound, as if a wave of surf had curled and crashed.

Leveret asked, 'What's that?'

'The roof falling in,' Battie said.

'Good Lord,' Leveret said, and Blair heard him trying to backtrack.

Battie said, 'No, that was normal, Mr Leveret. That's the system.'

'System?'

'You'll see. A cave-in is a sharper noise, a mix of timbers and stone, usually,' Battie said. 'You'll see what I mean.'

On either side now their lamps lit not so much tunnels as a honeycomb of pillars of coal a little like the columns of a black mosque. At the edge of conscious hearing Blair became aware of a new sound: crystalline, percussive, distorted and amplified by the vagaries of rock. Battie led the way for ten more minutes, and suddenly he and Blair crawled out into a narrow tunnel, the length of which was populated by shadowy figures wearing only trousers and clogs, some only clogs, covered by a film of dust and glitter, swinging short, double-pointed picks. The men had the pinched waists of whippets and the banded, muscular shoulders of horses, but shining in the upcast light of their lamps what they most resembled was machinery, automatons tirelessly hacking at the pillars of coal that supported the black roof above them. Coal split with a sound nearly like chimes. Where the coal seam dipped, men worked on knees wrapped in rags. Other men loaded tubs or pushed them, leaning into them with their backs. A fog of condensation and coal dust rose from them.

Blair looked at his compass. 'You're working backwards.'

'Correct,' Battie said.

The miners were attacking the inner wall of the west face, working back towards the pit eye and not along the outer wall, as Blair had expected. The outer wall didn't exist, it was a low space that receded into impenetrable murk.

Battie opened his map. 'I think you'll appreciate this, Mr Blair. This is the Lancashire system. We drive the main tunnels, the roads, through the coal to the border of the vein. We cut smaller tunnels to connect the roads and circulate the air, and then we start working backwards, as you say, to get the rest of the coal, just leaving enough stone pillars and props to hold up the roof until we're clear. The props collapse and the roof does fall – that's the sound we heard – but by then we're gone.'

'This is where victims were burned?' Blair asked.

'Along this coal face, but about fifteen yards in.' Battie faced the worked-out void behind the miners. 'That's where we were two months ago. That's two thousand tons of coal. Anyway, no one is allowed in old workings. Those are pit rules.'

The line of miners swung their picks at a relentless pace. Blair had seen the same phenomenon around the world: deep-shaft miners worked as if sheer physical effort could mesmerize the mind. In this case, perhaps there was also a sense that they were cutting their way back to the shaft. A bull's-eye lantern might have cut the murk, but the dim glow of a safety lamp was hardly better than an ember and barely lit the man holding it. Beyond the perimeter of the coal face it was impossible to say how far the worked-out area extended behind the miners, or whether the roof was six feet or six inches high. Blair picked up a stone and threw it sidearm. The stone was swallowed by the dark, its sound lost in the din of the picks.

'How far in is the roof up?' he asked.

'Ten yards some places, a hundred yards in others. It could stay up a month, a year. It could come down while we're here,' Battie said.

Leveret caught up with them, gasping, the worse for wear in the last, low stretch of tunnel. Blood smeared his forehead, and sweat and coal dust made black soup around his eyes. 'What could come down?' he asked.

'Nothing. Leveret, I couldn't be prouder if you had found Livingstone.' Blair gave him a handkerchief. 'A few minutes and then we'll head back.'

For every man with a pick, another shovelled the coal and loaded it in tubs. Every twenty yards the track split into short parallel lines so that tubs could pass. Into a coal pillar a man cranked a drill that was a barrel of cogs steadied by an iron brace that reached from floor to roof. He was a head taller than any other man along the coal face, and though the drill must have weighed forty pounds, he handled it easily. Black powder poured from the bore hole. The rod turned so smoothly the man could have been drilling into cheese.

Because of the poor light and the fact that they were so black with dust, Blair didn't notice at first that the man wore bandages on both his legs. At the sight of Blair he stopped work. 'Still looking for Reverend Maypole?' Bill Jaxon asked.

'You never know,' said Blair.

He was amazed that Jaxon was capable of walking after last

night's fight behind the Young Prince, but he reminded himself that miners took pride in the amount of pain they could ignore. With his long hair tied back, Jaxon looked like a statue by Michelangelo, but carved from coal, not marble.

'Still got your clogs on?' Blair asked.

'Want to try them?' Jaxon answered.

At Jaxon's side appeared a gnomish figure that Blair recognized as an ebony version of Smallbone, his drinking partner from the Prince. Smallbone cradled a long tin box. Jaxon unscrewed the top leg of the brace and extracted the bore rod from the hole. From the box Smallbone took a long straw that he slid in the hole and puffed into with his eyes closed. A jet of dust flew out. Blair enjoyed seeing a specialist at work. Next, Smallbone brought out a ten-inch waxed paper tube from the box.

'What . . .?' Leveret asked.

'Gunpowder. He makes the shots himself,' Jaxon said.

Battie said, 'Smallbone is a fireman. On the surface a fireman puts out fires. Down here a fireman fires the shots.'

The bore hole had a downward slant. With a wooden rod Smallbone pushed the paper tube in as far as it would go, carefully punctured its end with a copper needle and fed in a fuse, a 'slow match' of rough cotton cord soaked with saltpetre. He led the cord out and tamped the hole with clay so that one foot of fuse hung free. Very homemade, Blair thought. In the meantime, Battie had moved his lamp along the roof in search of firedamp. 'It looks clear,' he said.

'Shot!' Jaxon yelled.

The shout was passed along. All the miners in sight gathered their tools and moved to the main-road tunnel out of the line of fire. Battie led Leveret and Blair. Jaxon followed with his drill while Smallbone stayed at the hole alone.

Battie advised Leveret, 'Look the opposite way, sir, and open your mouth.'

Blair watched Smallbone pass the lamp slowly along the roof and down the wall to satisfy himself there was no gas, a sign of intelligence better than any written examination. He knelt by the dangling fuse and blew against the flame of his lamp until it flared in response and tilted towards its protective gauze. He blew harder and the flame grew brighter and pushed until a tongue of fire penetrated the wire screen and reached out to the cord. On his third breath the fuse end reciprocated with an orange bud of light.

The fireman returned with quick, short steps and had joined the group for five seconds when the tunnel behind him erupted with a clap like thunder and swirling billows of black dust. The blast was more powerful than Blair had expected. The miners rocked like men on a deck, while the report divided into echoes that subdivided into other tunnels. One by one the men shook their heads and opened their red-rimmed eyes wide.

'Doubling up on the charge, Mr Smallbone?' Battie said. 'Do that again and you can find employment in another pit.'

It was the first hint of hypocrisy Blair had seen in the underlooker and Battie seemed uneasy at his own protest. Everyone – owners and underlookers – knew that miners were paid only by the tubs they filled, not by the time they spent picking at deep, hard coal. That was why firemen blasted in spite of firedamp. Smallbone's shot had dropped a wide shelf of coal to the floor and fractured the wall besides. The miners dug reviving snuff from their tins and returned to work. Jaxon shouldered his drill and brace and moved down the tunnel to start the next hole. As he moved, an avenue of admiration formed around him.

Smallbone, with no chagrin, lingered by the fallen shelf and expanded to Leveret. 'Yer German dynamite, well, it's a fart in t'wind.'

'I thought it was powerful,' Leveret said. 'I've read about it in scientific journals.'

'On German coal,' Smallbone said. 'This is English coal.'

Nothing like a pit as a leveller, Blair thought. Where else could you find an estate manager discussing explosives with a naked miner? He noticed that Battie was contemplating the worked-out void again, where airborne dust still shivered from the blast.

'About twenty more yards along the face, that's where I think the explosion was. How far in, Mr Blair, I don't know. I've thought about it a thousand times.'

'You think it was touched off by a shot?'

'No. Only Smallbone was firing shots at this end of the face. He and Jaxon, the man with the drill, would be dead, too. They lived to save a half-a-dozen men, thank God. There was a spark. Someone did something incredibly stupid. Some fool forced open his lamp to light his pipe. Or pulled the top off just for more light to swing a pick by. There *was* gas. A real "blower". And there was a complication. The blast unsettled some waste – stones and small coal – that we'd bricked in. Gas loves waste. After we aired the blower out, gas leaked from the waste until we bricked it up again. Had to if we wanted to bring in lamps to search.'

'How big a section did you rebrick?'

'Maybe two foot high, three wide.'

'Show me.'

Battie stared into the void. 'We had the Mines Inspector here and we had the inquiry. It's all done with, Mr Blair. So what are you after? Clearly you know your way around a mine but it's very unclear to me why you're in *this* mine. What are you looking for?'

'There's a man missing.'

'Not here. After the fire there were seventy-six lamps and seventy-six bodies accounted for. I made sure of that.'

'Each and every one identified? There was enough left of them to tell?'

'They were identified officially by the coroner – every one, Mr Blair.'

'All from Wigan? I saw some Irish in town.'

'There were some day workers from outside.'

'And nobody's been in there since?'

'It's against the rules. Anyway, nobody would go with you.'

'I hate coal mines,' Blair muttered. He held his lamp out to opaque eddies of suspended dust. 'Could you check the map one more time?'

While Battie was distracted with his satchel and sorting through it for the map, Blair stepped into the dark.

The way was surprisingly open for the first steps, and blackness swam around him. But within a few feet the roof lowered steeply and pressed him first into a crouch and then down to all fours, crawling on the floor and pushing the meagre light ahead, he and the lamp invisible from behind. Battie's blinded, furious shouts and curses chased after him ineffectually.

Dust rolled like waves before the lamp. Above the lamp was a faint nimbus, like a ring around a moon. It was the scope of Blair's sight and knowledge. He held his compass to the light, aiming west.

Once he stopped at the sound of an abandoned timber giving way with a slow tick, like a clock. The roof was settling, but easing down. That was why miners preferred wooden props to iron, for the warning.

Twice he had to correct around stone pillars. At one point

he had to squeeze on his stomach through a rockfall, but the other side was clear up to where a whole section of subterranean roof had collapsed and the air was foul enough for the flame of his lamp to start sputtering. He backed away and followed the line of the collapse south. Overhead, the roof was moist and glittered like stars. It was like navigating, he thought, in a world where everything was solid.

He struggled around gritstone slabs that had crept up from the floor. What he wanted to avoid was falling in a pocket and having his lamp go out.

His foot was caught. When he tried to pull free, he heard Battie's voice close behind him. 'You're a miner, Mr Blair.'

'I have been.'

He lay still and let Battie pull himself level. The underlooker had a lamp, though all Blair could see in its light was Battie's eyes.

'The Bishop's man, they say. Wants a tour. Not so unusual. The board of directors comes by. They turn around before we're a hundred yards into a tunnel. A big thank you. Other appointments, wrong clothes. Not you.'

'So I've broken the rules,' Blair said.

'You'll never be allowed back down this pit.'

'So I might as well see.'

Battie was silent for a moment, then hitched himself forward on his elbows. 'Bugger all,' he muttered. 'Follow me.'

For a barrel-chested man, Battie was an eel at sliding over and around rockfalls, rising boulders, holes. Blair scrambled to keep the irons of the soles of Battie's clogs in sight until the underlooker's progress slowed and became uncertain.

'Should be here. It changes all the time, though. I can't—'

Battie stopped. Blair pulled closer and set his lamp next to Battie's. The doubled glow showed a yard-high gap between roof and rubble that was filled by a wall of bricks of the maroon variety used for Wigan houses. About forty bricks in all. The mortaring looked sloppy – hasty might be a better word.

Battie asked, 'Have you ever had to rebrick after an explosion, Mr Blair? You don't know what's lurking on the other side. Could be firedamp, could be afterdamp, could be both. You do it in turns. Hold your breath, lay a brick, back out and let the next man lay his. Jaxon and Smallbone. Each with a rope around his waist.'

'This was where the explosion was?'

'Next to it as far as we could tell.' Battie craned to look at the roof. 'It will all fall in sometime. Not soon enough for me.'

Like a watermark, the impressed words 'Hannay Brickworks' appeared on a brick, then on a second and a third. Blair caught a rotting odour of firedamp, like marsh gas. As the lamps grew brighter he saw that the mortar between the top bricks was cracked, perhaps from Smallbone's shot or from one days earlier. Battie's face shone, his eyes widening.

In the lamps the flames lengthened to blue columns. The wicks themselves went out, but enough gas had already infiltrated to ignite and float in the gauze like plasma. Illuminated, Blair thought three thoughts. To blow the lamps out would press the fire through the safety gauze and set off the surrounding gas. To wait was useless because as the safety gauze heated the wire itself began to glow like an orange web of fuses. Third, he had worked very hard to kill himself.

As it didn't happen immediately, he remembered that methane was lighter than air. He started scooping out the rubble at the base of the brick wall and pulled out loose rocks and dust to a depth of a foot. He took a lamp by the base and, balancing the flame within, set it down in the hole as straight up and down as he could. Hairs burned off the back of his hands as he did so. Battie understood. Just as carefully, he did the same with the second lamp, so that they stood side by side in the little excavation, two brilliant spears of blue cupped by bristling red wires.

The spears burned steadily for a minute, then pulsed and shortened reluctantly, from the bottom to the top. Wires dulled from gold to grey. The first flame seemed to swallow itself in a gulp of tarry smoke. The other vanished a second later, leaving Blair and Battie in utter darkness.

'No gentleman would have thought of that,' Battie said.

Blair became aware of Leveret desperately shouting his name; he had forgotten about the estate manager. Miners were calling also. Stiffly, like two men swimming in black shallows, he and Battie followed the sound.

Chapter Six

HANNAY HALL WAS barely visible through greening branches. Between tree roots lay pools of violets. As always, after Blair had been down a pit, the colour of flowers seemed as intense as polished gems. Most miners were the same in this regard, and he sometimes thought it was a mercy for them to come and go in the dark, not to be tantalized by senses whetted by deprivation.

He followed a gravel path along a wall of yew trees and around a lily pond to the conservatory, an oriental pavilion of iron and glass. Entering, in one step he left cool England for a steamy world of palms, mangoes and breadfruit trees. Pink hibiscus unfurled. Spotted orchids hung from plaques of moss. A path edged with aromatic jasmine and orange bloom led to Bishop Hannay, who sat by a garden table on which lay newspapers and a cup of Turkish coffee. In his linen shirt Hannay resembled a viceroy enjoying colonial ease. Around him was subdued activity: gardeners tapping pots to listen for the hollow note of a dry fern, sub-gardeners spraying with water syringes the size of rifles. Above him a forest of date palms lifted glossy fronds as large as fans.

'All you need is a fruit bat,' Blair said.

Hannay gave Blair a long study. 'Leveret says you two were down in the mine. He came back looking like a casualty. I gave you permission to visit the pit, not to lead a chase through it. What on earth were you doing?'

'What you hired me for.'

'I asked you to look for John Maypole.'

'That's what I was doing.'

'In the mine?'

'It never occurred to you?' Blair asked. 'You have a curate who happens to disappear on the same day as seventy-six other men die in your mine and you think there's no connection? Then you happen to hire a mining engineer to look for the missing man? It seems to me you might as well have pointed where to go, so I went.'

At a discreet distance a boy sprayed a rainbow over banana palms. Each bead of water sparkled within a luminous arc of hues.

'And you found Maypole?' Hannay asked.

'No.'

'So he was never down there?'

'I can't say that. Your man Battie is a competent under-looker, but he can't identify everyone who comes down a cage at the start of a shift. Six days a week their faces are black.'

'Those men grew up together. They'd know each other in the dark.'

'But you also have day workers from outside Wigan, men whose real names no one even knows. Day workers arrive from Wales, Ireland, everywhere. They come into Wigan, rent a bed and look for work. Didn't Maypole like to preach at the mine surface?'

'He was fanatical,' Hannay said. 'Worse than a Methodist.'

'Well, he may have taken his preaching underground. When I came back from the mine I read the newspaper accounts again. Twelve of the dead were day workers. Another ten were badly burned. Maybe one of them is Maypole but you won't find out without exhuming the bodies.'

'Blair, all anyone in Wigan expects from life is a proper burial. Miners scrimp so that when they die they'll be drawn in a decent hearse with black plumes and matched black horses. And you suggest that a bishop uproot the recently departed?'

'If Maypole is in one of those graves, the sooner we dig him up the better.'

'There's a pleasant prospect. The last Wigan riot was less than twenty years ago. The miners looted the town and the police locked themselves in the gaol until the militia arrived. And that was over a small matter of wages, not the desecration of graves, thank you.'

'Or—'

'Or what?'

'Or Maypole took off and is happily spending your Bible Fund in New York or New South Wales, in which case I'll never find him. At least you know one thing: he's not in your mine now. That was the point, I suspect. You didn't want to reopen the inquiry into the explosion, but you didn't want your curate discovered dead in a Hannay mine. And the way you set me up by telling poor Leveret to omit obvious information like a disaster that took seventy-six lives on the same day, it all seems like my idea.'

Hannay listened without a change of expression. No, he didn't look like a viceroy, and certainly not like a bishop, Blair thought. Something far more powerful, a Hannay in his dominion. At a barely audible thump, Hannay looked down at his newspaper, where a drop of water had hit and spread; he looked up at panes clouded by condensation.

'Humidity. Maybe we should have a fruit bat.'

'Or a tapir rooting around the pots,' Blair suggested.

'Yes. What fun we could have here if you stayed. Don't you think you should linger in Wigan and search out your family background?'

'No, thanks.'

'As I remember from our campfire conversations, your father was anonymous and your mother died when you were young. Blair is not a Wigan name.'

'It wasn't hers. An American took care of me, so I took his name. I have no idea what hers was.'

'Which makes you a regular curiosity. You have no idea of who or what you are. A blank slate. Sometimes I think that's why you have such an obsession with maps, so that at least you know where you are. Well, that's fun for you, but what about poor Charlotte? She'll want more proof than your speculation.'

'I've done what a mining engineer can do. I want to be paid and I want to go back to Africa. That was our bargain.'

'Our agreement, Blair, was that you would conduct a diligent search, above ground as well as below. I think you're doing extremely well. If you could just find something more definite.'

'Do you want to dig up the graves?'

'Good Lord, no. We're not ghouls or resurrectionists. Carry on. Quietly. Console Charlotte. Speak to Chubb. I'll let you know when you're done.'

On his way back, Blair saw the same luminous carpet of violets. This time he noticed that the trunks of the beech trees themselves were black from coal soot. On the bark were moths as dark as miners.

Blair went from Hannay Hall to Wigan and John Maypole's room in the alley near Scholes Bridge.

He knew Portuguese traders in Sierra Leone – the worst men

in the world – who had plaster saints on bureau altars. These men sold liquor, rifles, still the occasional slave, yet they felt a commonality with saints who, before their enlightenment, had themselves often lived lives of deep venality. After all, saints included murderers, prostitutes, slaves and slave owners. A statuette was a reminder that no one was either perfect or beyond redemption.

A portrait of Christ, however, was a different matter. Who was going to measure up to that? Yet Maypole had risen from his bed every day under the ceaseless scrutiny of the character in this painting. The olives and thorns seen through the window and the wood shavings around His feet were rendered with better than photographic precision. The Saviour Himself looked less like a Jewish carpenter than a blue-eyed, underfed London clerk, but his gaze filled the room with limpid, impossible expectations.

Blair went through the contents of the room in the same order he had with Leveret. The closet with two suits. The range, chest of drawers, wash basin. Bible and books. The simple possessions of a dedicated curate. This time, however, he had murderous resolve. There was nothing like a visit to the Bishop to give him more faith in his own cynicism.

He had accepted Maypole's reputation as pure white, but no man was so good. Everyone had secrets. Saint Francis must have eaten a sparrow or two. Saint Jerome in his hermit's cave probably whiled away the hours with some private vice.

He riffled through *Re-Reading the Bible, Early Italian Poets, Sesame and Lilies, The Utilitarian Christian, The Athletic Christ, Taking the Gospel to Africa*, which sounded like good reading for the high-minded, though wasted on him. Ransacked and examined the backs and undersides of the drawers. Emptied the dry sink of bowl, knife and fork, tin and wooden spoons. Opened the ovens and groped inside. Upended the bed. Peeled back the edge of the linoleum. Turned over the painting and probed the frame with a penknife. Which left nothing but the brick walls.

Not that he was different, Blair admitted. If anyone examined his history, what would they find? He didn't have a history, only a geographic location. His memory wasn't a blank, but his English and American memory was a bare room compared with the richness of his African experience. English coal miners trudged through their tunnels; the black gold miners of Brazil sang in time to the hammering of their drills.

The African climate had a mesmerizing effect on him. The dry season and the wet season had rhythms – one of insects, the other of rain – that held him in thrall. His status as a white among the Ashanti kept emotional attachment at the right pitch, first testing and then acceptance, but never true inclusion, always a distance.

The apparent simplicity of his work – mapping rivers and examining rocks – masked its real intent from the Ashanti. Perhaps this was the lie that impelled him to help them, the knowledge that missionaries weren't the threat. The real threat was his surveys, which would lead to gold sluices, navigable streams and railway grades, and would change the Ashanti more than any Bible.

England, land of bricks. There were whitened Tudor bricks, red Elizabethan bricks, orange Georgian bricks, blue railway bricks and the blackened cottage bricks of Wigan. Maypole had scrubbed his walls, revealing their mottled colours and uneven surface. Blair could trace fault lines stepping from brick to brick, but testing each brick by hand might take all day and night.

He remembered the gardeners in the greenhouse tapping the pots. With Maypole's wooden spoon he started rapping the bricks, row by row, wall by wall. Well-mortared bricks responded with a solid sound, while the looser bricks were almost silent. Though more than a few were dislodgeable, they hid nothing.

Blair worked his way to the last wall until he had to remove the painting and lay it on the bed to continue. Below the nail, a brick in the centre sounded dead. Blair dropped the spoon and, fingers on the corners of the brick, drew it out.

Behind was an open space, a poor man's vault.

There were no coins or notes, no jewels or heirlooms, nothing but a leather notebook with a clasp. He opened the clasp and looked at the frontispiece, which read, in a modest and precise hand, 'This is the property of Revd John Thos. Maypole, D.D. If found, please return to the Parish Church, Wigan, Lancs.'

Blair leafed through the pages. They ran from the previous June to January and each week showed the same virtuous parade. On Mondays: Morning Service, call on parish sick and needy, Evening Service; Tuesdays: Morning Service, Young Men's Bible Study, Evening Service, Temperance League; Wednesdays: Morning Service, afternoon prayer at Home for Women; Thursdays: Morning Service, Bible Study at Ragged School, Evening Mass, Society for Improvement of the Working Class; Fridays: Morning Service, sick calls, workshop prayer, Evening Service; Saturdays: Morning Service, christenings and burials, miners' prayer, rugby, Workers' Evening Social; Sundays: Communion Service, Bible Study, Pensioners' Tea, 'dinner with C'.

Hardly a week of fleshly pleasures, Blair thought. 'Dinner with C' – which Blair took to mean dining with Charlotte Hannay – was the capper.

In the margin of every page were cryptic notations of a different tale: TSM–ld, Bd–2d, Ba–2d. Because Blair had himself come close to starving, the figures were easy to decipher. Tea with sugar and milk one penny, bread two pence, bacon two pence. In the midst of all his good deeds and while engaged to one of the wealthiest women in England, the Reverend John Maypole had been living on drippings and crust.

Maypole had also used the poor man's trick of writing both horizontally and vertically, economically filling every page with a dense, interwoven pattern of words and rendering the act of reading like unravelling a sleeve. Patiently Blair plucked out stern remonstrations like 'Unworthy Thoughts, Vanity, Denial'. The kind of cold shower a curate was expected to turn on himself.

In the first week of December, however, this had changed.

WED. C. ill and bedridden so instead of "Home" to prayer meeting at the pit, brief wds. on the 'Working Jesus'. My suspicions confirmed.

THURS. Mass. Ragged Sch., Soc. for Imp. Evening Service. At the meeting Oliver asked if I was well. (*That would be Leveret, Blair thought.*) I lied. Difficult to sustain concentration. In total confusion and shame.

SUN. After Morning Service confronted her. She is totally wo guilt. Accuses me of hypocrisy! Carried on, but can't confess, certainly not to Chubb. Spent the day in Hell.

What happened at the workplace meeting, and which women he had confronted, Maypole didn't say. On 23 December, however, the journal was clear enough.

SAT. Mass. She has a point. One cannot go among people as a Roman or a Pharisee.

SUN. Chubb ill and so allowed me to give the sermon, which was, I believe, the best I've delivered. On Job 30: 28–30 – 'I went mourning without the sun . . . My skin is black upon me, and my bones are burned w heat.' How like the miners' workplace! She was right.

Christmas! Infant Saviour, snowy day, starry night. First an innocent pantomime for the miners' children and then midnight service. Even Chubb cannot dwell on death at this great event. I feel reborn, at least in contemplation. A generative turmoil of the soul.

SAT. Mass. Rugby vs Haydock, played in mud and snow. Bill magnificent as usual. Afterward, I was accosted by a so-called 'sportsman' called Silcock, whom I had seen before at the fringe of matches. That I was a clergyman who enjoyed the sweat of honest games seemed to insinuate to him that I was also interested in more sordid entertainments, and he offered to introduce me to vices worthy of my interest. I offered to introduce him to the police and he left, shaking his fist and threatening to take my head off 'at the dog collar'.

MON. Mass. Parish calls. The New Year and Chubb warns again about the 'Sink of Pollution' that I am sinking into. That 'Sink' is despairing mankind!

THURS. Mass. Ragged Sch. I have been practising in the hole. Alone, only for an hour at a time but agony such as I have never known, and can barely lead the evening service.

FRI. Chubb now in a fury over 'insubordination', i.e. my going down to London and speaking to a Parliamentary Comm., where a cabal of reformers and the miners' union are trying to 'save' women from employment at the pits, in consequence of which they would be forced into the mills or prostitution. I knew Earnshaw at Oxford, now an energetic MP. Unfortunately his interest was not matched by his sympathy.

SUN: Chubb felled by another attack of croup and left

107

it to me to read the sermon. Trusting to let the Bible choose, the first passage I saw was Isaiah 45:3, and so I spoke on a divinely inspired message: 'I will give thee the treasures of darkness and hidden riches of secret places, that thou mayest know that I, the Lord, which call thee by thy name, am the God of Israel.'

Whatever the psalm was, the entries for the following days were code and in such an agitated tangle of lines as to be illegible, more the scribblings of a conspirator than a diarist. When Blair turned the page, he was back where he had started, the last week Maypole was seen in Wigan, starting on 15 January.

MON. The Song of Solomon has never been more apt:

> *'I am black but comely,*
> *O ye daughters of Jerusalem,*
> *as the tents of Kedar, as the curtains of Solomon.*
> *Look not upon me because I am black,*
> *because the sun hath gazed upon me.'*

The Queen of Sheba came to test Solomon, and he answered all her questions and she gave him gold, spices and precious stones. She was African and Solomon had, of course, black concubines.

TUE. 'There is nothing better for a man than that he should eat and drink, and that he should make his soul enjoy good in his labour,' says Solomon. What of the hellfire that Revd Chubb blows in the face of any miner who slakes his thirst with beer?

At one time I was like Chubb. I admired scholarship and single-minded preparation for the world to come.

Wigan has taught me differently. Now I would say that foremost are the warmth of family, friendship and the light at the end of the tunnel. All else is vanity!

We have two worlds here. A daylit world of houses with servants and carriages, shopping for kid gloves and fashionable hats, annuities, and rides across the countryside. And another world led by a tribe that labours underground or in pit yards so obscured by steam and soot that every hour seems like dusk. In circumstances of mortal danger and with the sweat of great physical effort, the second world wins wealth and ease for the first. Yet for the inhabitants of the first world, the second world is literally invisible except for the daily parade of black and exhausted men and women returning through Wigan to the alleys of Scholes. (*Here the writing again became almost impossible to read.*) How to enter that second world? This is the key.

The puffed-up barrister may have his house and parlour. But the miner, in the words of the Psalm, 'was made in secret and curiously wrought in the lowest parts of the earth'. The lady begs the praise of her maid. Instead, the pit girl lifts her eyes to the Lord and sings, 'I will praise thee; for I am fearfully and wonderfully made!' It is a wonderful, secret, most favourite psalm.

WED. Call on Mary Jaxon, widow. Home for Women. The duties of a curate suddenly seem small and safe. I feel as though I am setting off from a world of comfortable verities and travelling to another, realer land. Tomorrow is the great adventure!

The remaining pages were blank. Inside the back cover Blair found a photograph the size of a playing card. The picture was of a young woman, a flannel shawl angled gypsy-fashion to reveal only half her theatrically smudged face. She wore a man's rough work shirt and trousers. A skirt was rolled and sewn at her waist, and both hands rested on a shovel. Behind her was a crudely painted landscape of hills, shepherds and sheep. Printed on the other side was, 'Hotham's Photographic Studio, Millgate, Wigan'.

The photographer's magnesium flash caught the boldness of the subject's eye. In fact, the misshapen clothes accentuated the litheness of her body, the heavy shawl only framed the bright curve of her brow, and although she was half hidden and there was no identification of the subject either by the photographer or Maypole, Blair recognized no Queen of Sheba but Rose Molyneux returning the camera's gaze.

Chapter Seven

ROSE AND HER friend Flo were leaving the house; though they hadn't cleaned the coal dust from their faces, they had exchanged their shawls for velveteen hats. Even as Flo hulked in the door to block Blair's way, her eyes shifted impatiently over his shoulder to the brassy salute of a sweet vendor's bugle on the street outside.

Rose said, 'It's the African explorer.'

'Ah thought he was a photographer last night,' Flo said.

Blair asked, 'May I go with you? Buy you a round?'

The women traded looks, and then as coolly as a queen making plans, Rose said, 'Flo, you go on. I'll talk t'Mr Blair here for a minute and then I'll find you.'

'Tha sure?'

'Go on.' Rose gave her a push.

'Don't be long.' Flo balanced to polish a clog against the back of a trouser leg; she had switched to fancy ones with brass nails. A gay bouquet of silk geraniums festooned her hat. Blair made way for her and as she hauled herself out into the street he thought of a brightly dressed hippo hitting the water.

Rose let Blair in and quickly closed the door. The front room was dark, and the coals in the grate were dim bars of orange.

'Are you afraid of Bill Jaxon seeing you with me?' he asked.

She said, 'You're the one who should be afraid, not me.'

The rhythm of her words was Lancashire but it was obvious that she could leave out dialect when she wanted to, otherwise she would be speaking in ancient 'ah's and 'tha's. So she had some education. Most workers' homes had only a Bible. She had books on the parlour shelves that actually looked read. The coals produced a soft ringing. In spite of them, he shivered.

'You look pot,' Rose said.

Blair said, 'It's been a full day.'

She hung her hat on the rack. Released, her hair was a full Celtic mane. Coal dust gave her face a faint sheen and, like extravagant make-up, made her eyes look even larger. Without a word she turned and went into the kitchen, the same kitchen he had found her in two nights before.

'Should I follow you?' he called.

'Parlour's for company,' she called back.

He hesitated at the kitchen threshold. A kettle was on the stove; in miners' homes there was always a kettle of steeping tea on a hot stove. Rose lit an oil lamp and turned the flame low.

'And what am I?' he asked.

'That's a good question. Peeping Tom? Police? Reverend Maypole's American cousin? The man at the newspaper says he recognized you for an African explorer.' She poured tea and gin into a cup and set it on the table. 'So, Mr Blair, what are you?'

Rose kept the light so low that the air was smoked glass, and a scent of carbon lingered on her. Her eyes stayed on him as if to read his mind; likely she could predict the thoughts of most of the denizens of her small world. Probably she was the most seductive creature in it, and that was disconcerting, too, because it gave her confidence.

Blair supplemented the cup with quinine powder. 'Medicine.

I'm not contagious. It's just a reminder to us all not to sleep in tropical swamps.'

'George Battie says you're a miner. Or maybe from the Mines Inspector's Office.'

Blair drained the cup; the fever made him feel as if he had a slight charge of electricity. The last thing he was going to do was let Rose ask the questions. 'You told me that the Reverend Maypole talked to all the pit girls.'

Rose shrugged; her shirt was flannel, as stiff with soot as a snail shell. 'Reverend Maypole was very evangelical,' she said. 'A regular threat t'break into preaching any time. He was always about the pit yard. Men didn't want to come up for fear of an earful about the sanctity of labour. They'd stay down. Not just Hannay Pit, but at all the mines.'

'I meant pit girls, not men.'

'He preached t'pit girls, mill girls, barmaids, shop girls. Fanatical. But you knew your cousin, right? I mean, you rushed here from Africa out of concern.'

'I'm from the California branch of the family.'

'People say you were born in Wigan. You must be going round t'all your childhood haunts, knocking up relatives.'

'Not yet.'

'What was your mother's name?'

'I think we're getting off the point here.'

'You had a point?'

'When I started. Rose, you're a bit like a cross-current, aren't you? There's no straight sailing with you.'

'Why should there be?'

Blair realized it wasn't going to be quite as simple as he had thought.

Rose said, 'Now you're back, does Wigan seem smaller than you remembered? Or has it become a Garden of Eden?'

'I don't remember. Rose, Wigan is like Pittsburgh plunged

into eternal darkness, does that satisfy you? It is not the Garden
of Eden, it is either a city sinking into a volcanic pit or the rising
outskirts of Hell. Does *that* satisfy you?'

'You're blunt.'

'You asked.'

'Actually, Liverpool is the outskirts of Hell,' she said.

Blair shook his head. 'Rose. Rose Molyneux.' He could see
her in Hell, laughing, wearing a garland. 'Let me get back to
Maypole.'

'You have preachers in California?'

'Oh, yes. Bible thumpers pour over the sierras. Every fanatic
in America ends up in California. You said that Maypole wanted
to preach at the mine.'

'Maypole would preach at rugby games, at pigeon races, at
pantomimes. You like rugby?'

'From what I understand, it's like watching men run around
in the mud chasing a pig, except there's no pig. Is that all
Maypole wanted, just to preach to you?'

'He preached t'all the girls. I was just one more dirty face
t'him.'

'No, Rose. He had a special interest in you.' He laid the
photograph on the table. 'This was in John Maypole's room.'

Rose was so visibly surprised that he wondered whether she
would tilt to outrage or confession. Instead, she laughed. 'That
stupid picture? Have you ever tried t'pose with a shovel? That
card is for sale everywhere in England.'

'Men are strange,' Blair admitted. 'Some men like pictures
of undressed women, some men like pictures of women in
trousers. The Reverend had only one picture, though, and it's
of you.'

'I can't stop someone from having a picture of me. Flo saw
a book about you. It called you "Nigger Blair". Why do they call
you "Nigger Blair"?'

'The penny-dreadful writer is a low form of life. I can't stop them and there's no controlling them.'

'All the same, they don't come into your house and ask all about your personal life like they're the police when they're not. What are you? I'm still not clear on that. Why should I talk to you?'

'I'm just doing a job for the Bishop.'

'That won't do.'

Blair found himself at a loss. So far he'd learned nothing and this girl, this *pit girl*, was in control.

'I'm not police, not Maypole's cousin, not a Mines Inspector. I'm a mining engineer and I've been to Africa, that's all.'

'Not good enough.' Rose stood. 'Bill and Flo are waiting for me.'

'What do you want to hear?'

'Considering your first visit, you know more about me than I do about you.'

Blair remembered opening his eyes to the sight of her bathing. He conceded the point. 'Such as?' he asked.

'Any reason t'talk.'

'A reason? Maypole may be dead—'

When Rose stood and started toward the parlour, Blair grabbed for her arm. She was too quick and he only caught her fingertips, which were rough and black from sorting coal, though her hand was slender. He let go. 'I have to get back to Africa.'

'Why?'

'I have a daughter there.'

Rose smiled, triumphant. 'That's better,' she said. 'Is the mother white? Or is that why they call you "Nigger Blair"?'

'On the Gold Coast, it's women who pan for gold. They use pans painted black and swirl water around. Usually in riverbeds,

115

the same as anywhere in the world except that they don't have quicksilver to draw the gold. Still, they get an amazing amount. My job was to map the rivers, determine how navigable they were and find out where the gold was washing down from. The trouble is that the Ashanti don't trust the English because they aren't fools. Is this boring you?'

Rose topped his tea with gin and sipped some from her cup, her lips turned red from the hot drink. 'Not yet,' she said.

'The Ashanti capital is Kumasi. Orange-earth country, ferrous soil. Outcroppings of rose quartz. Very pleasant. Huts and guava trees and banana. The king's palace is the one big building. I stayed with Arabs because they're traders. Gold, palm oil, slaves.'

'Slaves for America?' Rose asked.

'Slaves for Africa. That's how anything is harvested, how anything is carried. By slaves. This Arab traded gold and slaves. He had a fifteen-year-old girl who had been captured in the north. She had unusually fine features. They thought she'd bring a good price in Kumasi. Obviously she wasn't being sold to carry bananas. But she cried. She cried all the time. Usually Africans accept their fate. They beat her, but not too much because that would damage the goods. She went on crying, and finally the Arab told me he was giving up and was going to sell her back to the raiders, who could make her their entertainment on the way south. That didn't sound very nice, so I bought her. You're sure this isn't boring you? Maybe you've heard this kind of story before.'

'Not in Wigan,' Rose said.

'I set her free. But how was she going to get home? How was she going to live? Unless I took care of her she'd have to sell herself back into slavery. I hired her as a cook – tried to teach her how to cook, how to clean. There was nothing she could do and I was afraid to leave her on her own in Kumasi, so I married her.'

'Did she ever stop crying?'

'At about that point, yes. I don't know how legal the marriage was. A mixture of Islam, Methodist, Fetish.'

'Was the Arab there? The trader?'

'Oh, yes. Best man. Anyway, she took being a wife very seriously and insisted on my taking it seriously: otherwise she said she'd be ashamed. Other people would know, and that would make her no better than a slave. So she got pregnant.'

'Was it yours?'

'Oh, without a doubt. A brown girl with green eyes? The Wesleyans said I had stained the white man's reputation. They closed down their mission. Maybe if they'd had women they'd still be in Kumasi.'

'You chased the Wesleyans out?'

'In a way.'

'You're better than the Devil.'

How much of this did Rose understand? Blair wondered. Did she know where the Gold Coast was, let alone what an Ashanti looked like? Or seen a nugget of gold in her life? He had started talking about Kumasi only because she was about to go and he didn't know what else to say. Now that he'd started on this disastrous course, on his disastrous life, it was hard to stop.

'I was never an explorer in the Gold Coast. There are Ashanti roads, caravans, toll collectors, unless you insist on cutting your way through the bush. There are lions, but the real dangers are worms, mosquitoes and flies. I was three years with the Ashanti. They were curious and suspicious because they couldn't quite figure out why a man wanted to look at rocks. The Ashanti think you find gold where there are giant baboons or smoke or a particular fern. I was looking for quartz reefs and diorite. Making maps and delivering them to the coast and the mail boat so they could be brought to Liverpool and then to here. But there was a war last year. Also dysentery. In Africa every disease hits like the plague. My wife died. The girl survived.'

'Did you love her, your wife?'

Blair couldn't tell if Rose was serious or not. He did see despite the low light that while each feature of her face was individually perhaps too bold, as a composition they had balance and her eyes were as bright as two candles.

'No,' he said. 'But she become a fact through perseverance.'

'So why did you leave?'

'I had to go to the coast because I had run out of medicine and money. However, the funds that were supposed to be waiting for me at the District Commissioner's office had been diverted to help celebrate the arrival of a distinguished visitor from London who had helped incite the war. I especially needed the money because I had squandered the Bible Fund on my porters, the men who carry my gear. They walked as far as I did, and carrying ninety extra pounds. Anyway, I was found out, which made me worse than a criminal on the Gold Coast.'

'A black sheep?'

'Exactly. So I am here to rescue my fortunes, to please my patron, to carry out this small mission and be reinstated.'

'Where is the little girl?'

'With the Arab.'

'You could have stayed.'

Blair contemplated his cup; at this point, it was less tea than gin. 'When a white man slides in Africa, he slides fast.'

Rose said, 'You were finding gold. You must've been rich. What happened t'that?'

'That went to paying for the girl. The Arab does nothing for free, but he's a relatively honest businessman.' He raised his eyes to hers. 'Now tell me about John Maypole.'

'Th'Reverend didn't know when t'quit. He was at us when we walked t'work and at us when we walked back. T'share our burden, so he said. But he grew into an irritation. Then after work he was at the door.'

'Your door especially,' Blair said.

'I told him I was pairing with Bill Jaxon and it was best for him t'stay away. Bill didn't understand at first, but they got on. Maypole was a boy. That was why he was so moral, he didn't know any better.'

'You saw a lot of him?'

'No. I'm Catholic. I don't attend his church or his do-good clubs.'

'But he sought you out. The last time anyone saw him, the day before the fire, he met you at Scholes Bridge. How far did you walk with him?'

'I was walking home and he followed me.'

'You were talking, too. What about?'

'I might have teased him. He was easy to tease.'

'As he was talking to you, he pulled off his priest's collar. Do you remember why?'

'I don't remember him doing that at all. Ask me about the blast, I remember *that*. The earth jumping. The smoke. Maybe it blew Mr Maypole out of my head.'

'But the last time you saw him, you just went home?'

'I was seeing Bill.'

'Have you ever seen Bill fight? Pretty bloody.'

'Isn't he fooking glorious?'

'Fooking glorious?'

'He is,' Rose said.

He thought of her watching Bill fight, the sound of wooden

soles on naked flesh, the gore smeared on skin. How did Bill and Rose celebrate afterwards? An interesting choice of words, 'fooking glorious'. And they talk about savages in Africa, he thought.

'Did Bill Jaxon ever threaten Maypole?'

'No. The Reverend only wanted t'save my soul, he didn't have any interest in the rest of me.'

'That's what you keep telling me.' Blair turned the picture on the table for her to see better. 'But that's not a picture of the soul.'

Rose studied it more closely. 'I extra washed and then I get t'studio and they wipe that muck on my face. I look like an Irish potato farmer.'

'You look ferocious with that shovel. Dangerous.'

'Well, I never touched a hair on Reverend Maypole. I don't know why he had a picture of me.'

'I like the picture. I even like the shovel. It's far more interesting than a parasol.'

'Gentlemen don't cross the street to meet a girl twirling a shovel.'

'I've crossed jungles to meet women with plates in their lips.'

'Kiss any?'

'No.'

'See!'

As coal collapsed it sent a shower of sparks up the chimney. Rose stared at the grate. She was small for moving steel tubs, Blair thought. Her face was as delicate at rest as it was wild when animated. What sort of life did a creature like her look forward to? Gin, babies, beatings from a man like Bill? This was her all-too-brief flowering, and she seemed determined to make the most of it.

'I should be getting on t'Bill and Flo,' she said. 'I don't think he likes you.'

'Bill didn't mind Maypole.'

'Bill likes t'rule the roost. Maypole let him.'

'Well, they played together.'

'You'd have thought the rules of rugby were laid down by Christ t'hear Maypole preach.'

'What did he preach to girls?'

'Chastity and higher love. Every mother had t'be the Virgin Mary. Every girl who sported was Mary Magdalene. I don't think he ever had a real woman.'

'Now, I'm not a gentleman—'

'We all know that.'

'—but I have the feeling that for a man like Maypole, there was nothing more attractive than a woman in need of saving.'

'Maybe.'

'Did he ever call you "Rose of Sharon"?

'Where did you hear that?' The question was so casual that it stood out like a half-driven nail, a small slip.

'Did he?'

'No.'

'You said he never had a real woman. You don't count his fiancée, Miss Hannay?'

'No.'

'You've met her?'

'I don't meet the Hannays any more than I've been to the moon. But I've seen the moon, I have an opinion about it. Have you met her?'

'Yes.'

'And what do you think?'

'She's thin on charm.'

'Thin on everything, but she has money, clothes, carriages. Going t'see her again?'

'Tomorrow.'

'Sounds like you can't resist her.'

'Compared with you, she's a thorn, an icicle and sour wine.'

Rose watched him silently from across the table. He would have liked to see her face clean. He'd seen her bathe, but what he remembered was her body within a glowing sheath of water. He hoped the image didn't shine from his eyes.

Rose said, 'You have t'go.' She added, 'You're not so sick as you say.'

Later, at his hotel, Blair asked himself if he was crazy. He had hidden the reason for his return to Africa from everyone with a right to know: Bishop Hannay, the Royal Society, even the innocuous Leveret, and now he had blurted everything to a girl who would spread this most irresistible of stories to all the pubs in Wigan, whence it would quickly work its destructive way to Hannay Hall. What a combination he had given her – slavery and racial mixing! The tragedy of the young black wife. The poignancy of a white father and his half-caste issue, set against the barbarism of an African jungle and the rapaciousness of Arabian traders. England itself would go to war to save that child if she were white. What was he thinking? To impress a coquette like Rose Molyneux by telling the truth?

Look at the lies she had told in return. The only treasure John Maypole possessed was a picture of her, and she said he only wanted to save her soul?

Consider the house. How was it that while all the other homes on Candle Court were stuffed with families and day lodgers like herrings in a net, Rose and her friend Flo had an entire, well-furnished house to themselves? How did honest girls pay for that?

Her secrecy. She'd made him quit the house alone and said she would wait till he was out of sight to leave herself.

Was it her revenge for his first visit, catching her in her

bath? Was it his fever? Though he didn't feel that ill. Sometimes a brain that was warm made inspired choices. The reason he hadn't told her about finding Maypole's journal was that the book was the only advantage he had over her.

He had to laugh, though. If she could do this to him, what had she done to Maypole?

Chapter Eight

'AN OUNCE OF quinine?'

'Two ounces,' Blair said.

'You're sure?'

'Quinine is what keeps the British Empire going.'

'Very true, sir.' The chemist added a second weight on one side of the beam scale and tapped more white powder on to the other. 'I could break this into any number of doses wrapped in rice paper for easier swallowing.'

'I drink it with gin. It swallows very easily.'

'I dare say it does.' The chemist poured the quinine into an envelope. He frowned. 'Might I ask if you are doubling up, though?'

'A bit.'

'Have you considered Warburg's Drops? A combination of quinine, opium and sloes. Plums to you, sir. Very smooth going down.'

'A little too sedative.'

'If it is a pick-me-up you're after, then might I suggest arsenic? Clears the head wonderfully. Some of our veterans have had excellent results.'

'I've tried it,' Blair said. Arsenic could be used for almost anything: malaria, melancholy, impotence. 'Sure, I'll take some of that, too.'

'The Bishop is paying, you said?'

'Yes.'

The chemist cleaned the scale on his apron and from the drug run, the long set of drawers behind the dispensary counter, brought out a jar of actinic green to mark it by colour as poison. The shop itself was tinged an underwater hue by cobalt blue bottles arrayed in the window. Dried botanicals scented the air and a coolness emanated from two creamware urns with perforated lids for leeches. The chemist poured out a pyramid of chalky powder. Blair dipped in his finger, licked it and let the bitter taste sting his tongue.

'You appreciate the importance of temperate dosage, sir?'

'Yes.' I'm eating arsenic in front of you, Blair thought. How temperate can a man get?

'A little coca extract for vigour?'

'I might be back for that. Quinine and arsenic for now.'

The chemist filled a second envelope and was giving them both to Blair when the scales swayed and glass stoppers jiggled. Starting at the top shelves and moving to the bottom, brass measures and stone mortars, poison rounds and perfume jars began to tremble as a heavy resonance shook the plate-glass front of the shop. Outside, a mover's steam-powered van lumbered by, a two-storey locomotive with boiler, black stack and rubber wheels that made the cobblestones of the street groan. Behind his counter, the chemist moved quickly from side to side to reach up and keep first one leech urn and then the other from falling.

Blair opened the envelopes, poured lines of arsenic and quinine across his palm and tossed them into his mouth. As the van passed he saw Leveret's carriage outside the hotel. He pocketed the envelopes and left.

*

'You seem revitalized today,' Leveret said.

'Yes.' And motivated, Blair thought. He had to show progress before any rumours were spread by Rose Molyneux. If she started to entertain friends with lurid reports of his half-African daughter, the news would not take long to reach Wigan's monitors of virtue, and then not even Bishop Hannay could ignore the scandal of miscegenation. What had he told Blair about the name 'Nigger Blair'? 'Discourage it.' The Bishop would drop him without paying another penny.

'Today's Wednesday?' Blair climbed up into the carriage seat.

'Right,' Leveret said.

'Maypole was last seen on a Wednesday. Wednesday afternoons, he always went to the Home for Women. You wanted me to pay a courtesy call on the Reverend Chubb, we'll do that. Then let's talk to the police. There's a Chief Constable Moon we should see.'

'We should at least inform Charlotte that we're going to the Home.'

'We'll surprise her.'

As they drove, Blair became aware that besides being uncomfortable about etiquette, Leveret sat a little stiffly.

'You're all right?'

'Yesterday's tour of the pit took a toll, I'm afraid. My grandfather was a miner. He always had stories, but now I know what he was talking about. Explosions, falling rocks.' He lifted his hat to show off bandages. 'Low roofs.'

'Nice. Gives you panache.'

Beyond the entrance to Hannay Hall was a smaller gate and a meandering path. As they progressed, Blair realized they had entered a private park. Trees – plane, chestnut and beech –

became regularly planted, footpaths were edged in purple crocus and the carriage joined a swept avenue at the end of which sat a small fortress. A mock fortress, he saw as they approached. Three storeys of brick with limestone parapets, decorative towers and loopholes filled with stained glass, the whole surrounded not by a moat but by various colours of primroses. Two young women wearing plain, grey dresses with no bustles sat in a garden arbour. A third girl, also in grey, emerged from the door with a swaddled baby.

Leveret said, 'This is the Home for Women. It was a Hannay guest cottage.'

'A cottage?'

'The Prince of Wales stayed here once. Hannays have always done things in the grand style. Wait here.'

Leveret went inside. Through a window opened to the warm air Blair saw young women in grey uniforms around a blackboard scribbled with rows of arithmetic. He was aware of being an interloper of the wrong gender, and he wondered how, even armoured by a clerical collar, Maypole had felt. Through the next open window he saw a class huddled around prosthetic limbs wrapped in bandages. Some of the students had the robust frame and red cheeks of pit girls, others were sallow from life in the mills. They sat stiffly and unnaturally in their uniforms, like girls posing in paper wings for a Christmas pageant.

Leveret returned and followed Blair's gaze. 'Charlotte wants them to have professions. Nursing is one. She insists that they read, too.'

'Poets?'

'Economics and hygiene, mainly.'

'That sounds like Charlotte.'

Leveret spoke hesitantly, as if about to commit an act he knew he would regret. 'She's in the rose garden.'

They went around a side of the Home where a lawn sloped

down between rounded masses of rhododendron to the terminus of a boxwood hedge. From the other side rose two sharp, familiar voices.

Earnshaw was saying, 'It is simply my conviction, Miss Hannay, that charity can be overdone and that the best intentions often lead to the worst results. Your father tells me that you have argued for paying pit girls and mill girls *not* to work during the last stage of pregnancy. What is that if not an invitation to immorality and sloth? Don't you think women, as much as men, should suffer the consequences of their acts?'

'Men don't get pregnant.'

'Then consider the inevitable outcome of educating women above their husbands and above their class.'

'So that they might be dissatisfied by life with a drunken, ignorant lout?'

'Or by life with a perfectly acceptable and sober man.'

'Acceptable to whom? You? *You* marry him. You speak of these women as if they were cows waiting for a bull with four good legs.'

Blair came around the hedge to a garden of pea-gravel paths and rosebushes so bare and severely pruned that they looked like iron rods. Charlotte Hannay and Earnshaw stood at the central, circular bed. Was this the woman 'black and beautiful' who had invaded the mind of John Maypole, the figure who led the curate to suspect that a pit girl in corduroy had more life than a lady? Blair doubted it. Charlotte was an example of how silk could subdue a small woman, her bosom compacted by stays, her legs swimming somewhere within a bustle of purple silk, pruning shears poised in a hideous purple glove. Blair removed his hat. Did her eyebrows arch at the sight of him or were they pinned high on her forehead because her hair was combed so tautly under a sun hat as black as crêpe? He saw a coppery flame at the nape of her neck, but she could have been a novitiate for all he could tell of her hair's colour. At her side was Earnshaw's beard shining in the sunlight. Behind them at a respectful distance was a nurseryman in a smock and straw hat holding a sack of dripping liquid manure.

Leveret said, 'If we could beg your indulgence, Blair has a question or two.'

Earnshaw suggested to Charlotte, 'I can return later. Or would you rather I stayed?'

'Stay, but I can manage visitors by myself,' Charlotte said.

'She could probably geld visitors by herself,' Blair muttered to Leveret.

'What was that?' Earnshaw demanded.

Blair made a vague gesture towards the building. 'I was just saying that this must be a golden opportunity for all these women.'

'If you were a reformer or a pedagogue, Miss Hannay might conceive some interest in your opinion. Since you are a con- fessed associate of traders in flesh, your opinion could not be less welcome.'

'Wrong,' Charlotte Hannay said. 'Since Mr Blair is such a depraved individual, his opinion is all the more valuable. Blair, speaking from your wide experience, what will more likely keep young women in a condition of financial need and sexual peril, the ability to think as an independent person or, as Mr Earnshaw insists, training for domestic service so that a penniless, ignorant maid can bring a brandy to her master in his bed?'

She was remarkable, Blair had to admit. Like a sparrow chasing men around a garden. 'I've never had a maid,' he said.

'Surely in Africa you had female servants. You must have taken advantage of them.'

Had rumours from Rose already reached her? Blair wondered.

'Sorry, no.'

'But you have a reputation as a man who will try anything at least once, from ostrich eggs to snake meat. Supposedly no man in England knows more about African women than you. Mr Earnshaw, who knows nothing about either African women or English women, says it is unnatural to educate a woman above her station.'

'To make her unfit and unhappy in her station,' Earnshaw explained. 'It's unfair to her and unhealthy for England.'

'Like God, he proposes to create women fit for only one station. Like a politician, he presumes to speak for England when, in fact, he speaks only for those allowed to vote – men.'

Earnshaw said, 'If I might ask, what has this to do with Blair?'

'Blair,' Charlotte asked, 'is there another tribe anywhere that degrades women as thoroughly as the English?'

Earnshaw protested, 'Miss Hannay, think of any Muslim country. Polygamy, women dressed like tents.'

'While in England,' Charlotte said, 'a man is allowed by law to beat his wife, force himself physically on her and dispose of her property as his own. You've been in Africa, Blair. May the most vicious Muslim legally do that?'

'No.'

Charlotte asked, 'What better witness than a man who has infamously used women of every race? Testimony from the Devil!' She moved on to the next bare stems and asked the nurseryman, 'Joseph, what do we have here?'

'Tea roses, ma'am. Pink Carrière. Dooble-white Vibert. Red General Jacqueminot. Wi' mulch an' gravy.' He indicated the sack he held. 'Cow droppings soaked wi' ground hoof an' horn. It'll be beautiful, ma'am.'

White, red, yellow, pink; it was amazing what future blooms were expected. Yet it was clear to Blair that Charlotte at a young age was already everything she would be, a prickly armature of thorns.

Over her shoulder she asked, 'Oliver, why are you bandaged like a veteran of the Crimea?'

'I went down the pit with Blair yesterday.'

'Be glad you weren't a girl.'

'Miss Hannay, why *do* you dislike me so much?' Blair asked. 'I haven't had a chance to earn so much contempt.'

'Mr Blair, if you saw a slug on a flower petal how long would you let it stay?'

'I've done nothing—'

'You're here. I told you not to come and yet you did. You either have no manners or no ears.'

'Your father—'

'My father threatens to close the Home for Fallen Women at the first sign of scandal, but he is willing to hire you, a man who would embezzle a Bible Fund. The story is well known, along with tales of foul habits and black harems. My father did not choose you for this task because you possess any investigative skills; he chose you because you are the most loathsome individual on not one but two continents. He chose you because the choice of you is in itself an insult to John Maypole and me.'

'Oh.' Blair felt wound in the web of an industrious little spider. 'So where do you think John Maypole is?'

Charlotte dropped the shears into a pocket of her skirt and turned to Earnshaw. 'I might as well get this over with, otherwise we'll have him following us for ever like a tradesman with a cigar.' She faced Blair. 'Where the Reverend John Maypole is at present I have no idea. Until it is proved otherwise, I assume he is well and that he will make the reasons for his absence known when he cares to. In the meantime I will carry out the work we began together in the full anticipation of his return.'

'The last day he was seen was a Wednesday. Meetings for the Home were on Wednesdays. Did you see him there?'

'No. I happened to be ill that day.'

'Miss Hannay has a frail constitution,' Leveret said.

She didn't appear frail to Blair. Small of frame, but not frail. 'When was the last time you saw him?' he asked.

'Sunday Services.'

'Sounds romantic. And not a word since?'

'No.'

'Did he ever talk to you about his visits to the coal mines? To the Hannay Mine?'

'No.'

'The pit girls there?'

'No.'

'Or indicate any frustration that he couldn't extend his ministry down into the mine itself?'

'No.'

'He liked to preach, didn't he? At the drop of a hat?'

'He felt he had a calling,' Charlotte said.

'And wanted to be part of the working class, at least long enough to preach. Did he ever mention a miner named Bill Jaxon?'

'No.'

'Did he have any history of melancholia?'

'No.'

'Did he like to roam the countryside? Swim in the canal? Take lonely walks on slag heaps or high cliffs?'

'No. His only pastime was rugby, and he did that to reach the men.'

'But you didn't spend much time with him outside meetings, did you? You had a spiritual relationship.'

'I hope so.'

'So he could have a tattoo of the Royal Navy and you wouldn't know.'

'No, no more than you would know whether any of the women you debauched had a brain or a soul,' Charlotte answered passionately, toe to toe. Put a pair of clogs on her and she would be a dangerous creature, Blair thought. Earnshaw and Leveret faded from his conscious view.

'Was Maypole intelligent, would you say?'

'Intelligent and sensitive.'

'So he knew he would break your heart if he disappeared and didn't even drop a line?'

'He knew I would understand whatever he did.'

'Lucky man. That's the kind of woman *I've* always needed.'

'Stop it,' Earnshaw said from somewhere, but Blair felt an accelerating rhythm of mutual loathing and knew Charlotte Hannay felt it also, like a crescendo heard by two.

'Did he mention wealthy relatives who might be old and sick?' he asked.

'No.'

'Pending lawsuits?'

'No.'

'Spiritual crises?'

'Not John.'

'Anything pending but your wedding?'

'No.'

'Mail is delivered twice a day. I understand that lovers write to each other every post. Did you keep his letters?'

'If I did, I'd rather put them in the hands of a leper than deliver them to you.'

'No sense he felt he might have been missing out on simple pleasures?'

'Simple as in animal? No, that particular depth is your level, Mr Blair.'

'I meant simple as in human.'

'I don't know what you mean.'

133

'Human weakness. This is the Home for Fallen Women, Miss Hannay, so there must be some humans here. Maybe Maypole met one.'

Charlotte stooped to snip a long stem with her shears. With more force and speed than he expected, she stood and whipped the stem across Blair's face, which immediately burned.

'You will leave now,' Charlotte said. 'I will have dogs here next time and I will have them set on you if you ever dare return.'

'I personally will set on you if you return,' Earnshaw said.

Blair felt blood wet his cheek. He plopped his hat back on.

'Well, regretfully, I must be going. Thank you for all your help. My best to your father.' As he walked away he paused by the nurseryman. 'Knew a man in the Gold Coast raised roses. Retired sergeant major. Roses big as a platter. Used guano. Guano's the key.'

Leveret retreated in reverse, leaving excuses. 'I had no idea, no idea. So sorry.'

As they went around the hedge, Blair used a handkerchief to mop his face and motioned Leveret to stop and be silent. They heard a furious Charlotte Hannay on the other side.

'And you, Mr Earnshaw, do you have any idea how obnoxious it is to offer your protection before it's asked?'

'I was merely supporting you.'

'When I'm so weak that I need support I will let you know.'

Smiling through the blood, Blair walked up the lawn.

'Now you've set *them* to arguing,' Leveret said.

'It doesn't matter how much people like that argue, they're moralists. They were made for each other.'

*

At the river, Blair washed his face. The clouds were high and edged sideways by the sun, and although the cuts on his face burned, he felt strangely braced.

Leveret was distressed. 'You can't speak to people like Charlotte like that. That was a terrible scene. The language was unforgivable, Blair. You goaded her.'

Blair picked out a thorn. In his reflection on the water's surface he saw three gouges, otherwise only scratches, and felt a hot sense of satisfaction.

'I goaded her? That's like accusing somebody of goading an asp.'

'You were cruel. What were you getting at with insinuations about John being human?'

Blair dried himself on his jacket and put a dab of arsenic in his palm. 'What we are, Leveret, is a sum of our sins. That's what makes us human instead of saints. A perfectly flat surface has no character. Allow some cracks, some flaws and short-comings, and then you have contrast. It's that contrast with impossible perfection that makes our character.'

'You have character?' Leveret asked.

'Tons.' Blair put his head back and threw the powder into his mouth. 'It turns out that Maypole might have, too, in a demented, religious sort of way.'

'Questions like that can ruin a man's reputation.'

'I'm not interested in his reputation. I'm more of a geologist, I look for feet of clay. So I find it interesting that a penniless curate managed to connect to a girl with so much money.'

'Everything in Wigan is connected to the Hannays. Half the people work for the Hannays. Besides the Hannay mines, the Hannay Iron Works manufacture boilers, iron plate and loco-motives. There are the Hannay Cotton Mills and Hannay Brick Works. They build their own chimneys to burn their own coal to spin their own yarn on a quarter of a million spindles. I haven't travelled the world like you, but I would venture to say that the Hannays are one of the most efficient industrial complexes anywhere.'

'And making a fortune.'

'And providing employment. Well-paid employment compared to average wages. But there's more to the Hannays than commerce. The family supports the Church, which means paying for clergy and organs and pews. The Ragged Schools for poor children. Evening Schools for men. Dispensary for the Sick. The Explosion Fund, the Widows and Orphans Fund, the Clothing Society were all started by Bishop Hannay himself. Without the Hannays there would be less work in Wigan and very little charity. Everyone is connected to the Hannays, including you. Or did you forget?'

'The Bishop doesn't let me forget.'

'Charlotte has probably gone to him already and told him about our disastrous visit. He'll have to discharge you now.'

'I won't spend any more delightful days with the sanctimonious Miss Hannay? Bring my money and I'll be gone.'

'You don't understand her situation.'

'I understand that she is a rich young woman whose hobbyhorse is a charity for poor girls she dresses up in Quaker grey. She probably knows as much about real life in Wigan as she does about the moon. It doesn't matter because she'll be the richest spoiled brat in England when her father dies.'

'Not quite.'

The way Leveret said it made Blair pause.

'You just described the Hannay empire.'

'Yes, but Bishop Hannay is also Lord Hannay. When he dies, the estate will pass with the title. A woman cannot inherit the title. Everything – land and properties – will go to the nearest male heir, her cousin, Lord Rowland, who will become the next Lord Hannay. Charlotte will be well settled, of course.'

'You mean rich.'

'Yes, but whoever she marries, John Maypole or anyone else, would have full disposition of whatever she inherits.'

Blair watched bees buzz by with golden satchels of pollen. Which explained Earnshaw, he thought, though he hovered by Charlotte Hannay more like a beetle than a bee.

The visit of the Municipal Committee for Health and Sanitation to Albert Court, a U of two-storey red-brick housing, was a form of war. All the residents stood in the middle of the courtyard as disinfectors dressed in white smocks and caps rolled in caissons bearing bright pumps and canisters of polished brass. At every third or fourth house, a disinfector manned the pump while his partner unreeled the hose, dashed into the front door and sprayed a poisonous mist of strychnine and ammonia. The stench was choking, but the Reverend Chubb, in command, a red committee sash over his cassock, issued directions like a general oblivious to the smoke of battle. The residents were women and children; Blair noticed that a number cradled bird cages. Among the committee matrons in official sashes he recognized Mrs Smallbone, her skirt of black bombazine adding a menacing bounce to every stride. She dug into a boy's head with a comb and signalled to two other committee members, who bore down on the boy with water and carbolic soap. Chubb acknowledged the arrival of Leveret and Blair in the courtyard with no more than a flicker of his concentration.

Blair remembered having his own head clipped and washed, hands clamping his neck to hold him still as if he were a dog. It was the smell of the soap that did it.

'Medicine doesn't taste good,' Chubb said.

'It wouldn't be medicine if it did, would it?' Blair asked. 'Shouldn't there be a medical officer in charge?'

'He's ill. Fumigation can't wait. If these people insist on crowding five in a bed with lice-ridden bedclothes, not even bothering to use the sanitary facilities the landlord provides, creating a miasma from which spread cholera, typhus and smallpox, then community measures are called for. A sink of pestilence affects us all. Think of the mince rats.'

'Mince rats?' Blair didn't want to think about them.

'Some of the houses will have to be sealed and left with sulphur candles.'

'Where do the people from those houses go?'

Chubb marched ahead. 'The children should all be in school, where they can be properly inspected.'

Certainly some of the residents had crusted bare feet and ragged clothes, just as some houses had split doors and broken panes. Most, however, looked merely angry, rousted from homes that showed lace curtains in the windows and thresholds that must have been zealously scrubbed with stone to be clean at all. Chubb seemed to send in the fumigators on an arbitrary basis.

'How does he know which houses to attack?' Blair asked Leveret.

Leveret whispered, 'Simple. He wouldn't dare break into a miner's house. The miners would break into the town hall. In defence of the people here, there are only two privies for two hundred occupants.'

Chubb returned. 'Sufficient, if there is social discipline. Look at their clothes. Rags, probably infested. If it were up to me, we'd burn them.'

'Too bad you can't have an *auto da fé*,' Blair said.

'That's a Papist practice. There has always been an obstinate core of them here. The Hannay family, as the Bishop told you, was once, long ago, Roman. And of course we have Irish among the miners – Irish and pigs.'

'They go together?'

'Filth and immorality go hand in hand. Squalor breeds disease. No doubt, Mr Blair, in your travels to the sinkholes of the world you have noticed that smell itself is pestilential. I know that in time these people will come to appreciate the effort we make on their behalf.'

'Maypole used to do this?'

'He was on the Committee for a time.'

The cart rolled forward, leaving in the air an acrid taste that coated the lips.

'Reverend, you're a born missionary. You mean Maypole quit.'

'He was disobedient. He was young. Rather than stamp out pollution, he sheltered it.'

'You mean, the Home for Women?'

'Home for Women Who Have Fallen for the First Time,' Chubb corrected him. 'As if in Wigan there is such a thing as women who have fallen *only* for the first time. It is a dangerous thing for even the most hardened man to save a fallen woman. A young curate's interest in such a pursuit has to be suspect. Philanthropy has masked weakness more than once. It is not the woman who is saved but the saviour who goes under.'

'Are you thinking of any particular woman?'

'I don't know any women that *particular*. I washed my hands of Maypole and his "Magdalenes".'

Blair walked to stay abreast of Chubb and the disinfection carts. 'Otherwise he was satisfactory? He conducted services, did sick calls, that sort of thing?'

'Yes.'

'He seemed to have little money.'

'Men do not join the Church to make money. It is not a trade.'

'He was broke.'

'He didn't yet have a living, a post as a vicar and the remuneration that comes with it. He was of good family, I was given to understand, but his parents died when he was young, leaving him little. What did it matter? He was about to marry far above his station.'

'Did he give you any indication that he was considering some sort of adventure, that he might leave?'

'Leave? When he was engaged to the Bishop's daughter?'

'He seemed happy?'

'Why shouldn't he be? As soon as they married it was pre-ordained that he would rise to the highest ranks of the Church.'

'What about his preaching at the mines? Do you know anything about that?'

'I warned him that open-air sort of thing was for Wesleyans. Unfortunately Maypole had low-church leanings. Like his play-ing at rugby. What I needed was a man to serve Communion, visit the sick, take food to the deserving poor. That is enough work for two.'

'What do you think happened to him?'

'I don't know.'

'Did you ask the police?'

'We don't want to overly bother the police. It's not a scandal unless we make it one. If Chief Constable Moon hears anything, he'll tell us.'

'Tell me, do you still want to find Maypole?'

'I don't know that I care. Saint Maypole, here and gone. I serve at the Bishop's pleasure, of course. We all do. But tell him when you see him that I've waited long enough. I need another curate.'

The cart rolled ahead, sunlight smeared over brass, and Chubb hurried to keep pace.

*

Chief Constable Moon had an indentation in the middle of his forehead. 'Brick.' He pulled a sleeve back from a white scar that ran the length of a meaty forearm. 'Shovel.' He lifted a trouser leg. His shin was cross-hatched with scar tissue and punched in as if shot. 'Clogs. Enough to say that today when there's a set-to with miners we wear stiff leather leggings. And what happened to you?' He peered at the scratches on Blair's face.

'A rose.'

'Oh, well, we can't report that, sir.'

'No.'

Moon's uniform was blue, embroidered in silver at the collar and cuffs, and he had mobile features that suggested he enjoyed authority dispensed with nudges and winks. Blair himself enjoyed the luckless state of mind of a man with nothing to lose. Arsenic coursed through his veins like a secondary fever. Leveret had left to plead Blair's case to the Bishop. By now Charlotte Hannay must have gone to her father and demanded his dismissal. Moans issued from holding cells of whitewashed stone and straw bedding across the corridor, but the Constable's office offered the comfort of a tile firegrate, a desk of mahogany, deep chairs of Russian leather, gas lamps that illuminated maps of the worlds of Lancashire and Wigan. There was the prosperity of a new business to Moon's office.

'Nice, isn't it? The old station and town hall were damaged by the miners when we had some troubles a few years back. The Hannays, of course, were major contributors to the improvements.' Moon allowed himself a pause. 'We want to set the Bishop's mind at ease. It's just a little late in the day. What with the Hannay explosion, the rescue, identifying bodies, accident inquiry, funerals, no one mentioned Maypole to us until long after. Well, I think they wanted to be quiet about it, don't you? Young curate engaged to the Bishop's daughter. Best solved privately. Never been a formal complaint, not in the log.'

'But you did ask about Maypole?'

'Using discretion. At railways, in case Maypole bought a ticket. Walked the ditches and canals. Sad business, but you never know. Of course it's coal country. Old shafts everywhere. If a man walks in the dark and doesn't know where to stop, then he might never be found.'

'Maypole had trouble with a man named Silcock. Is that name familiar to you?'

'An expert with a cosh. Preys on hotel guests, gentlemen who've had too much to drink. Has a fair, square-rigged look. That's his guise.'

'Like Maypole?'

'Now that you mention it, in a general fashion. Anyway, we were on top of that. We ran him out of Wigan the same day we saw him bother the Reverend.'

'You arrested him?'

'No, but we put the pressure on. Had to warn him twice, but he disappeared.'

'Have you located Silcock since then?'

'No.'

'Don't you think you should have?'

'Someone else's problem.' Moon shuffled his jaw back and forth. 'Mr Leveret couldn't be with you?'

'He went to Hannay Hall to report on the day's progress. Chief Constable, do you recall seeing Maypole the day before the explosion?'

'You have so many questions you could be a regular detective. No.'

'When was the last time you talked to him?'

'The week before. He was always bringing an excuse for a drunken miner. I understood. Forgiveness is a young curate's job, after all.'

Moon made it sound like the drooling stage of a baby; Blair felt a dislike for the man.

'Do you remember which miner it was that week?'

'It was Bill Jaxon.'

'Jaxon and Maypole played on the same rugby team, didn't they?'

'Ah, Bill's a famous boy. He gets in scrapes. Miners do. That's why they're so good at rugby, what does a split nose mean to them? They say if you want a good rugby team in Lancashire, just shout down a shaft.'

'What had Bill done to attract the attention of the law?'

'He broke another man's head for squeezing the wrong girl. I couldn't blame Bill myself. You see, we get travellers who don't know Wigan ways, who get confused.'

'By what?'

'Pit girls.'

'How so?'

Moon had his front teeth, but not the side ones, which made his smile wet and gummy. 'Well, they do what they want, don't they? Drink like men, work like men, live like men. And draw a certain sort of gentleman who travels up here by train to see an Amazon in trousers. That sort of gentleman thinks he can take liberties, and then finds himself squaring up to someone like Bill.'

'Who was the Amazon in Bill's case?'

'A girl named Molyneux.'

'Rose?'

'The same. A pit girl, attractive in a sluttish way. A fairly new arrival in Wigan.' Moon appeared taken aback. 'However do you know her?'

'She was on the list you supplied Leveret of the last people to see Maypole.'

'That's right. I never liked it that the Reverend Maypole wasted time with her. I warned him about over-socializing with miners, letting them drag him down to their level.'

'What level is that?'

'They're good folk but they're primitive. A fact, sir.' Moon shifted his attention to Blair's cheek. 'Know what miners use to clean wounds? Coal dust. So they end up tattooed like savages. You don't want to look like them.'

From the police station Blair walked so that Leveret would have time to bring word of his dismissal to the hotel.

The night clerk poked into message boxes. 'Sorry, sir, nothing for you.'

'There has to be.' Blair couldn't believe that the Bishop would not at least warn him after Leveret's report or Charlotte Hannay's complaint. 'Look again.'

The clerk ducked under the desk. 'There *is* something, sir.' He brought out a heavy, unshapely package wrapped in brown paper and string. Written on the paper in a thick pencil was, 'For Mr Blair. From a friend.'

'Do you know who brought this?'

'No, it was here when I came on. A gift, I suppose. Seems to be in two pieces.'

The clerk waited expectantly for Blair to open the package. Instead he carried it up to his room, set the parcel on the sitting-room table, lit the lamps and allowed himself a quinine and gin. He told himself he had done his best, at least as much as the police had done for the saintly John Maypole. Tomorrow he would be in Liverpool booking passage, even steerage, to escape. In a year his three nights in Wigan would seem a passing dream.

Reinforced with another gin, Blair loosened the string of the package and unwrapped the contents, which proved to be a pair of shoes. Not shoes. Clogs with stout leather uppers attached by brass nails to solid ash soles edged on the underside by horseshoe irons. Shamrocks were stitched into the leather and extra brass heads studded the toes. They were the clogs that Bill Jaxon had won from the Irishman.

Out of curiosity, Blair sat down and pulled off his boots. He slipped on the clogs, closed the clasps and stood. Because wood didn't bend, his feet rocked within, lifting at the heels. The sound of the clogs on the floor when he stepped was like rolling balls. But they fitted.

Chapter Nine

WHEN BLAIR ARRIVED at the Hannay yard, miners on the day shift were already below, but Battie, the underlooker, had come up in the cage to supervise the lowering of a pony, a mare with a milk-white mane and tail. The pony was in blinkers and trailed a harness with two extra-long cinches. While Battie attached a chain and hook to the bottom of the cage, a stableman with hay lured the little horse close to the platform.

The underlooker noticed Blair. 'Are you planning to take another tour of the pit? We won't be crawling on our hands and knees again, will we?'

'No.' Blair dropped his pack from his shoulder to the ground.

Battie finished hooking the chain and stepped back. He wore a dusting of carbon powder. He shielded his eyes from the sun to peer at Blair's face. 'You've been crawling through brambles?'

'I met a human bramble.'

'Mr Leveret with you? I don't see a carriage.'

'I walked out on my own.'

'Carrying your pack all the way? You're not still asking about the Reverend Maypole?'

'Still,' Blair said, although he had left a note at the hotel desk saying where he was headed and hoped to see Leveret roll into the pit yard at any moment with word that the Bishop had fired him. 'Did Maypole come here often?'

'Yes. He was a preacher of opportunity, very good at drawing parallels from the Bible – workers in a vineyard and men in a pit, that sort of thing. I feel bad now.'

'Why?'

'I'm afraid I told him that a pit yard was not a church. You can't preach around rolling wagons and tubs. He was welcome to visit as a friend of the Hannays, but not as a minister. That was a week before the explosion. I should have kept my mouth shut.'

The cage rose, trailing its extra hook below while workmen laid planks across the shaft. The stableman was wiry as a boy, with a beaked nose and a fierce moustache. He walked the pony on to the planks, forced her to her knees, and then to her side. He folded her front legs into the forward cinch and strapped them tight, then did the same with a second cinch around the rear legs so that only her four hoofs were free. He yanked the cinches to test their tension before he connected a ring in the harness to the hook hanging from the cage. At his shout, the cage rose and lifted the pony to a sitting position and then over the hole. The workmen pulled the planks aside, opening the shaft.

'Pretty little horse,' Blair said.

Battie nodded. 'And expensive. I like Welsh ponies, but they're in short supply. This one is all the way from Iceland.'

'White as the proverbial snow.'

'Well, the poor girl won't be white for long.'

The pony hung, trussed, between cage and shaft. Though the stableman tucked hay under her nose and held her reins, she rolled her eyes. A shadow of horse, cage and tower stretched across the yard.

147

'It's her first time. She'll quiet,' the stableman called. 'We don't want her bucking when we send her down pit.'

'Some of the ponies die their first month down,' Battie told Blair. 'Maybe lack of light or air or proper mucking. A mystery. You forgot something?'

Blair stepped on to the platform. 'No, it was just something you said the other day. You showed me where you found the victims of the explosion, the ones who suffocated and the ones who were blown up. You said you'd "thought about it a thousand times".'

'Anyone would, a fire like that.'

'It was the word "thought". As if there was something you were trying to figure out, going over it in your mind. You didn't say "remembered", you said "thought".'

'I don't see the difference,' Battie said.

'There may not be.'

'That's why you came out here?'

'One reason. Was there something you were thinking about?' Blair asked.

The pony didn't calm. Instead, she began to thrash until the cage above her swung against the guide wires like a jointed pendulum. Loose hay spilled, straws of gold sucked by the downdraft into the shaft. Once a pony went down a pit it wouldn't come up again except once a year for a week, until it was finally lame and hauled up for the knacker's cart. In spite of her reins and all the stableman's pulling, she twisted her head to bite the cinch. The cage ticked the tower's wooden props.

'I think about everything that goes on below. That's what an underlooker does,' Battie said.

'I'm not talking about accusations, but maybe something that didn't make sense.'

'Mr Blair, perhaps you haven't noticed, but a dark tunnel deep in the earth is not where you find sensible men.'

The cinch broke. As the pony kicked more freely, she gyrated, which caused her to kick more violently. The stableman ducked her hoofs and tried to pull her back over the platform by her reins so that if she broke or reared out of the bottom cinch she wouldn't pour herself into the open shaft.

'Pull her clear,' Battie shouted.

But the weight of the pony started to drag the stableman towards the shaft. The irons of his clogs slipped across the platform. Battie grabbed him by the waist. Blair removed his jacket, threw it over the pony's head and then held on to Battie.

The three men clung to the reins as the pony thrashed and tried to shake the jacket off. Slowly the kicking stopped. The pony spun but ever more idly, sedated by blindness. Battie took the reins while the stableman fetched a hood, which he expertly slipped over the pony's head even as he snatched Blair's jacket off. Blair took it and staggered against a prop. Activity in the pit yard had ceased around the spectacle. Blair's heart kicked. He was as covered in the pony's lather as if he had rolled in foam.

The stableman was furious. 'Tha' shouldna' done that. Think Ah don't know me job?'

'Sorry,' Blair said.

'You made him look a fool,' Battie said. 'He'd prefer to die.'

More stablemen arrived to pull the pony to the platform and truss her with a new cinch. Across the yard, men again began to weigh tubs, drivers to back their engines into wagons, blacksmiths to beat iron. Battie shouted to the winding house. A tremor ran the length of the cable as it rose, but the pony in her hood was pacified. As the cable reversed and unreeled, she dropped from sight down into the hole, followed by the cage, which stopped momentarily at platform level for Battie to get on.

The underlooker hit the cage bell and said, 'The numbers

agree, Mr Blair. Seventy-six lamps, seventy-six men. That's what matters.'

Blair was still trying to get his breath. 'It's hardly a mystery.'

'What?' Battie called back.

'Why the ponies die. Fear.'

An unhappy smile stole on to Battie's face. Then he disappeared under the top of the cage as it descended, gathering speed but moving smoothly, anchored by the pony hanging underneath.

Blair went over to the sorting shed. A locomotive was shifting a train of loaded wagons away from the siding. Connected only by chains, the wagons slapped together as they transmitted the stop-and-go of the engine. Pit girls walked alongside, collecting larger pieces of coal that fell.

Over the shed itself a cloud of coal dust glittered in the sun. Blair didn't see Rose Molyneux at the siding tippler or among the women picking rocks and dirt from the belt or tending the coal as it cascaded through the grates. The first time he had seen them at work had been in the dark. In daylight their uniforms – work shirts and trousers, head covering of flannel shawls and rolled-up skirts – were neither male nor female but fashion for hermaphroditic drudges. He did recognize the large form of Rose's friend Flo as she disengaged from other women at the bottom of the chute and came his way.

'It's t'gentleman caller,' she said and nodded towards the tower. 'Ah saw thi ride t'carousel.'

Blair swung the pack off his shoulder. 'I have something for Rose. Is she here?'

'She is, but she got hurt. Not bad. She'll be back later, Ah can't say when.' Flo put out a black hand. 'Give it t'me, Ah'll pass it on.'

'I want to give this to Rose myself. I have to talk to her.'

'Well, Ah can't say when she'll be back.'

'When do you quit work? I'll talk to her then.'

'Five. But it wouldn't do for her t'talk then, not when t'men are up.'

'Then I'll meet her in town.'

'No. T'best place is Canary Wood. It's t'trees closest t'pit. She'll meet thi there after work.'

'I'll look for her in Wigan if she's not there.'

'Rose will be there.'

Flo seemed pleased with the negotiation. Also, suddenly afraid to trade more words. 'I mun t'work,' she said.

'If you mun you mun.'

'Aye.'

She edged towards the coal chute. She was too large to slip away on light feet, though, and no shawl or black smudges could hide the satisfaction in her backward glance.

Blair had walked halfway back to Wigan when he came to a halt. Most of the road was by fields black with fresh-turned earth. His plan was to find the widow, Mrs Jaxon; according to Maypole's journal, he called on her the day he disappeared. Other people saw him later, but maybe he had said something to the woman.

Yet Blair found that he had stopped walking, as if the power to do so had left his legs. Rather than the dark fields, he saw the pony thrashing on the chain. Fear welled up like the dark of the shaft, but it wasn't fear of falling. Something worse the way the mare whipped its head back and forth as it struggled to escape. The sweat of its terror covered him still.

He found himself on the ground on his knees. It wasn't malaria. The horse was gone, replaced by a memory of a paddle steamer pushing between black seas and a grey sky. The hoarse sound of the waves vied with the uneven churning of side wheels as the ship made way, wallowed, made way. The captain held the Bible flat to read in a wind that was strong enough to lift beards. Six sailors shouldered a plank on which lay a body wrapped in a muslin sheet. They lifted the plank and the body shot out like a wingless angel through the air. The little boy pulled himself up on the railing to watch.

Above the water the descent stopped. The plank had snagged the sheet and it had unwound in a fluttering white arc down to the knot that secured the body within the first turn of the cloth. As the ship plodded forward, the body sank into a wave, reappeared and swung into the side of the ship, sank into a wave, reappeared again. Because she was weighted with lead he heard her hit the ship.

A sailor cut through the sheet. Released, it immediately trailed behind and, dropping, whipped as if escaping grip after grip. The body, covered by a foamy wave, was quickly out of sight, although he thought he saw the sheet on the water for a minute more. Blair, a gold miner whom the boy and his mother had met on deck, patted him on the head and said, 'These things happen.' It was young Blair's experience as he grew that things like that happened all the time.

Now he bent over and sobbed. The goddamn pony, he said to himself. The sheet unwinding from the plank, his jacket whipping back and forth. The cage slamming against the guide wires, her hitting the side of the ship. He couldn't remember the last time he had cried, except that now memory was born kicking painfully from the inside out. The fucking pony.

'Are you all right?'

Blair raised his head. A blurry Leveret looked down from a carriage that Blair hadn't heard come.

'Sure.'

'You seem upset.'

'Leveret, you are one sharp observer.' Blair rolled on to his back; he wouldn't have been surprised if his eyes flowed out. His ribs were racked as if they weren't used to this form of exercise. He'd been walking along, remembered that burial at sea and suddenly turned into a fountain.

'Can I help you up?'

'If you want to help, tell me that I've been dismissed, that the Hannay family no longer needs my services.'

'No, the Bishop says he is very satisfied with your work. He wants you to continue just the way you are.'

Blair sat up. 'What about Charlotte Hannay? He wants me to stay away from her?'

'The opposite. The Bishop wants you to talk to her again.'

'You told him what happened?'

'He says you should turn the other cheek.' When Blair laughed through his wet face, Leveret added, 'However, the Bishop says that if you don't possess sufficient sympathy to do that, you should feel free to defend yourself from attack.'

'The Bishop said that? He knows that his daughter despises the sight of me?'

'I told him what happened. Charlotte and Earnshaw had already reported to him in detail. The unpleasantness of the episode in the garden has been thoroughly described.'

The episode in the garden! What an English way to describe anything from murder to a fart, Blair thought. He pulled himself to his feet. 'Hannay is mad,' he said.

'The Bishop says that the Reverend Maypole's disappearance is too urgent and important a matter for any personal considerations to interfere. He seems to be more convinced than ever that you are the right man for the job. He said there may be a bonus for you.'

Disgustedly Blair threw his pack on to the carriage and

climbed up to the seat next to Leveret. 'I don't want a bonus and I have no idea how to do "the job". Your Chief Constable Moon thinks Maypole will never be found. He's probably right.'

Leveret sniffed. 'Have you been riding? Were you thrown by a horse?'

Blair thought the question over. 'Close.'

He changed clothes at the hotel. He felt strangely invigorated and cleansed. Colours were rawer, fresher, more vibrant to his eyes. He bought a magnifying glass at a stationer's for reading Maypole's journal. He even had an appetite and talked Leveret into visiting a Scholes eating house for rabbit pie and pickled eel.

The air inside was a cloud of pipe smoke so sharp it made the nose wince. Crutches and a cripple's cart parked by tables where old men in caps and stained scarves played games of dominoes between arguments, mixed with younger workers taking the day off. They ate their pies with clasp knives, an etiquette that made Leveret stiff and fastidious. Blair was used to Arabs and Africans eating with their hands. He also had a weakness for this sort of tableau, the timeless scene of luckless men gambling, the same here as in Accra or Sacramento. With the games came two rhythmic choruses, the pop of men drawing on their clay pipes, the slap of ivory tiles.

The beer was dark and sent an almost visible ripple through Leveret. He still wore stamps of plaster and appeared slightly crimped, as if he had been posted. He whispered, 'I haven't been to one of these places since I used to sneak in with Charlotte.'

'She used to come here?'

'When we were children. We both loved eel pie.'

'Charlotte Hannay? I can't see that.'

'You don't know Charlotte.'

'A grim little mollusc.'

'No. She . . . at least she used to be the opposite.'

'A fish?'

'Adventuresome, full of life.'

'Now she's full of opinions. Isn't she a bit young to be so much smarter than everyone else?'

'She's educated.'

'What does that mean?'

'The classics, science, French, Latin, a little Greek—'

'I get the idea. Does she know anything about the miners and pit girls?'

'It's a Hannay tradition to slip into town. When he was young, the Bishop himself was always in the working part of Wigan. Boys used to leap over old shafts. It was a dare, you know? Some wouldn't jump at all. Hannay was the champion.'

'Well, they were his shafts, weren't they? Maybe that should be a requirement for ownership, jumping over an open shaft. Did Maypole come here?'

'For a time. He wanted to eat like the miners and suffer with them. But he told me that he discovered that miners actually eat quite well. Roast beef, mutton, ham, and of course great quantities of beer. John couldn't afford it and he went back to living like a curate.'

'Most people went to his church?'

'No. I don't know if you noticed, but in the newspaper office there was a book called *Lancashire Catholics: Obstinate Souls*. That's because Lancashire has remained the most Catholic county in spite of the Reformation. We're also the most Methodist. We're the most at whatever we are. In the Middle Ages Wigan was a refuge for runaway slaves. In the Civil War we were Royalist. Not like Southerners.'

'Southerners?'

'London people. Southerners are convenient people, they do whatever is convenient for them. Mining is not a convenient sort of occupation.'

'Did Maypole ever wear clogs?'

'For rugby, yes, because the other men did.'

'I didn't see them in his room. Do you ever wear clogs?'

'Good Lord, no.'

'Did you as a kid?'

'My father would never let me. Remember, he was the estate manager before me. Being the son of a miner, it was a great step up for him, starting as a clerk, rising to assistant manager, then manager. He said, "No more bow legs for this family." My grandfather had legs like hoops from hauling coal as a boy when his bones were soft. In one generation the Leverets sprouted up.'

'Like evolution?'

Leveret thought. 'Improvement, my father said. My mother's father was a lock-keeper and I would spend all day at the canal – a canal's a fascinating place for a boy, between fishing, horses and boats – until my father put an end to the visits. He was a great friend of Chief Constable Moon, and Moon always believed in the improvement of workers in general and miners in particular. Although Moon says improvement starts at the end of a stout club. An intimidating man. A chief constable is an important figure in a town like Wigan.'

'Moon is a goon in a uniform.'

'Rather catchy.' Leveret suppressed a smile.

Blair nodded towards a corner table. 'See the man cutting sausage? Face black with coal. Coal in his hair, his nails, every crevice of his skin. Moleskin waistcoat falling off his back. Speaking a language unintelligible to any other Englishman. Wearing clogs. Bring him back an hour from now, washed, shaved, in London clothes, sounding like a London man, in shoes, and you wouldn't believe he was the same man. He couldn't convince you. But is that improvement?'

'The clothes make the man?'

'And soap,' said Blair.

'Do you know what people believe here? People believe that English woollens are the best insulation for tropical heat. They do. They think it's the advantage that English explorers have. You have to be English to understand.'

'No doubt. That's why I don't understand why the Bishop is more convinced than ever that I'm the right man for the job. If I'm not finding Maypole, what am I doing right?'

Leveret strained for a positive answer. 'I don't know,' he confessed. 'Although I think your approaches are imaginative, I can't say that I feel we are any closer to finding John or discovering what happened to him. After the argument you had with Charlotte I was certain that the Bishop would let you go. Instead he was quite clear that it was her duty to cooperate. In fact, he wanted me to tell you that while Charlotte might resist at first, you mustn't be discouraged.'

'Maybe I can catch his daughter where there are no weapons. Or roses.'

'Charlotte can seem difficult because she has so many causes and takes them so seriously.'

'Like Maypole. Tell me, what kind of relationship did she have with him?'

'They shared the same ideals: to better Wigan through education, sobriety, sanitation.'

'If that doesn't win a girl's heart, what will? What I meant was, did they ever hold hands, kiss, dance?'

'No, nothing the least coarse or physical.'

Sometimes Blair wondered whether he and Leveret spoke

the same language. 'Were Maypole and Charlotte happy? I'm not talking about the higher contentment of doing good, I mean the lower contentment of another warm body.'

'They didn't think that way. They were allies, fellow soldiers fighting for the same social goal.'

Blair tried a different tack. 'Tell me, did you ever see any disagreement between them? We're talking about a woman with a, let's say, flammable temperament.'

Leveret hesitated. 'Charlotte could be impatient with John, but that was because she wanted to help so many people.'

'Maybe also because she's the daughter of a bishop and he was a lowly curate?'

'No, she has never had anything but contempt for class distinctions. That's why she doesn't live in Hannay Hall. She refuses to have a servant.'

'Exactly, she just orders everyone around. How did John Maypole get on with Hannay? What did the Bishop think of his daughter marrying someone who wasn't an aristocrat?'

'A bishop and a curate don't ordinarily have much to do with each other. Also, John is a reformer, which the Bishop does not necessarily approve of. The marriage *was* going to be an enormous step down socially for Charlotte. However, since she couldn't inherit the title or land, the question of whom she married wasn't all that important.'

'Tell me, how is it that Hannay is both a bishop and a lord?'

'Well, there were three brothers. Being the second, the Bishop went into the Church and Rowland's father, the youngest brother, made a career in the Army. When the older brother died without issue – sons, I mean – the Bishop succeeded to the title.'

'And after the Bishop?'

'Charlotte's brother would have been next in line, but he died in a riding accident two years ago. Rowland's father died in India a dozen years ago, so it would appear that Rowland will be the next Lord Hannay.'

'Charlotte's out of the picture?'

'As a woman, yes. The Bishop never mentioned any of this to you?'

'Why would he?'

'After his son's death he was distraught. That was when he went off to Africa with you. It might be why he thinks of you so fondly.'

'"Fondly"?' Blair had to laugh at that.

'Charlotte changed too. She was riding with her brother when he fell. It was after the accident that she began to turn into someone more serious – which was what appealed to John, of course, when he came to Wigan.'

'Of course.'

Blair actually felt a twinge of sympathy until Leveret added, 'You're not unlike her brother in a way. I can't think why she despises you so.'

'Kismet. Did Maypole pick Charlotte or did she pick him? You don't have to explain mating rituals, just tell me who asked who.'

'Considering their different social stations, it would have been impossible for John to ask her. But he worshipped Charlotte.'

'So you can't imagine Maypole in love with someone he might have met in a place like this? A flesh-and-blood dirty working girl from Wigan?'

'That's a peculiar question to ask.'

'What's the weekly rent for a Hannay company house at, say, Candle Court?'

'Three pounds.'

'The weekly wage for pit girls?'

'Ten pence a day. Before deductions. After, just under five shillings a week.'

'Who said England was against slavery? Which leaves a couple of pit girls nearly three pounds short of making the rent, let alone paying for food and clothes. You're sure Maypole never helped a girl in that kind of situation?'

'There was no one but Charlotte. Blair, there must be other lines of inquiry.'

'Other lines? To really question people would take a police campaign, which would be public and which the Hannays refuse to do, so I follow the feeble lines that I have.'

'Which are?'

'Envy. Reverend Chubb dislikes his overly fortunate curate so much that he brains him with a candlestick and hides him in a crypt.'

'No.'

'I don't think so, either. Money. Mr Earnshaw, Member of Parliament, listens to Maypole's passionate appeal for pit girls, but what really catches his attention is that his friend is engaged to a wealthy woman. Earnshaw secretly takes the train to Wigan, slits Maypole's throat, goes back to London and then returns to Wigan as the white knight of temperance to court the grieving Miss Hannay.'

'No.'

'Probably not. Then there's you, honest Oliver Leveret, who always loved Charlotte Hannay and must have been shocked when she perversely chose your best friend to share her bed and bank account. You, who are supposed to help me and have done nothing but describe a saint who never existed. That Maypole I never could find. But John Maypole wasn't a saint. He disobeyed Chubb. He lusted after pit girls. Most likely he considered Charlotte Hannay an expendable witch. You suspected something was happening. One week before he disappeared you asked him about it, and when he said everything was fine, you knew it was a lie. You are my last line, Leveret.'

Leveret reddened as if he'd been slapped. 'John did tell me not to be concerned. How did you know I asked?'

'What made you ask?'

'He was so agitated.'

'Exactly what did he say?'

'That he was experiencing a spiritual crisis. That miners were closer than priests to the ideal of Heaven. That minute to minute he swung from ecstasy to despair. But he did assure me that he was fine.'

'That sounds fine to you?'

'I knew John was human. So am I. If I loved Charlotte, I never aspired to her. No one was happier for John when their engagement was announced.'

'Let's get back to ecstasy and despair. Was the ecstasy a working girl? Was the despair Charlotte Hannay?'

'There was only Charlotte.'

'Both? Quite a woman.'

'Blair, do you actually suspect me?'

'No, but I think it's time you started helping. Can you do that?'

Leveret's colour rose to the roots of his hair. 'How?'

'Get me the inquest for the Hannay explosion.'

'That would be the Coroner's Report. We discussed this before. There is a copy at our offices here in town, but to be kept there at all times, as I told you.'

'Bring it to my hotel.'

'Why?'

'It makes me feel I'm doing something. I don't understand England. I do understand mines.'

'Anything else?'

'I need your carriage.'

'That's all?'

Blair remembered King Solomon. 'You haven't had any

black women passing through Wigan, have you? African women?'

'No.'

'Just a thought.'

As Blair drove towards the Hannay tower, miners and pit girls trudged home in the opposite direction beside the road. Riding in Leveret's carriage literally put him in a class above. He saw neither Flo nor Bill Jaxon. No one raised their eyes. They might have been sheep or cattle in the gloaming.

He missed an equatorial sun and a sharp division between day and night, but he admitted that English light had eccentric charms. Thunderheads towering so high that a train of coal wagons looked like a fold on the landscape. Sparrows that tumbled from high to low, from light to dark, around hedgerows and chimney towers. There was a stillness that no locomotive could shake, a stirring that no veil of soot could hide.

Everything was contradiction. Bishop Hannay, who didn't care for Maypole, wanted him found. Charlotte Hannay, Maypole's fiancée, wouldn't help. The more Blair infuriated her, the happier the Bishop seemed to be. Leveret was correct when he said that Blair didn't understand. Day by day, he understood less.

Close to the Hannay yard was a rise of leafless, dun-coloured willows and oaks swaying in the wind over a lower canopy of brambles and gorse. Blackthorns showed white buds; otherwise this last remnant of Wigan forest was as drab as a feather duster. There was no access by road and no sign of Rose Molyneux. Blair tied the horse and found a footpath that wandered between bushes. As thorns reached out he pushed them away with his leather pack.

The wood was nesting for moles, foxes, stoats; there was little wild woodland left around the mines and Blair could almost feel the concentrated animal activity around him. Within minutes he reached what he judged to be the centre of the little wood, a small clearing around a silver birch, and saw a finch sitting on a branch pour forth a stream of musical notes. He was dumbfounded, as if while touring an urban ruin he had stumbled into an ancient, miniature chapel, and the finch itself was pulling the bell ropes.

'It's a canary,' Rose said.

She slipped out from the shadow of a willow, though with the fading light, her shawl and so much coal dust on her face she was a shadow of herself. A food tin hung in her hand.

Blair asked, 'How is that?'

'They escape from the pit, or sometimes they're let go and this is the first wood they fly to. They mix with the birds here.'

'That's hard to believe.'

'Not for me.'

Her hair hung loose in red-brown coils, her corduroy coat was velvet with coal dust and she wore a satin ribbon around her neck to balance her ensemble. One hand was bandaged and he remembered Flo had said she'd had an accident.

'You're hurt?'

'We weren't serving tea t'day, we were sorting coal. Sometimes there's a sharp stone on the belt. What did you have t'tell me?'

The birch lit up. Startled, the bird flew away, followed by a clap of thunder. In that moment of illumination Blair realized that he had never seen Rose Molyneux before in a good light. She was always half covered with dust or weakly lit by a candle or lamp. The lightning showed a forehead as high as Charlotte Hannay's but over brighter eyes, and as fine a nose but with a more relaxed and fuller mouth, red against her black cheek. She seemed taller than Charlotte, but beyond that she was more physically present, a civet compared with a domestic cat.

'I want you to return something for me,' Blair said. From

his pack he took the pair of clogs that had been delivered to his hotel. 'These were left for me by Bill Jaxon. I saw him win them off an Irishman he kicked half to death. I know Jaxon is your beau. I think he has the idea that I have designs on you and these clogs are a warning that if I don't leave you alone he will kick *me* half to death. Tell Jaxon that I got the message and that I don't need any clogs.'

'They're handsome ones. Shamrocks.' She looked at the stitching and the brass-studded toes.

'Well, they didn't bring the Irishman any luck.' He held the clogs out but Rose still didn't take them.

'Bill scares you?'

'Bill certainly does scare me. He's violent and he's not half as dumb as he looks.'

'Oooh, he'll like that description.'

'You don't have to repeat it to him.'

'Maybe it's clogs that bother you? Are you getting grand now? You'd prefer pistols or swords?'

'I'd prefer having no trouble at all. The only reason I talked to you in the first place was to ask about John Maypole.'

'You came twice,' Rose said.

'The second time was because of the photograph Maypole had of you.'

'And you said you wouldn't bother me again.'

'I'm trying not to bother you, believe me.'

A few raindrops began to fall through the trees. Rose was oblivious, picking up spirit like an actress on a stage. 'If I was Miss Hannay it would be different. If I was a lady, you wouldn't come throwing clogs in my face. You wouldn't be badgering me with questions like a poor-house inspector.'

'Rose, your friend Flo arranged for us to meet here. I'm not throwing clogs, I'm trying to give them to you. And as for Miss Hannay, you're twice the lady she is.'

'Just say you're a coward. Don't give me sweet words.'

Blair lost patience. 'Will you take the damn clogs?'

'See? Is that how you speak t'a lady?'

Nothing with Rose went as he hoped. As the rain began to beat down, hair stuck to her sooty brow, yet he was the one who felt bedraggled. 'Please?' he asked.

She placed her hands behind her back. 'I don't know. A famous explorer like you, you can answer t'Bill yourself. You have all the world to hide in if Wigan isn't safe enough.'

'What do you want, Rose?'

'Two things. First, a ride t'town. You can set me down when we're close. Then you must promise never t'come t'my house or bother me at work again. I don't need another Maypole.'

Comparison with Maypole was an unexpected sting.

'Rose, take the clogs and I will never bother you again.'

'I'll take them on that account only.'

While Blair led her out, the storm arrived with a heave of tree boughs. He asked himself why he was leading the way when Rose knew the path through the wood better than he did, but she seemed to expect it, like the princess of a tiny kingdom.

Chapter Ten

'AH WENT DOWN PIT when Ah were six. They lifted us oop an' down in baskets. Ah worked a brace o' canvas an' frame t'let air in. Otherwise folk below coodn't breathe, they'd die.

'When Ah was eight Ah was big enough t'draw coal. That means drag it. Ah had a chain went around m'neck an' between m'legs t'sledge, same as me mum an' all m'sisters. Ah was a strong lass an' Ah'd draw forty, fifty pound o'coal. No ponies in that pit. So tight tha could barely squeeze through.

'Was it hot? Up face, where they took t'coal, everyone was stripped. Like Adam an' Eve. Tha were crawling through water an' muck. Things happened t'girls. That's wha there was t'big Reform an' Parliament put all t'girls on top o'pit. Not because of our work but because of our morality. That's how Ah become a pit girl.

'Ah didn't mind t'work. Sortin' coal. Tipping tubs into wagons. Cold in t'winter. Tha danced just t'stay warm. There's worse than freezin'. M'first girl, when she coom t'work on the brew she was caught b'tween wagons an' was crooshed. She was ten. T'owners an' t'managers coom by t'give us five shillin's for her. That's t'death rate. Five shillin's fur oldest girl, three shillin's fur each girl after.'

'What did you do?' Blair asked.

'Tha genuflect an' say, yes sir, no sir, three bags full, sir.'

When the kettle rattled, Mary Jaxon moved it to a cold burner and put in a tea ball to steep. The centre of any miner's home was a cast-iron range. Its fender was polished to a shine. The smell of bread emanated from the oven. The design of the house was the same as Rose Molyneux's, but in Mary Jaxon's kitchen there were a dozen children packed on the stairs to stare at the visitor.

Around the table were Blair and a circle of neighbours, men with the black necks and red-rimmed eyes of miners, no one Blair knew except the little stableman who had cursed him at the Hannay Pit. Behind them stood their wives; it was understood that men home from work had the first rights to chairs. Though the women had covered worn dresses with their best shawls, from the way they folded their sinewy arms and narrowed their eyes Blair detected a higher general level of suspicion. Like Mary Jaxon, they had gone from the pit brow to a terraced house, bearing children one a year on wages that dried up in the summer when coal prices dropped or stopped completely during strikes. Mary Jaxon made a curious hostess, like a mother of a wolf pack, a combination of ferocity and hospitality. Blair had returned the carriage to Leveret and come alone on foot to draw as little attention as possible, but Mary Jaxon had at once stepped out of the back of her house and summoned neighbours from the entire alley. She said Scholes was the sort of community where interesting visitors were shared.

'Tha like tay?' Mary asked.

'I'd enjoy some, thanks,' Blair said.

'Art tha really from America?' a girl asked from a middle step.

'Yes.'

A boy from the bottom of the stairs asked, 'Art th'a Red Indian?'

'No.'

They watched him fixedly, undiscouraged, as if he might turn into one.

Blair asked Mrs Jaxon, 'The last time the Reverend Maypole came by, what did you talk about?'

'About t'boons God's given t'workin' man. Patience, sufferin' an' all t'wee angels we supply. For a woman t'boons are dooble.'

The miners shifted uneasily in their chairs but nods from the wives said that Mary Jaxon spoke for them.

'Anything else?' Blair asked.

'Reverend Maypole wanted us all t'kneel an' pray fur t'health of t'Prince of Wales, who'd got a sniffle. There's that Queen with her huge German family, an' that we don't hang them Ah think is mercy enough.'

A titter went up the steps.

'An' he was a great one fur Christian sports,' one of the men offered.

'Which are?' Blair asked.

A small boy on the stairs said, 'Cricket.'

'Rugby,' a larger boy said and hit the first.

Mary Jaxon said, 'Remember, t'following afternoon, seventy-six men was laid like burnt matches around pit head at t'Hannay Mine. No one noticed a priest comin' or goin'. Not unless he could raise t'dead. Tha understand everythin' Ah'm sayin'?'

'Yes.' Blair also understood that he would be getting no information. Maybe it was the explosion, he thought. Every family had lost a son, father, husband, brother – at the least a close friend. Perhaps that was why they were in the kitchen, because front parlours were used for laying out the dead. Possibly Mrs Jaxon and her neighbours were upset about his questions. In any case, he was ready to leave even though everyone else in the kitchen continued to stare at him with dumb anticipation.

'Tell us about Africa,' Mary Jaxon said.

'Africa?'

'Aye.' Her eyes shot to the stairway. 'T'babs know nothin' of t'world. They plan t'be ignorant aw their lives. They think they can't be bothered t'read or write 'cause they're goin' down pit.'

'A lecture for "the babs"?' Blair asked.

'If tha don't mind.'

Entertainment from the outside was rare in Wigan, Blair knew. This was a world where a hurdy-gurdy drew a crowd. Still, it also struck him that other travellers on their return from Africa delivered their talks in the Map Room of the Royal Society. Gentlemen travellers, of course. Celebrated explorers. In formal clothes with official guests, champagne, toasts and a silver medal from the Society. Blair never imagined they would give him one, but the disparity was telling. The Society had his maps and reports, even a monograph or two, and here he was at his début in Wigan, in a kitchen suffused by the close smells of stew and wet wool, accompanied by the occasional knock of a child's clog against a stair.

Blair stood. 'I have to go. Thanks for the tea.'

'Tha art *the* Blair from Africa?' one of the miners asked.

'Maybe not. Good night.'

'I knew it. A fake,' the miner's wife said.

On his way through the dark parlour to the front door he walked into a table. Stopped short, he looked at an oval mirror beside the hat rack and saw a gaunt man in the bent hurry of a thief, although he hadn't taken anything but their decent opinion of him. Of course the decent opinion had nothing to do with him. It was a gift because they had little else to give. What did it matter? It had nothing to do with him at all.

'Something does occur to me,' Blair said as he returned to the kitchen. The adults were still trading expressions of outrage over his departure. Half the children had trooped down the stairs; at the sound of his voice, they climbed back up. Blair took his seat as if he hadn't left. 'If you do go to Africa or anywhere in the world, you will need to write legibly and read with understanding, a perfect case in point being the late governor of Sierra Leone, Sir Charles Macarthy, who led a thousand Fanti troops against the Ashanti of the Gold Coast. Although the brave Macarthy was warned by scouts how badly he was outnumbered by Ashanti warriors, he spurned retreat and so the two armies clashed at the Battle of Assamacow.'

His audience, even the stableman, resumed their earlier seats and positions. Mary Jaxon poured more tea.

'The Fanti were stalwart soldiers drilled in the British manner, but the Ashanti were from a kingdom that had not only conquered other African tribes, but withstood the Danish, Dutch and Portuguese. The fate of West Africa stood in the balance. Although Macarthy was a courageous general, the enemy host swarmed on all sides. The fight was close, first with riflery, then with spears and swords. Then the worst possible thing that could happen to Macarthy did happen: he ran out of ammunition.'

Blair paused to sip from his cup. From the stairs a diagonal of eyes watched every move.

'Fortunately, he had an excellent runner. Macarthy wrote a message to his ordnance-keeper demanding the ammunition and the runner ran off with it, dashing through a momentary breach in the Ashanti lines. Macarthy and his Fanti allies held on grimly, harbouring every shot. You can imagine their relief when, following the bank of the river, the runner returned leading two pack mules laden with crates. And then imagine their disappointment and disbelief when they opened the boxes and found not ammunition but macaroni. The ordnance-keeper had not read Macarthy's request correctly. Hunched under enemy bullets, Macarthy wrote a second note. Again the runner slipped into shifting mists of smoke. Again Macarthy and his loyal, dwindling troops held out, this time with no ammunition of their own at all, defending themselves only with steel. And again the runner broke through the siege and returned with yet two more mules and crates. They broke open the crates.'

Blair sipped again, very slowly, and set down his cup.

'More macaroni. The ordnance-keeper simply could not make out anything Macarthy wrote. The rest of the story gets pretty nasty. The Ashanti completely overran them. The Fanti were slaughtered almost to a man. Macarthy fought as long as he could, propped himself against a tree and shot himself rather than be captured. It was probably wise. The Ashanti cut off his head and boiled his brains. They roasted the rest of him, and his skull they took back to the capital of Ashantiland to worship along with a pile of skulls of other enemies they admired, because Macarthy was a valiant fighter although he was an unusually bad penman.'

A silence followed. Around the table faces were warm and flushed.

'B'gum, that was a gripper,' one of the men said and sat back.

'T'ole story was macaroni,' a woman said.

''S true?' the man asked.

'Pretty much, for an African story. In fact, it's one of the truest I know,' Blair said.

'Gor,' said a boy.

'Watch tha mouth,' a mother said.

A miner hunched forward. 'Is there gold mines in th'Gold Coast?'

'Yes, and deposits of granite, gneiss and quartz that suggest there is a good deal more gold undiscovered. A person who learned some geology would have a great advantage.'

'We're aw geologists here when it comes t'coal.'

171

'That's true,' Blair said.

'Did tha shoot a gorilla?' the smallest boy asked.

'No, I've never seen a gorilla.'

'Elephant?'

'Not shot one.'

'Real explorers do,' the boy maintained.

'I've noticed. But real explorers travel with as many as a hundred porters. Porters may carry shaving soap and fine wine, but it's the explorer's job to get fresh meat for the expedition. Besides, he has the rifles. Since I only had a few men with me, I shot only antelope, which are like deer.'

The stableman finally spoke. 'So a man could make a fortune in gold down there.'

'Absolutely. More likely, though, he'll die of malaria, Guinea worm or yellow jack. I wouldn't send any man there who had a family or a chance of happiness nearer home.'

'Tha went.'

'With blinkers on, if you know what I mean.'

'Ah do.' The stableman's face split into a grin.

Blair told them how to prepare dried rats and bats, drink palm wine, weather the winds of the dry season and the tornadoes of the rains, wake to the screams of monkeys and go to sleep to the mad laugh of hyenas. How to address the Ashanti King, which was through an intermediary, while the King sat on a golden stool under a golden parasol and pretended to hear nothing. How to back away from the King, staying low. How the King moved slowly and majestically, like Queen Victoria, but bigger and browner and in flashier clothes.

The questions around the kitchen had none of the archness of a salon. Their interest was so pure and intense that it lit faces – both parents' and children's – as if a window to the sun had been thrown open. If his answers weren't the lecture he'd ever imagined giving, but more like the sort of shapeless baggage of

172

impressions that a traveller opened for assembled relatives, the experience was still curiously enjoyable.

When he left Mary Jaxon's door an hour later, he found that he had forgotten about the rain, a cold, steady deluge that ran off the rooflines in ropes. Shops had closed their shutters. Beerhouses and pubs were muffled by the downpour. The streets were almost cleared of wagons and there were certainly no cabs. He pulled his hat brim low and set off towards his hotel.

Lamps lit only the corners of long, dark blocks. Lakes appeared where streets had sunk over old mine shafts. He found himself making a detour through side streets and back alleys to find his way to the centre of town. The further he went, though, the narrower the alleys got and the more ash pits and fewer people he saw. He seemed to be trapped within a maze of backyard fences, pigeon lofts and pig sties. The locals obviously knew a better route but, by the time he'd decided to ask, there was no one else around.

Blair had spent half his life trying to find his way. He never minded asking where he was. Africans loved giving directions; African etiquette could turn simple instructions into an inescapable hour of sociability. He was trying to find his way now and there wasn't even an African in sight.

As he came out of the alley he found himself at a field of high grass and thistles that rose to a horizon edged with the sulphuric glow of mill ovens fading in and out of the rain like chain lightning. He climbed the ridge and discovered that it ended abruptly at a black dune stretching into the dark in either direction. The dune was coal slag, the mountain of rock and dirt and carbon dust left after the lifetime of a mine, after it had been driven, worked out and abandoned. The slag had dropped down with its own weight into the collapsed workings of the mine like the caldera of an ancient volcano. Like a volcano there were lingering, opalescent signs of life, votive candle glimmers as coal dust heated and ignited spontaneously within the slag, producing relatively harmless blue flames that worked their way through dirt to dart here and there – a second in each place – as evanescent, almost animated imps of fire. Rain couldn't quench them; in fact, low pressure brought them out.

There was light enough for Blair to see an abandoned brick kiln with the stub of a chimney teetering on the edge of the grass and, in the deepest point of the slag pit, an inky pool with the rest of the chimney standing diagonally up from the middle. How deep the water was depended on how tall the chimney was. There was even enough light for him to use his compass.

'Lost?'

It was Bill Jaxon's voice. He was the only person Blair would have expected to see. He finished reading the compass and discovered that he'd changed direction and was headed north. If he skirted the slag to the west he could reconnect with streets that would take him directly back to Scholes Bridge.

'I said, are you lost?' Bill emerged from the shadow of the alley and walked up the ridge to where Blair stood.

'Not any more, thanks.'

Jaxon topped Blair by half a head. With his cap and longish hair, bunched-up woollen jacket and white scarf trying to fly in the wind as it swept up the face of the slag, he looked even larger. Or was it the clogs? Blair reminded himself to add an inch for them.

'I asked you to not bother Rose Molyneux, but you keep at her. Now you're at my mother. Why are you doing this?'

'I'm asking about the Reverend Maypole, the same as I asked you. That's all.'

'You think Rose or my mother did something to Reverend Maypole?'

'No, I'm just asking what Maypole said, what he seemed like, the same as I ask everyone else.'

'But I told you not to.'

That was true. Blair had faith that he could talk himself out of a pinch. The main thing was never to make an adversary – Ashanti, Fanti, Mexican, whatever – lose face. It also helped to have no self-respect. All the same, he put the compass in his pocket to keep his hands free.

'Bill, the Bishop hired me to do this. If I don't, someone else will.'

'No, they won't. This has nothing to do with finding Maypole.'

'For me it's just Maypole.'

'But you've put me in a position. People hear about you socializing with Rose and it puts me in a position.'

'I understand. Bill, the last thing I want is to put you in a position. You're the champion here, ruler of the nether world. I'm not even a challenger.'

'You're not a fighter.'

'Or a lover. I'm a mining engineer, and there are some mines calling to me from the other side of the world right now, but I can't go until I've found out what happened to Maypole.'

Rivulets of water ran down his neck and under his collar. Under his cap, Bill's face was blank as marble. He looked down at Blair's feet.

'What are you wearing?'

'Not clogs. I'm not going to fight.'

'Afraid?'

'Yes.'

Bill seemed to think the problem through. 'I wish I had a choice.'

'You do.'

175

'But you got the clogs?'

'I got your gift. No, thanks. I gave the clogs to Rose to give back to you.'

'So you did see Rose again.'

An unanswerable question. Blair had the sense – the sense of falling from the top of a tall ladder – that words, no matter how glib, would never replace wings.

'To give back—'

He didn't see the kick. His left leg felt paralysed from the hip down. Bill bounced back quickly, lightly for a big man, and using his other foot like a scythe, scooped up both Blair's legs. Blair landed on his side and rolled away from a kick that raked his back.

'I told you to stay away from Rose, didn't I?' Bill said.

Blair got to his knees, his left leg numb. Bill feinted from side to side, and Blair ducked as a clog swung at his face and crawled backwards from the kick that followed that. There was something ignominious about the situation, he thought. He had survived attacks with spears and guns in the most exotic parts of the world, and here he was on the verge of being kicked to death in an English coal town.

A clog caught him above the ear and he saw beads of blood fly to the side. Jaxon skipped playfully from right to left, manoeuvring Blair so that he slipped over the edge of the grass with one knee in the slag. Wind stung his eyes with carbon dust.

'Bill, if you kill me, they'll come right after you.'

'Not if you disappear.'

'You want me to leave Wigan, Bill? Give me a couple more days and I'll be gone.'

For a moment, Bill Jaxon seemed genuinely uncertain. His gaze travelled down the slag to the water at the bottom. 'They won't find you,' he said.

Bill pretended to pull his foot back. Blair dodged and the

move sent him sliding over the lip of grass and down the slag, which was warm, almost hot. When he half swam, half clambered up, Jaxon stomped on his hand.

'You should have brought clogs,' Bill said.

Blair grabbed Jaxon's ankle. Instead of merely stepping back, Bill tried to kick free, and Blair changed his grip to the cuff of the other ankle. The harder Bill kicked, the more off-balance he became, until he toppled next to Blair on to the slag and the two slid down together through waves of black dust. Flames touched them briefly, harmlessly. They rolled down to the bottom of the slope, by the edge of the water.

The slag pit was like a cup, boggy at the base, worse footing for clogs than shoes. The chimney rose like a sunken cannon aimed at the sky. When they stood, Blair didn't let Jaxon get room to kick. He hit Bill in the face, moved forward and hit him again until Bill backed into the water and went under, immediately out of his depth. It was a tall chimney, Blair thought.

Jaxon struggled in the water and gasped, 'I can't swim!'

Blair gave him a hand, and as he was pulling him up, hit him and watched him sink a second time.

Bill surfaced. 'For God's sake.'

Blair let him bob for a while before waving him out. He offered Bill help, and as Jaxon swung up the bank he hit him harder than before.

A minute passed before Bill floated to the surface again, face down. Blair fished him out by his hair and dragged him up on the sandbank. He wasn't breathing. Blair turned him over and pumped his back until Bill's mouth discharged an eruption of rank water. Satisfied that he was alive enough, Blair removed Bill's clogs and threw them in the pool.

Blair crawled up the sand, wearing a second skin of black dust, losing half his progress in sliding for every inch he rose.

On either side, flames popped out of the slag like flowers, and as quickly disappeared. His left leg was not functioning well; neither was the hand Bill had stomped on. At the end he was feebly clawing his way towards the same ridge of grass he had fallen from. He saw waiting for him, obscured by rain and dark, the roofline of terraced houses and chimneypots and what appeared to be a looming, headless figure.

'Is 'e dead?' it asked Blair.

Blair gained the ridge and swayed to his feet. 'No.'

There was momentary stupefaction in the dark. A latch swung open and the focused light of a bull's-eye lantern blinded him, though he glimpsed the pit girl Flo, her head and shoulders covered with a shawl that sparkled in the rain.

'Then tha best run,' she said.

Blair kept his weight on his good leg; he could just picture himself hopping on one foot through the alleys. 'I don't think I'm running anywhere.'

'Ah'll help.'

Flo offered her back to lean on; it was like holding on to an energetic locomotive that carried as much as led him, the beam of her lantern aimed ahead. It made sense to him that she chose the alley instead of staying anywhere near the sand, but she continued to guide him between backyards rather than cut to the streets even when they had the chance. Through fence boards he saw the white flash of a pigeon loft. At this point, he didn't need a compass to know she was not taking him towards his hotel.

'Where are we going?'

Flo didn't answer. Like an engine, she pressed forward on a track of mud, slats and perpendicular turns until she pushed open a gate Blair never would have noticed. A pig squealed and scurried around its corner sty. Brick steps led between wash tubs to a back door that Flo rushed him through.

Inside, she let him sink into a chair. The room was dark except for a fire grate and she played the lantern on him. 'You're black an' bloody, too. But you're safe now.'

Blair's leg was numb and vaguely throbbing. He put finger-tips to the side of his head and felt matted hair and a spongy flap of scalp. A little safety sounded good. While Flo lit the lamp he leaned back and let his eyes close. He listened to her stoke the grate. The smell of warm sugar and sweet milk penetrated his headache. He sat forward and looked. The grate was in an oven. A pot simmered on the range. By the stairs stood a full-length mirror that was familiar. From her knees, Flo turned to footsteps descending the stairs.

Rose Molyneux came down into the kitchen in a plain muslin blouse and skirt that made her hair, unbrushed and damp from a bath, appear like coppery knots. Her eyes were dark, charged with anger.

'What's he doing here?'

'Ah followed Bill, like tha said. They had a brawl an' Ah didn't know where else t'take him, Ah didn't. He's hurt.'

It was a wonder to witness, Blair thought. Rose dominated the room in a way that made the bigger girl quail. 'You were stupid t'bring him. Mr Blair looks black as a miner, is all. He only needs water and soap t'change back.'

'Believe me, this is the last place I want to be,' Blair said.

Rose said, 'You're the last person I want t'see, so we're even.'

'Rose, all you had to do was give the clogs to Bill, as I asked you to, and tell him that you're his and his alone, and that I didn't want to fight. Then Bill wouldn't have tried to kill me and I wouldn't be here now.'

'I'm not a maid t'do your errands.' She pointed with the poker to a corner of the kitchen. 'There are the clogs. Take them yourself.'

Flo said, 'He's not walkin' anywhere. Take a look at 'is head.'

179

Rose took the lantern from Flo and ran her hand through Blair's hair, roughly to begin with and then with more care. He felt her stiffen at the sight of something. 'Maybe water and gin,' she said.

Flo fed the fire to heat water. Rose fed Blair the gin. One item of trade you could always get in Africa was good Holland gin, so there were constants in life.

'Why don't you get a doctor?' he asked.

'You need a surgeon. At this hour he's so drunk I wouldn't trust him t'sew up a cat.'

Blair felt light-headed. The scene of the two women and the bright oven grate seemed to float around him. The lid of the pot began to rattle.

'Water's ready.' Flo pulled a zinc tub across the floor to the oven.

Rose tied on an apron and waited, hands on hips. 'Well?'

'I can bathe myself.'

'You've more than dirt t'worry about. Anyway, I've seen naked men before. And you've seen me.'

Which was true, although Blair was sure that she was far more attractive undressed than he was. He pulled off his boots and socks and stood shakily, supporting himself with the table to unbutton his shirt. Looking down, he saw how coal dust had collected down the centre of his chest. He opened his trousers and long johns and stepped out of them, feeling not so much bare as embarrassed. In the Gold Coast he had always been aware how pale and scrawny he appeared. In Wigan, too, as it turned out.

Moving made him dizzy. Flo gave him an arm to help him kneel on the ribbed bottom of the tub. Rose opened the oven grate. With a cloth she took an iron pan from the coals and from the pan she removed a needle glowing orange that she dropped into a bowl of water. He heard the hiss.

'You really make ten pence a day? Serfdom has not come to an end.'

'That's none of your business,' Rose said.

'And pay three pounds a week in rent? How do you manage that? Maybe you're tipping more than coal.'

'Drink this.' Flo gave him a second cup of gin.

Scissors appeared in Rose's hand.

'You're giving me a haircut?' This seemed the final indecency.

'Just t'see what I'm doing.'

He listened to the click of the blades and was aware of matted hair falling to the floor, but he didn't seem to have any sensation on that side of his head. Nothing was making sense. He should be in a proper surgery, Blair thought. Wasn't that one of the glories of civilization, trained medical men? He noticed that the gas lamps of the kitchen were suddenly turned to their brightest.

'You're not going t'cry like a bab, are you?' Rose asked.

He was wrong, he did have sensation on that side of his head. When she tipped the bowl of cold water over it he had to lock a scream inside his teeth. Flo gave him a twisted rag to bite on, and handed Rose a needle and red thread.

Rose said, 'Think about Africa.'

Blair thought about Bill Jaxon. If Jaxon had wanted to kill him before, how much more implacable an enemy would he be once he heard where Flo had taken Blair? The more he thought about it, he realized he couldn't even go to the police. Chief Constable Moon would ask first what the fight was about, and second where he had gone afterwards. It would sound like a sordid Wigan romance. As the needle tugged he gripped the edges of the tub.

Flo mixed hot and cold water in a pitcher. Rose cut the thread, put the needle down and again emptied the pitcher over

Blair. Water felt like an electric shock. Then she began washing his hair, which was no worse than massaging a wound. He spat the rag from his mouth because he couldn't breathe from the water running into his nose. He didn't shake so much as quiver with every muscle in his body.

Flo refilled the cup of gin and said, 'Ah best find 'im clothes.'

'Then hurry,' Rose said.

As Flo left, Blair reached for the cup and finished it in two swallows, trying to rush sedation. He felt isolated in a shroud of pain, trying to keep his balance, awash in water that was black and red.

Rose rinsed his hair, poured a pitcher of hot water over his shoulders and started to rub him with soap and a sponge. He rocked from the effort of her scrubbing. Steam rose around them.

'Flo says you beat Bill. You don't look it.'

'I don't feel it.'

'You could have left 'im for dead, she says.'

'Is that why you're taking care of me, because I didn't? Is he in love with you?'

'Quiet and sit up.'

Although her hands weren't broad, they were strong, and when she washed his neck he let his head loll back drunkenly. In the mirror by the stairs he saw himself, the tub and her. Her hair was loose and wild; all she needed in it, he thought, was a briar rose to be a muse of summer. Add a lute and a silvery streak and she could be a model. Between the steam and washing him, she was almost as wet as he was, damp muslin clinging to her arms. Her hair brushed his cheek. It was the sort of deep brown that became red with the looking. No fizzy orange but threads of sable, copper, sienna, gold.

She poured more water over him to sponge his chest. It was the heat of the water combined with the gin in his veins, but he

182

felt himself start to harden. The tub water wasn't so soapy that she couldn't see. He was astounded and ashamed. The rest of him was bruised and dead, yet this single part was unmistakably alive, rising like Lazarus, a traitor from the water. He shifted on his side to make the physiological fact less evident. Rose washed around the bruise on his hip, a circular motion repeated by her breasts against his back. From their friction he became aware that they had stiffened, too.

He felt his blood pound, but Rose didn't break contact, as if they were both mesmerized and complicit in the steady rhythmic motion of the sponge in her hand and the heat of the stove.

'Understand, you can't come here again,' she said. Her voice was thick.

'Too bad.' He had meant to say it sarcastically but it didn't come out that way.

'Bill won't rest until he has you down.'

'It's you and Bill, then?'

'In Bill's mind.'

'Which is enough?'

'Enough for everyone else.'

'For you?'

He felt her breath on his neck as her hand came to a stop. He was amazed that through the pain and gin he could be so aware of her touch, of her heartbeat through the slight tremor of her breast, the very air of her.

'You don't want the answer,' Rose said.

'I do.'

'Not really. You're Nigger Blair. You make your mess and move on. Maybe you sneer at the Hannays, but you sneer at everyone. At least Bill left his mark on you, I'll give him credit for that.'

'I don't sneer at you.'

He didn't. Rose had seemed a liar and coquette before. Now

she was a different person. She had become real. Being real, she didn't have another ready word. Neither did he. They were trapped like two people who had encountered each other in the dark, neither wishing to back away. He felt her soft exhalation and the brush of her hair on the side of his cheek. The sponge in her hand rested motionlessly on his thigh. He didn't know who would have moved first if Flo hadn't returned.

'Success,' she announced as she marched down the stairs, oversized trousers hanging from one hand and a cap and shapeless jacket in the other. 'Everythin' but a silk scarf.'

Immediately Blair felt himself subside into uncomplicated pain. Rose sat back silently and wiped her brow while Flo bustled around the kitchen. Blair didn't understand what had transpired but he did know that the moment was gone and that without its tension he was progressively more drunk.

Rose got to her feet and gave the sponge to Flo. 'Dry him, dress him, take him back t'his hotel.' She untied her apron and went up the stairs that Flo had just come down.

'Sure.' Flo was surprised by Rose's retreat but still full of momentum. She said to Blair, 'Your shoes are full o' muck, but you can wear clogs.'

'Great.' It was his last coherent word.

Chapter Eleven

IN THE MIDDLE of the night Blair woke and lit the lamp in his hotel room. The flame burned away some of his stupor, though the oversweet taste of gin coated his tongue.

The visit to Mary Jaxon and her neighbours, and memories of being bodily transported by Flo, had the quality of dreams rather than actuality. The fight in the slag pit, especially, seemed more hallucination than fact, except that his hands were raw with scrapes and one leg was bruised black.

When he approached the mirror he saw that the hair above one ear had been cropped. He lifted the hair and turned to see out of the corner of his eye a semi-circle neatly stitched, the edge faintly coloured blue from coal dust that couldn't be removed. Not Bill Jaxon's mark. Her mark.

While his head throbbed, Blair opened Maypole's journal, attempting for a second time to make sense of the entries the curate had written the week before he disappeared. The weave of vertical and horizontal lines was a maze of Indian ink and they were in transposed letters. If the lines had simply been in Latin they would have been safe from him. Codes were different. Miners knew codes; old Blair had kept a notebook of claims before they were registered, hidden in a variety of ciphers: keyword, picket fence, Porta's and pigpen.

'Jbn uif spt fpg tib spo . . .'

Blair had it. The Augustus code, a one-letter shift in blocks of three – baby's play. Maypole was an Oxford man? He should have been ashamed of himself.

> I am the rose of Sharon, and the lily of the valleys.
> My beloved spake and said unto me, 'Rise up, my love, my fair one, and come away.
> 'Let me see thy countenance, let me hear thy voice; for sweet is thy voice, and thy countenance is comely. Take us the foxes, the little foxes, that spoil the vines: for our vines have tender grapes.'
> These are words I wish I could say to her.

As there were no vineyards around Wigan, Blair assumed that Maypole had slipped into the Bible, and while he could easily identify Charlotte as, say, the murderous Judith, who cut off the head of an Assyrian and hung it on a bed, he didn't see her as a vixen.

> She tells me how people visit the pit yard to gawk at the women as if they were another race. Can coal dust and trousers make people so blind? Don't her intelligence and spirit shine through that disguise? She charges that my cassock is a stranger costume than any trousers she might wear, and though I rebuff her accusation, in private I begin to agree.

Blair remembered the last time Maypole was seen, running after Rose Molyneux and pulling off his ecclesiastical collar.

> 'Thy lips are like a thread of scarlet . . . Thy two breasts are like two young roes . . . which feed among the lilies.

'How much better is thy love than wine! and the smell
of thine ointments than all spices!'

Why was Maypole coding what was in the Bible? Blair
wondered. Unless it had some particular power for him. The
Song of Solomon really shouldn't be placed in the hands of
young curates, he decided. The Good Book ran like a railway
engine on a track of sanctified slaughter, and then, out of
nowhere, came Solomon's verses of love. He pictured conduc-
tors shouting, 'Don't look out of the windows at the naked man
and woman! We'll be pulling into Isaiah and the degradation of
Zion in five more minutes!'
The lines switched to plain text.

'It is the voice of my beloved that knocketh, saying,
Open to me ... my love, my dove ... for my head is filled
with dew, and my locks with the drops of the night.
'My beloved put in his hand by the hole of the door ...
I rose up to open to my beloved; and my hands dripped
with myrrh, and my fingers with sweet smelling myrrh
upon the handles of the lock.'

The next entry shifted to a different cipher, too much for
Blair's headache. One thing was clear, though. If this was the
fiancé of Charlotte Hannay, he was a man in trouble.

Chapter Twelve

BLAIR LIFTED A leech from a jar and set it in a row of its companions feeding on his bruised and swollen hip. Not that he expected leeches to draw anything but subcutaneous bleeding. He lay on his side to keep deeper blood from pooling, wearing only a loose shirt and socks, his skin red from the overstoked fire of his hotel sitting room. Since his veins swam in aspirin, arsenic and brandy, he expected the worms to soon swoon and drop.

Leveret had delivered a bound copy of the Coroner's report, and Blair had sent him off for a list of pit girls who had attended the Home for Women. Where else could Rose have learned how to stitch a wound? What better place to meet John Maypole?

The report weighed an imperial pound.

Being the Inquest of the Coroner's Jury into the Circumstances and Causes of the Explosion at the Hannay Pit, Wigan, Lancashire, held at the Royal Inn, 21 January 1872.

The site didn't surprise him. Inquests were held in a local public room, which usually meant any inn with space enough to seat the jury, witnesses, bereaved families and interested parties.

The first page was a fold-out map of the Hannay Mine,

the scale fifty yards to an inch, marked with arrows to show how fresh air arrived from the downshaft, branched from the tunnel called the main road, and circulated through cross tunnels to the far periphery of the coal face. Ventilation returned through the back-road tunnel until it was sucked up a diagonal channel called a 'dumb drift' to join the upshaft far enough above the furnace so that the tainted, gassy air wouldn't explode.

The map was also marked from '1' to '76' to indicate where men had died. There was a capricious quality to mine explosions because blast and smoke underground could multiply like a dozen locomotives racing through tunnels, suddenly swerving from a likely victim to chase down a less fortunate man half a mile away. Also, in the insidious alchemy of a blast, the methane that fuelled a fire was always followed by afterdamp – carbon monoxide – and no man was safe until he had reached the surface ahead of the spreading gas.

Death certificates followed. Blair's eye skipped around because there were so many.

1. Henry Turton, eight years, pony tender. Attempting to aid his pony, Duke, he became tangled in the reins and was carried to the bottom of the shaft . . .

23, 24 and 25. Albert Pimblett, sixty-two; his son, Robert Pimblett, forty-one; and grandson Albert, eighteen, found side by side and apparently unmarked in the main road. It is surmised that as one succumbed to gas, the others stayed to help, and so all perished. They were identified by their wives . . .

45. In the main road, an Irishman called Paddy, no other name known. Age unknown. He was identified by a Fenian tattoo . . .

48. William Bibby, fourteen. Identified by his brother

Abel, who had not gone to work that day because of a headache . . .

53. Bernard Twiss, sixteen. Burned. Recovered at the coal face by his father, Harvey, who failed at first to recognize him. Identified later by a red cloth he used to hold up his trousers. . .

66. Arnold Carey, thirty-four. Found burned and disfigured at the coal face. Identified by his wife, who recognized his clogs . . .

73. Thomas Greenall, fifty-four. At the coalface. Burned and mutilated, recognized by the fact that he had previously lost a finger . . .

74 and 75. George Swift, twenty-one, and John Swift, twenty. Burned and mutilated. Identified by George's belt buckle and John's watch . . .

76. A day worker known as Taffy. Age unknown. Identified by a black tooth . . .

A missing finger, a watch, a tattoo. It was enough to make a man take a personal inventory.

The thirteen members of the jury were listed: three bankers, two retired Army officers, a builder, one insurance agent and six shop owners, all of a social caste that turned to the Hannays the way flowers heeded the sun. A jury of one's peers.

George Battie was the first witness.

Coroner: As underlooker, you are one of the employees most responsible for the day-to-day safety of the Hannay Pit and the men who work in it, is that not true?
Battie: It is, sir.
Coroner: Last week seventy-six men died in that mine. Every home in Wigan lost a husband, a father, a brother. Their widows are gathered here today, asking how it is

possible that such a mass calamity could have been allowed to occur. We will hear testimony and opinion from survivors and rescuers, experts who were called immediately to the scene of the disaster, as well as experts who visited the pit later, agents for the mine owner and miners' union, and finally from Her Majesty's Mines Inspector. However, you may be the most important witness of all, since you were the individual charged with the safety of those victims.

Blair could see Battie strapped into a Sunday suit, facing the questions like a pony staring down a shaft.

Coroner: What did you do on the morning of 18 January to ensure the safety of the men in the Hannay Pit?
Battie: I am always first man down pit at four in the morning to hear the report of the night underlooker whether there have been accidents or complaints since the previous day. There were none. I then checked the barometer and thermometer.
Aaron Hopton, Esq., Counsel for the Hannay Pit: Why is that?
Battie: If the barometric pressure falls, gas creeps out of the coal. When that is the case, I caution the men against setting off any shots that might ignite the gas. The barometric pressure did drop that morning and I issued such a caution as the men came down in the cage. I then visited workplaces to make sure that the caution was understood, paying particular attention to districts of the coalface I knew to be fraught with gas. As I did so, I also examined the ventilation to be sure that every part of the mine had access to good air, and that every workplace had two routes of escape.

Miles Liptrot, Esq., Counsel for the Hannay Pit: Did you examine where the explosion originated?

Battie: Yes, sir. That is, I believe I can estimate where the explosion took place, and I did inspect that area the morning of the fire.

Enoch Nuttal, Esq., Counsel for the Hannay Pit: Did you detect gas that morning?

Battie: Yes.

Isaac Meek, Esq., Counsel for the Hannay Pit: Determined by?

Battie: Passing my lamp across the coalface and observing a lengthening of the flame. I moved a brattice—

Hopton: Brattice?

Battie: A frame of wood and canvas for directing ventilation. And I told Albert Smallbone—

Liptrot: That would be the fireman at that location?

Battie: Yes, sir. I told him to watch the gas and not to fire any shots.

Nuttal: To set off any gunpowder for the easier getting of coal?

Battie: Yes, sir.

Meek: Describe, Mr Battie, where you were and what you did when you became aware of an explosion?

Battie: I was at my desk at the bottom of the shaft at two forty-five in the afternoon when the floor jumped and hot clouds of coal dust shot from the tunnels. The ponies were in a turmoil. One carried a boy to his death in the cistern beneath the cage shaft. The cage arrived almost at once, seconds too late for the poor boy.

Hopton: Go on.

Battie: I wrote a note for the pit manager, explaining the situation, and sent the cage back up. Then I took men with rescue supplies that are always at the ready – picks and shovels, litters and splints, brattices and timber, block and tackle, canaries in cages – and started with them into the main road because that is the main artery of fresh air. The first men and ponies we encountered were rushing out. I soon began to find brattices that had been blown out of position, disrupting the inward draft of good air and allowing afterdamp to spread. We repaired the canvas to improve ventilation and push the gas back. Only as the quality of air improved could we move forwards. It is one thing for fate to take a life; it is another matter altogether for the leader of a rescue party to endanger more lives through recklessness or haste.

Five hundred yards in, we found men who had succumbed to gas and fallen face forward unconscious to the floor, a sign they had fallen while running. We turned them on their backs so they could breathe and tended some twenty men in this fashion as proper ventilation took hold. All survived. Another fifty yards on, however, the canary in the cage I held dropped, and we now started to find men stretched out on the floor, unmarked by violence but beyond any ministration. We also started to meet cave-ins and were forced to dig through obstructions, propping up rock as we went, rigging block and tackle to move fallen props. There were pockets of good air as well as gas, and we were able to extricate another eighteen men alive, besides finding the bodies of thirty-five more.

Coroner: What about the canary? Canaries are sensitive to carbon monoxide, hence their use in mines. You said the canary in the cage you held dropped to the bottom of its cage. Were you progressing with a dead canary?

Battie: We had three cages. Only one was in the lead. When it dropped, it was handed back to revive while one of the other canaries was handed to the front. We were indeed slowed by thicker concentrations of gas, which required men as well as birds to take turns in the lead. Five of us were overcome and had to be carried out. However, we were reinforced by survivors who chose to participate in the rescue rather than to run for safety. Smallbone had been injured by a rockfall and was being assisted to my office by William Jaxon when the explosion took place. Both joined us and took such extreme risks I had to restrain them.

Hopton: They heard cries for help?

Battie: After an explosion, timbers make all manner of sounds. However, from a thousand yards on there were no more survivors.

Liptrot: And you advanced quickly?

Battie: It was three forty-five when Jaxon and Smallbone joined us, but our progress slowed despite their efforts. If you can't see the bird in the cage and the flame in your lamp sinks to a nub, you order everyone back until fresh air lifts the flame again because dead rescuers are no help at all.

Nuttal: You cite the zeal of Smallbone and Jaxon. Why do you think they pressed so hard?

Battie: The explosion was at their district of the coalface. When we emerged at the near end of the face, the bodies there were singed. With every step, the destruction was more severe. Midway, the victims were burned. Some were buried under coal tubs thrown off the track, others blown by the force of the explosion into old workings. The far end of the coal face was Smallbone's and Jaxon's station. Had they been there at the time of the explosion nothing would have been left of them.

Meek: Who was the last victim recovered?

Battie: A dayworker, a Welshman we called Taffy.

The black tooth, Blair remembered.

Coroner: At least we can trust that the death of these men was mercifully swift. The watch later identified as that of John Swift was found with its crystal shattered and its hands stopped at two forty-four, the very moment of the blast.

Progressing with a dead canary was an accurate description of Blair's own life. He shuffled stiffly across the carpet to feed the fire grate. Since they were along for the ride, he decided to name the leeches on his leg Famine, Death, Conquest and War after the Four Horsemen of the Apocalypse.

Blair was self-taught. What had there been to do in a Sierra winter but read through the old man's library of classics? Sober, old man Blair had no conversation beyond engineering or, drunk, the Revelation of Saint John the Divine. The women the boy saw were either Chinese or whores. To win attention he told them stories that he stole. His favourite was a version of *Robinson Crusoe* in which the castaway was a woman instead of a man, and Friday was a boy instead of a native. They lived so happily on the island that they let ships pass rather than wave them down.

Hopton: I appreciate that you and the other members of the rescue party were operating under strain and emotional upset. Did you, however, immediately examine the coalface for evidence that a worker had fired a shot contrary to your caution?

Battie: Not immediately.

Liptrot: Why not?

Battie: There was more gas.

Coroner: From what?

Battie: From old workings, sir. Waste stone and unusable small coal that we'd bricked to help support the roof. It's normal practice but, unfortunately, all sorts of gases accumulate in waste. The explosion had cracked the bricks. The whole tunnel lit up when our lamps felt the gas. The choice was to abandon the coalface with any bodies in it that we hadn't found or stop up the leak.

Nuttal: What was the condition of your lamps?

Battie: Red, sir. Too hot to hold.

Nuttal: Because of gas?

Battie: Yes.

Meek: What access did you have to this leak?

Battie: Poor. The gas was blowing from a bricked-up area deep in the coal seam under a low shelf, and the way was partially blocked by debris. While we tried to ventilate as best we could, I sent for bricks and the makings for cement that we store in side tunnels, and when they arrived I sent everyone out but Smallbone and Jaxon. We mixed mortar at the face and they took turns crawling with two bricks at a time in almost total darkness to repair the wall. They succeeded, and as a consequence I was able to bring lamps to that area of the coal face that I most wanted to examine.

Hopton: Why that part?

Battie: It was the area where I had detected gas that morning.

Hopton: Did you suspect that, contrary to the caution you issued, one of the victims had set off a shot?

Battie: No, sir.

Liptrot: Perhaps you feel it would be uncharitable to speculate?

Battie: I couldn't say, sir. Besides, sir, the only fireman in that district of the coalface was Smallbone.

Nuttal: And he was with you. So it was unlikely that Taffy or the Swift brothers or Greenall or any of the deceased set off a shot of gunpowder in the absence of Smallbone.

Battie: Yes, sir.

Meek: But if they did, they would be less expert.

Battie: Yes, sir.

Hopton: Isn't it true that Greenall had been reprimanded in the past for lighting a pipe in the mine?

Battie: Ten years back.

Liptrot: It's true, though?

Battie: Yes.

Nuttal: Any heavy drinkers among the men at the coal face?

Battie: I wouldn't say heavy.

Nuttal: Weren't John and George Swift reprimanded by police only last week for carousing on the street?

Battie: John was just married. They were celebrating.

Hopton: Does drink affect a miner's judgement?

Battie: Yes.

Hopton: Miners drink.

Battie: Some.

Nuttal: Do you drink?

Battie: I'll have an ale on the way home.

Nuttal: An ale or two?

Battie: The temperature down pit is one hundred degrees. You sweat off five pounds in a day. When you come up, you need something to drink.

Hopton: Are you suggesting that ale is purer than Wigan water?

Battie: You said it, sir, not I.

Meek: You are involved with the miners' union, are you not?

Battie: I am a miner and I am in the union.

Meek: More than that. An active leader. A defender, is that right?

Battie: I suppose so.

Meek: With no insinuation intended, would it be fair to say that the last thing a union leader would admit was that one of the unfortunate victims was himself to blame?

Battie: I don't know what happened down pit that day. I do know mining is dry and dangerous work, that's a fact of life. Nothing is ever going to change that.

Blair felt dry himself, and the ache from his head was crowding out his ability to focus. He drank a brandy, wished it was ale, set down the report, peeled off the leeches and napped.

He lunched on cold beef, cheese and wine, keeping in mind Battie's warning about the water. The leeches lunched on him. A different foursome now. Juliet, Ophelia, Portia and Lady Macbeth.

He hated coal mines. Gold was noble and inert. Coal, which had been living material, was still alive, exhaling gas as it changed into rock. Of course all the easy, shallow coal was long gone. As mines went deeper, coal was harder, air fouler, firedamp stronger. For what? No nugget of gold.

Coroner: Mr Wedge, you are the Manager of the Hannay Pit. Were you aware of a danger of explosive gas at the coal-face on the day of 18 January?

Wedge: I was so informed by George Battie, and I agreed with Battie's caution against firing shots. That's what an underlooker is for, to take such precautions and protect property.

Coroner: As Manager, where were you and what did you do when you became aware of the explosion?

Wedge: I was in the yard and knocked almost off my feet by the explosion. With my very first breath, I sent runners for medical assistance and help from the nearby pits. A bad fire requires the transport of injured and dead for long distances underground at a time when your own miners are incapacit-ated. Next, I looked after the cage, which was, thank God, operative although a volume of smoke rose from the shaft. A messenger had come from Battie to say he had started rescue operations below. Although we had to wait for the cage to return to the surface again, we immediately sent volunteers down with lamps. It is a sad fact that in mine disasters rescuers are often among the victims. That is why we strictly count lamps, so that we know by simple arithmetic when *everyone* is out of the pit. The worst for a family is not knowing if someone is found.

Blair wasn't certain of his own age and had no idea of his birthday. Old Blair, however, taught him geometry, and when Blair was probably no more than nine he figured with a protractor – using the average time of an Atlantic crossing and taking into consideration trade winds and winter seas – the approximate latitude and longitude where he last saw his mother. Since then he had crossed the same position only once. He had stood at the rail and looked down at dark swells that moved under sheets of foam. The sense of cold and isolation was overwhelming.

Coroner: Your name is?
Jaxon: William Jaxon.
Liptrot: You are the miner who usually drills holes for the fireman at the coalface where the explosion took place?
Jaxon: Yes, sir.
Nuttal: Did you drill any holes that day?
Jaxon: No, sir. When Mr Battie issued a caution against shots, no one drilled any holes.
Hopton: But you were not at the coalface when the explosion erupted?
Jaxon: No, sir. I was helping Albert Smallbone to the cage because his pick hit a rock that shot out and hit his leg. We

were in the road when it gave a shake like a rope. Smoke blew us along until we rolled into a refuge hole. We couldn't see, couldn't hear, because of coal dust and because we were concussed, like. We worked our way through side tunnels and that's when we met Battie and the others.

Meek: And decided to return to the coalface with them rather than seek your own safety?

Jaxon: You could put it that way.

Coroner: Your name is?

Smallbone: Albert Smallbone.

Liptrot: And you are the only fireman for that district of the coalface where the explosion took place?

Smallbone: Yes, sir.

Liptrot: Smallbone, were you given a caution about gas from Battie?

Smallbone: Yes, sir.

Nuttal: You must feel fortunate to be alive.

Smallbone: I would feel more fortunate if my friends were alive.

Meek: Was your leg badly injured when the rock hit it? When you chose to return with Jaxon and Battie?

Smallbone: I disregarded it, sir, in the heat of the moment.

In spite of aspirin, Blair's head still throbbed. Good stitching only went so far. He felt like Macarthy of the Gold Coast after his head was severed, boiled and stacked with the other honoured skulls.

Molony: My name is Ivan Molony. I am Manager of Mab's Pit, one mile distant from the Hannay Pit. On the afternoon of 18 January, I saw smoke rise from the Hannay Pit and knew that an underground explosion of some sort had taken place. I gathered a party of volunteers and rushed to the Hannay yard.

Nuttal: It is a tradition among Lancashire mines to lend assistance at the first sign of a fire?

Molony: Yes, it is a form of mutual aid.

Nuttal: And at the yard you proceeded down the shaft into the pit?

Molony: With other volunteers.

Hopton: You were the first expert to arrive at the coalface where the explosion is believed to have originated. Describe the scene as you found it.

Molony: A smooth wall at one end and a tangle of burned bodies and wagons at the other. Terrible carnage, like soldiers mown down by grapeshot. In the midst of it, Battie and two of his men had erected brattices for ventilation and were just setting the last brick in the wall to stop a secondary leak of gas.

Liptrot: You are aware from previous witnesses that there was a caution in effect at the Hannay Mine before the explosion. In your expert opinion, what besides a shot of gunpowder might have set off such a disaster?

Molony: At Mab's Pit we search miners to prevent them from taking pipes and matches underground. We lock the lamps and keep the keys. It doesn't matter. They bring pipes anyway, and if a miner doesn't detect gas and unlocks his lamp to light up – which they do, in spite of every warning – he could certainly kill himself and all his mates.

Hopton: I would like to ask you, as an expert, how miners regard cautions against the discharge of gunpowder underground?

Molony: They're not happy about it.

Liptrot: Why not?

Molony: A shot of gunpowder will loose more coal face than a day's worth of swinging a pick. It's a matter of economics. Miners are paid by how much coal they send up, not how much time or labour they put into it.

Nuttal: Are there other ways in which a miner can undo the best efforts of a mine owner?

Molony: Any number. The first impulse of an improperly trained man, if he finds himself in a gas-saturated tunnel, is to run. If he runs fast enough, the flame will bend through the safety mesh of his lamp and ignite the very gas he is trying to escape.

Nuttal: Considering the force of the explosion at the Hannay Pit, was the tunnel necessarily saturated with gas?

Molony: No. A small initial explosion would do, considering that miners recklessly stuff every coalface in Lancashire with canisters of gunpowder waiting to be used in charges. Once initiated, the canisters can set themselves off in a series of explosions the length of the tunnel.

Hopton: From your long experience, what do you feel was the more likely cause of the Hannay explosion, inadequate supervision on the part of the owners of the pit or a breach of safety regulations on the part of a miner?

Molony: As there was no deficiency in the regulations or their supervision, nothing is left but error on the part of a miner, is there?

According to the report, at this moment a disturbance broke out among the families attending. The uproar continued until a representative of the miners was given permission to speak. The name was familiar to Blair although he had met the man only once, clumsily chasing peas around a dinner plate at Hannay Hall.

Walter Fellowes: I am Agent of the Miners' Union and Mutual Insurance Fund. Acting in those capacities, I went

down the Hannay Pit the day after the explosion, and while I
agree with Mr Molony that it was a heartrending scene of
hellish destruction, I am outraged by his attempt, familiar to
us from past inquests of this nature, to lay the blame for a
mining disaster on the very victims who suffered its fatal
consequences. I would like to remind Mr Molony that it is
not mine owners who are brought up lifeless and disfigured
to the grief of their widows and children but the miners sent
down by those owners. As to whether there is culpability on
the part of the owners and compensation due the victims'
families, this is a matter for the Civil Court and I would
appreciate it if Mr Molony kept his opinion, expert or
otherwise, to himself. I would also like to remind Mr Molony
that a man who does not bring a certain amount of coal from
a pit will soon be unemployed, so it is hardly the miners'
greed that leads to the extensive use of gunpowder. I would
like to ask Mr Molony a question.

Hopton: I object.

Meek: Fellowes has no standing with the Court.

Coroner: Nevertheless, would Mr Molony entertain a question from Mr Fellowes?

Molony: If Fellowes wants to. Go ahead.

Fellowes: Mr Molony, at all the numerous inquests you have
graced with your opinions, have you ever found a wealthy pit
owner, rather than a poor miner, responsible for an explosion?

Molony: No, for the simple reason that you do not find
wealthy gentlemen swinging a pick or lighting a tube of
gunpowder. I would, however, consider them very dangerous
if they did.

The report said that, 'General laughter relieved the tension
in the room', preparing the way for the most expert and
indisputable witness in the realm.

Coroner: The inquest welcomes the comments of Benjamin Thicknesse, Her Majesty's Inspector of Mines.

Thicknesse: I have listened to the testimony delivered today. I have studied the ventilation map and cross-section details of the Hannay Pit. I have some thoughts and conclusions that duty and conscience urge me to share.

First, I offer the sympathy of the Queen and the Royal Family. A disaster on a scale of the Hannay explosion touches the entire nation. Her Majesty mourns with you.

Second, that the mining of deep coal is the most hazardous occupation short of war, has always been and likely always will be.

Third, that the prompt and intelligent actions of the underlooker George Battie and the rescuers he led were the salvation of numerous miners overcome by afterdamp. The swift bricking up of a second gas leak by Battie, Smallbone and Jaxon possibly staunched a second disaster.

Fourth, I cannot take issue with the opinions of any of the expert witnesses. They may all be right; they may all be wrong. A miner might have rashly opened his lamp to light his pipe, but we will never know. A spark, a flame, a gunpowder tin may have contributed singly or collectively to the force of the explosion. The answer is buried at the coal face. Was ventilation sufficient to clear the gas? After all, fresh air had to travel down a full mile from the surface, and then circulate through eight miles of tunnels and cross-tunnels. Based on safety standards as we currently know them, our calculations say that the ventilation was sufficient, yet a boy and his pony could have knocked one piece of canvas down and disrupted the whole carefully planned flow of air. It is a fact that the Lancashire coalfield is a 'fiery' coalfield – that is, particularly given to the accumulation of explosive gases. This fact is exacerbated by another one. The deeper the coal, the more fiery the coal. Yet the deeper the coal, the harder the coal, making gunpowder more necessary.

Finally, there is one more element: coal itself. Coal dust that lingers in a tunnel atmosphere and reddens the miner's eye and blackens his lung is, in proper ratio to oxygen, almost as explosive as gunpowder. This is, of course, a controversial point. No matter, one might ask how any man would chance work in subterranean chambers so fraught with known and unknown perils? How could any father kiss his children goodbye in the morning with the knowledge that by the afternoon they might be orphans?

This would, however, be an emotional and short-sighted response. It would bring British industry to a halt. Mills would lie empty, locomotives would stand and rust in their yards, ships would idle at their docks.

It is also an insult to science. British technology is improving every day. As knowledge increases, safety assuredly follows.

Finally, a single human error, one breach of orders, may well have been to blame for this catastrophe.

Tragically, the answer is buried. We will simply never know.

The record indicated that the jury deliberated for fifteen minutes, then returned with their verdict.

We the jury find that seventy-six men came to their deaths by an explosion of firedamp at the Hannay Pit on 18 January; by what means or by whom the gas was ignited there is insufficient evidence to show.

The jury is also unanimous in stating that the mine in which the calamity has happened has been properly conducted, and that there is no blame to be attached to the proprietors of the said company.

Not that the jury had been asked about the company's blame, but in a sentence they had effectively destroyed the chance of any victim's family bringing a claim against the Hannay Pit.

Blair raised a bitter toast of arsenic and brandy. What a surprise.

Appended to the report was a copy of the lampman's ledger for anyone who had signed for a lamp the day of the explosion. The list included survivors and rescuers as well as victims.

Battie, George	308
Paddy	081
Pimblett, Albert	024
Pimblett, Robert	220
Twiss, Bernard	278
Jaxon, Bill	091
Smallbone, Albert	125

The names went on at numbing length, but the point was, as Battie had said, that there were seventy-six lamps for seventy-six bodies.

Blair wore blankets like a Turkish pasha to make himself decent when dinner was brought by a girl with popped eyes who set out grilled chops and claret.

'Everybody's talkin' about what tha said.'

'What did I say?'

'About t'Africans an' t'macaroni. Ah laughed an' laughed.'

'It's not a bad story.'

'Art feelin' well or pot?'

'A little sore, thanks. Definitely pot.'

'It's terrible out, a night t'stay in.'

'I'm not stirring.'

'Oh, an' there's a letter, too.'

The girl produced it from her apron. Her hands lingered so long on the creamy envelope and raised monogram that she dropped it, but Blair caught it on its way to the floor. He tore the flap open and removed a single page that said, 'Come to Theatre Royal tomorrow at noon. Prepare yourself for a cultural occasion. H.'

A typically imperious summons from Hannay, with no chance to beg off. A Wigan 'cultural occasion'? What was that?

When Blair looked up, he saw that the girl's eyes had popped even more, and he realized that in saving the letter his blanket had slipped from the leeches that formed a row of dark, fat commas along his flank.

'Sorry. They're not pretty. Of course at this point they're practically family.'

'Nawh.'

'Yes. They even have names. Hopton, Liptrot, Nuttal and Meek.' He covered up. She was on tiptoe, as if he might next reveal a tail or a horn on his head.

She folded her thin arms and shivered. 'Gives me goosepimples.'

'I hope so. It's girls who don't get goosepimples that come to a bad end.'

'True?'

'It's the last form of decency.'

Give me leeches rather than lawyers, though, Blair thought. Despite what Hannay's Counsel claimed, miners did not make certain mistakes. Experienced miners did not open safety lamps or run recklessly through gas. If in those last seconds they had noticed their lamp flames start to float, they would have hastily organized brattices to clear the gas. Or, failing that, made an orderly retreat through the fresh air that was still blowing through the main road.

Which raised other questions. Before the explosion, why did Jaxon and the injured Smallbone choose to make their way from the coal face through the fouler air of the back road?

Something even more curious had emerged. George Battie told the inquest that his first act after the explosion was to send messengers up in the cage. Wedge, the Manager, testified that after the messenger arrived on the surface the volunteers there had to wait for the cage to come up again. Why had the cage gone down? Who took it? Was it possible, Blair thought, that he had finally caught sight of John Maypole?

It was strangely pleasant to engage in an intellectual puzzle. His mind had raced ahead so fast that he had not noticed that the serving girl was still standing at the door.

'Something else?' he asked.

'Just everyone's talkin' abowt how tha beat Bill Jaxon. That's never happened before.'

'Is that so?'

'And how he's looking for tha.'

The inquest vanished from Blair's mind. 'Now *I've* got goosepimples. Anything else?'

'That was all.' She backed out.

Blair waited a minute, pushed the tray away, peeled off the leeches one by one and dressed.

Chapter Thirteen

RAIN GAVE BLAIR AN excuse to pull his collar up. Curtains were drawn and the pavements empty except for urchins chasing through the water that rushed out of the gutters. He pounded on her door to be heard over the downpour.

When Rose finally opened, he hobbled through and leaned against the jamb, resting his weight on one leg. The kitchen was lit only by an angle of lamplight from the parlour. Why did she always keep the house so dark? Her hair was wild, spilling from a comb. Skin olive from coal dust, in a skirt and blouse of patched muslin, sleeves too short for her wrists, the same as she had worn the night before. There was no sign of her friend Flo.

'I told you not t'come back,' she said.

'I didn't want to, but word is going around that I beat Bill Jaxon in a fight. I'd rather hear that Bill beat me, or that there was no fight at all.'

'I couldn't care either way.'

'Someone is spreading this story.'

'Not me. I haven't thought about you or Bill all day.'

From the open doorway, neither in nor out, he glanced around as if he might have missed Bill sitting on a kitchen chair in the dark. The house seemed as empty as ever, which again made no sense in the Calcutta conditions of Scholes.

'Tell Bill I'm not his rival. I have no interest in you.'

'Such pretty words. You're no more a poet than a gentleman.'

'I just want to leave Wigan as soon as possible. I don't want to get involved.'

'Involved in what?'

'Anything. I told Bill I was a coward.'

'Well, he should have listened.'

'Tell him—' Blair started when the sound of the rain on slate roofs accelerated to a drumming that drowned out his words and, without thinking, he moved away from the open door. Without conscious intent, he found his hand on her waist. By itself it drew her close. Rose could have hit him or driven her comb into his hand. Instead, she raised her mouth to his and gave him the taste of coal.

'Take off your hat,' she said.

He let it drop to the floor. She turned his head to the side to see the shaven patch, then turned it again to study his eyes. How he had gone from one point to another, Blair didn't understand. Some sign had passed that he hadn't caught, only acted on.

'That must hurt,' Rose said.

'It should.'

Through his hand he felt her heart, beating as hard as his. He couldn't hear the clock over the rain, but he saw the pendulum stirring by the grate. If he could have stepped back in time a mere minute and undone his touch, he would have. He couldn't. Besides, at a moment when her usual coquetry could have been expected and would have set him free, Rose seemed as astonished as he was. Or she was a better actor.

Upstairs, her room had an unlit lamp, the shadow of a chest of drawers, a bed with cotton sheets as worn as cambric. In his arms she was more slender than he had expected, and paler. He caught the flash of her back in a long mirror.

A year of deprivation made the slightest touch feverish, as in a reverie. Need was a form of insanity, he thought. He entered her with desperation, as a drowning man rises to the surface. She couldn't have been more than nineteen or twenty, but she waited for him with patience. He felt like a satyr upon her younger body, until, when he was firmly set, her face coloured and he felt her legs around his back.

What would the first drink of water in a year be like? What is water to the soul? What is astonishing about a primal act is the wholeness of two bodies, as he was astonished to find himself in a bed and made complete by a mere pit girl. He was aware of her sooty hands and face, and of his hands and face growing as dark, but mostly of her eyes, which watched him with a glow of triumph.

Sweat shone on her brow and welled around her eyes, making the lids darker, the whites brighter, avenues to a gaze that drew him in. Should an ignorant girl be shallow? There was a depth to Rose he was unprepared for, but now had fallen into. More than fallen: plunged.

Pain washed away. Or he had gone to a level where pain could not follow, a level that was all Rose, where he felt himself gladly disappear then reappear, his whole body hard as a stone she clung to, then shudder and dissolve from stone to flesh.

'How old are you?' Rose asked.

'Thirty, thirty-two, somewhere there.'

'Somewhere? How can you not know?'

Blair shrugged.

She said, 'I hear people go t'America and start over. I didn't think they forgot that much.'

'I started early and I forgot a lot.'

'You know where you are now?'

'Oh, yes.'

She had lit the smallest blue flame on the lamp and sat against pillows packed against the pipes of the headboard. She exhibited – if that was the word – a complete lack of shame. Quantitatively – and he was an engineer, after all – she had a slim, almost wiry body with sharply pointed breasts and a twist of brown, not red, hair at the base of her stomach. Her eyes, in turn, looked across her body and met his gaze with an unblinking assertion that there was yet more he would have to recognize and contend with.

'I don't mean Wigan,' she said.

'I know.'

He sat against the foot of the bed, his bad leg trailing to the boards on the floor. Flo might be out another hour or all night, she told him.

'You have a house to yourself? How do you manage that?'

'That's my business.'

'You're not a simple girl.'

'You wanted a simple girl?'

'I wanted no girl at all. That's not what I came for. That's not what I thought I came for.'

'Then what happened?'

'I don't know.' He couldn't explain to himself what had guided his hand to her. 'All I know is that your madman Bill is out in the rain looking for me.'

'You're safe here.'

'That doesn't sound likely.'

'Do you want t'go?'

'No.'

'Good.'

In their voices was the excitement shared by two people who

had cast off from shore in a small craft on to high seas in the dark with no plan at all. She wasn't his equal, he reminded himself. He had seen four continents; she had spent her life close by the mines. Yet from the platform of this bed they seemed to be equals. Now her claims of distinction – like the velvet ribbon she wore, even in trousers – didn't look ridiculous. Was he misleading himself, or was it intelligence aimed from her eyes?

'You've been living like a grandee. Can you bear t'spend the night here?'

'I've been living like the dead. Yes, I'd rather be here.'

'"Living like the dead"? I like that, I know what you mean. Working at the pit, sorting coal, I feel like a chambermaid in Hell.'

'Do you hate it?'

'No. Working in a mill, that I'd hate. The noise? I've friends who hardly hear any more. Air so full of cotton you can't breathe? Wearing skirts around all those spinning gears? You lose a leg, choke t'death or die of consumption. And for less money. I'm lucky.'

'You could be a domestic.'

'Be a maid? I know that's more respectable, but I'd rather have my self-respect.'

Talk died for a second because they didn't know each other, he thought. They had nothing in common, had gone through no period of wooing, only found themselves impelled towards each other, like planets falling into a mutual gravitational pull.

'How many maids have you seduced?'

'How many men have you seduced?'

She smiled, as if that erased the questions. 'Was it different, having a white girl again? Or is it true what they say, that all cats are grey in the dark?'

'I haven't had all that many women, but all were different.'

213

'How?'

'Touch, smell, taste, motion, heat.'

'God, you're a scientist. And what do I taste like?'

He ran his hand over her flank and across her belly, then licked his palm.

'Rose. A slightly burnt rose.'

She shifted to one elbow. Though her brow hid in the tangle of her hair, the jet picked out in her irises scattered bits of brown and green. And though coal dust lay like a resident shadow across her face, her body had a redhead's extreme fairness, with veins so blue around the swell of her breasts that he could almost watch her pulse.

She ran her hand up his leg and held him there. 'I see you're alive again.'

Rose was no ordinary girl, Blair thought. He had brought a year's hunger to her bed and yet her passion matched his, as if a single night would have to feed the rest of her life, too. She had the abandon that willingly, consciously accepted damnation if she could find someone to be damned with.

As *she* was *someone*. Not dismissable, not a tourist's photographic curiosity, nor a silhouette standing on a slag heap. As real as any Hannay.

Was it love? He thought not. Their bodies beat together with a ferocity more like anger, like crazed, sweating cymbals. He felt his eyes starting, the muscles of his shoulders straining as her nails travelled the groove of his back.

White smeared black, the sheets spread infinitely from side to side. Above the bed was ordinary space. Within her a deeper place. Not Wigan. A different land altogether.

*

'You're starting t'heal.'

She straddled him and parted the hair from the cut on his head.

'That's my plan,' he said.

'It's a brilliant plan if you can stay away from Bill.'

'That's the major part of the plan – at least, it was.'

She hopped off Blair and was back a moment later with a shawl. She sat on his chest and turned his head to the side.

He asked, 'What are you doing?'

She spat on the wound and blew on coal dust from the shawl. 'What miners do,' she said.

Chapter Fourteen

A PIANO PIECE by Mendelssohn was followed by a brass band playing 'Onward, Christian Soldiers' while children costumed in huge paper collars and cotton beards as martyrs of the Reformation marched on to the stage of the Theatre Royal.

'The children are orphans of miners. The benefit is for them,' Leveret whispered to Blair. They stood in the rear of the theatre, under a bust of Shakespeare with pen in hand. The theatre bowed to all the Bard's plays, with murals of tragic figures and ardent lovers, on the proscenium the sight of Othello the Moor poling a gondola across the Grand Canal.

Blair had arrived late and kept his hat on the blued stitches on his head. He saw Hannay in a box seat; the Bishop seemed to be looking down from his height at a simple-minded but profoundly amusing comedy.

Leveret explained, 'Queen Elizabeth has the prettiest dress and all the red hair. You can tell Bloody Mary by the blood on her hands.'

'Reminds me of Charlotte.'

'Wyclif, the martyr, is tied to a stake, naturally. That's why most of the children are carrying torches.'

'That's the way I feel.'

'There will be two tableaux, one religious, one cultural.'

'Wonderful, but why did Hannay ask me here?'

Leveret was evasive. After some hesitation he said, 'I have the list you asked for.'

'Of "Women Who Have Fallen for the First Time"?'

'Yes.' Leveret handed him an envelope as covertly as if he were passing French postcards.

Two executioners in black hoods led the martyrs out. A string quartet played 'Drink to Me Only with Thine Eyes', J. B. Fellowes of the Miners' Union reported on the status of the Widows' Fund, and the quartet finished the first half of the programme with 'Annie Laurie'.

During the interval, Wigan gentry moved down the staircase to the lounge. This was the class whose coaches stood outside the drapers and milliners on Wallgate and Millgate, whose servants polished the brass and swept the pavements every morning, who invested in government funds at 5 per cent; in other words, people who wore shoes instead of clogs. When Blair thought of the effort involved in dressing for a charitable event such as this – the lacing of corsets, the mating of hooks and eyes on boned bodices, the hoisting of crinoline cages to squirming waists and laying of petticoats on top – every woman represented a battery of chambermaids with bloody fingers. The final effect was a flow of ladies in watered silk, foulard and grosgrain in hues of fuchsia and grenadine, accompanied by men who in their cravats and black suits seemed as static as burned trees. Some of the younger women affected the 'Alexandra limp', after the princess left lame by rheumatic fever. As Blair's own leg was stiff, he felt to some degree in style.

He was mystified about what was supposed to transpire in the theatre, although he was aware that around him there was a whisper of anticipation. In the centre was Lady Rowland, wearing the erotic glow of a woman accustomed to masculine attention. Her black hair, veined with silver, pillowed a hat with a green stone. Blair couldn't hear the banter, but he saw the way she skilfully led it with her fan, rewarding each sally with the appreciative smile of a mature and extravagantly attractive woman. On an outer ring of her solar system bobbed Chief Constable Moon, resplendent in a black frockcoat with black silk braids that hung from his shoulder to his cuff, carrying a dress helmet with a black ostrich plume. Blair didn't think word of his nocturnal visit to Rose Molyneux could have reached Moon already, but he kept a distance from the Chief Constable anyway.

A coterie of younger admirers surrounded Lydia Rowland, and if the mother glowed, the daughter, with less effort, glittered. A circlet of white roses framed her golden hair and blue eyes, with their gaze of crystalline innocence. Was it innocence or complete blankness? Blair asked himself.

He was so mesmerized that it took him a moment to notice Charlotte Hannay and Earnshaw in a corner. It had to be punishment for her to be in the same room as Lydia Rowland, for where her cousin shone, Charlotte was a pale figure in a dour, purplish gown, her hair a margin of angry red under a tangle of black lace. Here she was, the local heiress, and she could as well have been a governess or an émigrée from some cursed Middle European state. Earnshaw was at her side, his beard looking as brushed as his suit.

Charlotte's response to some riposte from Earnshaw was a basilisk stare that would have plunged a normal man into silence, but the Member of Parliament maintained a confident air of satisfaction. Which was why politicians were assassinated, Blair thought, because nothing else would faze them.

'So the benefit is for orphans?' he asked Leveret.

'A special subscription for their pageant.'

The band had come downstairs and lined up in front of

bowls of punch and trays of meringues. The blue serge and brass buttons of their uniforms brought out the English pinkness of their cheeks. Behind the table hung oversized paintings on uplifting themes: *The Sermon on the Mount, The Quelling of the Waves, Judith Bearing the Head of Holofernes*. Blair became aware of Bishop Hannay and Lydia Rowland at his side.

'*The Sermon* is such a peaceful painting, Mr Blair, don't you agree?' Lydia asked. 'The crowd, blue skies and olive trees, and Jesus in the distance.'

'The wrong painting for Blair. He's not a man for fair weather,' Hannay said. 'He's one for storms and sharp knives. We don't want him too tame. I wish we had more than Temperance punch, Blair. From what I understand, you've earned it.'

'How is that?'

'Rumours have reached me that you are actually beating people to extract information.'

'That would be terrible, Your Grace, but he hasn't, I promise,' Leveret said.

'Why not? If Blair is finally getting interested, that's good.'

Blair looked at the black worn by other guests. 'I should have dressed differently.'

'No, you're blending in very well,' Hannay said. 'Leveret, don't you have a little surprise to see to?'

'Yes, Your Grace.' Leveret rushed off.

From different points across the gallery, Blair sensed the icy regard of Lady Rowland and an electric loathing from Charlotte Hannay. He felt the cut on the side of his head. He didn't feel that he was blending in.

Although Hannay drew Blair aside, the presence of a bishop created a kind of vortex. All heads turned to the Bishop, though few guests were secure enough in social status to approach. It did strike Blair as a public place to hold a private conversation.

Hannay said casually, 'Give me the benefit of your opinion. Who among the women here would you say was a shining light? Who is a diamond among dull stones?'

'Lydia Rowland, I suppose.'

'Lydia? Lydia is a stunning girl in an ordinary way. Next month the London season starts. My sister will take Lydia down to London to present her at Court, pay calls at the right houses and drive in the right carriages and dance at the right balls until she attracts a husband. No different from the customs of tribes we've met. No, I don't mean Lydia. What do I care about Lydia?'

'You mean Charlotte?'

'You can't see it? Of course, she is my daughter. She also used to be the brightest, most amusing child in the world. A dazzling princess. When she went down to London for her début she wouldn't have any of the Horse Guards or fops strutting in Court, and I didn't blame her. Now I hardly recognize her. It is as if she pours ashes over herself every morning to hide how bright she is. Look at her next to that sack of gas, Earnshaw. A professional politician. He defeated an old friend of mine, Lord Jeremy. Jeremy was a fool to run. He stood for office on the whimsical platform that his family had served the country since the Black Prince and that he employed ten thousand men and paid a hundred thousand pounds in wages, whereas Earnshaw was a nobody who employed a single clerk. Earnshaw won and now proposes that peers not be allowed to run for the Commons at all, that they be confined like relics to the House of Lords. Serves Jeremy right.'

'Why?'

'You don't run against professional politicians, you buy them.'

'Earnshaw is bought?' This was a different view of the champion of moral reform, Blair thought.

'It's been a great waste of money if he isn't.'

'Even for a bishop that sounds cynical.'

'As a young man I preached the Golden Rule, in middle years I tried to persuade by reason. I don't have that sort of time any more.'

'What did you pay Earnshaw to do? He seems to be a suitor for Charlotte.'

'Earnshaw is not a suitor, he is a locomotive. He will huff and puff, and then, when he's scheduled to, will disappear down the track.' Hannay stopped to welcome an ancient matron cobwebbed in veils, inquire after her health, direct her to the meringues. He returned to Blair. 'Orphans always draw a crowd.'

'There were a lot of orphans on the stage today.'

'Orphans are the price of coal.'

'I read the Coroner's report. Seventy-six men died, and your lawyers succeeded in making sure that the mine was held blameless. You don't want the inquest reopened.'

'I believe everything is back to normal now.'

'Not for the dead, not for widows who weren't allowed a legal claim against you.'

'Blair, as I remember, the Coroner's jury indicated that one of the dead miners was responsible. We lost two weeks' production. I made no legal claim against the widows for my financial losses, which were substantial. Please don't feign compassion. You merely hope that I will be so frightened of reopening the inquest that I will declare you done and send you happily away. But I won't do that.'

'You don't mind if I ask more questions about that report?'

'On legal grounds? I have no anxieties.'

Blair saw Hannay's quick look through the crowd towards

four men huddled by the stairs. They were all in their thirties, balding, edgy as whippets. Four dowdy wives in flowery dresses stood close by.

'Hopton, Liptrot, Nuttal and Meek?'

'Hopton, Liptrot, Nuttal and Meek, *Esquires*. Very good. Yes, I feel adequately represented in the courts.'

Blair caught enough of their return glances to tell that the lawyers would not be so comfortable with his questions as Hannay claimed to be. Inquests, like the dead, were best buried. He also sensed the approaching glare of Charlotte Hannay. 'Why did you ask me here? Why do I feel that the orphans aren't the show, that I am?'

'Well, you are. Half.'

Charlotte brought Leveret, who had returned. 'Mr Blair, I understand that you bullied Oliver into stealing the names of women who have sought help from the Home. Do you have any sense of privacy? What good purpose could a morally debased individual like you have for those names?'

'It's to find John,' Leveret said. 'It's for you.'

'On my behalf? Inform me, then. What villains has the famous Blair encountered in his investigation? Footpads, assassins, highwaymen?'

'Just miners,' Blair said.

Like a man dropping a pin, sure that it would be heard, Hannay asked, 'Any women?'

Lydia had returned, just in time to catch her breath. 'Uncle, that's an outrageous suggestion.'

'Is it?'

'Not with John,' Leveret protested.

Hannay said, 'I want to hear Blair's answer. As Charlotte's father and as John Maypole's bishop, I should want to know if he was involved with another woman. Blair?'

'Maypole was involved with a lot of women, especially

women in trouble. Whether that meant something besides good works, I don't know.'

'You wanted names, so there was someone,' Hannay said.

'It's too soon to say.'

'One of those girls from Charlotte's Home? A pit girl, a mill girl?'

'What does it matter?'

'Mill girls are consumptive and ethereal, pit girls are robust. I see Maypole as being more attracted to the consumptive type.'

'I really don't know.'

'Well, one thing is clear,' Hannay announced. 'Blair is making progress. Charlotte, it's time to give up Maypole. Either his ghost or, worse, his sins will emerge soon. Blair has the bit now and I will whip him on until he finds your little curate or his bones. It's time to rearrange your life.'

A moment passed before the Hannays and Rowlands noticed that the rest of the lounge was watching, rapt. Not that the Hannays or the Rowlands ever seemed to care particularly; it had occurred to Blair before that the Bishop and his family set their own laws of conduct, and that for them other people existed no more than as faces daubed on a backdrop. In that distorted context, Hannay seemed to have especially staged this event.

The Bishop turned to all. 'Now for the surprise. In the first part of the programme, a pageant of children engagingly portrayed the martyrs who suffered gloriously for their mission: to spread the Bible and the Word of God throughout England. Today Britain has a mission to lift the many new peoples of the earth out of their ignorance and to take to them that same Word. Fortunately, we are blessed with new heroes, as you shall see when we reassemble upstairs.'

*

223

In the middle of the stage was a closed mahogany case as tall as a man. While the band played 'Rule, Britannia!', the orphans returned to the stage in blackface, black wigs and 'leopard skins' of spotted muslin. The boys held bamboo spears and cardboard shields; the girls carried coconuts. Their eyes and teeth shone.

'Africans,' Lydia Rowland told Blair.

'I can see that.'

A solemn girl in a tiara and an ermine robe of braided wool rolled over the boards on a canvas ship pushed by two 'Africans'.

'The Queen,' Lydia said.

'Right.'

'Rule, Britannia!' quavered to a finish, and Queen and ship trembled to a halt next to the case. When the applause diminished, Bishop Hannay joined her, thanked her and the other orphans, and let a second round of applause die.

'This is the dawn of a new age. We are exploring a new world, bringing it light in exchange for dark, freedom in exchange for shackles and, instead of primitive survival, a share in a trade that brings tea from Ceylon, rubber from Malaya, steel from Sheffield and cloth from Manchester on steamers from Liverpool that burn Wigan coal, never forgetting that our enterprise is blessed only when the Bible leads the way.

'As you know, my nephew, Lord Rowland, has manifested a passion for this dangerous task. Particularly on the Gold Coast of West Africa, he has laboured to free natives from the yoke of slavers, to bring those natives under the protection of the Crown, and to deliver them from superstitious ignorance by the lamp of the Church.

'Only this morning Lord Rowland arrived in Liverpool from Africa on an Atlantic mail ship. He was on his way at once to London to address the Royal Geographical Society about his explorations in the Gold Coast and the Congo and to report to the Anti-Slavery League about his efforts to stamp out that inhuman trade. Telegrams flew back and forth until we persuaded him to honour this benefit not with a formal speech, but with his presence. He will go immediately from this theatre to the station. I know that London is anxious to receive him, but Lord Rowland shares the family sentiment that Wigan comes first.

'During his travels in Africa Lord Rowland has incidentally gathered artefacts and curiosities that he deemed worthy of study at the Royal Society. He has consented to a first public exhibition of one such specimen here today for this benefit before it travels with him to London. Perhaps I do so with special pride, but I know I speak for us all in welcoming Lord Rowland.'

A slim man with golden hair appeared on stage to take Hannay's handshake. As the Bishop left him on stage alone, every row in the theatre stood to applaud. Lady Rowland proudly rose on tiptoe. As Lydia Rowland clapped, her fan spun on her wrist. The band roared back into 'Rule, Britannia!' with more fervour than before.

'Explorer! Emancipator! Missionary!' the girl Queen started to read her scroll. The rest of her words were overwhelmed by acclamation.

Rowland accepted the homage with an absolute stillness that focused all the more on him. It was a natural theatricality that had worked in Africa as well, Blair remembered. He was a little changed from the more robust man who had first arrived in Accra. That was the effect of Africa, Blair thought. First the skeleton came home, then the flesh, then the shock of leaving equatorial weather for the cold piss of the English spring. He almost felt sorry for the man.

Rowland's hair fell in wings at his forehead and was matched by a wispy beard. The stage lights seemed to lean towards him, to illuminate a balance of even features. Staring towards the rear of the theatre, he had the beauty of someone philosophical, Hamlet before a soliloquy. Like Hamlet, responding absently to adulation as if it were irrelevant, which provoked it more. Hannay made his way back to the front row. Rowland's attention followed the Bishop; his eyes found his sister in the crowd and focused on her for a moment, then on Charlotte, whose arms were stiff by her side. His eyes moved restlessly on until he located Blair in the row behind. There was a glitter to the gaze, a shifting of light within.

'Rule, Britannia!' ended with a flourish of horns, followed by murmurs throughout the theatre. Rowland stepped in front of the mahogany case and executed a diffident nod that seemed to be interpreted as a hero's modest bow. Still sharing the stage, the orphans were a line of white smiles on dark faces. Of course if they really were Africans, Blair thought, they would be running for their lives.

'That is too kind, much too kind. The Bishop has asked me to say a few words.' Rowland paused as if reluctant to intrude. His voice filled the theatre effortlessly. Which was important for explorers; they made their fame with books and lectures as much as exploration. Perhaps he was being petty, Blair told himself, just because he himself hadn't been invited to lecture anywhere but Mary Jaxon's kitchen.

'The journey itself', Rowland said, 'was not remarkable. Passage from Liverpool on a mail ship of the African Steam Ship Line bound for Madeira, the Azores, the Gold Coast, Sierra Leone. Endless trip until we transferred to a frigate of the Royal Navy on patrol to interdict slave ships. Thence to Accra, on the Gold Coast, to pursue slavers on land.'

Rowland brushed his hair from his eyes and took note of the 'native' orphans for the first time. 'On land. The worst feature of coastal Africa is the proliferation of mixed bloods. While Portuguese half-castes are superficially attractive, English blood mixes badly with the African and produces a muddied, mentally enfeebled race. It is one more reason for an Englishman to remember that he has a higher mission in Africa than the Portuguese or Arab trader of flesh.'

What about a mix of Celts, Vikings and Normans? Blair thought.

'Imagine, if you can,' Rowland said, 'a world of profuse and untamed nature, peopled with slaves and slavers, infested by every kind of predator that God in his curiosity could create, infected by a spiritual ignorance that can worship the baboon, the chameleon, the crocodile.' He touched the mahogany case. 'Animals were, in fact, another objective, with the aim to further science – British science, through the study of rare specimens. I repeat that this exhibit is purely scientific and pray that it does not offend.'

Rowland opened the doors of the case. Inside, bedded on white satin, were two black hands cut off at the wrist. Spiky black hair covered the back of one hand. The other was reversed to show a black, deeply creased, leathery palm with flat, triangulate fingers. The wrists wore bands of beaten gold.

'These are the hands of a great soko, or gorilla, that I shot near the Congo River. I had surprised him and his group while they were feeding. I felt deeply privileged to see them because, despite their great size, sightings are so rare. This is only the third specimen brought from Africa.'

Blair heard Charlotte Hannay whisper to Earnshaw, 'You approve?'

Earnshaw said, 'Absolutely. Not only on scientific grounds, but also for national prestige.'

Blair saw Charlotte's eyes darken with revulsion.

'What do you think, Blair?' Earnshaw turned and demanded.

'Maybe the rest is coming in another box.'

'Imagine a gentleman like him standing up to savages and

apes.' Chief Constable Moon insinuated himself next to Blair. 'He seems to know you.'

'I think we know each other.'

'He must cut a figure in Africa.'

'Excellent posture, beautiful clothes.'

'Something else, surely.'

Charlotte looked to catch Blair's answer. Blair saw Rowland look down from the stage at the same moment. 'Totally insane.'

Blair's words were swallowed as the brass band picked up the self-satisfied strains of 'Home Sweet Home'. Rowland listened in the distracted manner of someone listening from a distance. Or about to escape.

Moon tugged on Blair's sleeve.

'What is it?' Blair had to shout to be heard.

Moon shouted back, 'I said, I've found Silcock.'

'Who?'

'Silcock, the man you were after. If you want. It's your investigation.'

Chapter Fifteen

THEY RODE ALONG the canal in the Chief Constable's carriage, all black lacquer and brass like an undertaker's coach. Blair kept his hat on despite the pricking on his temple where the stitches rasped against the hat band. Leveret had come along at Moon's insistence. The afternoon had narrowed to a tunnel of dark clouds. Mill chimneys were lit sideways like columns along the Nile.

Moon was still thrilled by the event they had left. 'Quite a sight, those hands. Educational, as Mr Earnshaw said. What do you think, Mr Leveret? Should we show those hands to every naughty boy in Wigan and scare some improvement?'

'Is that what you'd do?' Blair asked.

'Made all the women take a step back, didn't they? I'd say having a pair of hands like that to show would improve behaviour all the way around.'

'Ask Lord Rowland. Maybe he could get you another pair. The Royal Society could have one pair and you'd have the other. Use them at school or in the home.'

'You're being humorous? Is Mr Blair being humorous?' Moon asked Leveret, who squirmed on his seat like a tall man trying not to be noticed. 'One of the things I liked about your father was that he had no sense of humour at all.'

'He didn't,' Leveret agreed.

'I always knew where he stood, and I'd like to think I know where you stand.'

Leveret looked out of the carriage and nodded.

'I wasn't joking,' Blair told the Chief Constable. 'You're at least the scientist that Rowland is.'

Moon swung the weight of his attention from Leveret to Blair. 'But it must deeply impress the natives when Rowland stands up to a giant ape.'

'It does, I'm sure. He not only stands up to the ape, he tracks it, traps it and blows its head off.'

'Lord Rowland is a marksman, I hear. And specimens, as Mr Earnshaw was saying, are the beginning of zoology.'

'Taxidermy.'

'Well, whatever you call it, it's the start of science and civilization, isn't it?'

Blair let it go. He had thought Rowland was in Cape Town or Zanzibar, halfway round the world. It was a shock to see him in Wigan, hailed like the Second Coming. He also smarted from the idea that he had misread Earnshaw. If the man wasn't a suitor, why was he wasting Charlotte Hannay's time? He poured powder across his palm.

'Arsenic?' Moon said. 'I don't believe that in his expeditions Dr Livingstone uses that, does he?'

'He uses opium.' Blair tossed the dose down and felt a bitterness spread through his mouth and brain. 'Tell me about Silcock.'

'Sort of a thug, sort of a sport. If he didn't take your money at cards, he'd catch you in the alley afterwards. I warned him off Wigan twice in January, the second time after the fire. Anyway, we have him in a corner now.'

'Has anyone asked him about Maypole?'

'No. Have you ever been in trouble with the law yourself, Mr Blair?'

'Why do you ask?'

'Because you have the look. Not quite a wolf in sheep's clothing. More like a wolf with a scarf around his neck. Someone might say, "Oh, he's wearing a collar." I would say, "No, he's planning to eat." When I hear you had a dust-up with Bill Jaxon and got the better of him, it inclines me to think my instinct was right.'

'Where did you hear that?'

'Everywhere. I hear he thinks you're after a favourite girl of his. You're not so stupid as that, are you?'

Blair felt a frying along the sutures that Rose had sewn. Could be arsenic, could be Moon.

'Not so stupid, surely, as that?' Moon repeated. 'The women are worse than the men. A fact. Are you aware that in the infirmaries of the British Army most of the beds are filled with victims of venereal disease passed on by prostitutes and loose women?'

'It's passed both ways, isn't it?'

'But innocently or professionally, that's the difference.'

'In peacetime I thought it was the soldier's profession to pass venereal disease.'

'You have your joke again, Mr Blair, but in the south of England loose women are isolated in special hospitals for their own good. Here in the north there is no control.'

'How would you identify them? Bare arms? Trousers?'

'It's a start.'

'You mean pit girls?'

'I mean that pit girls are females who have reverted to the wild state. It's not just a matter of dresses or trousers. Do you think Parliament would investigate these women if it was just a matter of trousers? Trousers are merely a symbol of civilization. Do I care whether they wear trousers or sea-shells or go about stark naked? Not a fig. But I care about the rules. I can tell you

231

from sad experience that civilization is nothing but rules adopted for the general good. I don't know how it is in the South Seas, but once an Englishwoman has dressed in trousers she has divorced herself from decency or the considerations due her sex. Granted it's only a rule, but it's what separates us from the apes. The pit girl has her allure, there's no denying that. The Bishop himself, when he was a young man, before he was a man of the cloth, used to slip into town through the old Hannay tunnels to call on the girls. Was it Saint Valentine said, "Give me chastity, Lord, but not yet"?'

'Saint Augustine.'

'Well, that was Hannay. More than one girl had to leave Wigan with her ticket punched, if you get my meaning.' Moon leaned forward intimately. 'I ask you, how do Africans civilize their women?'

Blair sat back. 'I've never heard it put that way before. You're a regular anthropologist.'

'A policeman has to have an open mind.'

'They scarify them, put plugs in their noses, plates in their lips, weights on their legs, cut off part of their sexual organs.'

Moon pursed his lips. 'Does it work?'

'The women think it's normal.'

'There you are,' Moon said. 'Best rule of all.'

Canal traffic had to stop at locks to rise or fall to the next stretch of water, but it was clear to Blair as he scrambled down to the towpath that the last lock in Wigan was not functioning at all. Boats idled bow to stern in long lines on either side of the lock, and on the towpaths a crowd had gathered, boatmen joined by patrons from canalside beerhouses, boat children spread out on the banks above.

The boats themselves were marvels of design; fifty-foot

narrow boats were capable of carrying twenty-five tons of coal or, for pottery factories, flint and bones. More, each boat was a home with a six-foot cabin into which a family of seven typically squeezed, the bows of their boats decorated with fanciful white castles or red Lancashire roses. Despite the imminence of rain there was an atmosphere of a crowd diverted by a street pantomime. Tow horses, Clydesdales, stood forgotten at their lines. Dogs raced back and forth on boat decks. Moon, Leveret and Blair had to push their way through.

A boat aimed upstream was in the south lock. Its crew – father, mother, two boys, three girls, agitated dog, goat with enormous teats, two moulting cats – were on deck and looking over the stern tiller at a man chin-deep in water. His clothes swam around him.

A lock was a simple affair of two basins – one for up traffic, the other for down – each with two pairs of gates. The dimensions, however, were exacting; the boat was seven feet across and the lock was eight feet across, leaving six inches of clearance on each side and about a foot at each end. The boat was tied forward until the bow fender nudged the gate, otherwise the man in the water couldn't have been seen at all.

Water level in the locks was controlled by paddles built into the lock gates; these had to be cranked up or down. But it was an old lock, pounded by boats every day; the up gate leaked in noisy sprays and the level was perceptibly rising. It wasn't a bad problem in normal circumstances; the water level would equalize with the down gate open. Now the motion of the water rocked the boat against the walls and thumped it against the downstream gate. Each time the man in the water had to go under and then climb back up to a tenuous handhold on the punched and splintered oak of the gate or the slime-covered bricks of the lock wall.

Moon said, 'Somehow Silcock seems to have caught his foot

in a paddle in the down gate. The lock isn't big enough for Silcock and the boat, but we can't open the up gate without raising the water and drowning him. We can't open the down gate because the boats behind are packed so tight. He's trapped himself very smartly.'

'Why don't you crank the paddle off his foot?' Blair asked.

'That's the obvious solution,' Moon said. 'Every boat carries a crank – a "key" we call it, as Mr Leveret could tell you, one of his grandfathers being a lock-keeper – but the boatman managed to rip off the ratchet nut the key fits on. We could have a hundred keys, but none will work.'

Blair saw divers in the water outside the downstream gate. Moon said, 'The men are diving for the nut but this canal, with all the coal dust that's fell in it, is black as the river Styx. We're waiting for another; in the meantime, how does the old saw go: "For want of a nail a horse was lost, for want of a horse a battle was lost"?'

'How long has Silcock been in?'

'Since six this morning. I told you we'd warned him off twice before and he wouldn't admit to the men who he was until just before the ceremonies.'

'You could have told me as soon as you got there.'

'And miss Lord Rowland? I only trust you'll remember to tell His Lordship and the Bishop how helpful Chief Constable Moon was to you and brought you personally to carry out your private investigation. Mr Leveret, will you make sure of that?'

'Of course.'

'How did it happen?' Blair asked.

'You'll notice there's no bridge here. We tell them not to, but some fools will cross by walking on the gates, usually when they're staggering out of a beerhouse. Silcock must have fallen in. He makes an example, doesn't he?'

'The Chief Constable likes examples,' Leveret said.

'It's what people remember,' Moon said.

Across the top of Silcock's skull wet hair splayed from a gash that was open to the bone.

'How'd he manage that?' Blair asked.

'The boat was tied up in the lock for the night. He must have hit it on the way down.'

'Didn't the boatmen see him?'

'No.'

'You're telling me that the boatman cranked the paddle on to a man's leg and didn't notice?'

'I'm telling you that the boatman was so drunk he wouldn't have noticed the parting of the Red Sea. He was drunk, his wife was drunk, their children were drunk. Probably the dog and cats were drunk too. Right, Mr Leveret?'

Leveret, however, had vanished. As the boat wallowed, a jet of water arced from the up gate the length of the basin. Blair realized that if Silcock's leg wasn't jammed in the paddle and draining the lock to some extent he would have drowned already. Of course if he wasn't trapped he wouldn't drown at all. One of those ancient conundrums. And Wigan did seem to be the sort of place where people slept on the tracks and slipped down old shafts, so why not swim in a canal lock?

Moon shouted down until he got Silcock's attention. 'Silcock, there's a man here with questions for you.'

Fish-eyed, Silcock gasped up from the water.

Blair tried to imagine him dry, with a bowler and a deck of cards. 'Can you move the people away?' he asked Moon.

'These people get little enough entertainment. No pageants, no lords or bishops, no great apes.'

True enough, this was the sort of audience that appreciated public dramas, be it a train wreck or a hanging. This was a tribe the Bible did not mention. Men in plug hats, the descendants of gypsies and Irish navvies, the dark captains of the waterways, and women in blowzy skirts white with ground bone or orange from iron ore. They had assembled before Blair's arrival and were intent on staying for the duration of the performance. Which wouldn't take much longer.

Blair told Moon, 'While I talk to him, you can send for a fire pump or a pump from a mine.'

'And try to lower the Leeds–Liverpool Canal? I think not.'

'Back up the boats and open the gate.'

'Rehitch twenty horses and twenty boats? Not at this point.'

'Amputate,' shouted a man in the crowd.

'Underwater?' another voice asked reasonably.

'Help me.' Silcock grabbed for a diver and almost pulled him under.

Moon said, 'Mr Blair, I'd say you have the stage. If you have any questions, there's no time like the present.'

Blair asked, 'Can you at least get me a rope?'

A boy on the deck eagerly volunteered a mooring line. Blair made a noose and lowered it to Silcock, who slipped his head and arms through, gaining a quarter inch above the water, and fought off the tiller as it swung his way.

'Let the tiller be,' Blair called down. 'Don't think about it.'

Silcock focused on Blair. 'What should I be finking about?'

'Who did this to you?'

'I don't know. I only come back to Wigan last night and I fell in, I suppose, and split my head. I don't remember.'

'Were you drunk?'

'I hope so.'

'What pubs did you go to?'

'I don't know. I was drunk after the first one.'

This drew a laugh from the men on the far side of the lock, which lifted his spirits.

'After the last?'

'I slept for a while, I fink. Then I got up and fell in.'

'Can you think of any enemies?'

'I can fink of a lot,' Silcock claimed, playing to the crowd.

The boat wallowed sideways and chased him under. Being the objects of public attention, the family on board gathered close and watched with acute interest, father and mother both soberly sucking pipes now, the girls lined up with bows in their hair, the boys preening for friends on the bank.

'It's a wonderful example,' Moon said. 'A felon brought down by the hazards of trespass on private property.'

When Silcock came up on the rope, he had lost the little ground he had gained. Blair gave up on subtlety. 'What about Maypole?'

Even *in extremis*, Silcock was baffled. 'What?'

'You saw a Reverend Maypole here in December. You approached him after a rugby match and caught the attention of Chief Constable Moon, who ran you out of town.'

Silcock squinted at the Chief Constable. 'I might've made conversation wiff the man, that's not a crime.'

Blair said, 'You offered to introduce him to a variety of vices. Which vices in particular?'

Silcock took cognizance again of his greater audience; it was an age, after all, of gallows orators.

'Entertainments, maybe. One man's meat, anover man's fish.'

'Girls or boys?'

'Buggery's a bit upper-class for me. Anyway, cards was what I had in mind.'

'Why would you approach a clergyman at all?'

'He played rugby. That's a queer taste for a churchman. If he liked that, maybe he'd like somefing else.'

'You threatened him if he told the police.'

'Never. I fink I said, "No harm done." Those were the words. But not a minute went by before the Chief Constable here had me by the neck. For doing nofing but passing the time wiff a priest. Is that fair?'

He went under. Blair dug in his heels and hauled. When Silcock came up, the rope screwed his head into his shoulders and he had to twist his head to talk. 'This is a difficult fing, being saved.'

The diver outside the lock surfaced and rolled, exhausted, on to his back.

'Are you still game?' Blair asked.

'I'm drowning,' Silcock said.

'Are you game?'

'Yes. I'm game.' His eyes clung to Blair's as if they were hands.

'Did anyone in Wigan point out Maypole to you?'

'The people I associate wiff do not attend church. Not in my circles.'

'Your circles?'

'Travellers, sportsmen, men who like the fancy.'

'The "fancy". You mean fighting circles?'

'Pugilistic circles.'

'With gloves?'

'Bare knuckle. Gloves take away the featrical aspect.'

'The blood?'

'Where there's blood there's silver. When you stop a fight for cuts, you bet again. Makes for more action all around.'

'Rugby?'

'Not a real better's sport. More for miners. I like dogs, cocks, dogs an' rats, ferrets an' rats.'

'Purring? You know, the way miners fight with clogs?'

''S good.'

A diver hauled himself out, walked to Moon and shook his head. Silcock watched as water lapped his nose, the shelves of his eyes.

'Get some other men in,' Blair told Moon.

Moon said, 'There's no point warning a man off if I treat him like a bab when he does come back.'

'Ask me somefing else,' Silcock said.

'Who's the best at purring you ever saw?'

'A poser. Overall, Macarfy in Wigan.'

'You never saw Jaxon?'

'Not in action. I've heard of Jaxon.'

'What did you hear?'

'He's best, according to some. At purring.'

'Who said so?'

'A man named Harvey said he worked wiff Jaxon.'

'Was Harvey his first name or last?'

'I don't know.'

'A miner you played with?'

Silcock went under and his hair lifted like underwater grass. Blair pulled him up, though he felt Silcock's arms almost wrench from their sockets.

Silcock said, 'I wouldn't play wiff a miner. Get me cards all black and bent?'

'Harvey was too clean to be a miner?' To Moon he added, 'Get some divers in the water.'

Moon did nothing but magisterially motion for no one else along the lock to move.

'Clean and unlucky.' Silcock lifted a smile. 'Never knew a man wiff a worse run of luck. I stuck to him like his best friend.'

'He was clean but he worked at the mine with Jaxon? How did you meet Harvey?'

'Cards. If I could do nofing but play cards wiff Harvey, I wouldn't be here.'

He went under again. Silvery bubbles erupted from his mouth. Blair wrapped the rope around his back and heaved, to no effect. The drowning man's eyes were wide above ballooning cheeks, purple from Blair's pulling.

Blair didn't see Leveret return, didn't notice the Hannay estate manager at all until he fitted a foundry wrench the size of a man's leg on to the shaft of broken nut and hauled on the handle as if he were pulling an oar. He adjusted the wrench jaws and hauled again. A deep sound issued from the bottom of the lock and the boats lined up outside the gate shifted from side to side. Moon looked at him and coloured while Leveret turned the wrench more furiously.

Other hands helped Blair pull Silcock out and pump the water from his lungs. Out of the lock, Silcock was a small, sopping figure, a rag still wrapped around the rope. Water had magnified him.

Leveret walked across the lock with the wrench. 'That's what my grandfather, the lock-keeper, would have done.'

Chapter Sixteen

WHEN BLAIR GOT back to his hotel room, he went to the brandy on the stand by the bedroom window. Because the room was lit, he was faced with a reflection that looked like a man underwater.

In his all-but-last moments, when Silcock had claimed whatever dignity he could, bantering from his end of the rope like a sailor on the yardarm of a sinking ship, until only his nose was above water and then only his hands were trying to climb the rope, he had telegraphed his fear to Blair. Blair's hands trembled as if he were still getting the message.

The sluice gate had been so tight it had broken Silcock's ankle bone. He was no innocent victim, God knew; by Silcock's own account, he was a thief, a cheat and a drunk when he hit the water. Though Blair had talked to the family on board, all of them had been inside the cabin because the lock always filled so slowly, it was dark, and no one had heard a sound like a head bouncing off a gunwale.

Someone had laid open Silcock's head, dragged him down into the water of the lock, cranked the gate paddle on to his ankle like the bar of a rat trap and removed the crank. Or, as Moon maintained, Silcock fell head first from the gate, hit the gunwale on the way into the water and was swept into the draining paddle before it could close. As Silcock boasted even after his rescue, he couldn't start to list his enemies. He had never seen Bill Jaxon, and Blair knew from his own experience that Bill couldn't swim. Nothing had been gained by saving Silcock except that the wretch was alive, and that Blair's palms burned from the rope.

First the horse at the pit, now Silcock. Nothing was safe. One moment they were prancing along the green grass, and the next they were sucked under, as if water and mines were alive. He had a comic image of himself roped to everything in sight: Saint Blair, patron of the disappeared.

He carried his glass to the parlour and to the Coroner's report. There was no Harvey, first name or last, among the listed victims of the Hannay explosion, though he was sure he had seen the name before. He went through the list of survivors. No Harvey. Through the witness list. No Harvey. Which pointed out how peculiar it was for Silcock to say that anyone who worked with Bill Jaxon was clean enough to play cards. Men in a coal mine weren't clean. Even brake men and wagon men who worked on the surface were dusted black.

Did it matter? Silcock had nothing to do with Maypole aside from a single conversation after a rugby match and some suggestions that the curate had turned down.

He laid the Coroner's report aside to study Leveret's list from the Home for Women Who Have Fallen for the First Time. Rose Molyneux's skill at surgical stitching was not something picked up by the annual lacing of a Christmas goose. Someone had trained her. Not at the Home, though; no Molyneux had ever registered there.

He was at a dead end. A day with nothing to show but a new enemy in Chief Constable Moon. That was his talent, as Earnshaw had said: making enemies. A bizarre day illuminated by the deliverance of Silcock and the even more miraculous emergence of Rowland. Who had been in the wilderness. Before whom all bowed. Who by now would be in London.

Gorillas had been discovered only thirty years earlier. The first gorilla hide had been shipped ten years ago. Now there were gorilla hands in Wigan. And the wreck of 'Nigger Blair'. Not washed up on the sands of Zanzibar, but on a bishop's leash.

Why should he care? No one else cared about Maypole. He wasn't a detective or a patron saint. It wasn't like him at all.

He returned to the bedroom for the brandy. Rather than face his reflection again, he turned the light down and saw a wall of wrecked, soiled, ruined clouds falling on the town. On the street, specimen bottles shone in the chemist's shop, stacks of tinware towered inside a hardware store, blank faces loomed in the milliner's window. In the alley by the milliner's, a piece of metal caught the street lamp. He thought it might be a coin on the ground until it shifted and he recognized the brass toe of a miner's clog.

Blair stepped back and watched for ten minutes, long enough for his eyes to see legs in the shadow of the alley. It didn't take a man that long to answer a call of nature. He wasn't smoking, so he didn't want to be seen. He could be anyone, but if it was Bill Jaxon that was fine, because now Blair knew where Bill was. Jaxon wasn't about to batter down the doors of Wigan's most respectable hotel, as long as Blair stayed in the Minorca, a ship in port, he was safe.

He filled a glass of brandy and tried to concentrate on Maypole's journal. The sight of densely interwoven lines made him think of the priest bent over the page, like a giant doing needlepoint. He still hadn't decoded the ink-spotted entries for 13 and 14 January, and the only reason to think they might be worth the effort was that they were such knots. Untangled, they were still nonsense, but he reminded himself that Maypole was only a curate, not a devious miner. The lines looked like a Caesar code of transposed letters in blocks of four, which should have been no more than middling difficult, starting with the most frequently used letters, doubled letters, common combinations. The problem was that some combinations seemed so different as to be in another language. Ignoring the blocks and reading the lines again and again for the rhythm, he felt a familiar voice in his inner ear and then the first small words provided the vowel that evoked a name that turned a key that unlocked the rest.

> But King Solomon loved many strange women, together
> with the daughter of the Pharaoh, women of the Moabites,
> Ammonites, Edomites, Zidonians, and Hittites.

So a childhood listening to religious fanatics hadn't been wasted. Brandy didn't hurt, either.

> His wives turned away his heart after other gods, for
> Solomon went after Ashtoreth, the goddess of the
> Zidonians, and after Milcom the abomination of the
> Ammonites.

The abomination of the Ammonites? There was a title for a lawyer's card, Blair thought. Maybe Milcom could join Nuttal, Liptrot, Hopkins and Meek.

> Love undid Solomon, the wisest of men. But is it love or
> clear vision? Solomon saw these women for how beautiful
> they were. As I feel my own eyes open I sense how

dangerous clarity can be. If I have been blind, so has everyone else in Wigan. Perhaps blindness is safety, but now my eyes are unsealed, what can I do?

Blair wished his eyes were opened. At what point had Hannay switched from a quiet inquiry into Maypole's whereabouts to public humiliation of his daughter? Charlotte Hannay might be a nasty bundle, but the process made Blair feel small.

If, instead, it is my imagination and not my eyes, is that wrong? Was it a sin for Solomon to see the beauty in another skin, darker eyes, a fuller mouth? Some day, perhaps, C. and I will see the Holy Land. Every night, though, I am visited by the dreams of Solomon. It is not the Holy Land of Our Lord's blessed agony, which I have imagined like a series of lantern slides, each scene motionless and serene, an awesome progression from Gethsemane to Golgotha, which is a contemplation, in fact, on death. Instead, every sense of mine is alive, and each dream has the colour and tactile vibrancy of revelation.

To Blair, English middle-class character was a coin. Heads: cool, asexual persona. Tails: the visions of the sexually deprived. If Rose Molyneux batted her eyes at Maypole, as a flirt casually bats her eyes at any male, who knew what romance a curate could create in his mind? Unless, of course, they read his journal.

In my dreams I am as dark, sweat as hard and laugh as freely. And escape with her, slipping all the weight of class and learning. If I had the courage to follow her.

A curate refusing a bishop's daughter for a coal-yard belle? Not likely, and yet . . .

Each morning, before light, I hear them pass. Her and a thousand others, with the sound of their clogs like a river of stones. As the Psalm says, they seem 'made in secret, and curiously wrought in the lowest parts of the earth'. It is a Psalm written for Wigan. I found the sound of their passing so odd when I first arrived, and now it seems as natural as the dawn that follows. Later, as I prepare for Low Mass, a counter tide of sheep floods the streets before carriage traffic starts. Christ was a carpenter, he knew the labour and sweat of the men to whom he preached. All morning I attend my rounds with half the heart I should, ashamed that I have never shared the work of Wigan miners. I have the man and only lack the place in which to gain sufficient skill to pass as one of them. Just for a day.

At night, of course, a different agony awaits, when I would, as Solomon said, 'rise now, and go about the city in the streets' and seek her whom I love. I would if I dared.

Two hours later, brandy made a little puddle at the bottom of the glass. The last entry was a weave of lines in a more complex code. Credit was due. Maypole had recapitulated the progress of ciphers, from most primitive to most maddening. The last entry suggested a numerical system. Numerical ciphers were simple puzzles – a matter of transposing letters according to a pattern like 1–2–3, repeated over and over – 'Cat' became 'Dcw' – but it was impossible to break without the key. When the shortcut of birth dates didn't work, Blair understood at once and with a groan from the heart that the key would come from that wellspring of Maypole's inspiration, the Bible.

Number of Apostles, years of Methuselah, cubits of the Holy Tabernacle, or something more divinely, manically obscure like Nehemiah's census of Jerusalem; the children of Elam, numbering 1254, or the children of Zatu, 845.

The second hand of his watch twitched under the crystal, the arrow of a compass seeking a new north.

Blair put the journal in a hiding place behind the mirror, left the lamp on, let himself into the hall, then went down the hotel restaurant stairs and out of the rear entrance through the steam of the kitchen. He didn't feel like a wolf, as Moon had described him. He felt like a goat walking in the track of another goat. Wasn't that his method of finding Maypole?

Flo said, 'Tha can't come here.'

'I want to see Rose.'

'Wait.' She blew out the kitchen lamp and left him to stand in the dark outside.

He waited on the back step, above the mud of the yard, surrounded by the smell of slops and ashpits. To the west, the clouds had ignited into an electrical storm too far off for audible thunder. He couldn't see individual strokes of lightning, only illumination in one valley of thunderheads and then another. Was it distance, he asked himself, or did the screen of smoke that rose from the overlapping lines of chimneypots cut Wigan off? The town seemed to exist as a world to itself – and, as always, to be slightly on fire.

Rose came to the kitchen door so quietly he didn't notice her at first. She wore a dress damp at the shoulders from her hair, and he saw the reason he hadn't heard her approach was that she had rushed from her bath in bare feet. A scent of Pear's soap surrounded her like an aura of sandalwood or myrrh.

'I took the alleys. I know the way now.'

'That's what Flo said.'

'Flo—'

'She's gone. Bill's still looking for you.'

'I'm still hiding from him.'

'Then run somewhere else.'

'I wanted to see you.'

'Bill will kick you t'death if he finds you here.'

'Bill is sure I'm not here. Did Maypole ever talk to you about different kinds of beauty?'

'You came t'ask me that?'

'Did he come seeking through the city, wandering through the streets to say he loved you?'

'Will you go?' Rose pushed him.

Blair leaned against her hands. 'No.'

A curious torpor spread through his body, and he could feel the same lassitude in her, so that she pushed without force and they leaned together. Her hand slid up to his temple and brushed the hair where she had stitched him together.

'I heard there was almost a drowning. They say you helped the man and ruined the Chief Constable's little show, which makes you more fool than hero. Now Moon or Bill will catch you and ruin my good work. You think it's worth it?' She bunched his hair in her fist so that the skin burned. 'Or d'you just want t'go back to Africa?'

'Both.'

'You're a greedy man.'

'That's true.'

Rose led him in. So much for Maypole, he thought. So much for Solomon, too.

Lovely was an inanimate word. Carnality was alive, and Rose had carnality from the thick, darkened curls of her hair to the fine coppery down where her neck sloped to her shoulder. It was the way the cheap dress shifted on her hips as she led him upstairs lit by the cat's eye of a kerosene lamp turned down to its slit. It was stupid animal poetry. Better than poetry because appreciation entered every sense. She was victory over the mind. The Greeks placed physical grace on a level with the arts. Rose would have done well in ancient Athens. Or in Somalia or Ashantiland.

Not that she was a beauty. Someone like Lydia Rowland outshone her easily, but outshone her as a diamond might outshine a fire. A diamond was mere reflection, a fire was alive.

Nor delicate. Her shoulders were wide, the calves of her legs muscled from work. Nor voluptuous. In fact, she was slight of body more than round.

What was it? The allure of the lower class? He didn't think so; he was too lower-class himself to find any erotic quality in rough hands or thin cotton.

But she was all of a piece. She was *there*. In the hall he felt heat on the floorboards where her feet had stepped.

She made herself a small throne of pillows while he rested against the headboard. The room had more variations of shadow than any real light, but to him she looked like a happy jinnee released from a bottle. His body stretched out, as pale and bruised as a body brought down from the cross.

'What would you do now if Bill came in?'

'Right now? I couldn't move, I know that.'

'Bill's big. He's not bright, though, not like you.'

'I'm so bright I'm here with his girl.'

She sprang forward on to his chest, her hair wild around her eyes. 'I'm no one's girl.'

'You're no one's girl.'

While she was on him, she turned his head and examined his temple where it was shaved and stitched.

'Where did you learn nursing?' he asked.

'Sewing cuts is a good thing t'know around a mine is all.'

She kissed him and sat back on the pillows, assembling herself with animal disregard for being naked. He became aware again of the fact that she seemed to have the house only for her own use. For all its age, it was built under a single slate roof that spanned the whole row of houses from corner to corner, looked out on a cobbled courtyard, and was surrounded by terraces of other, almost identical houses and courts.

'Where's Flo? She seemed to dematerialize.'

'That's an expensive word. You went t'school.'

'You did, too. There are a lot of books downstairs.'

'I'm not much of a reader. It's all rote in the schools here. Remember the answer or they whip you with a rule. They beat me all the time. Name a country, I'll tell where it is. I know a hundred words of French, fifty of German. You'll teach me Ashanti.'

'You think I will?'

'I know it. And dance like them, too.'

He had to smile because he could see only her, out of all Englishwomen, in a golden cloth with golden bracelets on her arms.

'You're laughing,' she said.

'Not at you. I like the idea. Tell me, did you know the man who nearly drowned today? Silcock?'

'"As I was going to Saint Ives, I met a man with seven wives." But I never met a man called Silcock.' It was as firm a denial as he had heard from Rose, and he was relieved. 'Tell me about the big affair today. The Hannays and Rowlands and a pair of murderous hands off a great ape, I heard.'

'It wasn't the ape that was murderous. They should have had the hands of the Liverpool ship owners who made their fortunes off the slave trade and now send Rowland to Africa to

250

shoot whatever moves and spread the word of God. The men looked like pallbearers, which is appropriate for the poor gorilla, I suppose. The women each wore a hundred yards of silk, and not one of them looked as good as you.'

'Well, I've nothing on.'

'A chain of gold would suit you fine.'

'That's the sweetest thing you've said so far.'

'If I ever get back to Africa, I'll send one to you.'

'That's sweeter yet.' She had the power to make her whole body look pleased. There were harems that could learn from Rose, Blair thought. 'You're not friends with our Chief Constable Moon.'

'Not quite.'

'I wouldn't let you touch me if you were. He's scary, isn't he, like a fright mask? They say he wears iron leggings for miners' clogs. I wonder if he takes them off when he goes to bed. He told you about pit girls?'

'A menace to the country.'

'Him and the Reverend Chubb. They think they're guarding the gates of Heaven and Hell. They want us crawling t'them for charity, so they can punish us by handing out one crumb instead of two. They say they want us on our knees t'pray, but they just want us on our knees. The union is with them is the sad part. As soon as they drive women off the coal chutes, the wages'll double. Then it'll be a blow for the working class, as long as the class is men. They ask me, "Don't you want a home and kids, Rose?" I say, "If I could have them without a great, slobbery man, yes!" Let them rave about my trousers. I'd shake my bare bum at them, too, if it made them madder.'

'You would, wouldn't you?'

'Then they'd lock me up as a lunatic, of course. Moon would personally swallow the key.'

'How did you know about me and Moon?'

'You've got your spies, I've got mine. Right now I spy a little lie.' She stretched her leg up his. 'You said you couldn't move.'

Lamplight was golden in her eyes. He thought of brass toes waiting in the dark.

She wasn't much more than a girl, but instead of fleshy weight and satiation, she offered abandon, the chance to leave gravity and exhaustion behind. As if he and she were crew and oars and, having made the trip once already, could now take longer strokes that dipped and left iridescent rings expanding in the air.

Why was this profound? Blair wondered. Better than philosophy or medicine. Why are we made to probe beneath the skin so far? Who was in control? Not him, but neither was she. What was frightening to him was how well they orchestrated, how tightly they *fit*, tumbling slowly until the master explorer did not know up from down, his hands on the bedpost, feet against the bar, their breathing grown hoarser and more rhythmic while a rope wrapped around his heart, stiffening with every turn.

There was one more twist. He asked himself, was he following Maypole or becoming Maypole?

'I'll think of you with native girls, won't I?' she said. 'I'll be with some hairy miner. You'll be surrounded by black Amazons.'

'When I am, I'll think of you.'

She wrapped herself in a sheet and hopped from the bed, promising to find something for them to eat.

Idly Blair rose on an elbow and turned the flame up a half turn. On the nightstand by the lamp, a mirror ball offered a smaller, foreshortened version of the room.

He leaned closer to the face in the ball. Africans had been trading with Arabs and Portuguese and Liverpool merchants for years, but there were people up the rivers of the interior who hadn't ever had contact with the outside. When he had shown them a looking-glass, they were first astonished and then wanted to protect the mirror at all costs because it was clearly a piece of them. Which impressed him, because he had always had trouble identifying himself.

He looked at the side of his head where the hair was shaved. Though the skin was black with a vitreous sheen, he could count eight stitches neatly sewn and could even see, despite dried blood, that Rose had used red thread. Which was how Harvey came to him.

Blair remembered the inquest for the Hannay explosion and the death certificate for Bernard Twiss, sixteen, 'recovered at the coal face by his father, Harvey, who failed at first to recognize him. Identified later by a red cloth he used to hold up his trousers.'

Harvey Twiss.

Chapter Seventeen

BLAIR RETURNED TO his hotel and slept until the pre-dawn clatter of miners passed below his window, followed by the muffled baas of sheep being herded into town, the tide and countertide that Maypole had written about in his journal. With this double alarm, he rose and dressed to ride to the pit.

At the Hannay Mine, the mist was a steady downpour in the dark that Wedge, the Manager, ignored. He had a ginger beard and brows that glistened like a hedgerow in the light of his lamp. Outfitted in mackintosh and wellington boots, he led and Blair splashed in his wake across the yard. Beside the tub rails and railway lines that ran to the sorting sheds, other railway lines stretched across the pit yard to the mile-long complex that was the Hannay foundry, brickyard, lumber platform. Hannay-built locomotives, six-wheeled and pony four-wheelers, their boilers cowled in water tanks, stirred blindly without lanterns across the yard, hauling in wooden-bodied wagons spewing sand or hauling out wagons spilling coal. As a train stopped with the rapid fire of buffers colliding, a man ran alongside the wagons, setting brakes with a shunting pole. Simultaneously, coal carts and wagons pulled by heavy horses steaming in the rain lurched over crossings. Miners emerged from the lamp shed

254

with safety lamps dim as embers. Kerosene lanterns hung on poles. A circle of smoke and dust rose from around the yard, from the surface stables, workshops and sorting sheds where coal arrived still warm from the earth.

Blair couldn't see Rose, and he had no intention of visiting her, playing the lord while she tipped coal, though Wedge saw where his gaze had wandered. 'Women are the most extraordinary creatures. Work as hard as a man, paid half as much. But thieves! One of those frail little maids will tuck a forty-pound lump of coal in her knickers and skip all the way home. Some managers try to run their yards from a desk. You have to do the paperwork, but that's what clerks are for. My experience is that if you're not in the yard, the yard will walk away from you. Coal, cable, lamps, you name it. I keep my eye on everybody, and I make sure everybody knows it, including Mr Maypole.'

'He came here often?'

'Often enough.'

'Maybe more than enough.'

'Could be. I tried to impress on him that a pit yard was not a pulpit, that sermons had their time and place. There are, I admit, among the miners, lay ministers who might lead meetings down pit, strictly during their tea. Methodists, in the main. The Bishop says if getting on their knees helps miners get out coal, it's all right with him. I'm afraid, however, that the Reverend Maypole took it the wrong way. Being a young clergyman and all, he thought it gave the other side an unfair advantage. I finally had to ask him not to come till end of day. Very embarrassing. But in the yard, spontaneous preaching can be a hazard.'

'You were in the yard when the fire broke out?'

'Yes, and thank God I was. Every second counts in a situation like that. Fortunately I was in a position to organize immediate assistance to the men below.'

'Exactly where?'

Wedge slowed for a step. 'Here, in fact. I remember the blast as good as knocked me off my feet right here.'

It was too dark for Blair to estimate distances. 'Was there any confusion?'

The manager splashed on. 'Not a bit. As I told the inquest, a properly run pit is prepared for the unexpected. With my first breath I sent runners for help and medical assistance. Then I organized a corps of volunteers and, with the emergency supplies we had on hand, sent them down in the cage. They were on their way in less than five minutes.'

'You know a miner named Jaxon?'

'Jaxon was one of the heroes of the fire.'

'Did you see him before the explosion?'

'Waiting to go down pit with the others. He seemed to be out of sorts, quiet, wearing a muffler. Of course it was a wet day, which brings out the methane, which makes miners glum.'

Something stood out in Blair's mind, though he wasn't sure what. 'There was a manager from another pit, a Molony, who said he saw the smoke from his pit.'

'No wonder.' Wedge waved his arms. 'Smoke like that is half coal dust. Like volcano ash. Here in the yard you couldn't see your hand in front of your face. Horses bolting everywhere. Trains still rolling, and you're trying to remember if you're standing on a track or not. It takes a while to stop a loaded train. Now that I think about it, it was a dark, nasty day, but Molony saw our smoke, no doubt about it.'

'A messenger arrived from George Battie, the underlooker, so you knew the cage was working. But you had to get rescuers organized and that meant have them each sign out a lamp.'

'From the lamp man, right. That's the purpose of the lamp system, to know who is down pit and who is up, especially during the mayhem of a fire.'

'But then the volunteers had to wait at the shaft for the cage to come up. Why was that?'

Wedge slowed and twisted his eyes back towards Blair. 'Pardon?'

'Where was the cage? Battie's messenger had come up. The cage should have been here, you shouldn't have had to wait. Why wasn't the cage still at the surface?'

'I don't see that it matters. It didn't hold us up for more than ten seconds.'

'When every second counted, as you said.'

'Not that much. It didn't matter at the inquest, and it matters less now. Ten seconds, maybe twelve, who knows, and the cage came up and the properly assembled and equipped rescue party went down.'

'No experienced miner, no experienced rescuer, would have tried to go down without your direction?'

'That's correct.'

'What about someone inexperienced, not a miner?'

'Mr Blair, perhaps you've not noticed, but I'm aware who's in my yard.'

'Where is Harvey Twiss?'

Wedge came to a halt. 'Not here, not any more.'

'Where can I find him?'

'Why do you want him?'

'Harvey Twiss was not on the list of rescuers, but according to the inquest report Harvey Twiss found his son. I assume you sent him down. I want to ask him about the explosion.'

'I didn't send him down.'

'The report says he went down.'

'I didn't send him.'

Blair was baffled. He didn't know what they were arguing about.

'Where is he?'

'Harvey Twiss is in the parish graveyard. The same day he buried his boy Bernard, Harvey laid his head on the railway track in time for the London train. Now they're both in the ground, side by side, father and son. But I didn't send him down.'

A rivulet of water ran off Blair's hat. Feeling immensely stupid, he started putting together the Pit Manager's hostility about Twiss and his touchiness about the cage. He squinted through the rain up to the tower, then followed the diagonal of winding cables down to the windowless brick structure of the engine house.

'Twiss was your winder?'

'The only bastard in the yard I couldn't see. The only man I couldn't keep my eyes on, and he abandoned his post.'

'When did you find out?'

'I caught him sneaking up with the boy in his arms. Both black as spades, but I was keeping a sharp look-out for him by then.'

'Then?'

'I discharged Twiss on the spot. No reason to be in the inquest report, nothing to do with the fire, but son or no son, he abandoned his post.'

Inside, the winding house was tall, built to accommodate a steam engine the size and design of a locomotive, although instead of driving and carrying wheels, the rods drove a single vertical eight-foot drum. As cable groaned off the drum and angled up through a door in the house peak, the slates of the roof resonated.

Winding houses appealed to Blair, their great stationary engines like something powering the rotation of the earth. The Hannay machinery was handsome work – a drum of heavy iron, twin pistons and rods of yellow brass, the boiler of riveted steel – all huge and intricate and dwarfing the winder, a man with a pinched face who sat in a mourner's dark hat, overcoat and gloves, a drop suspended from the tip of his nose. Levers at hand, his attention was so given to a white dial lit by two gas lamps that his only reaction to the entrance of Wedge and Blair was a tic of his eyes. Although he was in the centre of an industrial yard, he could have been a creature interred in a tomb. By the door a sign said, 'Admittance to the Engine House is Absolutely Restricted. Signed, The Manager.' Another sign said, 'Do Not Distract the Winder.'

'Don't mind us, Joseph,' Wedge said. He shook water from his beard. 'Joseph is watching the indicator.'

Indicators were familiar to Blair. It was a big word for a simple dial with a single hand. The face of the indicator was marked 'S' at three o'clock for Stop, 'T' at two o'clock for Top, 'B' at ten o'clock for Bottom and 'S' at nine o'clock for Stop. The hand of the indicator was perceptibly inching counter-clockwise to 'B', which meant that a cage of men or tubs was descending the shaft at a speed approaching forty miles an hour. When the hand reached 'B', Joseph would apply the brakes to slow the cage and stop at 'S'. There were no automatic brakes. If he didn't stop the reel, the cage would hurtle with undiminished speed into the bottom of the pit. The metal cage itself might be salvaged, but nothing inside it would survive. Or, going in the opposite direction, if he didn't apply the brakes at 'T', the cage would overwind, crash into the headgear and catapult its contents off the top of the tower.

'No one else comes in?' Blair asked.

'Not allowed,' Wedge said. 'The engine furnace is stoked from the outside.'

'No friends?'

'No.'

'No girls?'

'Never. Joseph is a Temperance man, not like Twiss. Free of vice and gossip and idle tales.'

As the indicator arrow hit 'B', Joseph switched to the brake lever until the dial came to rest at 'S'. The moan of the cable died. For a minute the cage would now stay at the bottom of the pit to be unloaded and loaded again.

Wedge said, 'Joseph, Blair here has a question for you. The day of the explosion, you were stoking outside. On his own volition, short minutes after we felt the force of the explosion, Twiss ran out of this building and sent you in to run the cage. I did not see him do so and I certainly did not send him down pit, isn't that true?'

When Joseph nodded solemnly, Wedge shot Blair a look of vindication.

'You have a clean job indoors now, don't you?' Wedge went on.

Joseph drew a handkerchief from his sleeve. Rain and the first grey, downcast light of day crept through the cable door. Blair wondered whether a little arsenic would be out of place. 'When Harvey Twiss grabbed you and made you winder, was that before the first party of volunteers went down or after?' he asked.

'After,' Joseph said.

'So it's all worked out for the best, hasn't it?' Wedge said.

Joseph blew his nose. Blair was ready to go, but as if his own internal flywheel had been started, Joseph added, 'Twiss was a victim of foul habits. Cards and drink. How Mrs Smallbone put up wi' him, ah'll never know.'

A bell by the dial rang twice, signalling that the cage was ready to be brought up.

'Why would Mrs Smallbone have to put up with Twiss at all?' Blair asked.

Joseph raised his eyes sadly, as if from a bier. 'Twiss roomed at Smallbone's. Making a penny is not a sin, but letting a sinner into a Temperance house never led t'good.' He pushed the cable lever and the drum began its counter-revolution, ponderously to begin with and then with growing speed.

Now that he had light, when he got back outside and was alone, Blair paced distances from the engine house to the shaft, to the overlooker's shed, then to the middle of the yard. Rain was falling too hard for him to see more than an outline of the sorting shed, and nothing of Rose at all.

He saw Charlotte as soon as he returned to his hotel. She was leaving the chemist's shop across the street, a small figure in a walking dress of an obscure colour that he couldn't distinguish as either purple or black. Her face wrapped in a bonnet and veil of the same inky hue, with matching umbrella and gloves, she could only be Charlotte Hannay or someone bereaved. What caught his attention was that she wasn't moving at her customary brisk pace. An unopened umbrella hung in her hand and she went only as far as the milliner's window before she stopped and stood in the rain as if unsure which direction to take. Or more likely, he decided, waiting for her carriage.

He avoided her the way he would walk around a spider, went up to his room, slapped off the rain, had a brandy for the circulation and spread out a map of the Hannay yard. What was clear to him now was that the yard had been a scene of blind confusion as smoke poured out from the explosion below. He was ever more impressed with the heroic efforts of George Battie in the tunnels underground, but Wedge was a poor witness as to what had happened above. The Manager claimed he had dispatched a rescue party in a cage within five minutes of the explosion. Adding the time it would have taken Wedge to get his bearings, find wagons with horses that hadn't bolted, collect volunteers and distribute safety lamps, Blair thought that fifteen minutes was a better estimate.

He opened Maypole's journal, flipping through pages until he found the entry he wanted. Because the lines ran across one another, he had misread the words for 17 January. Not 'How to enter that second world. This is the key,' but 'Twiss is the key.'

If the one place in the Hannay yard that Wedge's eye did not reach was the engine house, the possibility existed that, with the connivance of the winder Harvey Twiss, Maypole could not only have hidden there, but, obscured by the smoke of the fire, crossed unseen the short distance from the house to the shaft and descended in the cage to that realer world he craved just as it was exploding, an act equally idiotic and badly timed. In his fervour it might not occur to a would-be saviour like Maypole that in a mine fire anyone who was not a miner was, at best, an obstacle.

The slightest chill pricked the hairs of Blair's arms and he allowed himself another brandy. From the window he was surprised to see Charlotte Hannay still outside the milliner's shop. She could exchange her bonnet for a hat, he thought – something in barbed wire, perhaps. The milliner herself bobbed out under an umbrella to pantomime an invitation of shelter. Charlotte appeared not only deaf to the offer but blind to traffic as she stepped off the kerb. She crossed Wallgate in front of a milk cart, startling the driver. In his room, Blair threw up his own hand reflexively. A churn tumbled off the cart and spilled a white skirt over cobblestones. Without taking the least notice, Charlotte continued at the same abstracted pace into an alley on the hotel side of the street.

Blair had never had an opportunity to observe Charlotte Hannay apart from their confrontations, when she had always had the busy focus of a wasp. Perhaps it was the rain, but from the perspective of his window there was such a wet and beaten quality to her that he almost felt sympathy and there was something dreamlike about the way she glided out of sight.

He went back to the inquest report and spread out the underground map of the pit. If Maypole did go down, what happened there? Thanks to Battie's cautious advance on the main road, no rescuers were overcome by afterdamp. All the bodies were identified, all the workings searched. Had Maypole, covered in soot, come back up in the cage holding one end of a stretcher? Had he then wandered off in shock? The curate had preached so often about Hell, how had he liked his first taste of it? But wandered to where? Blair found himself back at square one. The more he speculated, the more far-fetched his theory appeared. On the other hand, no one had seen Maypole since. And it was all after the fact. Nothing Twiss or Maypole did or didn't do could have affected the explosion itself.

He returned to the window. Diluted by water, dashed by wheels, the spilled milk was still a visible lace among the stones. A little stone lady, he thought, was what Charlotte Hannay was. He didn't know why, but he picked up his hat and went out in search of her.

The alley was crowded with whelk and oyster stalls, sheep heads crowded together, tripe draped like rags. Blair pushed through to a row of fish barrows, salt cod stacked under canvas sequinned with scales. There was no sign of Charlotte; it didn't help that she was small and dark.

At the other end of the alley was an outdoor market of shoddy-clothes hawkers, mostly Irish, and tinsmiths, mostly gypsies. Stitched and restitched greatcoats and overshirts hung like wet sails. Where the market forked he chose the street that he realized led towards both Scholes Bridge and Maypole's room. In the mud he found the dull imprints of clogs and the single impression of a lady's shoe. Mixed in the mud were twists of sheep scat. He remembered the flock he had seen in the morning and the sheep Maypole had noted in his journal.

Beyond a court of small foundries was another track of clog-flattened mud and the imprint of a shoe so small it could have been a child's slipper. Brick walls bowed and, overhead, roof-lines almost touched, admitting a narrow sheet of rain that disappeared into shadow. He stopped at Maypole's door, sure he would find her visiting, but the room was as bare as he had left it days before, the portrait of Christ the carpenter still hanging in the dark, the boards of the floor dry except for the threshold, where someone had opened the door to glance in only minutes before.

Back in the alley, the way became ever more foul from sheep. Blair come to the knacker's house and pen he had noticed on his first trip to Maypole's. For all the signs of sheep, the pen was empty. Fluffs of sodden wool clung to the chute that ran into the house. Because the house was a terminus without shutters or door, he saw Charlotte within. He checked the impulse to call her name because he could tell she was standing on the edge of the knacker's drop.

What knackers did was to drive sheep off a drop of thirty feet or so to break their legs and make them that much easier to kill. Blair crept close enough to see that an enterprising Wiganer had used the shaft of an old mine. Work had just finished because a faint lantern revealed walls and floor that had been plastered and whitewashed, butcher blocks, meat hooks screwed into walls, and a blood trough that ran below the hooks and emptied into a pail. Blood and offal covered the floor and smeared the walls. What light reached up from the drop had a rose-coloured hue.

The toes of Charlotte's shoes were over the edge and she

leaned forward, headfirst. A dive at that distance would do the job, Blair thought. Although he saw her mainly in silhouette, he imagined her white brow pointing down, her dress snapping out behind her.

'The Ashanti don't have sheep,' Blair said. 'Goats, yes. Monkeys, guinea fowl, lizards, too.'

She balanced, eyes forward, concentrating like a tightrope walker on her next step.

'And grasscutters, which are giant rodents, and forest snails, also giant. A knacker in Kumasi would have a real menagerie.'

When he moved in her direction, she teetered more towards the drop. He retreated a step and she straightened. Magnetic repulsion, he thought, the best example he'd ever seen.

'The snails take enormous cunning. Set out cornmeal and lie in wait by moonlight.'

'And elephants?' she asked softly. 'Do you shoot them, or do you wrestle them to the ground?'

'Snails are more in my line.'

'But not gorillas. You didn't like Rowland's gift, or is it that you don't like my cousin Rowland?'

Although her voice was small, it had its usual allotment of contempt. Under the circumstances, he took this as a good sign.

'I just wonder what Rowland did with the rest of the gorilla.'

'You don't like him,' Charlotte said.

'And Earnshaw, what happened to him?' Blair asked. 'He's not interested in the abattoirs of Wigan?'

'Mr Earnshaw has returned to London.'

On schedule, as Hannay had said? Blair wondered. When he tried to look at Charlotte, she turned her face away. Her dress was spotted and soiled at the hem and her shoes were ruined. At least the draught rising from the old shaft seemed to press her away from the edge. He was surprised that the red reek – the oily, airborne taint wherever blood or animal matter was processed – didn't knock her back. She was tougher than he had thought.

'Blair, what kind of a name is that?' she asked. 'You are supposed to have been born in Wigan. I looked at all the church records. There were no Blairs.'

'It wasn't my mother's name.'

'What was her name?'

'I don't know.'

'Your father's name?'

'No one knows.'

'Haven't you tried to discover who they were?'

'No.'

'You're not curious? You're more interested in John Maypole than you are in yourself?'

'As soon as I find Maypole, I can leave Wigan. That's what I'm interested in.'

'You're the most anonymous man I've ever met.'

'The fact that I'm not interested in Wigan does not make me anonymous.'

'But you are. Not American, African or English. Perhaps you're Irish. Celtic hermits used to sail away from Ireland, letting Providence set their course, praying to be cast ashore in distant lands so they could become anonymous. Do you feel Irish?'

'Sometimes cast ashore, but not Irish.'

'Then there were penitential pilgrims who wandered to the Holy Land to atone for the worst crimes, murder or incest. Do you have something to atone for?'

'Nothing that grand.'

'You haven't been in Wigan long enough, then.'

He tried to circle and inch closer, but she seemed to sense his every move, like a bird ready to take flight. A little dark bird with an umbrella in one wing.

'You don't like anonymity,' Blair said.

'I envy it.' Her voice dropped. 'I envy it. How close are you to finding John?'

'Maypole? I don't know. It would help if you told me something about him.'

'I can't help you. I'm sorry.'

'Anything. He didn't hint about any big plans or fears?'

'John was always full of great plans. He had a great heart.'

'*Had?*'

'See, there you go, picking my words apart.'

'Only trying to understand whether I'm looking for someone dead or alive. Who left on his own or under pressure. Why do I feel I'm the only one who wants to find him?'

'What do you mean?'

'The Bishop hired me to find Maypole, but now he seems to care more about your forgetting him.'

'Is that what you're asking me to do?'

'No. Just tell me, do *you* want me to go on looking?'

'It doesn't matter. Let's not pretend it does.'

'You were engaged to him. You loved him.'

'No. John wanted to help me. I let him, and that was weak of me.' She spread her arms wide.

'Maybe I can help you,' Blair said.

'Is that pity I hear?' she asked as if he had offered her a handful of worms.

'How can I help?' He resisted the urge to try to snatch her back from the drop.

'Can you fly?' Charlotte took a deep breath, turned and planted her toes on the ground and her heels over the edge. With her back to the drop and the poor light, the draught pressed her dress around her so it appeared she was falling. 'When my father was young, he used to leap over shafts.'

'I heard. You're as crazy as he is.'

267

'You're hardly one to talk. Is it true that you're fighting with miners?'

'No.'

'And seeing a pit girl?'

'No.'

She lost her balance for a moment. Her arms wavered. Dirt ticked off the wall of the drop and a stone echoed from below.

'I'll leave Wigan,' Blair said.

'What makes you think I'd care whether you left Wigan?'

'I thought that's what you wanted.'

'My father will find someone else just as terrible as you. Worse, if possible. Thank you for the offer, though. It makes your lies complete.' She raised her umbrella with both hands as a counterweight and stepped from the edge. Blair offered his hand. She ignored it And walked through the dark and muck of the house as if she were crossing the rug of a parlour.

'You've done this before,' Blair said.

'As a girl, a hundred times.' At the door she looked back. 'Was the famous Blair afraid?'

'Yes.'

'Well, I don't think you're lying about that. That's something.'

Chapter Eighteen

IT WAS A WET dusk when the miners returned from the pits. The warming smoke of chimneys created a new layer of clouds, like the smoke of battle after a city had been razed to the ground.

From the belfry of the parish church, Blair focused his telescope from street to street, lamp to lamp. Rain had dissipated to a drizzle that made stone shine and reflected sound. What looked like white smoke rose from a crumbling wall, moved laterally in the wind, turned on itself, scattered, regrouped and wheeled around and around the roofs. Doves.

More doves appeared as miners opened more dovecotes. Dogs barked. A darker plume of smoke approached the London & Northwest station. Horse cabs rolled at a trot down Wallgate to the station. When Blair lifted the telescope he could follow the transit of coal trains across every quadrant of the horizon. It could have been the Russian steppes or the Great Wall of China for all it had to do with him, he thought. He was annoyed that Charlotte Hannay had tried to find his name in a church register. Why would she bother, unless the Hannays maintained a feudal interest and thought of everyone in Wigan as a serf and everyone who left it as an escapee?

He found the blue slate roof of Candle Court. The terrace was all Hannay houses. He had checked at the company office on his way to the hotel, and Molyneux had been the name on the rent book since the previous October. Every week, Rose and Flo paid in rent six times what they earned.

Doves returned to their yards. Night spread in grey and black bands of smoke and haze. In front of hardware stores, assistants cleared pavements of washtubs and hoes. Bone barrows made the rounds of stalls behind the Town Hall. Butchers locked their shutters.

Maypole had always intercepted pit girls at the Scholes Bridge, the main crossing between the miners' neighbourhood and the centre of Wigan. Blair borrowed the tactic with the use of a telescope. At six, he spied a row of black dresses with bustles making a snakelike parade that appeared and vanished at different points, to emerge finally on Wallgate and march to the door directly below him. A Church society that looked like a witches' coven, he thought.

The image of Charlotte on the edge of the drop continued to distract him. She had been so desperate that, in spite of himself, he had felt sympathy, until she stamped on it. Which was fine, he preferred his dislike pure.

At seven, Bill Jaxon passed under the lamp at Scholes Bridge. He was alone and, for all his size, moved quickly out of sight. Blair swept the streets and alleys with his glasses until he found him at the butchers' stalls. From the stalls he had an improved view of the front entrance and side exit of the hotel. Blair had left the lamps burning in his room so that Bill would have something to watch. The safe thing would have been to stay in his room. He decided that safer still was to plunge ahead, find Maypole and leave Wigan completely.

There was a flaw in this reasoning, he knew. It was a little like Charlotte Hannay standing at the drop.

*

Smallbone lived on a narrow street that had half subsided into ancient mines and left the remaining houses leaning as if arrested in the act of collapse. A shout answered Blair's knock and he let himself in.

Though the parlour was unlit, Blair was aware of the gaze of Mrs Smallbone multiplied in portraits and pictures of different Temperance assemblies; the smaller frames had rounded glass that magnified her severe, unrelenting eyes. Chairs were draped in crêpe. A table wore a black skirt, as if half of Mrs Smallbone were present. As he passed, he touched the keys of a harmonium. Ivory: the elephant's graveyard discovered in Wigan. The air itself was pungent with a gritty, oddly familiar scent.

Smallbone was at the table of a kitchen identical with those of Mary Jaxon and Rose Molyneux – a small room ruled by a massive range and warmed by the grate – except that his had been turned into a kind of bomb factory. A rack of strings soaked in great pots of saltpetre on the range. Rope lines of fuses hung from wall to wall to dry. On the floor was the source of the smell that Blair had recognized: small open kegs of gunpowder. Grains of it covered the floor planks and table, and a shadowy haze of it hovered in the air. On the table were empty flutes of waxed paper, a scale and coin-shaped weights, and a coffee mill. There was stature to the scene and to Smallbone, as if he were sitting in no mere miner's kitchen but was a business magnate among glowing foundries and volcanic chimneys.

If Smallbone was startled by his visitor, he recovered well. 'What a pleasant surprise,' he said. 'I wish Mrs Smallbone was here. She's out for the evening. She's a woman for good works. I think tonight it's the improvement of ladies of loose morals, or stoning them t'death. She runs the north of England for the Queen, that's all I know for certain.'

'May I?' Blair slapped rain from his hat into the basin.

'How are you feeling?' Smallbone asked. He seemed to think Blair should be crippled.

'Good.'

'You seem to be. Well, I wish I could offer you something on such a nasty night. Mrs Smallbone left me bread and tea t'dip it in. Us being a Temperance house.'

Blair had brought brandy from the hotel. He set it on the table. 'Is this a mistake, then?'

Smallbone's nose quivered like a root for water, as if it could smell through glass. 'Not that I don't deserve a drink, mind, after a day's work and the long walk back in the rain.'

'I know that Dr Livingstone, the missionary, advised red wine for chills.'

'Well, there you are.'

Smallbone found two cups and, with the interest of a fellow chemist, watched Blair pour. The miner's face was washed to his collar, his hands clean to the cuffs, the lids of his eyes red from the occupational irritation of coal dust. With his first swallow, his eyes teared with relief. 'Mrs Smallbone is probably praying over some heathen right now. The Reverend Chubb is probably kneeling at her side. They're pulling the oars for both of us, bless them.'

'To Mrs Smallbone.'

They drank to her.

'You don't mind if I go on?' Smallbone asked. 'I make my own shots and I make extra to sell on the side.'

'I wouldn't want to bring business to a stop.'

'Thank you.' He produced a long clay pipe and topped the tobacco in the bowl with an ember from the grate.

'You've got enough powder here to blow up half of Wigan.'

Smallbone said proudly, 'All of Wigan.'

'All?'

'Because of the old mines underneath. Firedamp creeps up

into closets and cabinets. We had neighbours who looked in the closet with a lamp and blew themselves up. But the rent is low.'

'They should pay you to live here.'

'I'll tell that t'Bishop Hannay next time I see him.'

'Those are Hannay mines underneath?'

'Hannay mines, Hannay workings. Going back hundreds of years. When the Hannays were Catholic, they used t'run priests underground all the way from Hannay Hall t'Wigan. Catholics knew where t'go for Mass because there'd be a candle in the window. Shall I show you my secret?'

'Please.'

Smallbone scooped gunpowder from the open sack into the funnel of the coffee mill and starting cranking. 'Any idiot can buy gunpowder readymade. It's a government monopoly – fuses, too. Which sounds t'an idiot like a seal of approval, never stopping t'consider that where there's monopoly, quality goes out of the window. Then he makes a shot and it fizzles or kicks up late and blows off his head. See, an anti-monopolist, an expert, understands that it's air between the granules slows down a proper detonation. That's why loose gunpowder will burn but won't blow. So I grind it again because fine grains mean less air and your more dependable blast. Look.'

Smallbone pulled out the drawer of the mill and stirred the powder inside with his finger. 'Fine as ground glass. Of course you need a brass mill or you'll blow yourself up. And you have t'use the powder fresh, especially in rainy weather, or it soaks up water. I've been considering a touch of ammonium nitrate for added punch. What do you think, Mr Blair?'

'I wouldn't bother. You want to break up coal, you don't want it to disappear.'

'An excellent point.' Smallbone emptied the drawer into his hand, poured a stream of powder from his fist on to a scale, sipped from his cup. 'It makes my hand steady.'

When the scales balanced, he poured the gunpowder into a flute, twisted the ends tight and laid his finished shot in the canister.

'Harvey Twiss lived here?' Blair asked.

'Yes. That was a sad case, Harvey and his boy, Bernard.'

'The fire?'

'Harvey didn't get over finding Bernard. We laid the boy out right there in the parlour. Closed coffin. Bernard wasn't a member of the Burial Club, but Mrs Smallbone throws herself into these things. It was all done in crêpe. Mauve. Ham and tea. Poor Harvey was already in his cups, half off his head at the funeral. We never should have let him wander off.'

'To lay his head on the track?'

'So they say.'

'It was Christian of Mrs Smallbone to allow a sportsman to room here.'

'It was,' Smallbone agreed. 'Also, the extra pennies didn't hurt. Saintliness is an expensive business. Between letting the room, selling the shots and winning the bets on Bill we're just able to afford Mrs Smallbone's attendance at Temperance rallies up and down the country. Of course, they would be empty exercises without her.'

'Of course. Twiss was a good mate?'

'We weren't close. A sportsman, but a reliable winder.'

'Were you surprised to hear that Twiss left the winding house to join the rescue? A winder never leaves the house because everyone else counts on him to run the cage. Twiss must have been through explosions before.'

'Maybe not with his boy down pit.'

'Maybe not.'

'In the confusion and all.'

'How's your leg?'

'Pardon?'

'The one you hurt in the explosion?'

'I wasn't hurt.'

'Before the fire.'

'Right, *before*. I'd forgot.' Smallbone relit his pipe. Tiny flashes lit his hands. 'Now that I think about it, tonight's issue was women of questionable morals. Mrs Smallbone wants t'lock them all into hospitals as a sanitary measure t'protect the men. The Reverend Chubb and the police say a loose woman is categorically identifiable by the exposure of her upper arms. The trouble is that all the pit girls in Wigan go about with bare arms.'

'That must keep Mrs Smallbone busy.'

'It does. I tell her she could spare herself the worry and the pit girls the aggravation if she would reclassify whores according t'more pertinent parts of the anatomy.'

Blair refreshed their cups while Smallbone filled another flute of paper. The charge looked like a church candle.

'Between Mrs Smallbone's good works and rugby matches, you must have seen a good amount of Reverend Maypole.'

'An earnest man, very sincere.'

'And a great admirer of miners. Did he ever ask you to show him how to wield a pick?'

'No.'

'Maybe go down an old pit?'

'No.'

'You're sure?'

'One quality I'm proud of is my memory.'

'Which leg was it?' Blair asked.

'Leg?'

'That you hurt before the Hannay explosion?'

'Left. It was my left leg.'

'I thought it was the right.'

'It could have been my right.' Smallbone attacked the crank

275

again. 'It was a terrible blow. I leaned on Bill and we started for the pit eye.'

'Which way?'

'The back road.'

'The main road was closer to your work station and it had fresh, incoming air while the back road had foul. Why would you take the back?'

'A tub was off the rails at the main road. It was easier to try the back.'

'You were lucky. The men in the main road didn't survive.'

'See, that was a good reason t'stay on the back.'

'But you *did* turn to the main road. That's the way Battie was coming with the rescue party, and that's where you met him.'

'Bill heard them.'

'Bill was concussed, he said so at the inquest. When your ears are ringing you don't hear much. Lucky again. Were you waiting for George Battie?'

'For George Battie?'

'I'm just wondering what took you so long? A watch on one of the victims stopped at two forty-four, when it was broken by the explosion. It took Battie more than an hour to locate bodies and clear the gas to reach the point where he met you and Jaxon. It was three forty-five when you and Bill emerged from a cross tunnel midway on to the main road and met up with Battie. I'm just finding it difficult to understand what happened. You must have been clear of the blast and gas, but you only got midway when you met Battie? I wondered what took you so long unless Jaxon was carrying you.'

'Where d'you get all this information?'

'The inquest.'

'I had a bad leg, that's for sure.'

'Yet when you met Battie, you shrugged off the agony of this injured leg to join in the rescue. You "disregarded" the pain, you told the Coroner. Even so, can you explain what took you so long before you met Battie?'

Smallbone filled his fist with gunpowder. 'You know, Bill Jaxon and I are heroes. Everyone agreed. The rest of that inquest is full of shite. Thirteen men in shoes deciding about miners? Lords and lawyers who know as much of us as Mrs Smallbone knows of natives south of the Equator? And expert witnesses who wouldn't know coal from caramels? No one pays attention to a Coroner's report and you shouldn't, either.'

Gunpowder streamed in a black line from Smallbone's fist into a tube. His hand *was* steadier, Blair realized.

'All I want to know is why you and Bill left the coalface, why you took the back road, and what you waited for after the blast.'

Smallbone stacked weights on the scale for a double charge. 'What you should do, Mr Blair, is go back t'where you came from, either Africa or America. You have no idea what you're stirring up.'

'You mean Bill Jaxon and Rose? Tell Bill from me that Rose is a lovely girl, but there's nothing going on between us – just questions about Maypole, that's all.'

'It's not so simple. You can't come t'Wigan and decide in a day who is who or what is what.'

'Unfortunately I can't get out of Wigan until I find Maypole.'

'Then you could be here for ever.'

On his way out the parlour, Blair noticed one picture not in the spirit of the sombre portraits, a photograph of the Smallbones on a beach.

'Blackpool,' Smallbone said from the kitchen door. 'On holidays. All of Wigan goes.'

On a shelf by the photograph was an engraved silver shaving cup. Blair held it to the kitchen light and read, 'A. Smallbone. 3rd Place. Aquatics.'

'Handsome. From Blackpool, too?'

'Years and years ago,' Smallbone said.

'All the same, swimming in the open ocean? Winning third place at Blackpool? Where did you learn to swim like that in Wigan?'

'Canals. In a straight line I can swim for ever.'

Afterwards, standing in the back alley, Blair resisted the impulse to go to Rose's house. He realized he knew the way too well.

Ashpits steamed in the rain. Although windows were shut he heard an oath, a hymn, children screaming up and down stairs. Wigan was a miniature landscape that kept adding new dimensions: clouds, echoes, subterranean chambers.

Smallbone as a swimmer was a new factor. The attack on Silcock was a two-man job. Not the hitting over the head, that was simple. But carrying him to the canal, and there one man to drag him into the water to the bottom of the lock while the other cranked the gate paddle shut on Silcock's leg. All next to a boat of witnesses who would swear they heard not a thing. That was sly, that was Smallbone's sort of work.

He went over the lies Smallbone had told, but he also heard his own dissembling to Charlotte and Smallbone, mostly about Rose. Why would he care what Charlotte thought? Why should he care at all for a pit girl? He could feel the pull, though, as if she were a luxuriant vine that grew at night and reached in his direction.

Chapter Nineteen

'BISHOP'S WEATHER,' Hannay said.

Which meant that the night's rain had evaporated into a morning of high, blue skies and green hills bright as glass. Atop his ecclesiastical gaiters and frockcoat, the Bishop wore a broad straw hat for the expedition. In the same spirit, the Rowlands dressed like a pair of bouquets, Lydia in a dress and sun hat of tulip pink, the mother in a complicated outfit of peony red. In the breeze their silks, tulle and satin trim emitted scents of lavender, and their parasols shuddered like blown flowers. Blair kept pace in boots still damp from the day before. Behind him followed Leveret with a brace of yapping spaniels, and game-keepers bearing wicker hampers.

'Poor Leveret, he does have his hands full.' Lydia covered her smile as Leveret prevented first one dog and then the other from racing up the path. 'Did you have dogs in Africa?' she asked Blair.

'No, too many things in Africa eat dogs.'

Hannay said, 'That's our Blair, always a cheery answer. Look around, Blair. Creation all fresh and new, literally humming with life. You were starting to look a little drawn, that's why I ordered this day up.'

They crested a hill where butterflies trafficked above drifts of small, early daisies. What was disturbing was that at some level Blair felt that the day had indeed been ordered by Hannay. A westerly wind not only polished the hills but pushed smoke east, so that they could not even see evidence of Wigan's chimneys behind them. The only thing that didn't fit was himself: he felt like a poacher who had wandered into a garden party.

He looked back at the oversized hampers. 'I'm surprised we didn't bring a piano.'

'We can next time, if you want,' Hannay said. 'It's all for you.'

'If you want to do me a favour, give me a berth back to the Gold Coast.'

'Forget Africa just for a second, can't you? Here we are on this glorious morning, surrounded by decorative lilies of the field, assured of a healthy outing and a good appetite.'

The spaniels yelped at the faint report of a shot.

'Think of Wordsworth,' Hannay said. '"Am I still a lover of the meadows and mountains and all that we behold from this green earth." Poetry, Blair, is the frame of life. England is a small landscape, but we have exquisite frames.'

The path led up the hill to higher hills of steeply sloping meadows divided by upright stones that enclosed flocks of ewes and lambs, the younger sheep marked with dyes of bright red and blue. A blush of pleasure showed on Lady Rowland's face, as if the climb had caused younger blood to fill her veins.

'We have a game,' she said.

'Daisies,' the Bishop said.

'"My thirst at every rill can slake, and gladly Nature's love partake of Thee, sweet Daisy,"' his sister-in-law said.

'Wordsworth,' Hannay told Blair. 'Too bad Charlotte isn't here. She always wins.'

The sheep started as one at a volley of shots, walked a few steps, then reassembled as an anxious still life. Blair looked for a hunting party, but the sound had drifted from a still higher ridge. The dogs whined for Leveret to let them free.

'You're making progress,' Hannay said.

'You think so?'

'The Reverend Chubb, Chief Constable Moon and Wedge, our Manager, have all complained to Leveret. If that's not progress, what is? Leveret, on the other hand, is your great supporter.'

'And Charlotte?'

'Oh, Charlotte thinks you are a plague. Aren't these butterflies wonderful? Called peacocks, as if we were in Babylon. Well, as close as we can come in England.'

'That Charlotte thinks I'm lower than the pox, is that progress, too?'

'It helps make up her mind. The sooner she helps you, the sooner you'll be gone and then you'll both be happy.'

The miniature peacocks led the way. If England didn't have the fantastical variety of life that Africa did, Blair admitted some relief on encountering insects that weren't intent on sucking, stabbing or boring into him. He looked at his compass and caught Lydia Rowland at his elbow.

'Have you been successful in your search for the Reverend Maypole?'

'No.'

'Do you have suspicions?'

The word was innocent on her lips. The butterflies circled her as if she were delicious.

'No.'

'But Blair has been working hard,' Hannay said. 'I understand he has been interviewing people from every level.'

'That is wonderful to hear,' Lydia said. 'I visited the poor once with the Reverend Maypole and his parishioners were good people with the most patience and the brightest children.

281

We sometimes forget while we go on with our daily lives that we are being made comfortable by men who are hard at work beneath the very ground we walk on.' She faltered at the thought. 'There might be men chipping at coal underneath us at this very moment.'

'That's profound to contemplate,' Leveret said.

'We're a bit far from the pits,' Hannay said.

'Violets,' Lady Rowland said to change the mood.

Lydia brightened gratefully. '"A violet by a mossy stone half hidden from the eye! – Fair as a star, when only one is shining in the sky." Another flower?'

'Hemlock,' Charlotte said. She had come up the path so quietly that no one had noticed. Or she had dodged from shadow to shadow, Blair thought, because she was in a sort of anti-sundress of black silk with matching bonnet, boots and gloves, a cross of the sporting and the funereal. A glare lurked within the shadow of her veil like a flame in a safety lamp. Blair was struck by how young she was despite such grim attire.

At a knoll where the jagged stones of a wall were set into high grass like dragon's teeth, gamekeepers unrolled a Turkish carpet and set out from a hamper a blinding service of silver and mother-of-pearl. The hampers disgorged rabbit pies, Cumberland sausage, potted duck, savoury pies, porcelain jars of chutney, sauce and mustard, biscuits, cheeses and bottles of wine. The gamekeepers imitated footmen, carving pies and handing out plates, and then retired behind the wall. Hannay bowed his head and asked God's blessing on people who were, it struck Blair, already generously blessed. Nevertheless, he felt the site's undeniable appeal, the walls of stone adding a backdrop to the roll and toss of high grass in the wind. A lark lifted from a nest and rose vertically, trilling like a waterpipe.

Air played with the ribbons on the brim of Lydia Rowland's hat as she bent her neck in prayer. When they began to eat and Lydia lifted her veil, kid gloves still on, she delicately cut her rabbit pie and raised each forkful to her bow-shaped mouth. In contrast to Charlotte, who refused to raise her veil to drink or eat.

'Do you ever eat?' Blair asked her.

'When I can stomach it.' She asked her father, 'Why do you persist in inflicting Blair on me?'

'To find my missing curate. You know that. To drag the Reverend John Maypole from wherever he is hiding. Or until it no longer matters whether we find him or not.'

'What do you have against John?'

'What do I have against Maypole?' Hannay repeated the question and answered it idly. 'Not his idealism, because that is a natural stage of a man's life. Not his stupidity, because the greatest fool can sound wise if he simply sticks to the breviary and the Bible. But one thing I did not appreciate was his obsession with reform. Which leads to social agitation, which is not welcome in a Hannay mine.'

'Your uncle means unions,' Lady Rowland told Lydia.

'Blair is going to find him, though,' Lydia said. 'I feel quite sure this will all have a happy ending.'

In the distance, two shots sounded as quickly as a fusillade. The dogs liberated themselves with a sudden tug and escaped in the direction of the sound, their leashes dragging after them.

'Cousin Lydia, what is a happy ending to you?' Charlotte asked. 'Marriage, baby, house calls, balls? Have you considered that it might simply be the chance to have your own life?'

'I do.'

'Pit girls are freer than you. They make a pittance, but have you ever made a penny? Would you uncover your arms, pay your own rent, wear trousers?'

'Who would want to?' Lady Rowland asked.

'Perhaps she wouldn't, but would she dare? Or would freedom crush her life like an empty hatbox?'

'She has all the freedom in the world. Also expectations and obligations,' Lady Rowland said.

'To keep her dance card full but not tiresome, to be bright but not clever, to order dresses from Paris but store them for a year so she will be fashionable but not French.'

'And to marry well and be a benign influence on whoever that man is, yes.'

'Well, cousin,' Charlotte turned back to Lydia, 'you can start with Blair. You pretend to be interested. Scrub him and groom him and teach his tongue softer words until he pads by your side like a lapdog.'

Lydia's eyes welled with hurt. A nearer round of gunshots approached. She shook at the sound and her tears spilled.

Blair said to Charlotte, 'Your father's paying me or I wouldn't be within a thousand miles of this hill. If you're so free, why are you here?'

'Who said I was free?'

Blair escaped. He left the Hannays and Rowlands, climbed the stones, hiked along the wall and watched clouds arrive from the sea. They could be ships bearing him away, he thought. As a boy he had watched clouds, wondering about their routes, and here he was again, as if a day hadn't passed. They sailed overhead while their shadows slid across the hills from west to east. A kestrel hung on the breeze, watching for mice. If the little hawk could stay at this latitude, Blair thought, what points would it pass over? Newfoundland, the Aleutians, Lake Baikal, Minsk, Hamburg, Wigan.

He sank into the grass, closed his eyes and listened to the

far-off trill of larks, the oboe calls of crows. Beneath him he could almost hear the trooping of ants, the tunnelling of moles and worms. He felt his eyelids and hands relax. Grass was better than a bed. He was only aware of falling asleep when he awoke to see a man with a shotgun silhouetted against the sun.

'"I wandered lonely as a cloud that floats on high o'er vales and hills, when all at once I saw a crowd, a host, of golden daffodils." And you.'

Blair rose to his elbows. Rowland had eyes as blue as the sky at his back.

'I see daisies, no daffodils.'

'No matter.' Rowland had hair of tarnished gold worn wild, old tweeds, high boots. He broke the breech, extracted smoking cartridges, and smoothly fed in new ones. *Dispassionately* – that was the word that came to Blair's mind – which carried both the denial and the residue of passion. Rowland reminded him of Maypole's painting of Christ the carpenter. Christ with a gun. The spaniels came running up, one with a bloody magpie in its mouth, the other with a lark.

'I wasn't really hunting. It's just that a gun lends punctuation to a walk.' Rowland patted the dogs and they nuzzled close, smearing his boots and trousers. 'You're somewhat far afield, aren't you? Dreaming of home?'

Blair had been dreaming of the hills outside Kumasi, of palm fronds shifting before a rain and the muezzin's call to prayer.

'Yes.'

'I often come here, too. Out of sight of human habitation. Sometimes I think of Adam. The hunting he must have had in the Garden of Eden. All the animals freshly created. We can search the earth and never know its like.'

'I don't think there was any hunting in the Garden of Eden. Adam survived on fruit, anything but apples. No sex and no blood – I think those were the rules.'

285

'No hunting?'

'Not at first.' Blair got to his feet. 'Remember, it was only after the Flood that God let Noah hunt and put the fear of man in animals.'

'You're with the Bible Society now?'

'With the Bishop.'

'So I'm told.'

Rowland's attention was distracted by sweat on his brow. From a snuffbox he emptied white powder into his palm, twice as much arsenic as Blair had ever seen in one hand before, and ate it in a single swallow.

'Malaria?' Blair asked.

'What a good guess.'

'No guess at all.'

But there was more. Rowland proceeded to wipe the wet residue from his palm on to his cheeks. Blair had heard of women using arsenic to lighten their complexions, but not men.

'White faces frighten the natives,' he said.

'I think in your case that's gilding the lily.'

'You look like Hell too, Blair.'

'White man's graveyard.'

'West Africa?'

'Wigan.'

Rowland brushed the muzzle across Blair's chest. 'You could be right.' His eyes trailed along the wall. 'Are my mother and sister here, too?'

'And the Bishop and your cousin, Charlotte. I thought you were going to bask in glory in London for a while, educate the Royal Society, write a book, entertain the Queen. Why are you back?'

'Something I saw.'

'What?'

Rowland smiled and said simply, 'Something wrong.'

When the two men joined the picnic, Lady Rowland and Lydia were overwhelmed with surprise and delight, but Blair saw nothing so innocent on Hannay's face. Charlotte's greeting to her cousin was a cold kiss through her veil.

It was all strange to Blair. He knew nothing about families. All the same, after the first flurry of excitement and when the Hannays and Rowlands had settled back down on the carpet, it struck him how distant they were with one another. Of course Rowland was at least ten years older than his sister. From what Blair had heard about the English of their class, children were almost instantly shipped off to school, so they might hardly be friends. Charlotte took the farthest corner of the carpet, a still life in black. Lady Rowland was the most natural; she sat close enough to her son to stroke his hand, as if to reassure herself that he had returned in the flesh.

Hannay distributed champagne with the mock solemnity of a Mass. 'The father of the Prodigal Son said, "Quickly, bring out a robe – the best one – and put it on him; put a ring on his finger and sandals on his feet. And get the fatted calf and kill it, and let us eat and celebrate; for this son of mine was dead and is alive again; he was lost and is found!" Even better than a Prodigal Son is a nephew who returns bearing honour and fame.'

Rowland said, 'That is me, I assume, not Blair.'

'That is not amusing. Please,' Lady Rowland said. 'How was London? Tell us about your reception at the Society. How did they like the gift?'

'Those frightening hands,' Lydia said.

Hannay said, 'Since you decided to return, Rowland, the Reverend Chubb would like you to meet some working men. Not a bad idea.'

'Blair says you must have shipped the rest of the gorilla in another box. Is that true?' Charlotte asked.

'Blair would hardly understand what an explorer does,' Lady

287

Rowland said. 'No disrespect to Blair, but he was your father's employee in Africa. He worked for money. Isn't that true, Blair?'

'Still am and still do,' Blair said.

'Such a wonderful familiarity with all of us,' Rowland said.

'Do you feel the slave trade will be coming to an end soon?' Lydia asked her brother.

'Only when Britain protects free men,' Rowland said.

'Britain shipped eight million slaves to the Indies and America,' Blair said. 'Walk around Liverpool and see the African heads carved over the doors. Britain is simply pulling out of the business.'

'If that doesn't show you the difference between idealism and the man who works for cash, what does?' Lady Rowland asked Charlotte.

'What happened to your head?' Rowland asked Blair.

Blair knew that, out of them all, Rowland would be the one to sniff out blood.

'Maybe he tripped in the dark,' Charlotte said.

'Which reminds me,' Rowland said. 'Is Maypole dead yet?'

Hannay said to Charlotte, 'Not dead, but almost buried. Until Maypole is, Blair will be hard at work.' He gave the gamekeepers a nod towards the hampers. 'My God, I've worked up another appetite.'

As soon as the hampers were open, the spaniels stole meat and raced around the perimeter of the party, dodging the efforts of the gamekeepers to catch them. Blair helped Leveret chase them up the hill, and when one of the leads tangled between rocks, free the leash and take the dog in hand.

'Leveret, what the hell is going on?'

The estate manager had been almost perky since the incident at the canal. His face fell at Blair's tone. 'What do you mean?'

'I was supposed to find Maypole. Now it's either find Maypole or look until Charlotte loses interest?'

'Breaks her engagement to Maypole. That's what the Bishop wants.' Leveret kept his head down and worked busily with the leash even though it was unsnagged. 'Then you can go on your way, I suppose.'

'Why wouldn't she? He's disappeared, missing for months. Sorry, Leveret, but I know there was no great romance there, not on her part. She has a walnut for a heart as far as I can see. Why shouldn't she get engaged to someone else?'

Leveret whispered in a rush, 'The Bishop wants her to marry Rowland.'

'Her cousin?'

'Nothing unusual about that.'

'Rowland?'

'The Bishop seized on this idea as soon as John disappeared. Charlotte is resisting. Rowland is a change from John.'

'From Christian martyr to mad dog.'

'Do you know the hundred and thirty-ninth Psalm? "I was made in secret and curiously wrought in the lowest parts of the earth." It seemed to John especially to evoke miners and pit girls. Lord Rowland does not share that sympathy.'

'The hundred and thirty-ninth?'

'It was John's favourite. He started every sermon with it.'

Leading the spaniel along the wall, seeing the black Hannays and the golden Rowlands together, they did seem complete to Blair. Like a completed puzzle, he thought, though exactly what the puzzle was, he still didn't know. Complete and beautiful, the Hannays in their sombre wool and ebony silk, the Rowland women in petal-like folds of crêpe de Chine on the little field of the Persian carpet, on the greater carpet of the hill.

Chapter Twenty

AT HIS HOTEL was a note from George Battie asking him to
visit him at home, but Blair went to his room, poured a brandy
by the lamp and read the final cipher in Maypole's journal by
the number of the curate's favourite psalm.

139139139 . . .

'*Ukn Bsxduhqkj* . . .' became:

> The Apocrypha speaks of Darius, the King of Persians,
> who was so great in his power that all lands feared to
> touch him. Yet he would sit with Apame, his concubine;
> she would sit at his right hand and take the crown from
> his head and put it on her own, and slap the King with her
> left hand. At this Darius would gaze at her with mouth
> agape. If she smiled at him, he laughed; if she lost her
> temper with him, he flattered her, so that she would
> forgive *him*. I have seen Rose do as much. Taunt and leave
> a man pawing the earth like a tethered bull. And now the
> Rose for whom I would give all does the same to me.

Blair could picture Rose Molyneux at the table of Darius the
Great, giving the King a tap, a pout, a steamy glance. She would
have left Darius spinning.

It was no shock to learn that Maypole didn't understand women. Someone in the Bible hadn't either. Blair knew he didn't, he hadn't met enough ordinary women to shape an informed opinion. There had been the crib girls, who were indentured, which meant practically slaves even if they were in California. Natives in Brazil, who *were* slaves. The Ashanti, on the other extreme, who all dressed and acted like the Queen of Sheba. It wasn't the normal range from which to make even a biblical judgement.

'*The Rose for whom I would give all.*' He checked the date on the entry. 14 January. Four days before Maypole disappeared. If Rose Molyneux had also disappeared, the vow would make more sense. Instead she had gone nowhere and denied any tragic romance with Maypole, no matter how obsessed he was with her.

> She says that the Hannays are crazy. Must be, for having ruled so long, since the Conqueror, eight hundred years in Wigan, by custom and by law for being bishops, sheriffs, magistrates, ready to send down or ship off any threat to their authority. It's not a way she says she'd live.

Bold stuff from a pit girl, Blair thought.

A sound like rocks rolling in a flood drew him to the window to see the miners fill the street, shoulder to shoulder, on their trudge home. Wagons and carriages made way. Shoppers and maids shrank into doorways to escape the touch of coal. Some of the miners had lit their pipes, embers bright in the dusk, little lamps for the road. A pebble rapped off Blair's window. He couldn't see who among the dirty caps and dark faces had thrown it.

That deserved a second brandy. The warmth of it grew as he deciphered Maypole's next words.

I have been toughening my hands with brine and secretly practising the walk and work of a miner in an old tunnel. Bill Jaxon, reluctantly, has been a help. His co-operation is essential, but it is based purely on his Rose's mood, not on my mission. I feel like the Pilgrim who sets out on the long journey through the Slough of Despond, into the Valley of Humiliation, to the Hill Difficulty. My muscles ache, even my bones are bent from training. I will only be going a mile down, yet I approach the day with as much excitement as if I were setting off for Africa, the price of my ticket the cost of a pick and lamp. Thus I put my trust in God.

Trust in God? Often a miner's last mistake, Blair thought.

And in my Rose.

Now, that was faith.

Chapter Twenty-One

THE BACKYARDS OF Scholes were black ditches with boilers, turnip plots, sties, ashpits.

George Battie was bent over a tub, shirt off, braces hanging to his knees, to wash his hands by the light of a paraffin lamp. His house was no larger than an ordinary miner's, but as a pit underlooker he was afforded a longer, flagstoned yard, with beds of bare rosebushes and what Blair presumed was a garden shed.

As he let himself in at the alley gate, Blair saw two small girls chasing back and forth on the stones, their frocks so long that they seemed to move without benefit of feet. Each time a rose thorn snagged them, the girls squealed and jumped with mock surprise. Battie was as huge as a statue beside them, his arms and torso grey from coal dust, face black and eyes rimmed red. Vulcan at home, Blair thought. At this time of year, the girls hardly ever saw their father in the daylight. In the dark he left for the mine and in the dark he returned.

'Mr Blair, good of you to come.' Battie applied a bristle brush to his palms. 'I'm sorry, you caught me "in between". When I was young and ambitious I used to have a proper wash every night. Almost died of pneumonia. Have you found the Reverend Maypole?'

'No.'

'You're still asking questions?'

'Yes.'

'Do you mind if I ask *you* a question? Why are you asking about Harvey Twiss? Wedge says you were at the pit.'

'Twiss was a winder who left his post.'

'Twiss had nothing to do with the cause of the fire.'

'He didn't sign for a lamp. According to the Coroner's inquest, the lamp system is foolproof. Every lamp is numbered. Each man was supposed to sign out a lamp before going down, even rescuers. Twiss proved the system didn't work.'

'Mr Blair, you know your way around mines, so you have to know a Coroner's inquest is a fine shower of piss. Girls!'

Battie dried his hands with rags and, still bare to the waist, motioned Blair to pick up the lamp and follow him to the garden shed. The girls trailed after. He opened the door and entered to a sound more like lapping water than clay pots. The girls held their breath until Battie reappeared with a white dove on each hand.

'Fantails. Some prefer acrobatic tumblers or racing homers, but I love the fancies. Each one thinks she's a queen, or a princess at the very least.'

The birds had delicate heads and extravagant tails of crisp snowy white. They preened and spread their feathers as if Battie were their mirror. He set them on the girl's shoulders, and immediately there was a flurry of wings from a hole in the roof of the shed and two more doves lit on Battie's hands.

'See, they fix on you. When you buy a new pair, you keep them in their nests, feed and water them until they mate, and then the family's yours. You cull the squabs for dove pie, but we like to keep as many as we can.'

'Pretty,' a girl said.

'Like miniature swans.' He turned to Blair. 'Harvey Twiss

was my wife's brother. Did you think Wedge would make anyone like Harvey an engine winder without a push?'

'I didn't know you were connected.'

'In Wigan everyone's connected.' Battie turned his hands so that the doves climbed his fingers. 'Did you know that Albert Smallbone's father was a poacher?'

'No.'

'Him and Albert used to sneak out at night. I used to sneak out with them. Pheasant was easiest because they don't roost high up and if you've gentle hands you can pluck them one at a time. Ferrets for rabbits. Albert and I had a pair of spades, and our job was to dig up the ferret before he ate the rabbit. My father would have tattooed me if he knew, but it was the most fun I ever had, flitting like a goblin in the moonlight.' He smiled at the girls as they chased each other, birds hanging on and flapping. 'The lamp system, that's just to make the company sound safe and the families feel better. There are times when we've had to brick in bodies and come up with a number later by sorting out lamps. Were we right? Who knows? But the women think we do. Or pretend to. Were the men dead when we laid the final brick? God, I hope so. But sometimes it's them or all the men in the mine. You hear a blower of gas and it's the breath of Hell. The funny thing is, the last thing you'll probably ever see is a dead canary.' Battie's smile came and went. 'It's a short dash through the smoke from the winding house to the cage. Twiss went down, took a lamp off a body he found in the tunnel and joined the crowd coming from the yard. When they caught up with us at the coalface, I knew at the sight of him that Twiss had broken the regulations. There was nothing to be gained by putting all that in an inquest. He'd lost his boy, and a few days later he had his head crushed by the London train. Anyway, he didn't cause the explosion.'

'What did?'

'I don't know. It was where a shot was going to be. But the fireman, Smallbone, wasn't there. Neither was Jaxon or they would have been dead.'

'Where were they?'

'As I remember, Smallbone says he was injured by a falling rock and Jaxon was helping him out.'

'He can't remember if it was his right leg or his left.'

'Because he's probably lying. If he doesn't have a shot to fire, Albert's a great one for nesting in holes where his sleep isn't bothered by the sound of picks. We'll never know because anyone who could tell us whether Albert left the coalface is dead. And it's a difficult subject to bring up at an inquiry when Smallbone and Jaxon were celebrated heroes. Anyway, what set off the explosion had to be a shot, a lamp or a spark. But no one was there. That's what I go over again and again.'

The girls balanced doves on their heads like plumes, pointed at each other and laughed.

'Twiss was killed by the London train?' Blair asked.

'On the London and Northwest track. It was night. A coal train might have seen him in time, but passenger trains go twice as fast. The Constable said poor Twiss was so drunk he probably didn't feel a thing. I don't see what any of this has to do with finding the Reverend Maypole.'

'It's the cage. After the explosion you sent messengers to the top. The cage should have been up there to bring rescuers back, but they had to wait because someone else had already taken the cage down. It wasn't Twiss, he went down *after* them. So who took the cage?'

'It could have gone down empty.'

'It could have been the Prince of Wales. You said Twiss took a lamp from a body in the tunnel.'

'I asked him because I knew no lamp man would let a

winder sign out a lamp. He took it off a dead man in the main road.'

'After the explosion, were all the lamps accounted for according to the numbers in the lamp man's ledger?'

'Every lamp for every man. This time the numbers matched. Why are you dragging in Maypole?'

'Because I think he got as far as the winding house and when the explosion happened he seized his opportunity. It was a short dash to the cage, as you said.'

'But the Reverend was not allowed in the Hannay yard, not during working hours. It's an easy thing for a miner to slip in, there are no guards and he's only one more dirty face, but a clergyman is something else.'

'That I haven't figured out,' Blair said.

'And where did Maypole go if he did take the cage? No one saw him in the pit and no one saw him come out.'

'I don't know.'

'Twiss stole a safety lamp. What lamp did the Reverend use if all the other lamps in the pit were accounted for?'

'I don't know.'

'Well, it's a fascinating theory, Mr Blair – up to a point.'

Considering the theory's shortcomings, Battie's reaction struck Blair as exquisitely polite.

'Maypole was training in an old tunnel to go into the mine. Where do you think those tunnels would be?'

'Anywhere. You could be standing on them. It's all a honeycomb underneath the houses and you can go for miles if you know how they connect.'

Which was the story with everything in Wigan, Blair thought. 'Twiss was drunk when he died. Who was he drinking with?'

'Bill Jaxon. Jaxon said Harvey went off by himself.'

'Ah. Very melancholy, no doubt?'

'And inclined to rest his cheek on a cold rail. You don't plan to drink with Bill, I hope.'

'I avoid Bill Jaxon when I can.'

'The first sensible thing you've said tonight.'

'I want to come out to the pit tomorrow. There *is* one place he could have gone.'

'Come early. I'd like to see, too.'

The girls circled Battie, crying, 'Daddy, Daddy, Daddy, Daddy, Daddy!'

'A second,' he promised them. He told Blair, 'I don't want to leave you with a false impression. The inquest isn't real, it's only an official version, a procedure for the owners to blame the miners and open up the pit. But on our side, if the pit was shut, if they said it wasn't safe for us, know what we'd do? Rather than starve? We'd fight to go back down again, so we're guilty too.'

The girls begged, 'Be an angel, Daddy, be an angel!'

Battie re-entered the shed. Dark smells of boiled beef and burned dripping drifted across the yards. From the direction of the street, calls to tea vied with the tin horn of a rag man. Battie reappeared with a line of doves perched on each black out-stretched arm. As he let his arms drop an inch, the doves fluttered, giving the illusion that he was taking wing.

'You just caught her. She was going,' Flo said.

'Going where?' Blair asked, but the big girl ducked inside the kitchen door, leaving him on the step. How he had gone from Battie's yard to Rose's he wasn't sure. He seemed to have dream-walked and found himself at her back door. It opened again with Rose on the threshold, a shawl round her shoulders, the velvet ribbon at her neck, a hat on red hair that was half pinned and wild.

'The siren herself,' he said.

'Did Bill see you?' She looked over Blair's shoulder.

'I don't know. We'll find out. There'll be kisses for you and kicks for me.'

She brought her eyes down to him. '"Siren"? I don't remember singing for you.'

'Well, I was coming here anyway. I am Odysseus ship-wrecked. Dante stuck in the ninth circle of Wigan, looking for a glass of gin. My feet led me.'

'I don't think it was your feet.'

'I get your meaning,' Blair admitted.

'My meaning is I don't need your condescension.'

The blue colour cast on her was more than an effect of the night. She had half washed after the day's work, leaving carbon dust like kohl around her eyes and a faint metallic shimmer on her brow. Rose Molyneux, the muse of industry, with a sooty sheen made visible by the pale skin underneath.

'If you want me, say so,' she said.

'If you put it that way, I do.'

'One minute. Then you're gone.'

'Then I'm gone.'

He had graduated to the rank of company because she took the gin into the parlour, perched on the edge of a chair and gave him the settee. She was unwilling to light a lamp that might show him to the street, so they sat in the dark except for the glow cast by the fireplace. Though there were no goblets of gold, she could have reigned at Darius' table, alternately giving the King kisses and taps. She made her own rules. Where Flo had gone to, or how two girls managed a house alone when every room in Scholes was stuffed with lodgers, he didn't ask. She flavoured the gin with tea, that was her nod to etiquette.

'You found the Reverend Maypole?'

'I'm getting to know Maypole, but I haven't found him.'

'How's that, getting t'know him?'

'From his journal.' This was the first Blair had told anyone. 'It's full of notes and thoughts. It's full of you. It's interesting, seeing you through two sets of eyes.'

'Different sets of eyes. You're nowt like him.'

'What was he like?'

She gave him the full pause and let him hang for a moment.

'Good.' In the shadow that hovered around her, the fire lit only her eyes.

'Rose, I don't even know what you really look like. I haven't seen your face clean except that first night, when I was too addled to notice. You're always in the dark or decorated with dust.'

'It's dark when I leave work, and if you have skin in Wigan you wear coal. Should I wash my face for you?'

'Sometime.' He sipped his gin and looked around the room. England was giving him the ability to see in the dark. Pasteboard photographs were stacked by a viewer on the sideboard. He leaned back to pick out the gilt title of *Every Gentlewoman's Guide to Poetry* on a shelf. In a carpetbag were balls of red and orange yarn.

Rose said, 'Flo makes her own hats and knits her own shawls.'

'I remember. But we were talking about you.'

'We were talking about the Reverend Maypole.'

'His obsession with you. The night before he disappeared, you were walking up Scholes Lane with him and he pulled off his collar. I'm still wondering what that was about.'

'I'm still saying it never happened.'

'Maypole wanted to go down the mine.'

'Is that so?'

300

'He was a pilgrim. He had the Hannay Pit confused with the Slough of Despond. He thought you were some kind of angel.'

'I won't be blamed for what men think.'

'But why would he think that?'

'Find him and ask him. That's what you're paid to do.'

'Actually, no. What I'm discovering is that Maypole doesn't matter, dead or alive, found or disappeared. Not to the Bishop. What matters to him is Charlotte. When she gives up her engagement to Maypole, the Reverend can rot and Hannay wouldn't care. He'll pay me, send me on my way and I'm done.'

'You sound pleased.'

'It's a relief if I don't have to find a body. Sometimes I think I've just been hired to drive her crazy.'

'Can you do that?'

'I seem to do it without even trying. She's cold, though. There certainly wasn't any passion between her and Maypole – not on her part.'

'Maybe she didn't want passion. Maybe she wanted a marriage where she was free.'

'Well, she won't have that with Rowland. I didn't believe it when I heard about an engagement to him. They're first cousins. I thought that was frowned on.'

'Not for them, not for nobility.'

'Well, it's what Hannay wants.'

'And Charlotte?'

'At least she'll be rid of me.'

'You'll be sad t'see the last of her?'

'Hardly. Anyway, she's as good as sold.'

'"Sold"? That sounds African.'

'It is. Here's to the upper classes.' He touched his glass to hers.

Rose watched him as she drank, then took off her hat and let it drop to the floor. Not exactly a commitment to stay. A gesture of her own royal interest, Blair thought, the same way Charlotte once dropped shears into a pocket of her skirt.

'"An angel"?' She allowed a smile to suggest itself.

'Well, we can't help what men think.'

'And himself a pilgrim? In the Slough of Despond?'

'The Slough of Despond, the Valley of Humiliation, the Hill Difficulty. What pilgrims need is some bouts of dysentery, malaria and yellow jack.'

'Said he like a devil. You're living up t'your reputation.'

'Or ill fame.'

'Rowland's the one with the great reputation, isn't he?' Rose asked.

'Oh, his reputation is glorious. Explorer, missionary, humanitarian. He took some troops and a guide and found a slave caravan in the Gold Coast. There were a dozen raiders with about a hundred captives from the north on their way to Kumasi. Men yoked together to stop them from escaping. Women and children, too. Rowland started picking off the raiders one by one. He's a hell of a shot.'

'Served them right.'

'When the raiders hid behind the captives, Rowland had his men shoot the captives, too, until the raiders tried to run and he finished them off. The rest of the captives were overjoyed about going home, but Rowland insisted they keep going to the coast so they could report to the Governor and ask for British protection. It's a glorious story, isn't it?'

'It is.' Rose refilled his glass.

'When the chief objected, Rowland shot him and named a new chief. So they went on to the coast. The guide released the women and sneaked them off at night. Rowland kept the men yoked, but every day a few escaped and he shot some to keep the rest in line. About twenty made it to the Governor on the coast to beg for English care, which is why Rowland's reputation has such shine. I was the guide, so I enjoy the darker, more African version of the tale.'

'And he's t'be the next Lord Hannay?'

'It seems that way.'

There was a masklike quality to Rose's face, only betrayed by the glint and roundness of her eyes. 'Maybe you're just envious,' she said, 'because you don't have a name like Hannay.'

'Rowland and Hannay. He'll have two names. Why shouldn't I be envious?'

'Blair isn't a Wigan name.'

'Blair was the man who took me when my mother died.'

'You don't talk about him.'

'He was a gold miner who wore a beaver coat and a bowler hat, confused Shakespeare and the Bible when he was drunk, and was silent when sober. I don't know why he took me when we got to New York, though I'm sure the shipping company was happy to have me off their hands. I think I was like a stray dog to him, and as long as I didn't cry too much or cost too much, he'd keep me. At that time, people with nothing to lose were going to California. He went and I went with him.'

'And struck it rich?'

'Not quite. He was a good enough miner, but it was as if he lived under a dark star. He staked a creek claim when he should have filed for the hillside, and filed for the hillside when he should have dug on the flat. Scientific principles stood on their head to spite him. Quartz led to gravel banks, and when he sold the gravel banks a flood would wash the gravel off a motherlode. That was a good time to steer clear of him. But I wouldn't see him for months at a time, once for a year.'

'A year? How did you live?'

'There were Chinese in the camp and he paid them to feed me. For a long time I thought my name in Chinese was "Hih!" Then I found out it meant "Eat!"'

303

'He was mean t'leave you.'

'I didn't mind. The Chinese were a big family, and the big brothers were explosives experts for the railway. They were my idols. Then there were the crib girls across the road, which was a "Home For Women Who Fall Hourly". It was fairly entertaining, and Blair was okay as long as I returned his books to the shelf after I read them and made him coffee when he was drunk. He gave me and the dog equal attention.'

'Did you love him? Blair, I mean.'

'Sure. I loved the dog too and to be fair, I have to say the dog was more lovable than Blair or me. The old man took me to the School of Mines the last time I saw him and then he went back to California and blew his brains out with a Colt.'

'You're hard.'

He could be harder. He had never pressed her on the issue of her house rent, how she and Flo managed on the wages of pit girls. The money came from somewhere, and Bill Jaxon – with bets won on purring matches – was a likely source. Blair realized that he was willing to preserve the illusion of her independence and the unreal quality of the house because he was afraid that one wrong word would drive her away.

'So you're going to be Mrs Bill Jaxon.'

'Bill thinks so.'

'Bill's still hiding outside my hotel. He'd make a good newel post.'

'Do you envy Bill?'

'A bit.'

'What I mean is, he's real, isn't he? You're some creature from the papers. From the shipping news.'

'I am.'

'Sprung from nothing, you say.'

'Self-created out of my severely limited social exposure to Chinese, whores and miners.'

'No home.'

'Always moving, out of place, *sui generis*.'

'Is that Latin for lonely?'

'Miss Molyneux, you could have made a lawyer.'

She topped his glass. 'What do you call your daughter, the one in Africa?'

'Ah. Her mother and I went around on that. She wanted something English and I wanted something African. We compromised on something biblical.'

'And what was that?'

'Keziah. It means "Rainbow". From the Book of Job.'

'It's a beautiful name,' Rose said.

'A beautiful girl. We're pretty far from the Reverend Maypole.'

'I hope so.'

An unbidden image of George Battie and his two girls came to mind. Blair had assumed plainness in Battie's life and out of a black hole George had scooped up doves.

'You'll be leaving us soon,' Rose said. 'What do you miss most about the Gold Coast, the women or the gold?'

'Hard to say.'

'Why's that?'

Blair picked up the orange ball of yarn from the bag, pulled free a foot of wool shot through with brilliant aniline dye, and tied the yarn into a series of knots. 'They're hard to separate.'

'Knots?'

'Women and gold.'

He cut the knotted yarn with his pocket knife, slid the shawl off Rose's shoulders and tied the yarn around her upper arm. In the light of the fire, with her skin shadowed by coal dust, the bright yarn stood out.

'From top to bottom, a head band of royal purple and golden cloth, necklaces of gold filigree, breastplates of gold threads, armlets and bracelets of glass beads and gold, a skirt of pink, black and gold thread, and anklets of amber beads and golden wires. We'll simply have to use our imagination.'

He cut another length of yarn, knotted it and tied it to her other arm, then cut and knotted more and tied them around her wrists.

'Some of the gold is gold thread and some of it is cast. Some into chains, some into shapes of disks, bells, shells, seeds, cocoons.'

He untied and slipped off her clogs and tied yarn around her bare ankles. He helped her stand. 'Completely covered,' he said.

Her dress was cotton with a vestigial print and shell buttons, as many split as whole. He undid the buttons carefully, not to break them, and revealed a chemise of thin muslin. He slipped his fingers through the shoulder loops and slid the dress and chemise down.

With longer yarn he tied thicker knots. 'Think of a mass of golden necklaces with amulets and Dutch glass beads so heavy that with every move they sway. Strings of golden talismans and animals and in the middle, large as a lump of coal, a golden nugget.'

'My hair?' she asked.

'Your hair's already gold.'

She had a single petticoat of muslin, the meanest cloth of all. She stepped out of that and spread her arms. Someone could look in the window any time, Blair knew. If they squinted, they could see. He tied a final strand around her waist as a golden belt and stood back.

'Am I naked?' she asked.

'To someone else. Not to me.'

*

He carried her upstairs. He sensed that she wanted no man who couldn't do that much. Their faces and mouths pressed together, he tasted gin and salt and coal dust that made him take the steps two at a time. She held him and wrapped around him like a knot. Then they were in bed, his face hot against her belly. Wrapped in gold. She arched and stretched across the bed so that they travelled together and as one.

In Rose, hard work had created grace, the curved muscularity of a wild animal, the lightness and, for her size, the strength. More lithe than thick, steel like a dancer through the legs, an arch to lift both their bodies. Then she turned and devoured him as he devoured her, demanding that nothing be held back. He was besotted with her, soaked, gilt in her black dust, her breasts washed pink from his mouth.

What were they now? English? African?

Lost, Blair thought. Something about making love muddled time and space, rearranged them like limbs. No past, no future, and the present so attenuated that he could breathe fifty times within a second. Bent over her, running his finger between her shoulderblades and down her spine, he could feel time shudder to a halt.

She turned. Her hair, a mop dark with sweat, swept back. The glint of coal dust on her face, her lips swollen, her brow white. Despite her darkness she was lit by a faint reflection of lamplight from his body, the way the moon was sometimes lit only by reflection from the earth, a ghostly illumination called an 'ashen glow'. In that faint light appeared – for a moment – a disturbing, secondary image of someone finer.

'You call this love?' Blair asked.

'I call it fair and equal,' Rose said. 'You're a mess, Mr Blair. You need someone like me.'

'And what would Bill Jaxon do?'

'Bill wouldn't know till we were gone. Then he could kick in somebody else's head for spite.' The flame guttered. She slipped from the bed, knelt by the night stand and lit a new candle. She didn't move like a woman who wore bustles. It was a paradox that hard work had given her so much grace. Fresh wick light in her hair, she jumped back on the bed. 'We could be gone before anyone knew.'

'Gone? I thought you were happy here.'

'I was until you dressed me all in gold. What do I need t'know for Africa?'

'Some pidgin English.'

'Not what we talk in Wigan?'

'Not really. Swahili for general travel. Twi is what the Ashanti speak. If you can read a map, shoot the sun and stay dry in the rainy season, you've pretty much got it licked. Then it's largely a matter of knowing the difference between pyrite and gold and taking quinine in every conceivable form.' He touched the stitches on his head. 'The surgery you've got. You'd do fine in Africa. You could be an Amazon.'

'Then I don't need you? I could go without you.'

'Of course. Just follow the trade winds. That's what trade is, just winds and currents.' He put his hand on her heart and slid his palm down. 'Coal south from Liverpool on the Canary current.' Diagonally up. 'Palm oil west from Africa on the equatorial current.' Across. 'Gold east from the Americas on the Gulf Stream.'

'It's very simple when you put it that way.'

'That's about all I know,' Blair said.

'And you know other routes?'

'Yes.'

'Take me.' She placed her hand on his. 'Take me from Wigan, Mr Blair, and I'll love you t'the day I die.'

308

Chapter Twenty-Two

THE FURNACE WAS as yellow as the vent of a volcano, its light so intense that Blair pulled down the brim of his hat to shield his eyes. The design was plain, a firegrate in an arch of bricks mortared three deep in the stone, an approach ramp lined in brick to separate the fire from a tunnel that ran to seams of Hannay coal. Although the furnace was a mile underground, its dimensions were outsized: two men abreast could have walked on to the grate, and the fire sucked air with a thirst that tugged at Battie and Blair.

Battie shouted, 'It always seems a contradiction to burn oxygen to build a draught, but that's what draws more air from the cage shaft and blows the foul air out. We have to draw fresh. If we introduced foul air full of gas directly into the fire the furnace would explode.'

'You drift it?'

'Right. We channel foul air in a shaft we call the dumb drift that joins well up the chimney, where the updraught's cool enough so gas won't ignite. Good air in, foul air out and that's our ventilation. Twenty-four hours we have to keep it going or the pit stops breathing and then any man down here would be dead.'

A golden plasma floated over a bed of brilliant coals that

seemed to shift as if animated by the heat. The furnace fed on Hannay coal mined from the Hannay seam, a dragon that thrived by consuming itself. A coal bunker had been hacked out of stone at the end of the ramp, where two stokers in gauntlets and sacks with holes cut for their arms waited with a tub of coal. There were always two stokers in case one swooned, Battie had explained.

'Six tons of coal a day we burn in there,' Battie said. Once again, the underlooker had left his hat in his office and tied a handkerchief on his head.

Blair squinted, trying to look into the furnace and protect his eyes at the same time. 'The ashes?'

'Fall through the grate to be collected and dumped. It's been emptied twice since the accident.'

'Could we look anyway?'

'For what?'

'Buttons, bones. Clogs would be burned, but clog irons might be caught in the grate. Maybe nails.'

Battie looked at the stokers, just out of earshot. 'That would be wonderful news down pit, that the Bishop's man is sifting for bodies.'

'Tell them whatever you want.'

Battie motioned Blair to follow him down the ramp to the stokers, who had been watching with gaping curiosity.

'Men, this is Mr Blair, a special visitor to the mine. He's an American who likes to examine every cranny and stir every pot. Do we have a spoon?'

The 'spoon' was a long shovel. Battie took off Blair's hat and replaced it with a canvas hood with a viewplate of smoked mica. 'Mr Blair, you are a great pain in the fundament,' he muttered. He shoved on to Blair's hands a pair of padded canvas gloves that reached to the elbow. 'You're going to have to do this alone. I won't roast a man for a lunatic whim. Wait.' He picked

310

up a wooden bucket and poured water over Blair's hood and gloves.

Dripping, Blair took the shovel and climbed back up the ramp. Despite the viewplate the coals burned white, too bright to look at directly. Like the sun. The heat was stunning, a physical blow.

When stokers threw coal they did it from a safe distance. Blair stabbed the fire directly at the grate. Superheated air forced itself down his throat. Coals rang like glass bells under the shovel's blade. Within his shirt, he felt the hairs of his chest stand and curl. But the beauty was overwhelming. Molten gold shimmering in its own consummation, fold lapping over radiant fold, sparking as he thrust the shovel, looking for what on the dragon's tongue? A gleaming thigh bone, a well-picked rib? Vapour exploded around him and he realized that someone had thrown water at him from behind. He dug away, trying to scratch down to the red of the grate. There was a tug at his arm, and at his side he found Battie in hood and gloves wrapped in steam. Battie pointed. What he was saying, Blair couldn't tell until the underlooker dragged him from the furnace and Blair realized that the shaft of his shovel was on fire and the iron of the blade was a dull, angry red.

The stokers met them halfway down the ramp, doused Blair's shovel and his hood with water. Only when he took off his gloves did he notice that they and his shirt front were scorched.

'Have you been to Hell before?' Battie asked. 'You seem used to the work.'

'I didn't find anything.'

'Nor will you, not without shutting down the fire. Is insanity a requirement for an explorer?'

Blair staggered down the ramp, dizzy from the flames, almost hilarious. 'Now I know what toast feels like.'

Battie followed. 'Absolutely mad. Mr Blair, I'll keep my eyes open. If I find anything more suspicious than the cinder of a cricket's dick, you'll be the first to know.'

A morning downpour greeted Blair at the surface and for once he didn't care because he felt as if he were still smouldering. The yard was an inky pond. Steam hung over engines and horses and the sorting shed, obscuring the screens and pit girls under the overhang. Smoke emanated from kiln, forge and engine chimneys. Devil's weather, he thought, and welcome.

He found his mackintosh under the carriage seat, pulled the coat around himself and staggered to the lamp man's shed. Battie had said that after the explosion all the lamps had been accounted for. Blair didn't doubt him, but there was a way to check. He didn't remember all the safety-lamp numbers listed in the Coroner's report but he recalled two: 091 signed for by Bill Jaxon and 125 by Smallbone. What if one or other lamp had never been signed out again? It was just an idea and he didn't know where it led, but he went through the lamp man's ledger until the pages were almost as wet as he was. Safety lamps 091 and 125 had been signed out every working day since the explosion. Blair decided he was about as good a detective as Maypole was a miner.

The window of the shed streaked with rain, and this reminded him of Maypole's journal, the lines reading down as well as across. What was it the poor son of bitch wrote the day before he disappeared? 'Tomorrow is the great adventure!'

Blair found Leveret at Hannay Hall, in the stables, a brick court with a tower and a portcullis, like a defendable castle. The estate manager was in the courtyard, kneeling on wet cobblestones in boots and great coat, intent on the task of grooming a giant Shire mare, combing mud from her feathers, the long hair around the hoof. The giant horse rested her muzzle on Leveret's back. Despite the rain, beast and man both looked content.

In a corner, a farrier hammered a red ribbon of iron on an anvil. As stalls were mucked out, horses clopped across open passageways; one side seemed given to workhorses, the other to hunters. It was a scene stately and bucolic, Blair thought, where gentry massed in hunting pink to ride to hounds. Maybe where generations of Hannays had deflowered maids. It was odd how he now looked at things through Rose's eyes.

He was feverish, whether from malaria or the furnace he couldn't tell. Rose kept coming unbidden to his mind because he didn't know if she had been serious or playing when she suggested leaving with him. It wasn't only his feeling responsible for someone's rash decision. It made her real. Perhaps what made her more than a series of moments all in the present was – because of her suggestion – a sense of her future. If it took the setting of her bed and a smudge of coal transferred from her skin to his – well, that was the coarse nature of man. He had promised nothing. Perhaps it had all been a joke of hers. Or a mystery, like her house. It left him distracted. Stabbing at the furnace, he had thought of her. He tipped his head back and let rain cool his face. '"The deeper the shaft, the greater the heat" is a miner's rule.'

'Blair!' Leveret blushed. 'I'd never heard that.'

'You don't have enough stablemen to do the grooming?'

'Yes, but I enjoy it. To manage an estate, you can't just keep your eyes open, you have to put your hands on.' Leveret snapped mud off the comb with each pass; where he had combed, the hair was white and silky. 'I've worked in every part of the estate. Farming, stables, sheep, gardens, even the brewery.

I was raised to be the estate manager. John used to say I was like Adam in the Garden of Eden, because Adam was put there to oversee Eden, not to own it. I feel fortunate that Bishop Hannay has so much faith in me. I've never aspired to be a Hannay, I wouldn't want to be a Hannay.'

'Maypole could have owned it – some of it.'

'Charlotte's income is all.'

'Quite a lot for a curate with two suits to his name.' Even as Blair spoke, Rose returned to mind. What dowry could a pit girl bring? Wages? A jar of coins, money she had earned, which lowered its value in the eyes of the world. Better an heirloom that came with family prospects, expectations a man could borrow against. 'When we went down the mine you said something I should have asked you about. You said you had been down a mine before, an old one about ten feet deep.'

'An abandoned pit on the Wigan side of the grounds.'

'Did you ever mention it to Maypole?'

'That's why I went down. He asked if I knew of one, so I took him.'

'When?'

'It was after the New Year. John was curious. There are a number of tunnels here, actually, some used as priest holes – hiding places – when the Hannays were Catholic hundreds of years ago. This tunnel is inside the grounds at the north gate, about fifty yards to your right as you leave.' Leveret shifted and picked up the opposite hoof. 'I feel I've served you badly. I've served John poorly, too.'

'You have been conspicuous by your absence. Except for the picnic yesterday and you were busy with dogs then. You're always busy with four-legged animals.'

'Just hiding my embarrassment because I didn't tell you everything when you first arrived on the train.'

'You didn't tell me about Charlotte. About the Bishop's getting her to give up on Maypole and agree to Rowland.'

'I'm afraid so. This gives you such a wrong impression of the Hannays and of Charlotte. You've caught them at a bad point.'

'And I'm sure the sun shines in England most of the time. So it's me or Rowland in a way. Charlotte is stuck with me until she agrees to marry him? In the meantime I'm stuck with them?'

'That's one way to put it.'

'Fine, I'll drive Charlotte to it.'

'That's beneath you. You wouldn't do that.'

'Nothing is beneath me. I'm wet, I'm burned and I'm ready to leave. Like Earnshaw. Earnshaw was a set-up, wasn't he? The great reformer? He was brought by Hannay to keep Charlotte entertained. You told me Earnshaw wasn't courting, so you knew everything.'

'Charlotte is wealthy and attractive.'

'Charlotte has the allure of a young asp. Anyway, I don't like being another Earnshaw, and I don't like being part of the set-up for Rowland.'

'He's the future Lord Hannay.'

'He is a homicidal maniac. What a family!' Blair combed his hair with his fingers, it occurred to him that the horse was better groomed. 'You told me that Charlotte has her own cottage in the grounds. Where?'

'Why do you ask?'

'I want to talk to her, to reason with her.'

'It's the quarry cottage. Back on the lane, past the Home, you'll see the quarry, and then you can't miss the house. What if she won't talk to you?'

'Well, I still have my original option. I find Maypole wherever he's rotting or hiding. Hannay didn't pay Maypole to disappear, did he?'

315

'John wouldn't, no more than you.'
'You never stop hoping, do you?'

The lane was two furrows in a blanket of last year's leaves. Beeches green with moss and black with soot held back a tangle of thorns dripping water. Half a mile on, one side opened to a meadow with a flock of sheep white against a backdrop of trees while the other side offered glimpses of houses on Wigan Lane, no longer distant but approaching the perimeter of Hannay Hall.

One last turn brought Blair over a hill and along a stone wall that protected the traveller from falling into an abyss where the entire other side of the hill had been carved out. He stopped to look from the height of the carriage he had borrowed from Leveret. The drop was at least a hundred feet, the gritstone wall overgrown with algae and desperately hanging shrubs, the bottom a dismal lake lost in shadow. The house that seemed to go with the quarry, though, made a contrast. Its bottom storey was built from dun-coloured quarry stones, but the upper façade was white Tudor, a chevron of black beams capped with a cheerfully coxcombed red-tile roof. Between cottage and quarry were a small stable, greenhouse and dovecote. Around the house itself was a border of rosebushes that were bare and daffodils just opening their hoods. Smoke trailed from a tall brick chimney. Everything about the house seemed inviting.

When Blair knocked at the door there was no answer. Since he had seen the smoke, he went back to the kitchen door. There was no response there, either. Through the window the kitchen was dark, a long table set for one, a pastry on a plate beside an exotic orange. In the hallway were candlelight and a young woman in a white dress that mirrored the flame. He saw her clearly only for a moment before she blew the candle out.

From her red hair he had thought at first that she was Rose, but her face was too round. In a way she resembled both Charlotte and Rose; yet Charlotte would have regarded him with cool outrage, Rose with the languid indifference of a cat. All he had seen staring out of this girl's eyes was panic.

He called through the door, again received silence in return, and he could almost feel the easing of floorboards as she retreated deeper into the hall. The quality of her dress, a watered silk, suggested a specimen of the upper class. Her fear, though, made him speculate that she might be one of Charlotte's charges from the Home for Women, a fallen pit or factory girl hiding in the cottage from a righteous father. Whichever, neither rapping nor calling could entice her to the door.

He gave up and drove away. Rain steamed off his horse. He remembered that he looked like a gypsy, a tinker, trouble of one sort or another. Not the kind of face that opened doors.

To a degree, not finding Charlotte at home was a relief. He didn't know what he had expected to say to her, whether to explain his relative innocence about the Bishop's motives, or to give the devil in himself full rein and whip her towards Rowland. If he had received anything but aristocratic contempt from Charlotte, detected a single heartbeat of human softness or warmth, anything like Rose, it would be different. At the knacker's drop he had offered to leave Wigan, and Charlotte had thrown the offer back in his face, as if she were picking up a rag on a stick.

His mood was accompanied by a darkening wind and a scrabbling of branches overhead. He lit the carriage lamps, though he trusted more to the horse's good sense than to what he could see. Why he had even contemplated a second offer of truce to Charlotte he no longer knew.

The grounds were coming to an end; by his compass, the lane was bearing north, away from Wigan. A gust picked leaves and swirled them around him like bats. When he was beginning to think he had lost his way, the road showed two brilliant, parallel lines of light and from far ahead came the low beat of thunder.

In that blinding instant it struck Blair how extraordinary in their different ways Charlotte and Rose were, and how nothing but the most ordinary prettiness shone from the face of the girl in the house. Charlotte and Rose were fashioned in opposite ways, but both were gold, just as the third girl was dross.

The north gate was of wrought iron that had long ago rusted open. Tall beeches had been replaced by evergreens limping in the wind. Following Leveret's instructions, Blair paced off fifty steps and found himself waist-high in bracken. In the beam of his bull's-eye lamp, over a wave of ornate ferns, was a birch, always the first tree growing on coal slag.

At the tree he heard a ping of rain on metal. He tracked the tapping to a three-foot iron square that he swung back on a hinge, and the ping was blown away by a draught rising from below. He lowered the lamp slowly. Methane loved old pits, and he wanted to leave Wigan on foot, not through the air. Unlike a miner's lamp, a bull's-eye lantern was not designed for reading gas because the flame was enclosed in metal and aimed through a lens. All he could go by was the colour. The light stayed a safe yellow as it picked out a tunnel floor ten feet down. There were no rails, placing the mine back in a time when coal was dragged in sledges. Blair went to the carriage and returned with a rope that he secured to the birch. He rigged the lamp through his belt and went hand over hand down the rope into the shaft.

The floor was wet and slick, the timbers of the walls and roof bowing from age and rot. The open area of the pit eye was supported by free-standing pillars of corrupted stone; he thought a hard breath might bring them down. The tunnel was a miniature operation compared to the Hannay Pit, but the genesis of Hannay industry. There were hundreds of mines like this around Wigan, and thousands of even earlier ones, 'bell pits' that were nothing but holes hollowed out for coal until they collapsed.

Feeling one-eyed, he followed his lamp into the tunnel. He saw no footprints, but the fact that the shaft cover had opened at all suggested that the mine had been visited recently.

As the tunnel dipped, water striped the walls at the angle of descent. Toadstools fringed the ceiling. On damper walls glittered a remnant of coal carved out and hauled away long ago. His light caught a tail vanishing into a hole; there would be rats, mice, beetles; nature abhorred a vacuum. As the roof lowered, he fell into a miner's stooped walk. Big men had trouble learning the gait. 'My muscles ache,' Maypole had written.

The tunnel ended fifty yards on, where the coal strata had abruptly dipped and dropped out of reach, and dust had accumulated against a gritstone wall. A free-standing pillar of coal was left in the middle of the tunnel and Blair imagined the temptation it must have been to miners who were paid only by the coal they brought out. Still, it was important to come out alive.

He searched in sweeps of the light. Pearly, half-formed hands of stalactites reached down from the roof. A blank pool lay underneath. In the ebony powder at the pillar's base was the horseshoe print of a clog iron. Scuff marks on the stone floor could have been made by someone trying to get used to the stiff, rocking action of clogs. But more than walking had been practised. The walls were scarred with pick marks that ran straight as a chord and then scattered in clumsy imitation.

The tunnel had the chill of a crypt. Blair shivered and

319

treated himself to a sip of brandy. When he put the flask away, he saw another curiosity, a brattice – canvas stretched on a wooden frame – leaning against the end wall. Brattices were used to direct ventilation between tunnels. This was a single, primitive tunnel with no need for brattices at all. Unless it was hiding something behind it.

As he approached the canvas a timber knocked off his hat. When Blair twisted to catch it, he was blown off his feet. He spun through the air and rolled end over end. The tunnel filled with powder smoke, he was choking on it even while he didn't know whether he was up or down. His eyes smarted, blinded. His head rang as if his eardrums had burst.

On hands and knees, he crawled around the floor, found the lamp, still lit, and burned his fingers before he got it upright because he could tell only by touch. He crawled in the other direction, feeling his way until he reached water falling through the shaft. He looked up into the rain with his eyes wide open until they were washed enough for him to see. His body felt slapped by a giant hand, though he found no blood or broken bones, only a round hole that ran through the oilskin of his raincoat, jacket and his shirt. He wet a handkerchief, tied it over his nose and mouth, and went unsteadily back into the tunnel.

In the atmosphere at the end of the tunnel, smoke and dust still swirled and eddied. The canvas had been knocked aside by a device with a fat, wooden stock and a short, flared barrel that sat like a cannon on a steel ring. It was called a spring gun. Below the trigger ran a chain with rings tied to strings. Blair brushed dirt away. The strings were attached to cords stretched across the tunnel floor. When a man tripped a cord, as he had, the gun swivelled in his direction and the trigger snapped shut. A spring gun wasn't for game, but for poachers. A mankiller, outlawed, but still used.

Blair aimed his lamp along the muzzle. In the coal pillar just behind where he had stood was a steel rod an inch in diameter, and driven so firmly into the coal that it couldn't be budged. But for his stumble, he would be bleeding to death. Born and died in Wigan. Funny when he thought about it. To leave, go around the world and come back home for this. With his penknife he cut off a piece of trip string. It was woven cotton, the sort for wicks and fuses.

Hearing returned as the sound of water insinuated itself, dripping with clocklike regularity from the roof to the smooth, pulsing surface of the pool below.

He had never before experienced the panic of being trapped underground. Standing in what should have been his grave, he felt fear blow down the back of his neck.

It was midnight when Blair got back to his room. He tore off his shirt. A red sear ran along his ribs.

He pulled off the rest of his damp clothes, poured himself a brandy and went to the window. The street was black and yellow, wet stones reflecting lamps. A constable in a helmet and cape shuffled up Wallgate as slowly as a sleepwalker. He stared into the void behind the shops. There was no reflection from brass toecaps to be seen, no knock of clogs to be heard.

Traps had an anonymous character. Anyone could have set the spring gun. Maypole's journal and the height of the pick marks on the tunnel walls indicated Jaxon. But the use of fuse string as trip wire and the slyness of the trap suggested Smallbone, that one-man factory of homemade explosives. As a former poacher, Smallbone would be familiar with spring guns.

This didn't exhaust the possibilities. George Battie had been a poacher and he didn't want the Coroner's inquest reopened.

And who had directed Blair to the tunnel but Leveret? He had proof of nothing. He could have been assassinated by the Temperance League or the Wigan Brass Band.

He touched the welt, proof of only one thing. It was time to go.

Chapter Twenty-Three

AT THE IRONMONGER'S, Blair bought the stout sort of luggage covered in American canvas called a Railway Companion, along with rope, bath towels, a four-inch length of one-inch-diameter rod, a pair of wrenches and a pound sack of gunpowder. He didn't buy one, but noticed miner's safety lamps at attention on a shelf. Then he drove out to Hannay Hall and detoured to the Home for Women.

This time he approached the mock castle of the Home from the garden side. Through the long windows at the stairs he saw grey uniforms rushing to class or catechism, a stir like doves in a stone loft. Damp weather had cleared the benches outside. No one, not even a gardener, was visible on the long slope of the lawn between the Home at the top and the hedge at the bottom.

On the near side of the hedge was one small, recognizable figure. In a black dress and leather gauntlets, Charlotte Hannay was again pruning her roses. Her wide-brimmed hat sagged in the mist and copper strands of hair stuck to her cheek. Between trees and garden was a space of twenty yards. Blair knew she saw him coming, though she didn't look in his direction. The raw welt on his ribs asked to be coddled, but he had the sense that no weakness should be revealed to Charlotte Hannay.

'Do they ever bloom?' he asked. 'You seem to get most of your pleasure from cutting them back.'

She gave him not a glance. The rose garden was a perfect setting for her precisely because there were no roses. A rose garden should have roses as pink as English faces, Blair thought. If there were, though, she would probably decapitate them. With her pruning shears' curved blades, Charlotte Hannay put him in mind of a figure from the French Revolution, one of those women who happily attended Madame Guillotine. Her dress glistened as if she had been in the garden all morning, although there were few clippings in the basket that straddled the path. Except for her pallor and habitual frown, she could have made a not unattractive young woman, he thought, though that was like saying a wasp made a pretty insect except for its sting.

'Didn't I warn you not to come here again?' Charlotte asked.

'You did.'

She snipped off a long cane with red barbs. Switch in one hand, shears in the other, she straightened up.

'You intend to whip me, neuter me, or both?' Blair asked.

'Whatever would serve as the best reminder.'

She tossed the cane towards the basket and bent over the next plant. She trimmed the top twigs, making a way to reach in and prune the middle stems. Though the gauntlets protected her to the elbow, the silk sleeves of her arms were torn.

Blair said, 'No need, anyway. I'm leaving Wigan. You're not the only one, apparently, who'd like to see me go.'

Charlotte didn't bother to respond. As she trimmed dead wood, he noticed that her work slowed to a meditative pace. He expected her to charge him with prowling outside her cottage too, but she said not a word about it.

Blair said, 'I think in time I could have found Maypole. What I have discovered already is that I'm more interested in finding him than anyone else. It's clear this is not about a missing man. All your father wants is for you to give up a dead

324

engagement and then I'm free to go back to Africa. Am I correct so far?'

'It doesn't actually matter.'

'You don't care if I find Maypole. You would have helped me if you did. I got interested in him and his fate, but that's not worth being killed for. It makes me feel stupid to admit it. Anyway, I apologize for being used against you. I had no idea this was about you. The main thing is, I want to go and you want me to go.'

Charlotte bent among the stems. With each snip, Blair pictured another red rose dropping. 'The main thing is,' she said, 'I won't marry Rowland.'

'Marry who you want. The problem is the longer I'm here, the more I find. He had another life besides you. I think you want me to go now rather than later. Just tell the Bishop you're no longer interested in Maypole. Then the Bishop blesses me and sends me on my way, and you and I are square.'

'You are a worm, Blair.'

'That's not the answer I was looking for.' He felt a rush of blood as if she had hit him. 'Very well, do you know a pit girl named Rose Molyneux?'

Wind pressed the brim of Charlotte's hat. Blair realized that she must be cold in her thin dress and shoes. But where was she colder, he wondered, inside or out?

'I don't recall the name.'

'Reverend Maypole was infatuated with her.'

'I doubt that.'

Blair glanced towards the Home. 'She has some skill at surgery. I thought she might have picked it up in one of your classes. Maypole might have met her here.'

'Describe her,' Charlotte said.

'Physically, I'd have to say she was ordinarily attractive. She has red hair and a great deal of spirit, and that sets her apart. I wouldn't say she was intellectual, but she's quickwitted and direct. A free spirit. You rescue these girls, you must have a fair opinion of them.'

'I rescue them because they are not free, because they are working girls who are abandoned by their suitors or abused by their fathers. Otherwise the babies go to the orphanage, and the mothers, who are usually not much more than children themselves, descend in three steps – from Reverend Chubb's care, to the workshop, to prostitution. We make them free.'

'Well, Maypole thought Rose was a free spirit without your care. He was taken with her.'

'And was this regard reciprocated?'

'No. I think Rose was flattered by Maypole's attentions, but that's all. I don't think she had anything to do with his disappearance. The affair was mainly in his head.'

'As if you knew John Maypole.'

'What I'm getting at—'

A cane snapped. Charlotte threw it lightly aside. 'Let me guess. That I will be embarrassed by revelations of the Reverend Maypole's romantic attachment to another woman – an earthy, working-class woman – unless you end your inquiry? Is that right?'

'More or less, since you put it that way.'

'Devoid of emotion as I allegedly am, I can work these things out.'

'Good. Do you remember what your father said about closing the Home if there was a public scandal? I think Maypole's infatuation would qualify as that. All your saintly work will be undone.'

Charlotte approached a bush with canes already pruned to the nub. While she removed her gauntlet to feel for shoots, a liqueur of water and compost swam into her shoes.

'Let us be clear. You would force me to marry Rowland so

that you could collect money from my father and go back to Africa? If that's the case, I'll give you money and the ticket.'

'But you can't give me the work in West Africa your father can, and that's what I need.'

'You are lower than a worm. You are an extortionist.'

'It's not hard. I haven't seen one tear, one sign of human sympathy from you for that poor bastard Maypole. Not one word of help for me. Now you can find him on your own, if you care.'

'Perhaps you are simply too ignorant to understand the dimensions of the damage you could do. This is the only haven in the north of England where women pregnant out of wedlock are not treated as criminals or outcasts. We turn them from victims into employable, useful persons. Can you grasp that?'

'This is a doll's house where you dress poor girls in grey dresses. Your little world. You're the grey princess, the coal princess. What fun they have, I'm sure.'

'You'd wreck it all to get at me?'

'Unless you tell your father what he wants and I get what I need. As soon as I'm gone, you can change your mind. Or don't.'

Charlotte turned her back on Blair and moved to a plant already cut to a single Y of bare canes. She ran her hand lightly over the barbs in a slow, reflective search for shoots, until Blair realized she wasn't going to say anything more to him, that he had been dismissed.

Blair lowered himself by rope down into the mine and followed the same route as the night before, wrenches in his belt, taking care to sweep the floor with the light of his bull's-eye lantern for new trip wires. The spring gun sat at the end of the tunnel, the rod it had shot still lodged in the coal. The gun looked more like a stepson of a cannon than a rifle, and the sight of it made him wince.

He studied the pick marks on the wall as if he were an archaeologist in an ancient tomb. Miners used short-shafted picks because they worked in cramped conditions, and, all things being equal, the height of the work tended to indicate the size of the man. The marks were unusually high from the floor, Bill Jaxon's height, and expertly straight as a taut string, except where they went suddenly askew. At the same height but off-line and badly hit: too hard, too soft, or off the point. As the mishits went on, however, they improved. Jaxon and Maypole were both big men. Blair imagined the miner instructing the curate on the stroke and rhythm of the ancient craft of hewing coal. But why? If Maypole just wanted to slip underground to preach, he needed only to look like a miner, not to attempt the work. Winning coal with a pick was not something learned in a day or a week. Real miners would turn him out as a fraud and a danger.

A mystery never to be solved, Blair decided. The spring gun was all he'd come for. It was an ungainly forty pounds of hardwood stock and iron barrel on a base made from an iron wheel. Even after he had unbolted the gun from its base, the barrel made hard carrying under a roof that stooped to four feet in places. He laid the gun near the pit eye, went back for the base and was returning when an apparition of a spider the size of a man dropped through the shaft and hung in mid-air.

'Who is that?' The Reverend Chubb blinked at the dark and made vaguely swimming motions with his arms and legs. His hair, tie and wattles swayed as he hung. A hand from above held on to his belt.

'Is it Blair?' a voice asked.

'It is too black down here,' Chubb said.

'It's me.' Blair set the base down beside the gun.

'Good work, Chubb,' the voice said, and the Reverend rose again like an angel on a wire. Blair pulled himself up the rope to the surface, where Chubb stood dizzily reassembling his loose parts. Rowland kicked the shaft cover shut and leaned against the birch in a negligent way, like a poet who happened to be carrying a shotgun rather than a poem. His yellow hair was uncombed, his eyes bright as crystal set off by red lids.

'Very disagreeable and uncomfortable,' Chubb muttered to his chin.

'The work of a moment,' Rowland said, 'for which you have my gratitude, which is no small matter when you consider that I will be Lord Hannay and your living will be dependent on my good will. Otherwise you will eke out your final years like a cockle sucking on a pier.'

'I was pleased to oblige,' Chubb said.

'That is the wonderful thing about the Established Church,' Rowland told Blair. 'They do oblige. What are you doing here? We found a carriage standing in the lane and began beating the bushes for the driver.'

'Looking for the Reverend Chubb's missing curate. Chief Constable Moon suggested that he might have fallen down an old shaft.'

'There are a thousand abandoned shafts in Wigan.'

'I can only try.'

'Well, we'll prove the veracity of your claim. Moon is with us. Besides, there's something I want to tell you about. You'll join the party.'

They moved through stands of larch and oak. Besides Rowland, Blair, Chubb and Moon ranged gamekeepers on either side. Amid a fine rain fell heavier drops from branches. Wet leaves muffled the men's steps and soiled their trouser cuffs.

After being underground, Blair enjoyed the open air in spite of the company. Rowland bragged about his shotgun, a gift from the Royal Geographical Society. It was the custom product of a London gunmaker, with narrow double barrels and a breech engraved with lions and elands like the head of an elegant cane.

A woodpecker made an undulating flight across a clearing and alighted on the trunk of a larch fifty yards ahead. The bird crossed its black and white wings behind its back and had started to probe beneath the bark when Rowland fired and nailed its head to the tree. 'A tight pattern,' he said.

A finch panicked across the clearing. 'Too far,' Blair said.

Rowland shot and the bird split like a pillow, golden feathers wafting to the ground.

The advantage with arsenic, Blair thought, was that it did hone the eye and induce illusions of omnipotence; he wished he had brought some himself. Of course the peak was usually followed by a trough.

The keepers ran forward to pluck the kills and stuff the fluffs and feathers into silk sacks.

Rowland reloaded as he walked. 'There is a use for everything and employment for every man. England's strength is specialization, Blair. One man collects iron, another tin, another rags, another bones. One man collects horse manure for fertilizer, another dog shit for dye works. Feathers make fish lures. Nothing wasted, everyone gainfully employed. I think it will be wonderful to be Lord Hannay.'

Moon loomed at Blair's shoulder. 'First you fish in the canals. Now, I understand you have been popping in and out of holes.'

'You told me Maypole might have fallen in a shaft.'

'I'm flattered you took my suggestion so much to heart. I have to warn you, though, that this side of Wigan is practically a Swiss cheese. There are tunnels, they say, that go all the way to Candle Court.'

'In Catholic days,' Chubb said, still smarting.

You don't put the local vicar down a hole like a ferret even if you are lord of the manor, Blair thought. Which would be precisely why Rowland did it, to establish his exception to all rules. It was the way the Hannays did everything.

Rowland said, 'I've been teasing Chubb about evolution. The problem with the Bible is that it claims we are all created in the image of God. It makes a great deal more sense that we share a mutual ancestor with the apes, and that the races of man show the same scientific evolution from Negroids and Asiatics to Hamites, your Arabs, and Semites, your Jews, to the modern Anglo-Saxon.'

'I've seen too many Englishmen tip over canoes.'

'There are different English, just as there are ladies and pit girls. There's a reason those women do that sort of work. It's natural selection. I forget, Blair, what was your mother?'

'I forget, too.'

'Anyway, it gives me a sense of welcome and confidence to have representatives of the Church and the Law at my side. To know that they look forward to a time when I will be truly home. Of course the Bishop will be Lord Hannay for many years to come, I'm sure. We wish him the longest possible life.'

A starling passed with the flight of a stone skipping on water. Rowland fired and the bird turned a cartwheel. He asked Blair, 'Take you back to Africa?'

'It certainly does. Too bad you can't have some dead pachyderms lying around the grounds.'

'Shooting is the pinprick of reality, Blair. Otherwise everything is dull. A little bang, a little blood, and things come to life. Are you following this, Chubb? You might be able to use it for a sermon.'

'I don't understand why you want Blair along, My Lord.' Chubb was stumbling after them.

'Because Blair knows what I'm talking about and you don't. Moon, do you?'

Moon swept a branch aside for Rowland. 'I have some appreciation, My Lord.'

'Then we'll have some interesting times. But, Moon, you should have seen Blair in the Gold Coast. There are plenty of English on the coast, but in the interior there was only Blair. And Arabs, but they don't count. Not much of a marksman, but he knew his way. Spoke the lingo like a pasha. See, there are two Blairs. The mythic Blair in Africa and the lifesize Blair here. Have I done your portrait, Blair? Is your nose too long or out of joint? It's just that in Africa you had a certain style. It's sad to see you so reduced. There you go, looking at your compass again.'

'Thanks for the walk. I'm off,' Blair said.

Rowland said, 'Wait.'

From the mine, they had gone east through the first stands of trees and south-east through a screen of willows to the slag heap of another abandoned mine. Birches, as if they preferred to slum, grew on the slag. Behind the trees was a box hedge and a house.

Rowland climbed the pile. The wind was warmer, and the sky, if anything, was lower and darker than before. His face had a malarial shine. He pointed to a greening copse of alders another fifty yards on and directed Moon to lead Chubb and the keepers in that direction and scare the game up. Again he asked Blair to wait.

'I didn't tell you about the reception at the Royal Geographical Society. I wish you could have been there. I think every member of the Society was. Some of the Royal Family, too, to show their interest in items African and geographic and anti-slavery. We began with a champagne and an exhibit of the maps and intriguing artifacts. The hands of the gorilla were a great success. They wanted more parts, of course. At the end they hung a silver medal and ribbon around my neck and presented me with the gun. A brilliant affair. I could have stayed in London and been fêted for the next six months, but I felt I should be here. You haven't found Maypole.'

'No.'

'But you've found something. Charlotte can't hate you this much for nothing. What is it?'

'You want to marry her?'

'That's the whole point of your exercise. Have you learned anything that would help force the issue? The Bishop is not the only man who can send you to Africa.'

'You'd do that?'

'I would describe how you came to me full of contrition, begging for a second chance. Just tell me about Maypole.'

'Miss Hannay would want to keep the Home for Women going.'

'Who cares about her Home for Women? Keep her busy. Why not? I could shut it when I want. What is this information?'

Rose's name was on Blair's lips , but a hooting and cranking of noisemakers broke out among the trees. Moon and the gamekeepers could have been boys let out of school, he thought. A flock of redwings lifted, sleek black with chevrons of crimson. Rowland fired twice rapidly. The keepers kept up the din and as the birds turned in confusion, Rowland reloaded and shot again while the men stamped through underbrush.

Blair walked around the hedge to the driveway of the house, noticing that the gravel was unraked and the flagstones leading from the driveway to the door were obscured by weeds. It was not a worker's house but a full three storeys of brick propriety isolated in a corner of the Hannay grounds; he would have said an estate manager's house or the residence of a pretentious Hannay company officer. Wrought-iron balconies too grand for their windows decorated the front. An oppressive pediment of stone, a cap from Athens, weighted the brick facade. Ugly, empty, perhaps, but not in disrepair.

Rowland fired and a window shattered.

Blair asked, 'Have you considered the possibility that someone's inside?'

'I don't think so. Do you know why I was in Africa?'

'I don't know why the English do anything.'

Rowland aimed his gift from the Royal Society, fired and a second pane split.

'I had no occupation, only expectations. I went to make a name for myself, and who was there to get in my way but you. I return home and here you are again. That's perverse.'

'I'm working for the Bishop, that's all.'

'He says you're helping us. I want you to prove it. What can this information about Maypole be?'

'Shall we go attack some barns?'

Rowland shot at two upper windows. One blew in, the other left a fang of glass.

'There's something I don't understand,' Blair said. 'You're the next Lord Hannay anyway. There must be any number of eligible women who'd like a title. Beautiful, talented, as avaricious as you. Why do you want to marry Charlotte?'

Rowland's eye wandered from Blair to take in the alders, the mist and the hills beyond, and a wistful expression appeared on his face. 'Because I have imagined it all my life. Because she comes with the property.'

He shivered. Blair caught an overripe mix of cologne and sweat and garlicky breath, the scent the body surrendered when arsenic burned to the bottom of the wick.

'No, I don't have any information. Nothing about Maypole

and as for Charlotte Hannay, she hates me,' he said. 'I don't think that's news.'

As rain drummed, ringlets drooped on Rowland's marble brow. Blair didn't think about the house with broken windows. He imagined the dimmed lights of the map room of the Royal Society, the white rows of evening clothes, a medal around Rowland's neck. He said, 'Let me see your hand.'

Rowland put out his left hand. White streaks lined his nails, and the heel of his hand was a horny callus, trademarks of arsenic addiction. Did any member of the Royal Family notice them on the reception line? Blair wondered. Would they have noticed antlers sprouting from Rowland's head? When he scratched the palm, Rowland yanked it back in pain. Burning palms were another sign of arsenic collapse. 'You'll be dead in a year,' he said.

'So might we both of our diseases or our cures.'

'We have that in common.'

'If I felt better I'd shoot you now, but I don't have the strength to drag your body anywhere.'

'It comes in waves. You'll feel better soon.'

'I expect so.'

Blair left Rowland on the driveway and went around the screen of the hedge, controlling the urge to break into a run. By the time he was past the slag heaps, though, his stride lengthened and, gaining speed, he dodged through the willows on the far side.

Reference points were different in the rain, but Blair followed his compass. Water poured in when he opened the mine cover. He let himself down, found the spring gun and, like a man putting the shot with both arms, threw it up through the shaft on to the ground, then swung the base up and hauled himself out. Carrying gun and base, he waded through bracken to where the carriage was still tied, the horse snickering in the downpour. He opened the suitcase, the Railway Companion, and packed the gun and base in towels. Soaked and covered in mud, he whipped the horse on to the path as if Rowland might ride one more wave of energy and fly after him.

At the hotel, he assembled the gun on the threshold of his bedroom with three separate trip strings stretched into the sitting room and rigged between chairs. He approached the bedroom from different ways; each time he touched a string, the snout of the barrel swivelled in his direction and the flintlock slapped shut. He rammed home gunpowder, a linen wad and the rod and sat down in the dark to have some of his own arsenic and brandy. But with the image of Rowland before him, arsenic lost its appeal. Brandy wouldn't help either. The problem wasn't malaria, he decided, it was fear. Between Bill Jaxon, Smallbone and Rowland, he was afraid to leave his room, afraid to answer the door without artillery.

He heard clogs marching home in the street below. The storm ended and the night went from dark to black, as if Wigan had been inverted over an abyss. He felt the fear lapping like water. Nigger Blair in a chair too afraid to move.

Finally, he stepped carefully over the trip strings, uncocked the gun's hammer, pushed the spring gun under the bed, opened his knapsack and from a chamois cloth unwrapped a gleam, the brass tube of his telescope.

He went out of the rear door of the hotel and took the darkest crossing of the street to the parish church, where the whisper of an evening service was taking place at the front pews. The Reverend Chubb shuffled around the altar. While the congregation muttered a response, Blair slipped into the tower and climbed the stairs.

From the parapet at the top, the lack of a moon revealed how little illumination street lamps actually cast. Wigan was a black lake, the pavements incidentally visible by the spill of window light.

For once, rain had succeeded in cleaning the air. Stars shone with a clarity and generosity that made the tower seem to rise towards them. He brought out both the telescope and a tripod of adjustable legs with brass fittings that he screwed into the bottom of the telescope and set on the wall.

It depended where a viewer was. Orion stalked the Equator, where the Gold Coast lay. The stars of the southern hemisphere gathered in white archipelagos, leaving dark seas in between. Wigan's northern sky was more evenly ablaze, a bed of burning coal. Where a viewer was, however, depended on the planets – on the Pole Star and the Morning Star, but most of all on Jupiter. It was white to the naked eye. To the telescope, though, the planet revealed rose-coloured bands and three moons. Io, a pinpoint of red, hung to the left of Jupiter, and to the right were the grey pearls, Ganymede and Callisto.

As his eye continued to focus and adjust, Jupiter grew and intensified into a disc of roseate paper. Features sharpened: the Great Red Spot and ribboned currents light and dark. With nothing but addition, it was possible to determine the longitude of any visible place on Jupiter. Better, with Blair's dog-eared book of Jovian tables and Jupiter's moons, he could determine his longitude on Earth. This was the way navigators did it before the chronometer. It was the way, without an expensive watch, that Blair still did it.

In an hour, the moons shifted. Io swung wider. Blair had once seen them through a big Newtonian telescope which

revealed colours that he had never forgotten, so that as Ganymede and Callisto overlapped they changed colour to bitter,
frozen blue. From Jupiter's shadow rose the fourth and largest
moon, Europa, smooth as a yellow stone.

'What are you doing?'

Blair glanced behind him. He had allowed his attention to
depend too much on everyone in Wigan wearing clogs or boots;
Charlotte Hannay had climbed the tower in shoes like slippers.
She seemed dressed the same as she had been in the morning,
perhaps a little more disarranged, although it was hard for him
to tell in the dark.

He put his eye back to the telescope. 'Finding out where I
am. What are *you* doing here?'

'Leveret told me the different places that you went.'

Which meant she had been looking for him, Blair thought,
although she didn't seem ready to say for what.

'Why are you doing that? You can look at any map,'
Charlotte said.

'It's interesting. It calms the nerves. Jupiter has four moons,
and they've been observed for centuries. We know when each is
supposed to rise according to Greenwich Mean Time. The
difference in time is where you are. The longitude, at least. And
it's a lovely fact: there's this clock up in the sky that we can all
check.'

Moons rose fast. Europa was already half into the light
shared by its sister moons. He made notes on paper.

'You're covered in dirt. Where have you been?' Charlotte
asked.

'Poking around.'

'Exploring?'

'Yes, "walking up and down in the earth". That's what Satan
says in the Bible, which proves Satan was an explorer. Or at
least a miner.'

'You've read the Bible?'

'I've read the Bible. When you're snowbound in a cabin for the winter, you read the Bible more than most preachers. Although it's fair to say I think missionaries are stooges for millionaires who are trying to sell Manchester flannel to the world. Of course that's just one man's opinion.'

'So what else have you gleaned from the Bible, aside from the conceit that Satan was a miner?'

'God was a mapmaker.'

'Really?'

'Without a doubt. Nothing but maps. In the beginning a void, waters, heavens, earth, and then He lays out the Garden of Eden.'

'That is indeed the reading of a small mind.'

'No, of a fellow professional. Forget Adam and Eve. The important information is, "A river flows out of Eden to water the garden; and from there it divides and becomes four branches. The name of the first is Pishon; it is the one that flows around the whole land of Havilah, where there is gold; and the gold of that land is good."'

'You are obsessed with gold.'

'So was God, obviously. Take a look.'

Blair moved to the side, but Charlotte waited until he was at arm's length before she took his place at the eyepiece. She looked through the tube longer than he expected.

'I do see little white dots. I didn't even know you could see that much,' she said.

'In Africa it's even better because there are no lights at all. You can see the moons without a telescope. Straight up is best, of course. Lie down and you can feel the universe move.'

She stepped back into the dark. 'You were shooting with Rowland today?'

'I watched him blast some inoffensive birds.'

'You didn't tell him anything?'

'No. I don't think you're quite so terrible that I'd put you directly into Rowland's hands.'

'So where are we? By the moons, I mean.'

'Well, I haven't figured that out yet. You didn't know about this escapade Maypole had in mind, to go underground with the miners, pursue them and preach to them during their miserable half-hour break for tea?'

'John wanted to preach in the yard.'

'No, down the pit, a mile down at the coalface. What I don't understand is what put it in his mind. Being a preacher is one thing; a masquerade is something else. You see what I mean? It's not unusual for a curate to join miners in sports, but it would be unique for him to try to pass himself off as a miner. He wasn't that imaginative. Where did he get the idea?'

'What else don't you understand?'

'Why anyone would help him.'

He waited for her to mention the fright he had given the girl in her cottage. Since this was the second time that she hadn't brought it up, he assumed that the girl hadn't reported his visit.

'You can't wait to get back to Africa, can you?'

'No.'

'It seems to have great allure. I'm beginning to understand how much you miss it.'

What is this? Blair wondered. A little light in the dark? Sympathy? Something besides withering scorn? It struck him that Charlotte's voice wasn't as tight as usual, and there was more shine to her eyes in the dark than in the day.

'You obviously care about the Africans,' she said. 'We are supposed to send troops to help them but all we do is shoot them.'

'The English are good soldiers. They're fighting for beer and silver-plated spoons and Pear's soap ... they don't know why they're fighting, they're just sent. But I know. I know the maps I draw bring more troops and railway engineers and hydraulic hoses to wash out the gold. I'm worse than a thousand troops or ten Rowlands.'

'At least you're doing something. You're out in the world, not playing with – what did you call it – a doll's house?'

'It's not a doll's house. I was impressed by the Home. You're helping those women.'

'Perhaps. I think I've educated a girl, and then she steps out of the door and goes right back to the man who ruined her. It doesn't matter whether he's a miner, a footman or a shop boy. I've learned that a girl will believe anything a man says. Anything.'

'Sometimes it's the other way around. I met a girl here who could convince a man she was the Queen of Sheba.'

'She convinced you?'

'Almost.'

'But that's a flirtation. I mean otherwise sensible women with babes in arms who listen to a man declaim that the moon is a round of bread that goes best with ale and a feather pillow.'

'That's not believing, that's wanting a man and a feather pillow.'

'So what other landmarks do you search for?' Charlotte looked up.

'I travel everywhere. A poor man's odyssey. I used to do this when I was a boy and made up stories. See Virgo chasing Leo, instead of the other way around? What did the ancient Greeks make of that? Then a swim across the Milky Way over to Orion and his faithful Canis Major.'

'You had a poor but loving family?'

'Yes, but it wasn't mine. A Chinese family fed me. Later I found out that the mother's greatest fear was that one of her daughters would fall in love with me, a barbarian.'

341

'Did one of them?'

'No, I was a barbarian through and through. I did fall for one of them, though.'

'You seem to have a weakness for exotic women.'

'I don't know that it's a weakness. You were never in love with Cousin Rowland?'

'No, but I understand him. A Rowland is a Hannay without money. Not poor as you understand it. Worse. You were poor among poor. I mean, to be poor when the society you move in is rich. The humiliation when the family money has gone into gowns so that your mother and sister might attend the proper balls. Without my father's assistance, the Rowlands would live in three rooms in Kew. Rowland doesn't see the stars, he sees only money.'

'Don't marry him.'

'My father will shut the Home if I don't. I'll never have sufficient funds to start another. I'm as trapped as Rowland.'

'It sounds as if you're more trapped than the girls in the Home. They may suffer the consequences, but they did have some fun. Did you have any fun with Maypole?'

'I don't think I gave John a moment's fun.'

'He still loved you.'

'I thought you said he was infatuated with a pit girl.'

'That's one more thing I haven't figured out. Are you cold?'

'No. What constellation is that triangle?'

He followed her hand across the stars. 'The Cameleopard.'

'What is a cameleopard?'

'A giraffe.'

'I thought so. I've seen pictures of cameleopards and thought they looked like giraffes. So they *are* giraffes. I can go to my grave with that question off my mind.'

'Were you going to jump? At the knacker's drop?'

'No, I didn't have the nerve.'

'Not that time, you mean?'

'I'm not at all sure *what* I mean.'

They were silent. The sound of a cab horse below seemed miles away.

She said, 'I abused John. He would have accepted such a meagre marriage and let me go my own way. He was too good, too pure, a Christian snowman.'

'Not a complete snowman.' He thought of Rose.

'Better than me.'

'Earnshaw?'

'Hideous. I wish I had made him suffer.'

'If you couldn't make him suffer, no one could. I mean that as a compliment.'

'Thank you. For your sake, I should tell you that you'll never find John Maypole. Where he is exactly I don't know, but I do know that he's gone. I'm sorry you became involved. You're an interesting man. I've been unfair.'

She came to the edge of the parapet. An ashen light from the street crept up to her face. 'I'll leave you to your stars,' she said.

He felt the briefest touch on his hand and then she was gone, swiftly descending the ladder to the stairs of the belfry.

Blair found Jupiter again. The moon Io was still suspended to one side. On the other side, Ganymede and Callisto merged into blue twins. Europa had risen clear of Jupiter like a stone cast by a giant arm.

But his mind still turned on Charlotte. When she had stood in the faint light from below she had been a completely different Charlotte, and a new thought had been born. He was too distracted to work out longitude by the Jovian moons. Now he had no idea where he was at all.

Chapter Twenty-Four

WHAT SWAM INTO Blair's mind was Rose, when he caught her paler than pale reflection. And the girl in Charlotte's cottage. How she had hidden in the dark like a maid caught trying on her mistress's dress. In silhouette there was a shadowy resemblance to Rose, but whether it was a matter of height or a glint in her hair he couldn't say. He saw again the interrupted tea on the kitchen table, a place without a book, without even a lamp. What struck him was that, in spite of her fear, she hadn't said a word to Charlotte about a strange man at the window.

He packed the telescope and tripod into his pack, climbed down into the belfry and rushed down the tower steps. The service was over, the church a barrel of black except for watery votive candles in side chapels. When he went out of the door there was no sign of Charlotte at the front of the church or among the gravestones at the back. Most likely she had a carriage near his hotel.

The fastest way was the alley by the butchers' stalls. Blair was running after her when he tripped and his hat flew. A foot come out of the dark and kicked him in the stomach. He rolled and tried to breathe while other feet continued to stamp and kick. An oil rag was pushed and tied into his mouth, almost stuffing his tongue down his throat. Hands tied belts around his wrists and ankles and threw him on to a wooden plank, which began to roll. A cart, he thought. Crossing the street there was enough light for him to see that the cart's side walls were red. Though it had no horse, the cart gathered speed to the sound of a dozen clogs on cobblestones.

Bill Jaxon looked over a side of the cart and said, 'He can see.'

A sack was pulled over Blair's head. Within it a pungent cloud of gunpowder stung his eyes and stopped what little breath he had. The cartwheels crushed shells, slid on sheep muck, raced from alley to alley. The procession squeezed through a door and flew down an incline. He hoped they would only roll him around town to scare him and let him go. Maybe it was a good sign that Jaxon wasn't alone. Heavy doors opened and the cart lumbered into the echo of a tunnel. Blair couldn't think of any functioning mine in the middle of town. His hand felt a loose peg on the cart floor. It was smooth and split on one end and woolly at the other, and he understood that the red he had seen on the cart wasn't paint, and that he was back at the knacker's drop.

The sack came off with a handful of his hair. This time he was at the bottom of the drop where, during the day, the knacker waited for sheared sheep to fall and break their legs, the easier to kill and butcher. There was no knacker now and no sheep, though the floor was ridged with crusts of accumulated fat and gore. A pair of butcher's blocks stood at the side, red as altars. Lanterns hung on meat hooks. On the walls, ancient whitewash was barely visible through layers of black and new sprays of pink.

Bill Jaxon stripped to a silk scarf and brass-toed clogs. Blair recognized Albert Smallbone. He could tell that four others were miners by the masks of coal dust on their faces, and a man with a brush moustache he remembered as the stableman from the Hannay Mine, the man he had helped with the pony. They

345

tore off his clothes, ripping his shirt so that buttons sprayed the floor. As they knocked him on his back and dragged off his trousers, he wished the miners wore real masks, which would have meant they worried about being identified. They didn't seem to think this was a problem.

'Tha've a dark face neow, like oos.' Bill gave his words the full local twist. Dark from the sack's gunpowder, not coal, though, Blair knew.

Bill made a muscular dancer prancing in anticipation. Pulled upright, Blair felt small and naked, daubed with blood from the cart and floor. The men forced a pair of clogs on his feet and pushed the clasps shut.

'Ah'll keep an eye for constables,' the stableman said and ran off.

Bill said, 'See what 'appens when tha messes with a Wigan girl? Tha wants t'be a Wigan lad, tha mun learn t'purr.' He told Smallbone, 'Pull t'cork.'

Smallbone drew the gag from Blair's mouth and held it high. Other men pushed his head forward while Bill looped his scarf around Blair's neck and tightened it until their foreheads touched.

Blair said, 'I could have let you drown.'

'Your mistake.'

Smallbone snapped the rag down and Bill kicked Blair twice before he had a chance to move. Each leg was numb and bloody. He sank to his knees in stupefaction.

'Need a hand?' Bill asked.

When Blair reached up, Bill hit him and Blair felt his nose split. Blood sprayed his chest. Two seconds, he thought, and he already looked like a sheep who had taken the high dive.

He pushed himself up. The problem was that as his clogs broke the crust of the floor they skated clumsily on the sheep fat underneath. Bill, on the other hand, moved with sinuous ease. He spread his arms, retied his scarf around his neck, feinted and, as Blair slipped, tapped him lightly on the centre of his forehead, slowly spun and kicked savagely at the same place, but Blair had rolled away.

'You're not going to stop this?' Blair asked the miners, but they pushed him back towards Bill, ringed around him like dogs in a pack.

Bill had the strut of a champion, the glory of a white body on a red floor, raking his long black hair with his hands. A massive torso pivoting on a pinched waist, with the smile of a man who was turning sport to art. He merely leaned and Blair backed away and fell.

'Need a hand?' Bill asked again.

Blair rose unsteadily on his own. Bill rushed him, lifted him clear of the floor and carried him into a wall. Blair was crushed, his arms caught on the other side of the bigger man's back. He pulled Bill's head back by the hair, butted him and twisted free.

Miners blocked the door by the cart. Blair looked up at the edge of the drop, where he had stood before with Charlotte, and where the stableman now stood. A scream would have to rise like a siren over the drop and above the pens to reach the houses around.

Bill shook his head and rolled his shoulders, showing no more than a blush on his brow.

'Have you noticed something?' Smallbone asked Blair.

'What's that?'

'You're not worried about Maypole any more.'

Bill approached almost on the toes of his clogs while Blair slid sideways in retreat. Bill feinted as if to scoop up Blair's front leg and as Blair leaned back, he took a second, longer stride forward and kicked Blair on the inside of the thigh, continued moving in, and with the other clog kicked Blair in the small of the back. Blair stepped in and hit him square on the mouth. It was as ineffective as punching a man armed with swords. Bill kicked him in the middle of the chest and he rolled against the wall.

Cats 'purr'. What did that have to do with kicking? Blair wondered. Or killing somebody with brass-tipped wooden shoes? He found himself standing up again, using the wall. He was as red now as if he had been skinned. He ducked and Bill kicked a white hole in the plaster. When Blair tried to tackle him, Bill skipped aside, tripped him and kicked him on the side of the head. Blair was still rolling, or the blow would have pushed his brains out of his ear.

'That's enough, Bill,' one of the miners said.

Smallbone said, 'Bill's not through.'

Bill's clog tagged Blair's chin – not squarely, but enough for him to find a tooth loose under his tongue. Buttons, teeth – he was coming undone like a rag doll. He was dizzy, while Bill was spinning like a whirling dervish. Another kick and Blair found himself against the opposite wall. He got up again. It seemed to be his role in the drama. A kick in the ribs propelled him halfway across the floor and into a butcher block. A cleaver would be handy now, he thought. He crawled up the block and held on.

'Are tha goin' t'kill him?' someone asked.

'He's still standing,' Bill said.

If that was the issue, Blair thought, he was willing to lie down. Before he could, Bill gracefully leaped through the air and kicked him so hard he felt he had been shot from a cannon. He folded over. Bill kicked out his knees from behind. Well, I'm down now, he thought.

It didn't matter. As he curled up, Bill kicked his side, his arm, his leg. This was the way iron was forged when it was cold, by pounding. Blair trembled and it wasn't from cold.

'Constable's coomin'!' the stableman shouted from above.

Not fast enough. Bill tore open Blair's knapsack.

'No,' Blair said weakly.

Bill unwrapped the telescope and swung it against the wall. As the brass tube bent, broken glass poured out like sand. He tossed the tube aside and gave Blair another kick in the head.

What Blair knew next was that the lanterns had gone. He lay without moving until he was sure he was alone in the dark. He didn't feel for damage. He didn't particularly want to know. Some of him was numb. He wished it all was.

It would have been simpler to push him off the drop. He remembered his mother falling from the ship. In retrospect the waves seemed warm and restful, certainly softer than the knacker's floor.

He told himself that if he could reach a wall, he could find the door, and if he could find a door, he could reach the street. But the effort of lifting his head made it swim, and his last conscious act was not swallowing the tooth in his mouth.

Water woke him. The stableman had returned with a lantern, bucket and sheets.

'There was no constable coomin', you know, but Bill was going to kick thi inside out. In fact, I think he did.'

Were those his own hands, Blair thought, so red and amphibious? He washed them with the last water in the bucket before he put his fingers in his mouth, found the empty socket and pushed the tooth back in.

The stableman towelled him with the sheets. 'You can go t'constable but it won't do thi any good. We'll all stick up for Bill and you were messin' with his girl, he says.'

'Rose?' Blair tried to speak without moving his jaw.

'Who else?'

The lightest touch on flesh felt like the edge of a blade. What Blair waited for was the more pointed response of a fractured arm or rib moving in separate directions.

'Your head looks lahk a meat pie.'

Blair grunted with nausea, agreement and lack of surprise.

'Ah washed the coal dust out of the cuts as best Ah could so you won't look like a miner for the rest of your life, but you'll want t'get up sewed up and on a train as fast as you can. Bill won't rest until you're gone. Ah've kept your clothes as neat as Ah could and saved your hat and shoes and pack. Ah'm truly sorry about the telescope. Can you stand?'

Blair stood and passed out.

When he woke again, he was in the cart. He was dressed and the cart was rolling, so that was progress. He held the slits of his eyes open to see a lamp pass overhead.

The stableman was pushing the cart by himself. He looked in and asked, 'Is there anything else I can do for thi, Mr Blair? Something Ah can get?'

Blair muttered, 'Macaroni.'

'Maca—? Oh, Ah get it. Macaroni. Lahk in Africa. That's a good one, Mr Blair. We're almost there. Ah'll get thi to thy room, don't worry.'

The stableman had made a bed of sheets, but the jostling of the cart made Blair feel as if he were being rolled directly over cobblestones. He struggled to lift his head. 'Maypole?'

'No one knows. Forget him. Ah'll tell thi, Mr Blair, Ah'll miss thi more.'

Chapter Twenty-Five

HE HEARD someone say,

> 'For oft, when on my couch I lie
> In vacant or in pensive mood,
> They flash upon that inward eye
> Which is the bliss of solitude;
> And then my heart with pleasure fills,
> And dances with the daffodils.'

It was better than last rites.

His eyes were swollen shut, his limbs distant and unresponsive.
If he raised his head, he was nauseated from a swelling on the
brain. He wheezed through a nose that had been broken at
leisure and reset in haste, and slept profoundly or couldn't sleep
for more than a minute before the work of breathing or the
prick of a stitch summoned his attention. When he heard miners
walk to work in the morning, he dreamed of clogs and winced,
as if his head were a cobblestone.

Tea and laudanum were forced through his lips. Laudanum
was liquid opium, and the images flowed through his mind, a
great unravelling of memory. One moment he was in bed in Wigan,

the next stretched at his ease on a red hill in Africa, and the next burrowed for safety's sake as deep underground as he could go.

A miner in uniform climbed down into Blair's pit, took off a brass helmet to protect its ostrich plumes and tentatively touched the wall.

'Can you hear me? It's Chief Constable Moon. You're living very high, Blair, very high. I've never had a room like this to myself. Look at this wallpaper. Feel the flocking. Soft as a virgin's bum. Am I right, Oliver? Soft as a virgin's bum? The maid wouldn't know, Blair. No more than you.' As he buffed his helmet with his sleeve the plumes turned every move into a flutter. 'Well, I suppose it was a slip on the stairs? An accident? I just want to be sure you aren't shamming, taking the Bishop's money and lolling about in bed with only a broken head and maybe a rib or two. Bad enough you should upset honest working people, accosting women and provoking the men, but when you take advantage of a local girl you can't come tugging the sleeve of the law for protection. The men here protect their own.' He leaned close. 'Fact is, I found it hard to believe you really were the famous explorer, but you certainly look like "Nigger Blair" now.'

Blair saw in his inward eye a field of daffodils with a pit girl walking through them, gathering a bouquet. She was at the crown of a hill; he was at the bottom, blinded by the sun. No matter how much he called, she didn't hear.

Leveret joined him in the hole.

'I don't know if you can hear me, but I wanted to tell you

that Charlotte has acquiesced to marrying Rowland. Actually, she agreed the day after you were found in your ... condition. The Bishop is very pleased, in good part thanks to you, and you're free to go as soon as you are able. I have recommended an extra bonus for you and a letter obliging the Bishop to sponsor your return to the Gold Coast. You've earned it.' Leveret knelt on the coal. 'I have a confession. I knew when you came that the Bishop's interest was more in forcing Charlotte's hand than in finding John Maypole. I did hope, though, that you might find him.' Leveret's voice dropped. 'So you got involved with a woman. You're only human.' He added, 'I envy you.'

An ember chimed the hour. He thought of Charlotte's cottage, where a red-headed girl hid in the dark.

Dark was comfortable. He heard in the tunnel not Leveret but someone more familiar, old Blair, of all people, stumbling in a beaver coat and a whisky fog, whistling and offering bits of song.

> *Maintes genz dient que en songes*
> *N'a se fables non et menconges ...*

He dropped into a chair and let his coat slide, revealing a black front and an ecclesiastical collar. A book of faded red hung in one hand, a lamp in the other. He screwed up the wick and held the light over Blair.

'More poetry. How is your medieval French? Not too good, you say? As good comatose as conscious? Fair enough. I'm told we should read to you to keep your mind alive in case it is alive.' He opened the book. 'Smell that?'

A rose, Blair thought.
'A dried rose,' said old Blair.

A pony fell down the shaft, its white tail and mane snapping like wings, ticking first bricks and then timbers on the way down. The horse's tail trailed out behind.

Old Blair returned. Blair was happy to see him not only back from the dead but trading up, exchanging his moth-eaten fur coat for the crimson-lined cape of a bishop. The old man was anxious. After offering some pleasantries and getting no response, he sat silently in the dark of the tunnel for an hour before pulling his chair nearer. A visitor to the comatose is practically alone and words have a licence they usually lack.

'You're right about Rowland. I only hope he breeds a son as fast as possible. Then he can poison himself, for all I care, but he will marry Charlotte first. She has the strength of the Hannay line. It either goes through her or becomes a feeble caricature and we've enough families like that, with heirs too dimwitted to speak to anyone but their nannies, or else as queer as Dick's hatband. Long after Rowland is food for worms, Charlotte will have Hannay Hall to run, like a republic if she wants. Old families have odd problems.' Blair smelled a soft scent of roses again. 'And curious prizes. Remember, last visit I was reading you the *Roman de la Rose*. I hope you weren't expecting the Bible. The *Roman* was the great poem of the age of chivalry.' Blair heard a rustle of pages. 'Once there were hundreds of copies, but we consider ourselves fortunate to have a surviving one that has been in the family for five hundred years. Too bad you can't see the illustration.' Blair imagined a brilliantly painted scene of an amorous couple in a canopied bed framed by flowers of gold leaf that glittered and shifted in the lantern's flame. 'It's allegorical, of course. Decidedly sexual. The poem is set in a garden, but instead of a Tree of Good and Evil, at the centre is a single rosebud that the poet passionately desires. You couldn't write like this now, nor publish it. All the Chubbs and Mrs Smallbones in the land would rise up against it, banish it, burn it. I'll translate as I go, and if you find it excruciatingly dull, lift a hand or bat an eye.'

Blair made a pillow of the coal to listen. It was the sort of antique, endless tale that grew like a concentric garden, and his mind wandered in and out, catching and losing sight of the story. Venus, Cupid, Abstinence played hide-and-seek from hedge to hedge. Narcissus paused by a pool.

> *Ce est li Romanz de la Rose,*
> *Ou l'art d'Amors est tote enclose.*

He tried to use his time in the dark to good effect by going over the day of the fire. He had a new advantage. The pieces of information he had were scattered like the tiles of a half-seen mosaic, and he had tried before to bring a perspective to the little that he knew. Now that his own brain was scattered, he let each small, separate glimpse expand.

He could see Maypole join the miners' early-morning trudge to work. It was black and wet, and the curate was dressed for the pit in clothes borrowed from Jaxon, his inadequate chin hidden in Jaxon's scarf.

They moved over Scholes Bridge through Wigan and, still before dawn, across the fields. Maypole hung back but stayed part of the group, identified as Jaxon by his size and by Jaxon's mate Smallbone walking at his side.

Blair lost them in the lampman's shed. Did Smallbone pick up both men's lamps? Did 'Jaxon' get his own, tucked into a scarf? From the murk of the yard they descended into the black of the shaft. Inside the cage, close bodies smothered the weak nimbi of safety lamps. 'Jaxon' coughed and everyone turned away their faces.

At the pit eye, miners gave George Battie, the underlooker, no more than a wave as they headed for the tunnels. 'Jaxon' and Smallbone were quick to move out of Battie's sight, although once they were in the tunnel, they stopped for 'Jaxon' to set something right with his clogs, while other miners, who might notice that 'Jaxon' was suddenly as clumsy as a curate, went ahead.

Better yet, the damp weather had brought methane out of the coal. Since Battie had prohibited shots until the gas cleared, the fireman and 'Jaxon' had a slack day, hewing coal for lack of their usual labour, but at a slow pace, not exerting themselves enough to strip. They worked at the farthest reach of the coalface where no one could see beyond his lamp for more than a few feet. On this day, Smallbone could have been working with anyone. The real Jaxon came into the yard later and slipped into the winding house in case of problems.

If someone on that coalface had noticed that the Bill Jaxon below was, so to speak, not himself, that his costume or acting had slipped in the dark even for a second, no one on the surface would ever know now that all those men were in their graves. There might be no mystery to Maypole's vanishing at all if so many hadn't vanished with him.

What happened then? He tried to imagine further, but he saw Maypole's journal, and the script of vertical and horizontal lines that filled every page confused his eye. Sentences looked not so much like words as a trellis of spiky canes that even as he watched began to show red buds.

*

Old Blair, as if he understood French, translated in Hannay's distinct, rolling cadence.

> 'I seized the rose tree by her tender limbs
> That are more lithe than any willow bough,
> And pulled her close to me with my two hands.
> Most gently, that I might avoid the thorns,
> I set myself to loosen that sweet bud
> That scarcely without shaking could be plucked.
> Trembling and sweet vibration shook her limbs;
> They were quite uninjured, for I strove
> To make no wound, though I could not avoid
> Breaking a trifling fissure in the skin.
>   'When I dislodged the bud, a little seed
> I spilled just in the centre, as I spread
> The petals to admire their beauty,
> Probing the aromatic flower to its depth.
> The consequence of all my play
> Was that the bud expanded and enlarged.
>   'Of course the rose did remind me of my pledge
> And say I was outrageous in demands,
> But ne'ertheless she never did forbid
> That I should seize and strip and quite deflower
> The bloom from off her rosy bower.'

Blair opened his eyes.

The curtains were closed, framed by light like shadow in reverse, stirred by a draught. Rain tapped on the windowsill. Coal shifted in the grate. He sat up carefully, as if his head might split. A pitcher and basin of water sat on the night table. Empty chairs were pulled close to the bed and the door to the sitting room was ajar.

He slipped his legs over the edge of the bed. His mouth was

dry, his tongue almost adhered to his palate, but there was clarity to his mind, as if a wind had blown away a film of dust. He stood, and, holding on to chair backs for support, hobbled towards the closet. He remembered Livingstone, who thought he wouldn't die as long as he kept moving forwards, which was why he stumbled further and further into the African bush until his porters found him dead, kneeling at his prayers. Blair decided he wasn't going to die quite yet, certainly not by making the mistake of praying.

Facing the closet mirror, he forgot about Livingstone and thought of Lazarus, who was four days dead before being miraculously raised. Which was what Blair looked like in the glass, a little ripe for resurrection. There were too many bruises to catalogue, blotches of aubergine purple, and overall week-old, decaying shades of yellow as if he had died of jaundice or the plague. His ribs wore a patchwork of plasters, and above both ears there were shaved hair and stitches. He turned his head to see. Good needlework. One eyebrow was split, but his nose was human size and the tooth had rerooted, so he was alive.

From the hiding place behind the mirror he took Maypole's journal and opened the book to the small pasteboard photograph of Rose.

'You're awake.' Leveret was rushing in through the sitting-room door. 'And up. Let me help you.'

As Blair slumped against the chair he clutched the book. 'If you want to help, get me out of here. I have to hole up.'

Leveret caught him and eased him back towards the bed. 'Africa? America? Where do you want to go?'

'Rowland showed me a house.'

*

The house was a sullen presence in red brick, as if it brooded on its isolation from every other structure in the Hannay grounds. Its driveway connected to a lane deep in weeds. Its hedge neither shielded the front windows from the western wind nor blocked a view of slag heaps. The rooms were empty of furniture. Thanks to Rowland, broken glass covered the floors. Dismal for a normal tenant, perfect for Blair.

Leveret set up a cot in the kitchen. 'I'm afraid you won't be able to do more than heat tea on the firegrate. The former occupants found it too wild and alone, and I can't say that I blame them. You can't grow anything in slag, not even your own vegetables, and without a proper windbreak you get the gales straight off the sea.'

'When's the great wedding?'

'In two weeks. It won't be as grand as the Bishop wished, perhaps, but he is eager to carry out the event as quickly as possible. He will perform the ceremony himself. You know, you're free to go now. I could get you rooms in London or Liverpool, and arrange for a medical man. I know you'll want to get away from Wigan as soon as you get your legs under you.'

As Leveret hurried to the grate to lay sticks and coals, Blair dropped on the cot's mattress into the smell of mouldy horsehair. 'Who were the former occupants?'

'Actually it was the Rowlands. The Bishop invited them to live in the main house only last year.'

'Up to then he kept them here?'

'Yes. I noticed that there's been some damage recently. I could have a glazier here tomorrow. In fact I could furnish it for you.'

'No. No one but you. Rowland grew up here?'

'Not often. He was away at school most of the time. When

he was here, he never got on with his uncle – or with Charlotte.' Leveret stared at flames, reluctant to rise from the grate into a chimney of cold air.

'So we were the cupids.'

Leveret waved smoke aside. 'It takes a while. Inefficient but there's more than enough coal, you don't have to worry about that.'

'How do you feel about it?' Blair asked.

'I despise myself.'

To test his legs, Blair tottered around the hedge to the slag tip and back. The great circle route, he told himself. A regular Magellan.

Inside, he studied maps of Wigan and the Hannay pit, both above and underground. At night he pulled the spring gun to the centre of the kitchen and rigged strings across the doors.

Leveret returned to remove Blair's stitches. 'From what I understand, the patient generally gets drunk first. This must hurt like the devil. I brought some "Invalid's Stout". It's what miners dose their children with when they have a cough or influenza. You know, the stitching is so good I almost hate to cut it.'

'Leveret, this is not the time to develop a sense of humour.'

'Well, doesn't it strike you as ironical that having been born in Wigan, you return only to be beaten almost to death?'

'Something that obvious isn't ironical.'

'What is it?'

'Something that stupid? It has to be the hand of God.'

Leveret drew out a thread. 'The Bishop has been asking about you. He wonders when you want to go. He is offering you your old position as his mining engineer and surveyor in the Gold Coast. You won't have to join an expedition in East Africa or worry about the Colonial Office. This is quite a triumph for you.'

'Does Charlotte ask about me?'

'She asks for a report on your health each time I see her. When will you leave?'

'When I'm done.'

Birches crowned the slag white. What birches did that other trees could not was to tolerate the heat that coal in the slag still generated. Not only tolerate but flourish, with delicate branches tipped in green.

Blair waited until dusk, the right condition for reconstruction. He tied a strip of cloth cut from a sheet on to a limb, paced thirty feet and knotted a strip on to another birch, paced another fifty feet and tied a strip to a third tree. The first strip was for the lamp shed, where a line of men stood in the morning gloom. Smallbone was inside, signing for himself and 'Jaxon', who waited outside the door.

The second strip was for the winding house, where Harvey Twiss, alone, oiled the ten-foot rods of the engine as they smoothly churned.

The third strip was for the winding tower and cage shaft, where Smallbone and 'Jaxon' boarded last and faced the wall.

He walked around the three strips of cloth from different points of view. As light failed, wind arrived. The strips shook, and Blair imagined the ground jumping. Black smoke poured out of the furnace shaft and, from the force of the explosion, from the cage shaft. The stokers underground fed coals as fast as they could to keep the furnace fire drawing air. Messengers from Battie arrived.

Standing in the dark among the slag heaps, Blair thought he

was starting to see how things had happened. The one individual that a sportsman like Twiss would have allowed into the engine house was his champion, Bill Jaxon. What had these two men said to each other when they felt the blast? Bill's rush through the smoke to the cage spoke of his fear of being found so far from the coalface where he was supposed to be.

Twiss would have feared for his son. Discipline might have been enough to keep the winder in the engine house except for Bill's race to the cage, an example Twiss would have found hard not to imitate as soon as he could wind the cage back to the surface.

Lamps, what about lamps? Twiss had to lift one off a body lying on the main road. Bill Jaxon didn't because he already had the lamp Maypole had paid for; 'passage to another world for the price of a lamp and pick', Maypole had said about his practice in the tunnel. The safety lamps at the hardware store were, except for the numbers scratched on the base, identical to the lamps at the Hannay Pit. Now that the answer fell into place, Blair saw that Jaxon also would have had to bring one because he knew that, in case of problems, he couldn't go to the lamp man.

Smallbone was easier. Battie had mentioned the fireman's habit of nesting in side tunnels whenever he could slip away from work. Since the underlooker had banned shots for the morning because of the presence of gas, Smallbone had all the excuse he needed to leave the coalface and, incidentally, to survive and meet Bill coming the other way. What induced Smallbone to join Bill? He would have followed Jaxon to the moon, Blair thought, and they were miners, not cowards. And, perhaps, they wanted to be the first men on the scene for other reasons.

But why? Why would Bill agree to Maypole's masquerade in the first place? Maypole had no money. Bill had little religion.

What persuasion was left then but personal, a mystery when there was no person whom Bill cared about except Rose?

Most of the grounds were a plantation of mature beeches striped with soot and emerald lichen. In the early morning, following his compass, Blair made his way a half-mile to the stable and then along the lane to the lip of the quarry, where he took cover behind a screen of hawthorn and watched the cottage of Charlotte Hannay.

Sun rested on the red tiles of the roof and, minute by minute, slid down the white upper face of the house. Wisps of smoke issued from a chimney. Dragonflies rose from quarry water on iridescent wings, while empty hay-wagons lumbered along the lane. Leveret drove by towards town at a smarter pace. An ice van came from the opposite direction. By nine, sunlight had moved down to the lower storey of the house and spilled into the garden. A boy in a pony cart arrived to open the cottage's stable and exercise a long-legged bay. An old gardener whom Blair recognized from the Home for Women wheeled a wagonful of compost to the greenhouse at the side of the garden.

In the afternoon the boy returned to lead the horse back into the stable. Alders overhung the quarry; a kingfisher hunched on a branch and studied the water below. By three, shadow had filled the garden and covered the front of the cottage. Full hay-wagons plodded back along the lane, slower than before. They had deep-dished wheels that made them waddle. Again Leveret appeared, glanced at the dark windows of the cottage and drove on. Darkness drew midges, which drew bats to the quarry pool.

Charlotte never showed herself. Once or twice he saw candlelight inside, so briefly that he wouldn't have credited his eyes but for the chimney smoke. He watched until well into the night before he hiked back to his own mean lodgings.

The following day he did the same. The routine was similar. A steam tractor drawing a cocked plough rolled by. The boy mucked out the stables and ran the horse on a long lead. The kingfisher returned and pondered the quarry water as before. One difference was that a baker's van stopped to leave a basket on the front step.

At midday the basket was still on the step. In the garden the daffodils nodded taller, brighter heads. In the hawthorns white buds spread by the hour. The horse was a four-legged statue in its enclosure.

The horse turned. At the house, the door opened as a woman emerged nimbly to pick up the baker's basket and slip back in. But she couldn't resist her moment of air, an opportunity to shake out her red hair in the sun, if only for an instant, long enough for Blair to recognize the girl he had seen inside the house a week earlier. Again she wore a silk dress and again she could not resist a treat. Smoke drifted from the kitchen chimney. For tea, he thought, with fresh bread and jam.

The boy came by to take the horse back to its stall. Shadows swung over the front of the house. Farm wagons plodded along the lane. The sun fell and clouds faded. Midges were succeeded by bats, followed by stars.

Light showed in the parlour, a second in an upstairs room – gas sconces by their yellow cast, not the shaded candle of someone hiding. After a third one lit the downstairs hallway, the front door opened and Charlotte Hannay stepped out with a lantern in hand. She was unmistakably Charlotte, from the dress of semi-mourning to the black lace smothering her forehead. She was Charlotte by her every brusque step and abrupt glance at the garden and the lane. When she crossed into the stable, he heard the horse's throaty chuff of recognition, the way a pet demands grooming from a favourite person.

While she was in the stable, he moved from the quarry down to the lane's stone wall for a better view. When she came out, she walked the length of the garden to the quarry's edge and looked at the water long enough for him to grow nervous for his partner in astronomy; it was safer to contemplate stars than deep water.

The lamp in Charlotte's hand brushed her features with a soft upward light, raising impossibilities.

Chapter Twenty-Six

ALTHOUGH IT WAS opposite Wigan's Market Hall, Hotham's Photographic Studio had the bright colours and curlicued woodwork of a carnival booth. Signs announced 'Hotham's Portraits, From Scientific to Pathetic' and claimed 'Machinery, Buildings, Groups, Children and Animals Our Speciality'. The upstairs window was hung in heavy drapes that suggested the dark required by art. Behind the plate glass at street level were photographs categorized as 'Natural, Comedic, Historic' and framed portraits of gentry and nobility with cards noting 'By Kind Permission'.

Blair had Leveret's carriage and had rolled over every hole on the way, or so his ribs said. He tied the horse and went through the shop door, ringing a bell above it.

'Busy, busy. Look around, look around,' a voice called down the stairs over a wail that sounded like a baby being bathed.

The population of Wigan, perhaps of the whole British Isles, seemed to inhabit the shop's walls, tables and multiplicity of frames. The usual personages gathered in unusually democratic assembly: the Queen, Royal Family, Wellington, Gladstone, plus such regional honorees as a lord mayor, Members of Parliament, local matrons in fancy dress, washed faces in a workshop, prize cows, atmospheric studies of fishermen and nets, London from a balloon, and a locomotive wreathed in garlands at a Hannay pit. An aquiline Disraeli faced a melancholy Lincoln; the preacher Wesley thundered to a music-hall Juliet. In a self-portrait a photographer with spiked moustache and brows smugly held a shutter cord. And everywhere were Wigan pit girls, in individual and group portraits, and in *cartes de visite* the size of playing cards. They posed singly and in pairs with a variety of shovels and sieves, with sooty faces and clean, but always dressed in trademark shawls, heavy shirts, vestigial skirts rolled and sewn out of the way of trousers and clogs. In one or two instances the same model was shown in matched pictures of herself in filthy working garb and cleaned up in a Sunday dress to show that one day out of seven she could be a female.

When the bawling had gone on for five more minutes, Blair climbed the stairs to what looked like the backstage of an opera. Peeling backdrops of Scottish highlands, ancient Rome, the Grand Canal, Trafalgar Square and turbulent seas leaned against one another in the illumination of a whitewashed skylight. Stuffed parrots and silk flowers drooped over file cabinets. Fake banisters, urns, mantels, chairs, rustic stumps and country stiles were arrayed along one wall. Along the other were a black curtain and posing stands that looked partly like calipers, partly like instruments of torture.

The window at the front of the studio was hung with cloths and tapestries, and here the photographer was posing two children, a girl of about ten who leaned against a balustrade as stolidly as an ox against a post, while a baby already half her size screamed and squirmed against the sash that secured it to a chair. A toy monkey on a wand was attached to the camera tripod. The photographer popped out of the camera's cloth to rearrange the girl's arms. He might have waxed his moustache *à la française*, but he sounded Lancashire to the core.

'Gentle curves, dear, gentle curves.'

Sitting to the side, out of the camera's view, was a heavy

woman with the glower of a duenna holding something wrapped in bloody paper. The butcher's wife, Blair thought, paying in kind.

'Watch t'monkey, please.' The photographer rushed back to his camera and jiggled the wand. Blair recognized Hotham from the photograph downstairs. Apparently self-portraits were easier; his hair was plastered forward in poetic curves, but he had the white eye of a drowning man. As he ducked under the cloth, the baby thrashed from side to side and howled.

'If we don't like the picture, we don't pay,' the mother said. 'No picture, no pork.'

'Lookit Albert.' The girl smirked as her little brother waved four limbs at once.

Blair lifted his hat and pulled down the scarf that had muffled him to the eyes. His face was shadowed with bruises and stubble, the cut on his brow livid, his hair cropped and the scalp tracked with dried blood where it had been repaired. The girl's mouth formed a mute and anxious 'O'. The baby ceased its noise, rolled forward and gaped. They remained in these positions when the shutter was released.

From under his cloth the photographer said, 'Not quite what I had in mind, but very nice.'

Hotham accommodated Blair as a customer who looked as if he might choose to shatter every frame in the shop.

Blair said, 'You photograph girls.'

Nervously the photographer patted his hair with fingers that smelled of developer and spirit lamp. 'Proper cards, in good taste. Portraits on request.'

'You also sell them.'

'I do *cartes de visite*. Visiting cards, if you will, sir. Very popular, sold at all t'stationers, passed between friends and business associates, collected by connoisseurs.'

'Of women.'

'All sorts. Religious tableaux, the Queen, all the Royals. Divas, celebrities of the stage. Gaiety ladies and ballet dancers, women in tights, very popular with the soldiers.'

'Working women.'

'Match girls, needle girls, fisher girls, iron girls, ladies' maids, milkmaids, whatever pleases your fancy.'

'But your speciality?'

'Pit girls. I should have known what you had in mind. For discriminating gentlemen there is nothing like a Wigan pit girl. Some say trousers on women are a social scandal. All I say is, buy a card and judge for yourself, sir, judge for yourself.'

'Show me.'

Hotham pointed to the different portraits and *cartes* on view. Blair had already studied them, and the photographer sensed his disappointment. 'I have hundreds more. This is the premier pit-girl studio in t'country.'

'I'm interested in a particular one.'

'Give me her name, sir. I know them all.'

'Rose Molyneux?'

A tentative smile. 'Red hair, very pert, classic vixen?'

'Yes.'

The photographer plunged into a counter drawer. 'I have them organized, sir, categorized and alphabetized.'

'She has a friend named Flo.'

'Yes. I even have some of them together. See?'

He stood and placed four *cartes* on the counter. Two were with Flo, Flo grasping a heavy shovel and Rose holding a coal sieve like a tambourine. Two were of Rose alone, one with the shawl pinned coquettishly at her chin, the other with the shawl open and her head tilted in coarse suggestiveness towards the camera.

Except that it wasn't Rose. Not Blair's Rose. It was the girl hiding in Charlotte Hannay's cottage.

Blair produced from his jacket the photograph he had brought. The Rose he knew with a scarf turned into a mantilla that hid half her face. 'Then who is this?'

'Unfortunately I don't know.'

'You took it.' Blair turned to the studio's name in elaborate scrollwork on the reverse of the card. He didn't mean it as an accusation, though the photographer took a cautionary step back.

'In December, yes. I remember her, but I never got her name. She was remarkable. I think she came in on a dare. The girls do, sometimes. I asked for her name because I did want her back.' Hotham cocked his head at the picture. 'What a tease. She had a flash, you know, a pride. She didn't even tell me what pit she worked at. I showed people the photograph and asked, but with the Christmas trade coming on and all, and then the explosion in January, I forgot about her. Sorry.'

'Did you ever ask the Reverend Maypole?'

'Now that you mention it, I showed him a picture because he did know so many of the girls. He said he didn't know her.'

'That was all he said?'

'Yes, but, you know, he was so taken with the likeness that I gave it to him.'

At the office of the *Wigan Observer* Blair searched through the book *Lancashire Catholics: Obstinate Souls* until he found the reference he was looking for.

During Elizabeth's reign, Wigan was the heart of Catholic resistance, and when the Hannay family was sympathetic to their cause, a veritable rabbit warren of priests not only hid in the 'priest holes' of the Hannay estate but were so bold as to travel through Hannay mines and hold services in the town itself. The tunnels were an underground highway, with the grandeur of Hannay Hall at one end and the most modest of working-class residences at the other. A burning candle placed in the window summoned faithful communicants to the house where the priest was expected, a beacon of religious courage that comes down to us now only in the names of Roman Alley (since demolished) and Candle Court.

The newspaper editor had been watching Blair from under his visor since he had entered. 'It's Mr Blair, isn't it? You were here two weeks ago?'

'How many Candle Courts are there?'

'Only one.'

'Built by the Hannays?'

'For miners. Some of the oldest houses in Wigan.'

'Still owned by the Hannays?'

'Yes. Remember, you were here with Mr Leveret reading newspapers about the explosion? I want to apologize because I didn't recognize you then. With your own book on the counter? I must have been blind.'

You're speaking to the blind, Blair thought.

From the distance of the alley, Blair kept pace with the miners' march home through the street. It was a Saturday, fun in the offing and a day's rest ahead. Between corners, he followed them by the sound of their clogs, a tide of rocks. The calls of street musicians and sweet vendors joined in. Overhead, doves took flight against the evening.

MARTIN CRUZ SMITH

Mill girls were going home, too, but they made way for the
pit girls. He saw Rose and Flo pass under a street lamp. Flo
pinned a paper flower to her shawl and danced a jig around the
smaller woman.

When Blair lost sight of them he was afraid that they would
turn off to a beerhouse or pub. Behind Candle Court, he
loitered in the alley until a lamp was lit in Rose's kitchen. Flo
looked out of the window – no, admired herself in the glass as
she replaced her shawl with a plush hat with velvet flowers. She
turned to talk, vanished from sight and returned a minute later
to the window, pensively at first, then with increasing interest in
her reflection, finally with impatience. She added the paper
flower to the garden in her hat and was gone. Blair was at the
back door in time to hear the front door open and shut. No one
answered his rap, and the back door was locked.

The neighbouring houses sounded like carousels of clog
stamping and shouts. He waited for a peak to drive in a
windowpane with his elbow. When no one appeared in alarm
waving a poker, he unlatched the window and climbed in.

No one had started tea. The parlour was dark, with no
candle in the front window to let the faithful know that a priest
had come to serve the Eucharist, so he lit his own bull's-eye
lamp. He opened the closet and kicked the floor for hollow
boards. He hadn't actually seen Rose either enter or leave the
house, but he was expanding the parameters of the possible, he
thought. Most people, for example, would think it impossible to
live in the dark or underground, yet in Wigan half the people
did.

There were no false boards in the kitchen, either, but the
pantry floor sounded like a drum, and under a hook rug Blair
found a trapdoor that opened up to a ladder and released an
upwelling of black, brackish air. He quickly went down the
rungs and shut the door before anyone in the tunnel could feel

372

a draught, and he aimed his lamp low so that the beam wouldn't carry far.

Laid long before the use of rails and tubs, the tunnel floor was polished from the ancient dragging of sledges weighted with coal. The walls, rock streaked by tracer seams of coal, transmitted distant reports of the life just overhead: the muffled slam of a door, the trotting of a cab against a sibilant background of subterranean water. Timbers propping the ceiling moaned with ancient fatigue. By the time he had paced off a quarter of a mile his compass said that the tunnel ran north-east, towards Hannay Hall. He knew that fresh air must enter along the tunnel or it would have been permeated with gas, and fifty yards on he heard street sounds filtering down from an overhead grate almost overgrown by bushes. After another fifty yards, the tunnel widened into confession stalls and benches carved out of the living rock. A remnant seam of coal was cut into a series of black chapels with crude altars, shadowy crucifixes and the perpetual attendance of black Madonnas carved in bas-relief. Ahead, where the tunnel narrowed again, he saw a lamp. He shielded his own light until the other lamp disappeared at a curve in the tunnel, which allowed him to move faster and chance more noise. He was aware that the person ahead was travelling silently and quickly, familiar with the way. He started running, dodging water that had collected in the middle of the floor. The tunnel dipped and bent to the side as he expected, but when he came around the curve he was confronted by two lamps aimed at him.

Blair's own lamp lit two women very much alike. One was the girl he had seen dressed in silk at Charlotte's house, though now she wore the drab clothes and trousers of a pit girl. The other was Charlotte in her usual ebony silk dress and gloves, but her hair was loose and red and her chin was smudged with coal.

The two were almost identical in features, height and colour, but totally different in expression: the girl from the house regarded Blair with the blank eyes of a rabbit caught in the light of a train, and Charlotte glared at him with pinpoint fury. Otherwise they were images in a distorting mirror that made each woman half of the other.

'It's him. What do we do now?' the girl asked.

Charlotte said, 'If I had a gun I'd shoot him, but I don't.'

Blair said, 'You probably would.'

The girl said, 'He knows.'

Charlotte said, 'Better go home, Rose. Now.'

'This is t'last day, then?' the girl asked.

'Yes.'

Blair made room for the girl to pass in the direction he had come from. As she edged by, he saw the subtle difference of less forehead and more cheek, and watched her fear melt to a pouty anger. 'Bill'll have yer skin,' she said.

'Third time's the charm,' Blair said.

She left him with the ghost of a spiteful glance. 'He'll bury you, too, where t'worms can't reach.'

Rose Molyneux slipped around the curve, and he heard her clogs hurry into the dark. His eyes stayed on Charlotte, waiting for an explanation. She twisted from the beam of his light.

'If that's Rose, who are you? Did I catch you in transition? Were you changing yourself from a flame back into a lump of coal?'

Charlotte said, 'It was all coming to an end anyway. The days were getting lighter.'

The tunnel was cool as a crypt. The steam of her breath was no more ephemeral than she was, Blair thought. 'That's true. I never saw the Rose I knew in the light. Except for the first time, when I was blind drunk.'

She started to go and he grabbed her wrist. It was disorienting for him to talk to a Charlotte with wild red hair and the strength of a pit girl, as if he had hold of two women at the same time.

'You're put out because I fooled you.'

'You did. I preferred *your* Rose Molyneux to the one I just met. More than Charlotte Hannay. How did you do it?'

'It wasn't hard.'

'Tell me. People have been trying to kill me, thanks to your game. I'd like to know.'

'Attitude. I covered my hair, dropped my shoulders, wore gloves so no one would see calluses from working at the pit. And I'm taller in clogs.'

'More than that. Your face.'

'Pinched for Charlotte Hannay, that was all.'

'And the language?'

Charlotte put her hand on her hip and said, 'As if tha knew owt aboot t'way we speighk in Wigan or at t'Home fer Wimmen. Ah've oonly heard it aw me life.' She added in her normal voice, 'I acted.'

'You acted?'

'Yes.'

'And Flo acted?'

'Flo is a pit girl. She was my wet nurse's daughter. We used to come into town together and play Wigan lasses.'

'It was fun?'

'Yes. In masquerades that's what I always was. Not Bo Peep or Marie Antoinette: a pit girl.'

'And the family always had the tunnel from the cottage?'

'My father used it for his visits to Wigan, for his girls and fights when he was young.'

'Does your father know about this charade?'

'No.'

She tried to wrench loose and he pinned her to the wall. In

375

the light, between her flaming hair and mourning dress, she was one woman, then the other.

'How did you find Rose?'

'She came to the Home for Women last year. She was from Manchester and she was pregnant. She'd just started working at the pit. She wasn't on the register at the Home. I couldn't persuade her to stay.'

'You noticed that you looked alike?'

'I was amused by our physical similarities and then I began to think how odd it was we could look so much alike and yet lead such different lives. Then she lost the baby and had a fever and would have lost her place at the pit, so I went in for her. She had no old friends here, the other girls hardly knew her. It wasn't as difficult as I thought it would be. It was just for a day and then for a week and after that we took turns.'

'Rose liked the idea of trading?'

'I put her in my house. She much preferred wearing nice dresses and eating sweets to sorting through coal.'

'What a social revelation. Bill Jaxon's sweet on *her*?'

'Yes.'

'Which was an arrangement I was upsetting, coming to the house in Wigan, but you didn't want to warn me. Why did *you* want to trade and play the pit girl?'

'Aren't you the one who said I was a princess, that I had no idea of real life? Admit it, you were wrong.'

'And that's where Maypole comes in. The poor bastard. That's why he had to be a miner, once he knew about you. I wondered where he got the idea.'

She sank against the wall. 'He came by the pit and saw me.'

'No one else ever recognized you?'

'No one else there knew Charlotte Hannay.'

'Then he had to match you. "My Rose," he wrote. That was you.'

'I'm sorry about John. I tried to talk him out of it. It was only going to be for a day, he said.'

'He went to Bill Jaxon to change places. Bill must have been upset to learn that Maypole had found out, but he was willing to help for love, for *his* Rose, the real Rose Molyneux, so she could go on eating chocolates while you went slumming.'

'It wasn't slumming. It was freedom to have a voice that asked for more than a cup of tea. To have a body that had desires and could satisfy them. Who wore her arms bare and cursed out loud when she felt like it.' She met his eyes. 'Who had a lover.'

'Some fool who knew no one.'

'Better than that.'

'How big a fool was I?' Blair asked. 'How many people knew? Flo, Maypole, Smallbone, Bill?'

'That's all.'

'Does Rowland know he's marrying a pit girl? That will please the new lord of the manor.'

'No.'

'Why *are* you marrying him? Why did you give in?'

'I changed my mind. What do you care? All you want to do is go back to Africa.'

'Not to leave you to him. You think Rowland's only an unpleasant cousin who will make an unpleasant husband. He's not. He's a murderer. I've seen him kill Africans who walked to the right instead of the left. And he's an arsenic addict. I'm half one myself, so I know. He's worse. He's insane. If he gets one glimpse of Rose in you, you're dead.'

'That was acting.'

'Not all of it. I liked the Rose in you. He'll hate it. A shrewish, prunish Charlotte might survive a year or two with him, but you won't.'

'I was pretending with you.'

377

'It was real. Enough was.'

'What does it matter? I don't have a choice. I'm not really Rose, I'm Charlotte Hannay, who is marrying in two weeks.'

'When you were Rose, you asked me to take you with me to Africa.'

'I remember.'

'I'll take you.'

Someone else seemed to be speaking for him, some other half of himself, because he was as astonished as Charlotte, who caught a hint of his self-surprise.

'You're serious?'

'Yes.' He didn't want to think about it, the subject defied rational thought.

'You liked Rose that much?'

'I was getting to.'

'You liked the girl who drinks gin and pulls you into bed. What about Charlotte, someone who keeps her clothes on and has a functioning brain?'

'She can come, too. I'm offering you an escape.'

'It's the strangest proposition I've ever heard. I'm flattered, Blair. I am.'

'As soon as I collect from your father we can go.'

She scooped hair from her eyes. 'What a pair we'd make.'

'We'd be deadly.'

She looked down the tunnel as if she could glimpse a picture of the future forming in the dark. Blair could almost see it himself, some vision looming closer, dissolving as it came into view.

'I can't.'

'Why not? When you were Rose, you wanted to.'

'That was Rose. I'm a Hannay.'

'Oh, that *is* different.'

'I mean, I have responsibilities. The Home.'

'No, you mean the class difference, education, you having a real name, Rose being a footloose girl from Manchester, and God knows what my real name is. How could you entertain a trip with me when you can lock yourself up in a grand hall with a killer? I must have been joking. Perhaps I was, but I did like your imitation of a woman. It was the best one I've ever seen.'

'You're impossible.'

'I think we both are.'

'Well, we didn't get very far, did we?'

'No.' Blair agreed. He ignored the sadness in her laugh. As far as he was concerned, they were back at that point where every word between them was a stab.

She looked away, this time at nothing. 'What are you going to do?' she asked. 'Disappear?'

'Your men seem to do that. I'll miss the wedding, but I'll leave you a wedding present.'

'What is that?'

'Maypole.'

'Do you know where John is?'

'Let's say I know where to find him.'

Chapter Twenty-Seven

NIGHT SEEMED TO have welled from the shaft of the Hannay Pit and flooded yard, sheds and tower, as if everything up to cloud level was silent and underwater. There was no clamour of railway wagons, no coal tubs ticking to the top of the sorting shed nor rush of coals down sorting screens, no bantering of women, no line of miners murmuring towards the cage. The contrast was a blackness where locomotives sat dead on their rails and the winding tower was an unlit beacon amid a ring of shadows.

A secondary light escaped from the small upper door of the winding house where cables ran to the top of the tower. The cables were still; the cage was below and probably hadn't moved for hours. Inside the winding house, the winder would be staring at the dial of the indicator, or puttering around the great, immobile engine, keeping himself awake by oiling pistons and rods .

Air escaped from the upcast shaft, the draught driven by the pit furnace a mile below. Whether miners worked or not, the fires of the furnace stayed fed or the draught would die and the ventilation of the mine would fail.

There were two furnacemen below, Blair remembered Battie saying, the winder and perhaps a stoker above.

The lamp shed was locked. He returned from the blacksmith's forge with a bar and jemmied the shed door open. He set his knapsack and bull's-eye lamp unlit on the counter and opened the grate of a potbellied stove to a bed of half-dead coals whose glow lit the shelves. In their cages, canaries shifted and fluttered anxiously as he took a can of caulking and a safety lamp.

He walked to the tower platform, pulled the signal rope twice and heard the bell ring inside the winding house for 'Up'. A winder was supposed to stay at his post, not even leaving for a call of nature. At most, the man might glance out of the door at the platform rather than assume the signal was coming from below; Blair doubted it, but he kept his lamp dark and stood behind a leg of the tower as the great wheel overhead began to turn and the cable stirred from the ground.

He waited for the cage to make its mile trip. The furnacemen wouldn't hear it; the roar of a pit furnace covered all other sounds. As soon as the cage rose and came to a stop level with the platform, he jumped on between the tub rails and pulled the signal rope once for 'Down'.

Every descent was a controlled plunge, especially in total darkness. Midway the cage seemed to float and tap against the guide wires, a sensation of flying blind, even while the mind knew it was dropping in a steel cage. As if he ever really knew where he was. He winced. What was the speech he had given Leveret about the method of triangulation and the making of maps? That was the way he had pursued his amateur investigation, except that two of his points, Rose and Charlotte, were the same.

Pressure rose from the soles of his shoes to his knees. Round iron wire stretched as the cage shuddered between the guides and touched down at the pit eye.

There was being underground and there was being alone underground, when there was no distraction from the fact that

381

a million tons of rock stood where the sky should be. The work of hookers and drawers pushing tubs, and farriers and stableboys tending the horses, usually created the illusion that the pit eye, underlooker's shed and stables were merely a subterranean village. Without this activity that reassuring illusion was gone and a person had to accept how far from the rest of the world he was.

A burning safety lamp stood in a pail of sand at the platform. The heat and smell of horses was, as always, overwhelming. He opened his box of matches – illicit in a mine, but who could stop him now? – and lit the safety lamp he had brought from the yard. A flame leaped behind the wire mesh. He shouldered his knapsack and found the central black tunnel called the main road. This was where a conscious choice had to be made to travel fearfully or to set off as if the earth were his.

He had studied the plan of the Hannay Pit so long that a copy was imprinted in his head. A map was everything when walking in a mine. Of course, there was also the simple method of keeping the draught at his back. He kept his head low and found a rhythm that put his feet on every second sleeper of the track. Wooden props creaked more audibly without the workaday sounds of horses and wheels. Timbers settled, dribbling dirt. He raised his safety lamp and the flame lengthened to suggest a hint of methane.

Travelling in a miner's crouch made his strapped ribs feel as if they were rubbing together, but without having to buck the traffic of ponies and tubs he made good time. He moved past refuge holes, side shafts and brattices, the canvas panels that directed air. Past where Battie had found the first two victims of afterdamp the day of the fire. Past where the tunnel plunged to the turnaround where a pony had dropped and trapped ten men on the other side. Into a lower, narrower tunnel another five hundred yards. To the coalface, with its pillars of coal and blacker void where the pillars had been stripped away.

Short-handled picks and shovels lay where they had been left the day before. Blair chose a pick and automatically moved his lamp along the roof, finding a pulse of gas with the flame at a crack or two. Nothing like the gas on the day of the explosion. Then it had been damp and unseasonably warm. As the barometer dropped, gas had seeped out of pillars, roof and shot holes. In the whole length of the tunnel, lamp flames had started to separate from their wicks, all the signs that a fastidious underlooker like Battie needed to ban shots for the day.

Sometimes men were pulled off a gassy stretch of the coalface, but evacuate the mine? Never. Men swung picks or pushed tubs, boys went on leading ponies, all aware that in a gas-charged atmosphere a single spark could set off methane like a bomb or, after the firedamp turned to afterdamp, smother every one of them. Miners always went on working. After all, a man who came a mile underground had already made certain decisions about safety. Besides, they almost always went home at the end of the day.

Two weeks had passed since Blair's first visit. In that time the coalface had moved backwards in that curious Lancashire system of retreat, leaving a gallery of coal pillars that would slowly collapse under the weight of the earth above. Slowly in the sense of not immediately. Sometimes in a week, sometimes in a year, sometimes seemingly never. When the workings finally did cave in, they did so with a thunderous clap that sent waves of coal dust rolling to the pit eye.

The roof where he and Battie had crawled appeared clear for the first few yards; Blair couldn't see further through the ambient dust. He took a bearing from his compass. Pick in one hand and lamp and compass in the other, he crept forward into the void.

He remembered Maypole's journal entry, 'I will give thee the treasures of darkness and hidden riches of secret places.' When the curate reached the coalface, did he understand how grudgingly the Lord opened the veins of the earth?

As the roof angled down, he went backwards through evolution – from standing, to crouching, to his knees. The knapsack made progress twice as difficult until he removed it and tied it with his jacket to his leg; even so, he could move only by pushing the lamp ahead and following, a one-man train through the rubble. Sections of the roof had fallen in tomblike slabs. At one place he felt no floor at all, so he crawled along an edge to firmer ground, where he wiped his compass to reorient himself. His hands and sleeves were coated in black dust; he breathed it, choked on it, blinked to keep his eyes clear. Everything was warm, coal heated from pressure.

By now Blair was sure he had veered to the right or left, gone too far or hadn't gone far enough. The stones had shifted like a collapsed deck of cards – roof fallen in one place, floor crept up in another. He was sure he had missed what he had come for until his lamp flame seemed to lift its eyes, and through the dust he smelled the aromatic 'rot' of methane.

Within the mesh guard of the lamp, the reddish-orange nub became a taller, yellow flame with ideas, a flame with aspirations. Blair set the lamp where it was. As long as the flame stayed a flame and didn't become a blue-white column, he was on the right side of an ephemeral line. He crawled forward and saw a hastily patched wall of bricks and mortar a yard high and two yards wide. He brushed dirt off a brick to read 'Hannay Brickworks' in embossed letters; they were the same bricks, the same wall that he and Battie had found before.

He hiked himself on his elbow and dragged his knapsack close. As Battie had described it, this was not a blower, merely gas that had accumulated in waste stones and coal behind the bricks. In the intensified light he saw the telltale crack on the upper row of bricks behind which methane, lighter than air, would lurk. Lying on his side, he pulled the can of caulking out of his knapsack. He levered open the lid with his pocket knife and scooped the resinous tar out of the can with the blade of his knife, smeared the crack and lay back to see the effect. If the caulking was 'Good enough for the Royal Navy!', it ought to be good enough for the Hannay Pit.

Slowly the flame of the safety lamp cooled to its usual modest orange. Blair tapped the bottom row of bricks with the tip of the pick. Since methane was lighter than air, explosive gas should be confined to the upper space behind the wall, and it would be safe to remove a bottom brick. Theoretically. Which was why mining was both an art and a science, he told himself, because miners, like artists, died young.

Lying on his side, Blair delivered a more solid tap to the base of the wall. As two bottom bricks separated, he saw his own shadow rise up the wall, and when he looked back at the lamp he saw a flame tall enough to lick the cap. He dropped the pick and pressed himself as deep into rubble as he could. Billows of methane lit softly in shades of blue, floating on the heavier air, lapping under the low roof, enveloping him in liquid light. He lay still. Waving a jacket helped when gas wasn't lit; when it was lit, oxygen fed it. He held his breath to keep fire out of his lungs until the burning gas spread, broke and scattered into imps that slipped into crannies and disappeared.

The flame of his lamp settled again, although the smell of methane was pungent, as if he had plunged into a swamp. He pulled out the loose bricks and reached inside. His fingers felt around until they found, buried by stones, something that was not a rock. He pulled it out and replaced and caulked the bricks, then rolled closer to the light to examine a charred and twisted safety lamp. The lamp was constructed so that it was impossible, short of disassembling it, to remove the safety gauze, but the gauze was gone, ripped out. He rubbed the lamp base and held it to the light. Scratched into the brass was a number: 091. This was the lamp that 'Jaxon' had signed out on the morning of the explosion. No wonder Smallbone and the real Bill Jaxon had volunteered to make their way back to the coalface, for fear of someone else finding the lamp or any other sign of Maypole. To have to rebrick a wall was a godsend to the two men.

The explosion was clear enough now. After Smallbone had brought Maypole down, he had taken the opportunity to 'lark' in a middle tunnel – his habit, Battie had said – leaving Maypole alone at the darkest end of the coalface when he had never been down a deep pit in his life. What kind of spiritual experience was that? Did he fall to his knees in prayer or did he start to feel the weight of the earth above him, listen to the timbers, sense the air start to thin? He had no friend to guide him as Flo had guided Charlotte, and he would have been warned to stay clear of other miners, so he had neither experience nor companion-ship as solace. And the miners, had they wondered how oddly 'Jaxon' was acting? But who would have dared question as volatile a character if he felt anti-social?

The first time in a pit, men were often so afraid of their lamp going out that they would wind the wick up until someone shouted 'Turn her down!' Then they would overwind the other way, snuff the flame and be left in the dark. Did Maypole strike a match? Was that what he had done? Or had he yielded to the temptation of setting off a shot by himself? Jaxon had bored holes into the coal the day before. Smallbone's tin box of prepared charges was at Maypole's feet. Had he slipped one of those paper tubes of gunpowder into a hole and experimentally tamped it with his pick instead of a fireman's rod of non-sparking brass?

Then there was such a thing as spontaneous explosion. From methane, from the heat generated in coal as it was crushed, from the combustibility of coal dust in the air. It happened.

But what Blair believed most likely had happened was that a careful, dutiful Maypole had done nothing worse than tap the coalface with his pick, hear the firedamp whistle out, and then instinctively, like the good man he was, run to warn the other men working the coalface. Which, as the Inspector of Mines had said, no experienced miner would have done, because running pressed the flame through the mesh of the safety lump to the very gas a man was trying to escape.

Probably that was what had happened. In his innocence, Maypole had tried to warn the other men, and probably they smelled the gas, saw Maypole running with his lamp towards them and begged him to stop. All it took was one blue tip of flame pressed through the safety gauze. The force that ripped out the gauze and twisted the lamp like toffee put him and no one else at the point of the explosion. Where was the rest of Maypole? There might be parts, atoms of the man, but not enough for worms. It was too deep for worms, anyway, as Rose Molyneux had said.

In his journal Maypole had cited Job. 'I went mourning without the sun. My skin is black upon me, and my bones are burned.' Well, that prediction was true enough and he had taken seventy-six other men with him. And when the heroic rescuers Smallbone and Jaxon found Maypole's lamp they bricked it away for eternity and scratched the same number – 091 – on to the lamp Jaxon had brought, so that the lamp system itself would *prove* that every man had been accounted for.

Blair replaced and caulked the bricks, stuffed the lamp into his knapsack and crawled back through rubble to the coalface. He got to his feet, looking not so much like a miner now, he thought, as a stick of charcoal. He didn't feel vindicated, he felt sad, because in the end he admitted they had shared so much in common.

He staggered to the main road, keeping the welcome draught in his face. After a taste of methane, even foul air was an improvement. He was climbing the incline to the turnaround when the rails began to vibrate underfoot. He thought it might be from a rockfall until he heard a squeal of metal wheels. Out of sight, a train of tubs was moving.

A train was half a ton of slackly chained iron-plate tubs that at first push rolled in a lethargic, uncoordinated way. Blair backtracked and looked for room to let them pass by. He heard the train drop into a straightway, smooth out and gather speed. He wasn't gathering speed himself. Between his strapped ribs and the weight of his knapsack, he stumbled over railway sleepers, outpacing the poor glow of his safety lamp. The rails resonated underfoot. Runaway trains were one of the more common causes of fatalities in pits; with momentum, tubs tended to carry and drag whatever they met. He saw them career around the head of the incline, chains banging, filling the low shaft. He dived into a refuge hole as the lead tub clipped his heel and the train whipped by in the direction of the coalface.

After the reverberation of the tubs receded, he heard a rhythmic scraping, like a knife being sharpened. He looked with one eye from the refuge hole. A figure in a skater's crouch, outlined in yellow, a lamp in one hand and a pick in the other, was sliding sideways on the irons of his clogs down an incline rail.

Blair pulled himself in as Bill Jaxon passed, silk scarf at his neck, his back to the refuge hole. He took one-legged strides and balanced on sparks that faded like a comet burrowing through the ground. Blair felt a burning stab and realized that the only reason he hadn't been seen was that he was lying on his own lamp. He unbent on to the track and patted out the charred circle on his jacket. He was halfway to the cage and could reach it long before Bill could turn around from the coalface. He had just topped the incline, however, when he heard clogs following at an easy lope. Jaxon hadn't gone to the coalface at all. He had just flushed him out.

'Rose told me she met you!' Bill called. 'I want to hear about it!'

There was no chance of outracing Jaxon the remaining distance to the cage, or of hiding. His lamp would lead Bill right to him, yet he couldn't put it out without being blind. He pictured the main road he was on, the back road, and all the short side tunnels that connected the two main tunnels. The next side tunnel was covered by a brattice to keep air flowing straight, and he slipped through it towards the back road.

A moment later he was joined by Bill's voice. 'Good try, but don't you think I know t'pit better than you?'

The back road carried return tracks and spent air to the furnace. An oily wind, directed by more panels of canvas, pushed Blair's back. He pulled panels into the tunnel as he moved to block Bill's view of his lamp. Doing so, he hit his head on a low beam and was so dazed for a moment that he didn't know which way to go. From a wetness welling in his ear he was aware that a scar had opened.

'All you had t'do was leave us be,' Bill called.

Blair moved as best he could while he heard Jaxon smashing the brattices he had left behind. He ducked through a side tunnel back to the main road. Through other side tunnels he heard Bill running parallel on the back road. There was a small advantage in that shoes were quieter than clogs, though an ant could claim the same edge. Within a few steps, Jaxon would be crossing to the main road.

A solitary coal tub stood on the track. Blair put his shoulder to it and pushed it downhill towards the coalface. As he looked over his shoulder, Bill's lamp appeared above him on the main road.

Blair put his lamp into the tub, let it go and ducked to the side. The grade was mild; the tub didn't gather speed, but it didn't stop either. The glow of Blair's safety lamp bounced along the roof. In pursuit, Bill skated down the rail in graceful, burning strides.

In the black, Blair fumbled through a side tunnel to the back road and lit the bull's-eye lamp from his knapsack. The match burned bright and the lamp's narrow beam shot ahead, fuelled by the tinge of methane in the air.

After a hundred feet he dared return to the main road. His feet were heavy as andirons, his lungs wheezing in imitation of punctured bags. The stink of the stables was sweet, though, and the dim lamp in its pail of sand was the candle of a sanctuary. The cage sat waiting at the pit eye.

He heard Bill returning up the main road, furious. How he had caught the tub and returned so fast, Blair didn't understand, but he had. Blair stepped on to the cage and hit the signal rope.

As the cage lifted, Bill ran at full tilt out of the road and raced past the stable stalls. From Jaxon's eyes, Blair saw that he was gauging a leap for the rising cage, at the last moment saw that he would fall short, and instead flew the width of the shaft.

Blair sank to the floor of the cage, cradling his lamp and knapsack on his knees as it rocketed up. Through its open side, the beam lit a blur of damp, undulating stone and even though he knew he was headed for a yard of coal and slag he smelled grass and trees.

As the cage slowed, he pulled himself to his feet. The approach seemed endless. Finally, the cage inched up to a lakelike glimmer of lamps and the touch on his face of a genuine breeze. Locomotives crouched, sphinxes in the yard. The flag on the tower was a crescent moon.

As he stepped on to the platform, Albert Smallbone slipped from a tower leg and hit him with a shovel.

Blair stretched out on his back, the square edge of the shovel pressed under his jaw, Smallbone at the other end.

'Have you ever hunted with ferrets?' Smallbone asked. 'Hardly worth it. Worse than criminals. The ferret chases t'rabbit to the end of a hole and then proceeds t'eat him. Not what you sent him down for. If the leash on him breaks, you have t'start digging with a spade t'save some supper for yourself. Anyway, you're my rabbit now and Bill will be up in a mo.'

The cable was reeling fast. Blair couldn't see how much was left because whenever he shifted Smallbone pressed the shovel blade against his neck. His upended knapsack and its contents were spread around Smallbone's feet.

'The first time you went digging with George Battie, I told Bill you'd be back down pit. He didn't believe me. Bill's not bright, but he's beautiful, an element of nature. Like his Rose. I'm a more thoughtful man, like you, but we have t'appreciate people for what they are.'

Blair grunted to hold up his end of the conversation.

Smallbone said, 'Rose told us what she told you, which wasn't the sort of thing t'say to a suspicious man. Weren't we lucky t'get here when we did? Like I was lucky t'be taking a rest from the coalface when the whole pit went t'hell. You know, people have always struck me as the most fascinating of subjects. Rose is not so persuasive to me, but she has her way with Bill. It's Samson and Delilah. I never would have let Maypole take Bill's place, but she liked her special days in the rich house all to herself, and once Maypole got wind of what was up, she was afraid he'd expose her and Miss Hannay. We didn't do anything wrong. None of us did. All we did was help a preacher get a taste of the real world.'

'He wasn't ready for it,' Blair whispered against the shovel.

'You're right there. All I asked him t'do was sit still while I took a rest. That wasn't too much t'ask, I thought. But now you see our situation. Bill, Rose and me, we've done nothing wrong, but we'd be charged for seventy-six deaths. Not even Mrs Smallbone would pray for me, and, believe me, she prays for everyone. God knows, we tried t'warn you off.'

'Like you warned Silcock?'

'That was a botched job. He leeched on to Harvey after the fire and we couldn't know what Harvey had said in his condition. Nothing as it turns out, I suppose. He didn't drown. No harm done.'

'Twiss?'

'We took him for a walk. In Harvey's grief and such, I think it was a mercy.'

'Bill tried to kill me.'

'Bill's heavy-handed, but the idea people might suppose his Rose and you were intimate was a provocation.'

'And the spring gun?'

'An inhuman device. I hated t'set it, but if nothing else it should have been a message. The truth is, you could have left Wigan any time, and you didn't, and now it's too late.'

The cable made an ascending note. Blair knew that if he called to the winding house, Smallbone would cut him off, and even if he didn't the winder probably wouldn't hear anything over the popping of pistons and valves. So what would it be? A trip to the railway line where he could lay his weary head on a track like Harvey Twiss?

The cage rose to the platform and shook as two clogs stepped off and blocked Blair's view. They were familiar clogs with brass caps that shone like spear points of gold. With them aimed at Blair, Smallbone immediately hit the signal rope and the cage started back down.

'That was a good run,' Bill said.

'Good as a Christian athlete?' Blair remembered his first conversation with Jaxon at the Young Prince.

'Almost.'

The winder must wonder why the cage kept going up and down, Blair thought, but it was all the more reason for him not to leave his post.

'You were with Twiss when the gas exploded,' Blair said to Jaxon.

Bill looked at Smallbone, who watched the shaft swallow the cage and said, 'It doesn't matter.'

They weren't going to march to any railway tracks or canal, Blair realized. When the cage hit bottom, they would just drop him in after and he'd be one more casualty of a late-night stroll in Wigan. He saw himself plunging down the shaft. 'I shot an arrow into the air, it fell to earth, I know not where.' Well, he would know.

'What do you think happened?' Blair asked.

'The explosion? My opinion?' Smallbone said. He kept his weight on the shovel and his eye on the descending cable. 'It's all a laugh. The Lord giveth and the Lord taketh away, and he's splitting his sides while he does it.'

Blair looked at the twisted brass that had been a safety lamp. 'Did Maypole know?'

'Maybe; he certainly had a bright light t'see by. The truth is, a miner who thinks he's not working in his own grave s'fool. I knew that of Maypole. I'm surprised t'find out you're one, too.'

He nodded to Bill, who drew back his clog to kick Blair over the edge, but was distracted by someone crossing the dark yard without a lamp.

Smallbone squinted to make the figure out and cabled, 'Is that Wedge? Battie?'

Charlotte answered, 'I talked to Rose.'

'Get rid of him,' Smallbone told Bill, who kicked Blair over.

Charlotte was in trousers and shirt and carried a long-handled shovel, the kind used for sorting coal. When she hit Smallbone the shovel blade made the sound of a Chinese gong.

Blair had caught a guide rope of steel and tried to climb back up. Smallbone was felled by another blow from Charlotte. She was a blur, wielding the heavy shovel like a two-handed sword. Blair reached from the rope to the platform, where Bill waited for him. Charlotte dug the shovel into Bill's back, and when he didn't budge she threw it at his head, getting his attention. He turned and backhanded her. Blair watched her drop as he crawled on to the boards. He picked up the loose shovel and when Bill turned back to him, he swung it with all his might at Bill's knee, like a man's first chop at a tree. Bill tilted to the side. Blair tossed him the shovel. As Bill caught it with both hands, Blair stepped forward and with his fist hit him at the point where his brows met. Bill stepped back where there was nothing but air and balanced, one foot on the edge. His scarf snapped around him in the downdraught. When he dropped the shovel, it rattled off his foot and moved him another millimetre over the shaft. The shovel chased the cage, the blade singing off stone.

'Ah got thee, Bill, me boy.' Smallbone wrapped his hand on Jaxon's.

Reaching for Smallbone had the effect of tipping Bill the opposite way. Despite Smallbone's grip, the angle continued to change the wrong way, and Bill's clog slid. The iron he had skated on was moving over the worn wood of the platform edge.

'Fooking Maypole,' Bill said. He added, 'That's it.'

His eyes rolled back and the rest of him followed. He made one stroke with his free arm and fell.

'Jesus,' Smallbone said.

He scraped crabways across the boards and tried to free himself from Bill's grasp, and then he disappeared over the lip too.

Chapter Twenty-Eight

A BREEZE MOVED ahead of Blair, making a froth of daisies. He had been on the trail before, so it was easy to follow, even easier when marked by a satin ribbon snatched from a skirt or by the cough of a gun ahead.

Meadows led to higher slopes of sheep separated by rows of black rocks. He wore a Harris-tweed jacket over what felt like new ribs, and he breathed without a twinge air that seemed to buzz with life, as if the opalescent glint of insects in flight was a low field of electricity that charged every object in sight. From time to time he stopped to slip the knapsack off his shoulder and focus his new telescope on a hawk hovering over a tumbledown cairn or a lamb nosing through heather.

He turned the glass to the final hill, where wind combed grass up to a picnic set under clouds as white and still as columns. The oriental carpet of the Hannays was spread out as before. Lady Rowland and Lydia again were dressed as genteel, animated flowers, the mother's ensemble the velvet mauve of an American aster, and the daughter in a lavender dress of crêpe de Chine, her golden hair gathered into a sun hat, the muted colours reflecting the ambiguous state the family now inhabited. The men – Hannay, Rowland, Leveret – were in black. Drowsy flies crawled over the remains of potted duck, savoury pie, biscuits and stirrup cups of claret. A musk of gunpowder lingered in the air.

At the sight of Blair, Lady Rowland blushed with irritation, and Lydia, like a gilded statue, looked around for a cue.

'The very man,' Rowland said.

Hannay sat up stiffly and shielded his eyes. Blair noticed signs of disrepair on the Bishop, a sugary stubble on the jaw.

'A face to cheer us up. Good. The rest of us are inconsolable, but you, Blair, seem fully recovered. Shaved, healed, in the pink.'

'Better yet, paid,' Blair said. 'Outfitted and on my way back to Africa, thanks to you. I'm sorry about your daughter.'

'It was unexpected.'

Lady Rowland said, 'It was a bitter disappointment.' She didn't sound disappointed. If anything, satisfaction lurked in the corners of her mouth.

Lydia shimmered like flowers, a table arrangement brought out of doors. She asked, 'When are you leaving?'

'Tomorrow. Your uncle has kindly employed me to finish my survey of Gold Coast mines, though I was thinking of staying a while longer to search for my mother's family. She was from here. I'll probably never have another chance.'

'I'm surprised you stayed as long as you did,' Hannay said.

'It's beautiful country.'

'From an old Africa hand, that's a compliment,' Rowland said. 'You have risen from the grave. I heard you stayed in our old house for a week before moving back to the Minorca. You have truly infested the complete environs. Sort of a black cousin.'

'The arsenic's holding out?'

'The pharmacist is a good man. You know him well yourself.'

'One more thing we share.'

'The last thing. How are you on irony?'

'Mother's milk.'

'Chief Constable Moon tells me about a pair of miners who fell down a Hannay shaft two weeks ago in the middle of the night. They were found in the morning when the cage came up. They were dead, mangled from the impact and from hitting walls on the way down, according to the Coroner.'

'What a gruesome story,' Lady Rowland said. 'Why would the Chief Constable bother you with a story like that?'

'He knows my interest in unusual phenomena.'

'Two drunks falling down a well doesn't sound unusual.'

'What's unusual is that two experienced miners could have fallen down a shaft at the very pit where they worked. The same two men were heroes in the explosion at that pit in January. If that isn't irony, what is?'

'Or a moral tale,' Blair said.

'What is the moral?' Lydia sounded lost.

Lady Rowland said, 'That's it, dear, we'll never know. The lives those people lead are so different.'

Rowland wasn't done. 'It was the same night, in fact, that Charlotte disappeared, so we have irony *and* coincidence. Perhaps it's the coincidence we should concentrate on.'

Leveret said, 'There would have to be a connection. Charlotte didn't know the miners, had probably never seen them.'

'She was familiar with pit girls. My uncle is closing the Home for Women at my insistence.'

'If that satisfies you,' Blair said.

'Nothing satisfies me. I have earned fame. I carry a great name; at least I will. But it is as if I have been promised a garden in the centre of which is a tree with a certain apple. All my life I have expected to bite into that apple, and now I am told that the garden is mine but that the apple has been stolen by someone else. My satisfaction has been stolen.'

'You still get the coal,' Blair said.

Hannay said, 'Blair had a fall of his own some weeks ago. I visited him. He was delirious most of the time. His recovery is remarkable.'

'Thank you,' Blair said. It was true, even the malaria had abated. No more brown piss, his water was pure as a mountain spring. 'Perhaps it's the air.'

Lydia said, 'You should take up residence in Wigan.'

'I'm tempted. Quit gold for the homelier pursuit of coal.'

'What precisely do you know about your mother?' she asked.

'Nothing precise. We were sailing to America when she died. She told people on the ship she was from Wigan. She could have been a maid, a mill or shop girl, a pit girl.'

Lady Rowland said, 'There must have been a name on the baggage or something.'

'She didn't have any baggage. If she had any papers, she tore them up or threw them away.'

Rowland said, 'She was in trouble. Or perhaps she didn't want you coming back to bother relatives.'

'That's what I always thought,' Blair said. 'Yet here I am.'

Hannay poured a glass of wine for Blair, who took it but remained standing. The Bishop said, 'You should see Rowland shoot. His aim is extraordinary. He has been decimating the animal population.'

'We went shooting together in Africa. He decimated the population there too.'

'Your health.' Leveret raised his glass to Blair. 'I'm glad you're still here.'

He had said not a word about Blair's visit to the stable or

taking a carriage two weeks before when everyone else supposed he was too damaged to rise from bed.

'A curious thing,' Hannay said. 'We always dreaded Charlotte's arrival at the table or at any outing. Now I've come to realize that she was, in fact, the centre of every event. Without her everything seems pointless.'

'Life goes on,' Lady Rowland said.

'But life is not the same.' Hannay watched Rowland open a box of cartridges. 'Nephew, your hands are shaking.'

'It's the malaria,' Lady Rowland said. 'We'll go to London, see the doctors and stay for the season. Rowland will be the most eligible man there. He'll have to run from the women.'

'And vice versa,' Blair said.

'It won't be the same without Charlotte,' Lydia said. 'I was always intimidated by her because she was so intelligent, but I was thrilled by her because I never knew what she would say next.'

'Whatever are you talking about?' Lady Rowland asked. 'Dear, you will have a glorious season of your own, and we won't remember any of this. Even Mr Blair will fade from memory.'

'Did the detectives find anything?' Lydia asked.

'No.' Her mother shot a glance at the gamekeepers and repeated more softly, 'No. Your uncle engaged the best private agency in Manchester. There wasn't a sign. You have to think of the family now.'

'Blair could look,' Lydia said.

'Yes, Blair was such a great success at finding Maypole,' Rowland said. 'Uncle, would you please read the letter that came today?'

The Bishop's eyes stayed fixed on the wall that marked the horizon. His hand fumbled absently for a letter he took from the breast pocket of his coat and handed it to Leveret.

'Go ahead,' Rowland ordered.

Leveret unfolded the paper. He swallowed and read aloud:

My Lord Hannay,

This is by way of both farewell and apology for the concern I have caused you. I claim no excuse for my behaviour; I do, however, have reasons that I wish to explain in hopes you may some day think of me with some understanding and forgiveness. If I disappointed you, I have disappointed myself tenfold. I was not the curate I could be, no more than Wigan was the simple parish I first took it as. It is, in fact, two worlds, a daylit world of servants and carriages, and a separate world that labours underground. As my work went on, I discovered that I could not be curate to both those worlds with an equal heart. At one time, like the Reverend Chubb, I honoured dry scholarship above the friendship of my fellow man. I can say now that there is no prize on earth greater than the good regard of the working men and women of Wigan. The vanity of the Church I will miss for not one moment. Wigan, though, will always be in my heart.

I begin a new ministry of my own tomorrow. Thanks be to God, I will not bear this burden alone, for Charlotte has joined me. I cannot share with you our destination, but please know that we are content as two who are armoured by complete trust in God. Tomorrow the great adventure begins!

With respect and love,

Your humble, obedient, John Maypole.

Leveret looked at the envelope. 'It bears a Bristol postmark from three days ago.'

Blair said, 'I would have sworn Maypole was dead.'

'Not according to that letter,' Rowland said.

'It is John's handwriting,' Leveret said. 'These are his most personal sentiments. I've heard him say some of the same words.'

Rowland said, 'Hundreds of ships have left the port of Bristol in the last three days. They could be anywhere in Europe by now, or playing missionary in any slum in the south of England.'

'Do you think they're married?' Lydia asked.

'Of course they're married,' Lady Rowland said. 'It doesn't matter, your uncle will cut her off. He has to. She spited the family to run off with a madman.'

Blair asked, 'That's all Maypole wrote? Nothing about why he disappeared or where he went?'

'That's all,' Leveret said.

Lydia said, 'We have been waiting for a letter from Reverend Maypole for months, haven't we?'

Lady Rowland said, 'He must have been communicating secretly with Charlotte all that time. We called off the detectives. There's nothing to be gained from finding two runaways.'

Leveret removed his hat as if discovering what a warm lid it was. Pinpoints of blue marked his skin at the hairline. 'Do you think you'll need help in Africa?' he asked.

'No. Sorry.'

'The question is', Rowland said, 'whether Blair was in on it with Maypole from the start. I saw the way Charlotte looked at him when I came with the gifts for the Royal Society.'

'The monkey gloves?' Blair asked.

'Earnshaw told me how Blair was always after her, turning her against me.'

'She didn't act overly fond of me.'

'You were both acting. You were Maypole's agent all along.'

'Your Grace?' Blair appealed for a rebuttal from the Bishop, but Hannay seemed hardly to be listening.

'You never found out about your mother?' Lydia tried to change the subject.

'No, I suppose not. Maybe I prefer the mystery.'

Rowland said, 'Some mystery. A slut gets pregnant by a shop boy, has the brat, is worn goods, gets with child again, though not by any man thick enough to marry her, begs a ticket to America and ends her short, ugly life on the way. I might be wrong on a detail or two, but I would consider this mystery solved. Don't try to lend her dignity by calling it that.'

Blair counted the two steps it would take to cross the carpet, one in the mustard and one in pie, to reach Rowland, who raised his shotgun and said, 'No palm trees or natives to hide behind now, are there? What do you think of my detective work? I think I finally have you. Your mother was a willing whore, a syphilitic, nameless nobody, the sort of garbage ships throw overboard at sea every day. Is that close enough?'

Blair shrugged. 'You know, I have often said the same – and worse – for years. Because I was abandoned, whether she could help it, whether she died or not. It helps to hear the words from you because it reminds me how stupid and venomous they are. Especially stupid. Because she was no more than a girl, and when I think about how abandoned she must have been, without a penny after she got her ticket, no baggage, friendless, power- less, fatally ill before she got on board and knowing that she would probably die at sea, I appreciate how much courage it took for her to escape from here. So the one thing I know about my mother is how brave she was, and since I didn't understand that until I came to Wigan, I suppose it was worth the trip.'

He finished his wine and set it down. It felt wonderful not to have every bone an aching worm. The shotgun started to transmit Rowland's tremor and sweat rolled off his face.

'You shoot too much, dear,' Lady Rowland said. 'It makes you feverish.'

Hannay leaned forward with a heavy whisper. 'Rowland, if you ate less arsenic, your hands wouldn't shake. If you were any whiter you could be a snowman, and if you were any more insane you could be the Archbishop of Canterbury. My advice is to marry while you still have the wits not to climb the drapes. Responsibilities come first; madmen are not admitted to the House of Lords. You can go mad once you're in.'

'May I?' Leveret eased the shotgun from Rowland's hands.

'Well, I hate to go,' Blair said.

He slipped the knapsack over his shoulder and started down the path the way he had come. He had gone a hundred yards when he became aware of someone wading through the grass after him. He turned and faced Hannay.

'Your Grace?'

'Thank you, Blair. So rare of you to bow to me in any way. About the letter.'

'Yes?'

Hannay had it in his hand. He unfolded the single page and scanned the lines.

'It's well done. All the Maypole tics and flourishes. The question is, do I believe it?'

'Do you?'

'Not for a moment.'

Blair said nothing. Hannay blinked. In his eyes was salt water. His coat shook in the wind, loose as a sail.

'Not literally,' the Bishop added.

'What does that mean?'

'Not word for word. People sometimes ask me whether to believe in Genesis. Were Earth and the Heavens created in six days? Was Eve fashioned from Adam's rib? Not literally. It's a message, not a fact. The best we can do is try to understand.'

'Do you understand?'

'Yes.' Hannay refolded the page and pressed it flat in his breast pocket.

Blair looked back from the path. Hannay rejoined the picnic and it continued, barely audible from this distance. The scene had re-established the languor of an English family set between English hills and English clouds, the sky as liquid as a pool.

From the bottom of the hill he looked back again and they were as tiny as figures in a bead of water.

Chapter Twenty-Nine

IN THE HAZE of a Liverpool afternoon, the African steamship *Blackland* parted from the North Landing and rode the ebb tide out of the Mersey. Heavy with goods, low in the water, it nudged through the coal barges and ketches of the Long Reach, bearing north to begin with, then bending west and finally south to the open sea.

The *Blackland* was a doughty ark of civilization fat with Manchester cloth, Birmingham buttons, Bibles from Edinburgh and, from Sheffield, pots, pans, nails and saws. From London came *Punch*, *The Times*, and communiqués from the Colonial Office issuing Imperial orders and franchises, not to mention the mailbags of personal letters that made foreign service bearable. Packed with excelsior in wooden crates were cognac, sherry and trade gin, as well as quinine, opium and citric acid. From the hold wafted the perfume of the palm oil it carried on return trips.

The captain made a bonus on the fuel he conserved, and at best the *Blackland* made eight knots, which seemed none as it fought the oncoming swells of the North Atlantic. At the Bay of Biscay, however, the Canary current would surface and sweep the ship towards Africa. The *Blackland* would visit Madeira, execute a cautious swing around the emirates of the western Sahara, where Europeans had for centuries believed that the sea boiled and the earth ended, and, borne by the warm equatorial current, begin its African calls.

Passengers gathered in the first-class cabin at four for dinner and at seven for tea and on their first night out stayed on deck late before retiring to their cramped berths. Coal soot spread by the engine stack made the ship into a locomotive under the ocean night.

Ahead of the stack, though, the rail was a balustrade for constellations as brilliant as freshly lit fires, familiar stars prized because they would soon be traded for the Southern Cross.

Finally, singly and in groups, the passengers tired and went below. Wesleyan missionaries already praying for Zulu souls. A doctor, not too well himself, dispatched to the smallpox epidemic in Grand Bassam. Salesmen versed in tinware, drugs, gunpowder, soap. A lieutenant headed for Sierra Leone to drill Jamaicans shipped for African duty. A new consul for Axim. Creoles in frockcoats and beaver hats.

And last on deck, bound for the Gold Coast, a mining engineer named Blair and his wife, whom he called Charlotte, except when he called her Rose.